# THE OBELISK

# The Obelisk

Robert Ingebo

**THE OBELISK**



*This is a work of fiction. All of the characters, names, incidents, organizations, and dialogue in this novel are either the products of the author's imagination or are used fictitiously.*

*iUniverse books may be ordered through booksellers or by contacting:*

*iUniverse*
*1663 Liberty Drive*
*Bloomington, IN 47403*
*www.iuniverse.com*
*844-349-9409*



*ISBN: 978-1-6632-3461-2 (sc)*
*ISBN: 978-1-6632-3463-6 (hc)*
*ISBN: 978-1-6632-3462-9 (e)*

*Library of Congress Control Number: 2022900377*

*Print information available on the last page.*

*iUniverse rev. date: 02/23/2022*

# Dedication

"I give all glory and credit to my Savior, the Lord Jesus Christ, who played an instrumental role in the creation of this novel."

# CHAPTER ONE

Contemporary jazz washed over the two young gentlemen in rippling waves of sound as they occupied a rear table of the bustling nightclub. With lots of brass railings, table lamps, expensive walnut paneling, oversize drinks, and top-quality entertainment, Curley's represented the essence of the Chicago nightclub experience.

"The band sounds great," David remarked. "I wish they had decent clubs like this back in Cleveland. The crowd seems really into it."

"Yeah, the nightclub scene is pretty hot around here," Alan concurred. "By the way, congrats on making the surgical team. Your residency at the Cleveland Clinic gave you some impressive credentials. I'm glad I was able to make the recommendation."

"Thanks, Alan. I can't believe I was hired by Dr. Lucas. It will be an honor working with such a renowned surgeon."

"I'll have a bourbon and press, please," Alan said when the waitress appeared.

"Make mine a martini," David said, giving her a friendly smile.

David Sholfield was a tall, handsome, young doctor with black hair and an athletic build. A pair of intelligent blue eyes added a hint of intensity to his appearance.

By contrast, Alan Lawson was short and pudgy, with red hair and a ready smile.

"So, how are things in administration?" David asked as the waitress hurried off.

"Things have been pretty hectic," Alan replied with a sigh, "but that goes with the territory. Compared to your schedule, though, I shouldn't complain. It must be nerve-wracking to be on call twenty-four-seven."

"It's a sacrifice I'm more than willing to make," David responded, grinning. "I hope I can maintain the high level of competency Dr. Lucas is expecting. I thought my residency in Cleveland was stressful, but being chosen for the premiere cardiac surgical team at Northwestern Memorial has put everything on a whole new level."

"Relax, Dave," Alan said with a reassuring smile. "In a couple of weeks, you'll be on cruise control." He raised his glass. "Here's to the start of a successful and lucrative career. Not to mention all the cute nurses you'll be dating."

"Here! Here!" David said, clinking his glass with Alan's. "The money and respect would be great, but what I'm really hoping for is something to develop on the romantic side. My life has been painfully devoid of women with all the changes I've been through lately."

"I understand completely," Alan said. "Unfortunately, I'm not doing very well in the love department either. Perhaps we can do something to rectify our mutually deplorable situations. Check out those babes over there. Would you like to meet them? I'll make the introductions."

"I don't know, Alan," David replied, glancing in the direction of his friend's nod. "I'm not in the habit of meeting strange women in bars. They could be bad girls for all we know."

"Bad girls suit me just fine," Alan said, laughing. "Look at that gorgeous one with the long black hair. I saw her checking you out a moment ago. I think she's interested. Besides, I want to meet that brunette cutie-pie she's sitting with."

Just then the music stopped, and the band went on break. "That's our cue," Alan said with a grin, pushing his chair away from the table. "What do you say, pal? Shall we introduce ourselves?"

"I guess there's no way you're going to let me out of this one, eh buddy?" Dave responded with a mock grimace. "What the heck. All they can do is destroy our pride and relieve us of our cash."

"Hello, ladies," Alan said, giving his most accommodating smile as they approached the women. "May we sit and chat for a few minutes?"

The young women exchanged glances. "I guess that would be okay," the brunette replied shyly.

"Thank you, ladies," Alan said in a courteous tone as they sat down. "I'm Alan Lawson, and this is my friend David Sholfield."

"Pleasure to meet you, Alan and David," the brunette said brightly. "I'm Mary Nelson, and this is Angela Stockman."

Angela gave David a friendly smile. "Nice to meet you, David."

David felt an immediate tingle of passion as he returned her smile. Although he recognized a hint of sensuality in her appearance, her demeanor was quite reserved. She was definitely a nice girl, a woman he could feel safe with.

"So, tell me, Mary," Alan continued. "What brings you here tonight?"

"The music!" Mary responded enthusiastically. "I love good jazz, and Curley's always has the best bands in town. They import them all the way from New York and LA."

"How about you, David?" Angela asked. "Do you like jazz?"

As David let his gaze linger upon the beautiful woman for a moment, he realized that it was the graceful curves of her nose and lips that created the underlying sensuality. More than anything, he wanted her to like him, but he wasn't sure he could pull it off. The thought entered his mind that beautiful women tired of their boyfriends quickly. He couldn't afford to get hung up on her, to open himself to the awful pain of rejection, to suffer the intensity of emotional turmoil that could threaten his budding career. "I like all kinds of music," he managed. "Unfortunately, I don't have time to listen to it."

"Really?" Angela said with a look of curiosity. "What do you do that keeps you so busy?"

"I'm a cardiac surgeon at Northwestern Memorial," David replied unassumingly. "I arrived a couple of days ago. I just completed my residency at the Cleveland Clinic."

"I'm impressed," Angela responded. "No wonder you don't have time for socializing. It must be great having a career that gives you the ability to help people in such a direct manner."

"It has its moments," David concurred, "but mostly it's a lot of stress.

"I'm an English professor at Columbia College," Angela said. "I like my career—teaching the students and the time off in the summers."

"What about you, Alan? Are you a doctor too?" Mary inquired.

"No, nothing quite so dramatic," Alan said. "I work at the same hospital as Dave—in administration."

"You make it sound like a second-class career," Mary said, grinning. "No need to be modest, Alan. Sounds to me like you have a job that most people would envy."

"Thank you," Alan said, looking down at his drink bashfully.

"I'm also in the medical field," Mary said. "I'm a clinical psychiatrist."

"You must be a very tolerant individual to deal with people that have so many problems," Alan remarked.

"I like helping people," Mary said. "The trick is not to bring your work home with you."

The foursome spent the rest of the evening listening to the excellent music. It reminded David of being at a concert.

"We need to be going now, guys," Mary said after the band concluded their last set. "We enjoyed meeting the two of you. Maybe we'll see you around."

"Thank you for the nice time," Alan said. "Perhaps we can get together again sometime?"

"We'll see," Mary replied.

The look on Mary's face told David that Alan had no chance with her.

He wondered how to proceed with Angela. Her beauty and charm made him feel anxious and nervous. He knew his feelings were irrational—she had done nothing to intimidate him. He couldn't read her though. Did she like him, or was she merely being polite? If he asked for her phone number, would he appear too forward?

Angela gave him a charming smile. "I hope to see you again soon, David. I really enjoyed tonight." She slipped a piece of paper into his hand. He stared at it blankly as she walked away, realizing that she had just given him her phone number.

"Hey, man!" Alan exclaimed a moment later. "You two hit it off, didn't you?"

"I guess so," Dave said. "I didn't think she was interested. I thought she was just being polite."

"That's great, pal. She's drop-dead gorgeous. This must be your lucky day."

Alan's expression fell abruptly, revealing his disappointment. "Unfortunately, I didn't have the same luck with Mary. You know, Dave, 'polite' is not what I was hoping for with her. Oh well, Chicago's a big town, and tomorrow's another day."

Being a member of Dr. Lucas's surgical team proved every bit as stressful and time-consuming as David had imagined. Two weeks passed before he found the time to call Angela. He sat on his bed, staring at the phone on his nightstand, wondering if she would be mad at him for not calling sooner. Then he finally dialed the number.

"Hello. Is this Angela?" he asked tentatively, hearing a female voice on the other end of the line.

"No, it is not," the woman said firmly. "To whom am I speaking?"

"This is David Sholfield. Angela gave me this number. May I please speak to her?"

"One moment, please," the woman said formally.

"Hi, David!" Angela said, picking up the phone a few moments later. "I'm glad you called. I was worried you might have lost my number."

"I'm so sorry," David apologized. "I've been totally swamped at the hospital. Was that your mother on the line?"

"No, that was our housekeeper. She answers the phone when Mom doesn't want to be bothered, which is always. So, how've you been, other than busy?"

"Great! Dr. Lucas gave me some time off this weekend. I was wondering if you like carnivals. There's one not far from the hospital."

"What a nice idea! I would love that. Can I meet you there?"

"Yeah, sure. How about tomorrow evening at eight?"

David arrived at the carnival ten minutes early, thoughts of Angela drifting through his mind as he waited at the front gate. He couldn't wait to see her again. The thought occurred to him that she would make an interesting conversationalist with her detailed knowledge of English literature. But, of course, that was not the important thing. The main thing was how she felt about him. Alan had counseled him not to worry, to be himself—and that if she couldn't accept him for who he was, he was better off without her.

David began recalling his past, beginning with his college years and his subsequent residency at the Cleveland Clinic. He had dated a number of women along the way but had never fallen in love. Looking back, he realized that he had never had any serious communication with any of them. Several had tried, but he had shied away—dating had always been just for fun. For the first time in his life, he desired a more serious relationship, to become more intimately acquainted with a woman. Of course, he couldn't assume that Angela would feel the same way. He would take it nice and slow and enjoy her company without any expectations.

"David. How nice to see you again."

The sound of Angela's voice abruptly roused David from his reverie. There she was, standing there and wearing that beautiful smile of hers. Although dressed in blue jeans and a T-shirt, she looked stunningly attractive. A young man stood beside her, smiling.

"Angela," David said, managing a smile. "It's good to see you too." Once again, he felt intimidated by her beauty. He took a deep breath, brushing aside his feelings of inadequacy, realizing that if she had not wanted to see him again, she would not be here.

"This is Tom Harrison, a friend of mine," she said. "I hope you don't mind that I brought him along."

"No, not at all." Dave masked his disappointment with a smile. Bringing a friend, especially a guy, meant that she was keeping her distance. Or maybe she didn't trust him.

He glanced at Tom. The man was tall—about six feet two—and appeared to be in his mid-twenties. He was very thin and pale, with brown hair and green eyes. Although plain-featured and dressed in casual attire, he radiated an indefinable charisma.

"Angie thought it might be good for me to get some fresh air," Tom said unassumingly.

A myriad of thoughts whirled through David's mind as they entered the carnival. Why was Angela afraid to be alone with him? Was she feeling him out, keeping things strictly on a friendship basis until they became better acquainted, or was she paranoid, scarred by some secret, dark events hidden away in her past?

"Is there any particular ride you prefer, Angela?" David asked politely.

"Oh, yes," she said, her lovely lips parting in a gentle smile. "Definitely the Ferris wheel. Don't you love the way it makes you feel, looking at everything from way up high? It's like being on top of the world."

David stared at her for a moment as a variety of emotions—curiosity, passion, and suspicion—coursed through him. She was definitely something special.

As they walked toward the Ferris wheel, David noted Tom's furtive glances into the crowd. "Is everything okay, Tom?" he asked concernedly.

"Everything's fine," Tom replied in a shaky voice.

As they approached the ride, David noted that Tom continued to stare into the crowd, as if looking for someone he didn't want to see.

When they arrived, David showed the attendant the pass he had purchased at the gate.

"Enjoy the ride," Tom said, glancing at him nervously.

"Nice timing, Tom," David remarked, noting with amusement that he and the attendant had spoken the same words at exactly the same moment.

"It happens to me all the time," Tom said with a frown. "I don't know why."

"Synchronicity," Angela said. "It happens to very bright people. Their subconscious minds seem to know what's going to happen in advance."

"You guys go on ahead," Tom said as the attendant opened the basket in front of them. "I'll take the next one."

David felt uneasy as he sat down in the basket. The close proximity to the strange, beautiful woman made him feel uncomfortable. "This is pretty cool," he remarked, trying to relax. "I must confess, though, I haven't done this since I was a kid."

"It's not really summertime until you've attended a carnival. I attend at least once a year. This was the perfect suggestion."

David felt a gentle tug in the pit of his stomach as the basket lifted into the air and then stopped, allowing Tom to board. He felt an emerging sense of self-confidence. Angela was pleased with his choice for their first date, and Tom's presence, which he had initially assumed would detract from the romantic ambiance of the carnival, was actually a welcome development. It took some of the pressure off.

After everyone had boarded the Ferris wheel, it began to rotate, gradually picking up speed as it lifted them high into the air. David glanced at Angela again, immediately feeling a passionate response as he noted how incredible she looked with the wind blowing through her thick, wavy, black hair. Her pretty lips turned upward in a pleasant smile, and her eyes sparkled with excitement. Just as they reached the top, the lights blinked out and the ride quickly slowed to a stop.

"Oh boy," David said, trying to remain calm. "Looks like the power went out."

"That's okay," Angela said with a grin, appearing unaffected by the unforeseen development. "It gives us more time to talk."

David glanced behind him. In the dim illumination, he saw Tom. He was very pale and seemed frightened, gripping the sides of his basket and trembling while mumbling something in a strange language.

"Is Tom okay?" David asked, looking at Angela with concern.

"I hope so." She glanced backward at her frightened friend. "I was hoping it would do him some good to come out with us tonight. He's been very upset lately . . . His girlfriend has cancer, and he's been spending all of his time visiting her at the hospital."

"I'm very sorry to hear that. I guess this isn't the kind of therapy he needs right now." David noted the distraught look on Angela's face.

"But it's not your fault. You couldn't possibly have known there would be a problem with the ride."

Suddenly the lights came back on and the Ferris wheel began moving again. David turned around and glanced at Tom. Although appearing somewhat shaken, the young man smiled and waved, a relieved expression on his face.

A few minutes later, they exited the ride. On the way out, Dave asked the attendant, "What happened to the power?"

The young man shrugged. "I don't know. Everything was plugged in and no fuses were tripped. None of the other rides lost power. It must have been a fluke."

David turned to Tom. "Are you okay?"

"Yeah," Tom responded listlessly. "I'm sorry. I've been under a lot of stress lately. I think I'd better go home now. If that's okay with you, Angie."

"Sure," Angela replied with a reassuring smile. "Sorry about the problem with the ride. I was hoping the outing would help you relax a little. I didn't expect this to happen."

Angela turned to David. "I'm going to take Tom home. Call me later, okay?"

David called Angela the following Wednesday. Once again, the housekeeper answered the phone. "I'll get her," the woman said noncommittally.

"How's Tom doing?" Dave asked when Angela came on the line.

"I don't really know. I haven't seen him lately. I suppose he's spending all his free time with Joanne."

"His girlfriend, right?"

"Yeah. It's really a shame about her," Angela said. "He's very fond of her. Initially, he made several attempts to date her, but she turned him down every time. Then, strangely enough, a few months later, she had a change of heart and agreed to go out with him. It was like magic like she had discovered something about him that she had previously overlooked.

"After that," Angela continued, "just as they began dating seriously, she came down with lung cancer. That was strange since she'd never smoked. It's been really tough on both of them."

"I'm sorry to hear that. Bad things happen to good people, I guess. Have you guys been friends for a while?"

"It's a long story. Anyway, I'm sorry, David, but I've got to go now."

David thought quickly. He had intended to ask her out, but the timing seemed wrong. Realizing that it would be a long weekend without her, he decided to try anyway.

"I understand, but before you go, would you like to have dinner Friday evening?"

"I'm sorry, but I have plans for Friday."

"No problem," he managed, attempting to keep the disappointment out of his voice. "Shall I call you later?"

"Tell you what. I'm meeting some friends on the beach at Lake Michigan around noon on Saturday. Why don't you join us? I'll email you the directions. And bring your friend, Alan."

Dave tried to mask his elation. "That would be great. I haven't seen Lake Michigan yet. It'll be a treat."

It was a hot summer day, with the sun shining brightly out of a clear, blue sky as David and Alan walked along the beach toward the group of sunbathers.

"Everyone!" Angela announced loudly as they approached. "This is David and Alan."

David noted that there were six people there, merrily chatting amongst themselves, eating and drinking their fill. Coolers and picnic baskets surrounded them. Several large umbrellas jutted from the sand like guardian sentinels, shading them from the sun's burning rays. It was a pleasant, tranquil scene.

"So, this is how you do it in Chicago," David quipped with a grin, noting how ravishing Angela looked in her red-and-blue striped bikini. "I wish I had known you guys back in Cleveland."

"We teachers have a penchant for discovering various methods of occupying ourselves during the summer months," Angela said, laughing. "Anyway, you remember Mary from Curley's. And this is Ann, Becky, Chris, and Brett. They're all faculty members at the college." She smiled. "I see you brought your bathing suits. After you've changed, come and have something to eat."

A short time later, David and Alan returned, clad in bathing trunks.

"Fried chicken," Alan said, licking his lips as they sat down on two lounge chairs under Angela's umbrella.

"The food tastes home-cooked," David remarked as he tasted the savory fare.

"My mom's a good cook," Angela said. "She especially likes having my friends sample her wares."

"Have you heard anything from Tom?" David asked, allowing his gaze to linger on her full lips for a moment.

"Yes. I spoke to him just a few days ago. The incident at the amusement park gave him a pretty good scare. Fortunately, he's okay now."

"I hope you don't mind me saying so, but he seems a little paranoid," David remarked. "What does he do, anyway?"

"He's a professor of American folklore at the college," Angie replied.

"Well, I guess that explains everything," David remarked with a grin. "I guess I shouldn't joke, though," he continued, turning serious. "Tom must be going through a very hard time with his girlfriend. How's she doing?"

Angela frowned. "Not very well, I'm afraid. She's not responding to the chemo. They're going to transfer her to a hospice next week."

"That's too bad."

"I think that's quite enough bad news for one day," Angela said, her face brightening. "You guys finish your meal while I go for a swim."

She turned to Ann. "C'mon, girl. That water looks too good to pass up."

David gave Angela an appreciative gaze, admiring the lovely curves of her body as she ran across the beach.

"I second the motion," Alan remarked, noticing David's interest. "Angie looks drop-dead gorgeous in that bikini, man."

"Hold on, buddy," David said with a grin. "That's my girlfriend you're talking about."

"I don't know if you have the right to call her that just yet." Alan returned the grin. "You've only had one date with her so far, and it was cut short when that guy freaked out."

"Tom didn't freak out. He just got a little nervous when the power went out. His reaction was perfectly understandable, considering the shape his girlfriend's in. Actually, he seems very likable. He's got this compelling magnetism about him. You'll see what I mean when you meet him. And speaking of Angela, I'm totally nuts about her. I don't get the same feeling from her, though. She's not an easy read."

"Women aren't like books, man," Alan said, laughing. "In my humble opinion, she likes you, although I can't figure out why." He gave David a consoling pat on the back. "She wouldn't have invited us if she disliked you. Right, buddy?"

"But that's what I'm talking about, Alan. Both times I've been with her, it's been in a public place, surrounded by her friends, and she has yet to reveal anything about her past, her family, or anything at all, for that matter. It's like she's hiding something."

"What's wrong with a little mystery, my good man? It enhances a woman's desirability, in my opinion. It's not like you've been forthcoming with your family history either."

"Perhaps you're right, Alan. When it comes right down to it, I've been playing the same game, haven't I?"

Suddenly, David's cell phone rang. He listened for a moment, then shrugged his shoulders. "Sorry, Alan. The hospital awaits."

He rose to his feet and walked toward Chris, who was lying on a nearby chaise longue. "Nice meeting you, Chris. Tell Angie I'm sorry I had to leave so soon, okay?"

David walked into the living room of his apartment and threw himself down onto the couch with a sigh. He, along with the other members of Dr. Lucas's team, had just completed a longer than average heart transplant operation, lasting just over ten hours. More than anything, he needed a good night's sleep.

A few minutes later, he forced himself to stand up and trudged into the bedroom. Noting the message on the answering machine on his nightstand, he pushed the play button. "Hi, David, this is Angela. I couldn't reach you on your cell. Alan told me you've been tied up at the hospital, so I asked him for your home number. I hope you don't mind. Anyway, I'm meeting a few friends at Saphira's on Friday evening. I was wondering if you could meet us there around seven. It's no problem if you don't show—I'll assume you're working at the hospital. I'll email you the directions. Hope to see you there, okay?"

Although pleased to hear from Angela, David couldn't help feeling disappointed. Her tone sounded friendly but distant. She hadn't actually asked him on a date but was merely including him in another gathering of her friends. Was she interested in pursuing a relationship, or just being courteous because he was new in town?

David felt a sudden pang of loneliness. The only friend he had met since arriving in Chicago was Alan. David was crazy about Angie, but she made him feel like an outsider—there was no intimacy. Of course, his work at the hospital gave him little opportunity to socialize. He decided not to fall into the trap of self-pity. After all, he had a successful career going and the makings of a relationship with a beautiful woman. She hadn't blown him off yet. He decided to accept her dinner invitation and see where it might lead.

Saphira's was a trendy, elegant restaurant located near Wicker Park, packed with young, affluent professionals. David noted the open ceiling, giving full view to the bronze-painted ductwork and the electric power and gas lines, painted in black. A large fresco decorated the wall above the circular bar, consisting of blue squiggly lines representing the sea and yellow fishes. Although not an art connoisseur by any means, he knew the painting wasn't very good. Across from the bar were rows of spacious tables, complete with blue tablecloths and candles. Potted plants and incandescent lamps hung from the ceiling over the tables, suspended by guy wires.

Angela spotted David as he approached her table, led by a formally-clad hostess, and gestured to the empty chair on her right.

"How nice of you to join us for dinner tonight," she said, giving him a ravishing smile. "In case you don't remember, these are my friends—Chris Skinner, Ann Chandler, Brett Leman, and Becky Goodman."

Although David had met them briefly at the beach outing, it was the first time he had been formally introduced.

Chris was blond and thin, with a cleft chin. His blue eyes tended to wander distractedly when he spoke.

Ann was plain-featured and plump, with jet-black hair, and spoke with an English accent.

Brett was brown-haired and slightly overweight, but not to the point of obesity. He projected a friendly, charming demeanor.

Becky was a cute, dishwater blonde with large, hazel eyes. She appeared moody and high-strung.

"The sushi comes highly recommended," Brett remarked. "It's quite fresh, with decent portion sizes, and it's served with unique-tasting rolls. I'm not sure what they're made from." He abruptly rolled his eyes. "The place has lousy service, though. It takes thirty minutes just to get an appetizer."

"Now Brett," Ann admonished. "Be nice. David has just arrived, and we don't want him getting a bad first impression of our fine Chicago restaurants."

"You don't sound like you're from around here, Ann," David observed, noting her British accent.

"That's true," she replied, grinning. "I'm originally from London. I've lived here for the past ten years, though, so I've become somewhat Americanized."

"She's got a unique mind," Chris remarked with an envious smile. "I wish I had her talent for science. She could make a bundle if she ever worked in the private sector."

"I like molding youthful minds," Ann responded. "Some things are worth more than mere monetary compensation, you know."

"I don't think any of us are doing this for the money," Angela said.

"It's nice of you to join us, David," Chris remarked after the waiter had finished taking David's order. "You're the only one at the table who actually makes an honest living, you know."

"Yeah, it certainly feels that way," David responded. His face abruptly reddened with embarrassment in the ensuing silence. "I, I'm sorry, everyone," he stammered. "What I meant was, I've been putting in a lot of hours at the hospital lately."

Angela pecked him on the cheek. "We all knew what you meant, dear."

David looked down at his plate, attempting to mask his elation. She had actually kissed him! Sure, it was just an informal gesture, but it was the affirmation he had been seeking—that a romantic relationship was in the cards.

"So, David, as a surgeon, you must be somewhat acquainted with death," Becky said. "Do you believe in the afterlife?"

"Now what kind of a question is that to ask our new friend?" Brett gave Becky an admonishing look. "You don't have to answer that, David."

"I plead the fifth," David said, spreading his hands. "Let's just say that I have an open mind." He glanced at Angela. "When I was a teenager, I explored a few theories. One of my early influences was Ralph Waldo Emerson."

"Interesting," Angela responded. "Emerson began as a Unitarian preacher, eventually immersing himself in the exploration of alternative faiths after the death of his wife."

"I remember a little of that," David said. "He was considered a transcendentalist, believing that the outward world is an illusion, that the only reality is that of the mind, similar to Plato's philosophy."

"If he were alive today, he would be considered a pantheist," Angela explained, "believing that the universe is the ultimate focus of reverence, accepting things as they are. He venerated the beauty of nature and believed that paradise could be achieved in the here and now, not just in the afterlife. He accepted nature as his mother, his peace, and his security. He believed in a healthy mind, body, and earth.

If he were alive today, I suppose he would be a great environmentalist." She smiled shyly. "If I may quote the man himself?"

"By all means," David replied.

Angela's brow furrowed in concentration. "A leaf, a drop, a crystal, a moment of time is related to the whole," she began, "and partakes of the perfection of the whole. Each particle is a microcosm, and faithfully renders the likeness of the world...So intimate is this Unity, that, it is easily seen, it lies under the undermost garment of nature and betrays its source in the Universal Spirit...It is like a great circle on a sphere, comprising all possible circles, which, however, may be drawn, and comprise it, in like manner."

"Those are some novel ideas," David remarked. "Emerson seems to be saying that everything in nature is related to some central, creative source of power. I'll have to revisit his writings."

"Pantheism is not a new idea," Chris remarked. "Actually, it's older than both Christianity and Buddhism."

David listened patiently as the professors immersed themselves in a discussion of early religions.

During a break in the conversation, he turned to Angela. "It's interesting to hear a bunch of college professors discuss history and religion, but I'm more interested in learning about your personal history. Did you grow up here in Chicago?"

Angela fixed him with a piercing gaze. "I would prefer to get better acquainted with you before answering those kinds of questions, David. Why don't you come to my place on Sunday afternoon? We can talk then."

"That would be great!" David responded enthusiastically. "I'm off on Sunday—unless I get an emergency call, of course."

Suddenly, he felt exhausted—his hectic work schedule had caught up with him again. "I think I'd better head back to my place and get some rest, Angela. I enjoyed the dinner tonight. And the conversation. Your friends are an interesting group of people."

"I hope to see you on Sunday," Angela responded in a charming tone.

She reached into her purse and pulled out a memo pad. "Here's the address," she said, writing it down.

To David's surprise, after handing him the slip of paper, she gave him a parting kiss on the lips.

# Chapter Two

"Stockman Lake Road," Alan said, reading the sign as David turned the car down the wooded lane. "Isn't Stockman your girlfriend's last name?"

"Now that you mention it—yes," David replied.

"Looks like she's a somebody. There's even a road named after her family. This neighborhood looks very private—there are no other buildings around."

"Which way should I go?" David asked as they approached a fork in the road.

"Turn left. It looks like there's a cottage up there. That must be her place."

Alan whistled as David parked at the end of the driveway. "Will you look at this place?"

A pediment of timber rafters supported by beige stone columns created a delightful front entry to the spacious bungalow. Three cut-stone gables with dormers of varying heights, combined with wood and stone walls, gave it a charming storybook appearance.

"Looks like nobody's home," David remarked. "Maybe I got the date mixed up."

"I don't think so, buddy. I'll bet this is the guesthouse. Let's turn around and try the other road."

David was surprised by the size of the main estate as they pulled into the gated driveway. Built in the renaissance-revival style, the building's balanced, symmetrical façade was very pleasing to the eye. The cube-shaped structure stood three stories tall, featuring a hipped roof topped with balusters and wide eaves of ornamented brackets. Its beige-painted, smooth stone walls were constructed from finely cut ashlar, featuring horizontal banding between each floor. The arched windows on the main floor were trimmed with ornately carved designs. The rectangular second- and third-floor windows were much smaller.

They walked through the center archway—there were three in total—and David knocked on the door. Moments later, they were greeted by a maid who led them through the foyer into a great hall.

David noted the elaborate ornamentation covering the walls, floors, and ceilings, as well as the expensive furniture and accessories. They continued on through a number of other equally stunning rooms, eventually exiting through a pair of tall, French doors into an outdoor patio. The grounds were exquisitely manicured, complete with a large, English garden merging into a thick forest about ten acres away. Angela and her friends were joyfully engaged in a game of croquet in the center of the spacious lawn. He recognized the other guests—Brett, Ann, Becky, and Chris.

"Now I understand why Angie's been keeping me at arm's length the whole time," David said with a grin, squinting in the bright sunshine.

Alan laughed. "You can't really blame her, can you? She didn't want you to know she was loaded until she checked you out."

Angela abruptly dropped her mallet onto the grass and trotted toward them. David noted with appreciating her comely figure as she approached—her firm, full breasts jostling gently under her formfitting, rose-colored blouse; her curvaceous hips swaying from side to side in her tight white jeans; her beautiful, long, wavy black hair gently rippling in the warm summer breeze.

"Welcome, David," she said, giving him a dazzling smile. "I'm so glad you could make it. And it's nice to see you again, Alan."

"I love this place!" David remarked enthusiastically. "Thank you for including me in your plans. Is it yours?"

"It belongs to my parents," Angela replied proudly. "It was built in 1922 by my grandfather after he made his fortune in real estate."

She abruptly grabbed his arm. "Let's join the party, shall we?"

Angela led them to a circular, marble table, shaded by a voluminous, beige canvas umbrella. Tom Harrison was sitting in one of the thickly padded, brown leather lawn chairs.

"Have a seat, guys," she said. "Would you care for refreshments? We have iced tea, pop, and beer."

"Beer for me, please," Alan said.

"I'll have a cola," David said affably. It felt great being outdoors after another long stint at the hospital.

He smiled and turned to Tom. "How've you been? I hope you're feeling better."

Tom nervously looked over his shoulder. "Yeah, I'm okay," he eventually replied, gazing down at the grass. "But I have to watch myself."

David paused for a moment, unsure how to respond to Tom's eccentric behavior. He decided to ignore the cryptic remark. Why risk pushing the man into further paranoia by pressing the issue?

He turned to Angela. "You spend a lot of time with your friends, don't you?"

"I can't think of a better way to spend summer break," she replied brightly.

"You mentioned that this is your parents' place. Are they here?"

"Don't worry, David," Angela replied with a grin. "I didn't bring you here to meet my parents. They're overseas in Italy, hoping to discover some interesting new pieces for the house."

"Have you always lived here?"

"Yes. I love it here. When I was younger, I took vacations around the world, but I'm not interested in traveling so much anymore. Nothing beats home sweet home."

"I've done some traveling too," Tom interjected, interrupting the palpable chemistry developing between Angela and David. "I went to Africa once—the Sahara, of all places. I met some Bedouins there."

"Those are nomadic tribesmen, right?" Alan asked.

"They are. Actually, there aren't many left. Most of them have abandoned their nomadic lifestyles and moved into the cities of the Middle East. I was fortunate to have found one of the few remaining tribes."

"Now that you know something about me, I think it's time to tell me about yourself, David," Angela said, abruptly changing the subject.

"That's fair," David responded evenly. "I was born and raised in Pittsburgh. My father owns an oil service company headquartered there. As a young guy, I spent my summers learning the business, until I realized that I wanted to become a doctor. So, I finally ended up going to medical school."

"An oil service company?" Alan asked, raising his eyebrows quizzically. "Does that mean that you're rich too?"

"No," David replied, laughing. "It means that my parents are."

"I'm surprised you left the family business to spend your time cooped up in a hospital," Alan said. "You could have done some serious traveling working in the oil business, right?"

David responded with a serious expression. "I've always wanted to be a doctor. I like the idea of helping people. The world doesn't need another wealthy business executive."

"That says a lot about your character," Angela said with an approving smile. "Most guys would take the money and run."

"I think the same could apply to you as well," David said, gazing at her affectionately. "Why did you decide to become a college professor?"

"I've always been fascinated with books," Angela replied. "I also like teaching young people."

"Especially those with open minds," Tom said, speaking the words in exact unison with Angela. "It's happening again," he said apologetically, his face turning a shade paler. "The synchronicity."

"Does that happen often?" Alan asked.

"Unfortunately, yes," Tom replied, glancing over his shoulder.

"He has a gift," Angela stated. "It's just hard to find a practical use for it."

"It's quite a nuisance, actually," Tom said.

David noticed the young professor's hands were trembling. He thought about asking what was wrong but decided to refrain.

David turned back to Angela. "It's such a nice afternoon," he said gently. "Would you like to go for a walk? Perhaps you could show me the grounds."

"Maybe later," Angela replied. "It's time to return to my game. Why don't you join us? Have you ever played croquet?"

"When I was a boy," David replied, feeling a heady mix of disappointment and desire. Once again, Angela was giving him mixed signals. If her plan was to arouse his passion, she was definitely succeeding.

"It seems like a very civilized game on the surface," she said, "but it's actually quite cutthroat. Shall we?"

By the time the group finished their game, it was early evening. Although David was enjoying himself, his frustration was mounting. It was becoming increasingly difficult being with Angela in public, with no possibility of intimacy.

"It's time for supper," Angela announced.

David followed Angela and her guests into the formal dining room, noting that it was every bit as elaborate as the rest of the mansion. Two triple-tiered chandeliers hung at either end of the dining table from a lofted, sculpted ceiling. The walls, covered in finely crafted paneling of various woods and cornflower-blue velvet brocade, were adorned with fine wall hangings, paintings, and mirrors. Several large China cabinets stood against them, engraved with a variety of glyphs and carvings. A long, rectangular walnut table rose from a hydrangea-purple carpet, partially covering a champagne-colored hardwood floor.

"Please sit with me, David," Angela said in a gentle tone.

"All right," David replied, her sensual expression eliciting a renewed surge of passion. He was surprised at her abrupt change in demeanor. The woman was as perplexing as a Chinese puzzle box.

After several servers—pleasantly attired in rose and purple-flowered aprons—finished serving the first course with skill and efficiency, Angela stood from the table and made a toast.

"I would like to thank my good friends for spending the day with me. I hope you are having an enjoyable time. If you need anything, please feel free to say so." She glanced at David and smiled. "I hope the main course—surf and turf—is palatable to everyone."

"It reminds me of being back home," David replied with a grin, pushing his roiling emotions aside. "It's been a while since I've partaken of the finer amenities. I guess I've become used to fending for myself."

"Then I'll just have to see that you receive your proper nourishment," Angela said.

David's heart fluttered as he realized she was alluding to a more serious relationship between them. It wasn't the first time a woman had made her intentions known, but this time, instead of resisting the possibility of a deeper commitment as he had done in the past, he embraced it. The prospect of spending the rest of the summer with Angela was sublime.

"So, tell me, David," Brett said, smiling hospitably. "Have you given pantheism any more thought?"

David gleaned from Brett's demeanor that the man was aware of the budding romance between Angela and David. He quickly glanced around the table, noting the expressions and mannerisms of her friends—and they all knew.

"To be honest," David replied, "I've been so busy at the hospital, I haven't had time to study it."

"Actually, like Emerson, Henry David Thoreau was also considered a transcendentalist during his day," Angela said.

"I'm afraid I've forgotten the meaning of the term," David said.

"Transcendentalism was the name given to several philosophical ideas that emerged in New England around the mid-1800s," Angela explained. "The fundamental idea was the existence of an ideal spiritual state, transcending the physical. The transcendentalists were at odds with the established religions of their time. Have you read any of Thoreau's works?"

"Sorry," David replied. "It sounds interesting, though."

"I highly recommend his book Walden. It's his best-known work, based on an experiment he embarked upon called 'simple living.'"

"Simple living," David repeated with a chuckle. "I could use some of that."

"He lived for two years in a small house," Angela continued, "which he built himself on land that his mentor—Emerson—owned near Walden Pond. He lived completely independent of society—growing his own food and so on. I can lend you a copy from my library if you like." She gave him an alluring smile. "I will be your private tutor."

"And I will be your star pupil," David remarked, feeling the thrill of romantic expectation cascading through him like a waterfall spilling out of a mountaintop. There was no mistake about it — Angela had made her intentions clear.

The friends spent the rest of the meal discussing philosophy and literature, then dessert was served.

"There's something to be said for simple living," Tom remarked, lifting a forkful of cheesecake toward his mouth.

David gave him a look of concern. Tom's countenance was very pale and his hand was shaking. "It sounds like you're speaking from experience," David remarked.

Tom slowly lowered the fork to his plate. "I lived in my parents' cabin in the mountains of West Virginia for a while," he replied in a wavering voice. "It was quite thought-provoking, actually."

David thought he saw a fleeting shadow pass over Tom's face as he spoke. Suddenly, Tom's wineglass toppled over, spilling red wine onto the white tablecloth and giving it a blood-soaked appearance.

"Leave me alone!" Tom abruptly wailed, covering his eyes with his hands. Then he stood from the table and ran out of the room.

"Oh dear," Angela said. "I think Tom's having a nervous breakdown. Joanne's death has been really hard on him."

"Her death!" David exclaimed in surprise.

"It happened quite suddenly," Angela replied as she stood from the table. "He doesn't want to talk about it. That's why I didn't mention it earlier. I'd better go see if he's okay."

"I can perfectly understand his erratic behavior," Becky remarked as Angela left the room. "If I were in love with someone as much as he was with Joanne, you'd have to call the men in the white suits."

"I had no idea about his girlfriend," David said with a frown. "The poor guy's suffering through a terrible tragedy. By the way, did anyone notice his wineglass?"

"What do you mean?" Ann asked. "We all have wine glasses."

"Never mind," David said with a shrug. "It's nothing."

"I think that's my cue," Chris said, yawning. "I have a skydiving lesson in the morning."

"That's a little quixotic for a college professor," David remarked.

"Actually, it's my first attempt," Chris responded with a grin. "It's high time I break out of my cloistered shell before I was any older. Would you care to join me?"

David hesitated. "I don't know. I'm really not into exotic sports."

"Chicken," Ann taunted. "Tell you what. If you go, I will too. A daring adventure never hurt anyone."

"Why don't we all go?" Brett asked with a mischievous grin. "It's time to shake off the stodgy professor stereotype."

"Count me in," Becky said.

After writing down directions on a napkin, Chris stood from the table. "See you at the airport, everyone. Seven o'clock sharp."

"I had a nice time today," David said to Angela after everyone had left. He felt a rekindled sense of passion as they stood in the doorway—it was the first time they had been alone together. Although his desire for her was very strong, he was unsure how to proceed, afraid that she would think him too forward if he kissed her. "I'll call you soon, okay?" he said, smiling.

As he took the first step away from her, Angela grasped his arm. "Please stay," she said with an inviting smile.

"Thanks for meeting me here tonight," Alan said as David sat down at the table across from him. "I think both of us need to get away from the hospital for a while."

"That's for sure," David said with a sigh. "The last two weeks have been a tough haul. No disrespect intended, but I really miss Angie."

"I completely understand," Alan said with a chuckle, "but that's what friends are for, right? You need someone to cheer you up while she's away, celebrating her parents' return on their family yacht."

David glanced around the nightclub, Blue Sunday, noting how the large disco panels filled the trendy room with soft, blue light. Everything was glowing: the blue plastic strips bordering the dark grey, tiled ceiling, the pillars of stacked blue and grey plastic donuts rising from the shag carpeting at irregular intervals, and the white, cube-shaped plastic bases of the smoked-glass tabletops.

Complete with spherical-shaped plastic chairs, the place gave David the impression of the interior of an ultramodern spaceship. He noted the sad violin music emanating from the ceiling speakers, evoking feelings of loneliness—as if he was stranded out in deep space, far removed from his family and friends. "I miss her, Alan," he said with a melancholic expression. "If you're trying to cheer me up, why did you choose a sad place like this?"

"The reason should be obvious," Alan replied, smirking. "Look at those two hotties over there. I think they're on the prowl."

David glanced in the direction of Alan's gaze and beheld two young women — a strawberry blonde and a brunette — both clad in low-cut, silk blouses revealing their cleavage. Their skirts were very short and very tight. "I get the picture," he said with a chuckle, "but I'm no longer on the market."

Alan grinned. "So, you finally made it with Angie. I'll bet that was sweet."

"I can't believe it," David said. His eyes held a faraway expression. "She was so passionate and sensual. It was scary, in a way."

"Really!" Alan exclaimed. "Since when is a doctor scared of the human body?"

"I can't explain it. It was like she was starved for sex. She wouldn't stop. I finally had to ask her to quit."

"That's amazing! No wonder you've been acting so tired lately. Who would have ever expected that kind of behavior out of an English professor?"

"Yeah, she took me completely by surprise. She gave me a copy of the Kama Sutra and told me to start studying. She said she's going to test me on the material."

"Apparently, she teaches more than English," Alan said, laughing. Then his expression turned serious. "I wish I had your luck with the ladies, buddy. It's been very lonely around here lately."

"I can relate," David said with a sympathetic expression. "Why don't you hook up with one of Angie's friends? How about Becky? She's a cute gal."

"She wouldn't give me the time of day, man," Alan said with a scowl.

"How do you know that? Have you even tried? The trouble with you, Alan, is that you don't give yourself enough credit. You're a smart guy with a great job. I'll bet Becky would agree to a double date. I'll set it up with Angie. What do you say?"

"Maybe you're right. I just need a little self-confidence. Let's do it, man."

David watched with interest as the strawberry blonde from the adjacent table stood up and walked toward them, her bountiful breasts - obviously artificial - bouncing with every step. "How would you guys like to join us for a drink?" she asked in a confident tone. She stared unabashedly at Alan, giving him a friendly smile.

David and Alan exchanged glances. "Can you give us a minute?" David replied.

"Certainly," she said.

David noted Alan following her with his eyes as she returned to her table, her hips swaying provocatively from side to side as she walked.

"Well, what do you know?" Alan remarked, his features brightening with optimism. "I think she likes me."

"I told you there's nothing wrong with you, man," David said. "You just have to believe in yourself. By the way, are Chicago women always that forward?"

"Not that I'm aware of, but my dad always told me that there's a first time for everything."

"Before we meet the ladies," David said with a serious expression, "there's something I want to talk to you about."

"I understand," Alan responded with a perceptive smile. "You want to be true to Angie. I don't mind—really. I can handle this one on my own."

David grinned. "I'm glad to hear it—but that's not what I meant. Do you remember what happened at Angie's place at the dinner party?"

"You're talking about Tom, right?"

"Yeah. Every time I've been with him, something strange has happened. The first time I met up with Angela was at a carnival. She brought Tom along. When we rode the Ferris wheel, the power went out. I thought it was strange that none of the other rides were affected. I noticed that sometimes when Tom spoke, he would say the same exact words at the same time as someone else. It happened over and over. Angela called it 'synchronicity.'"

"Yeah, I remember reading about that in my psych class," Alan said. "The term was invented by Carl Jung. He called them 'meaningful coincidences.' It's like you dreamed about something, let's say a car—a classic Corvette, for example—and just as you're discussing the dream with a friend, the exact model you're describing drives right past you. Jung would say that you're running away from, or afraid of something. Maybe you're afraid to face the truth about yourself. The philosophical theories behind it get pretty deep."

"It sounds like it," David said. "Anyway, it was strange to see it happen with Tom, but what happened at Angie's place was even more puzzling."

"You mean his outburst at the dinner table? He acted extremely paranoid—like he thought someone was trying to harm him. Maybe his girlfriend's death pushed him over the edge."

"Maybe, Alan, but that's not what I'm talking about. When he was telling us about his parents' cabin, I thought I saw a shadow move across his face—like something passed in front of him. Of course, I could have imagined that. But I certainly didn't imagine his wineglass toppling over. His hands were nowhere near it when it happened. I've been unable to come up with an explanation."

"I would say a moth or some other small insect could have easily produced the shadow," Alan said. "They can dart around very quickly when they want to. As for the wineglass, he could have pulled on the tablecloth and toppled the glass."

"I thought of that, but I distinctly remember that his hands were resting on the edge of the table."

"He could have pulled it with his knees."

"True, but unlikely."

"And what's more likely?" Alan said, giving his friend a skeptical grin. "That he used telekinesis to tip it over? Or that a ghost did it? Come on, man. You're kidding, right?"

"Yeah, I see what you mean. There must be a rational explanation." David yawned and glanced at his wristwatch. "I don't mean to keep you from your next conquest, buddy. Go meet your new girlfriend. I'm going home and get some shut-eye."

"You're welcome to stick around," Alan said, grinning. "I think things are going to get interesting."

"See you at the hospital," David said, standing from the table. "By the way, this sad music is giving me the creeps."

# Chapter Three

"Hi, Angela," David said, picking up the phone on the first ring. "How was the homecoming party with your parents?"

"Hi, David. I had a wonderful time. It's the first time I've been on the yacht since last summer. The lake's sensational this time of year."

"How are your parents?"

"I told them about us, and they're dying to meet you."

"I guess the time has finally come to meet the parents," David said, chuckling. "I hope they won't be disappointed."

"Not at all. Dad thinks it's great what you're doing at the hospital."

"I'm relieved to hear that. My doctor's income is well below his pay grade."

"My parents don't judge people by the size of their bank accounts, and neither do I."

"That's good to hear. I really missed you these last two weeks. I had such a wonderful time at that dinner you threw at your parents' house. I especially enjoyed the dessert."

"I miss you too, honey," Angela responded in a sultry tone. "Have you been reading that book I gave you?"

"Oh yeah. Are you ready to test me on what I've learned?"

"That's the first time I've ever had a student actually ask to take a test, but yes, I think that can be arranged."

David was surprised by his passionate response to the sensual tone of her voice. "So, when can you schedule me in?"

"How about Wednesday evening? I've been invited to a Fourth of July party and I need a date. Can you come?"

"I think so. Dr. Lucas doesn't schedule procedures on holidays as a rule. Is it a formal affair?"

"Yes. A European duke is throwing it, and the mayor will be there, along with my parents. It will be the perfect opportunity to meet them. Meet me there at eight, and don't forget to wear a tux, okay?"

David jotted down the directions and hung up feeling euphoric, completely enamored by the lovely, young woman. She had known exactly the right words to say to excite him into a state of arousal. He couldn't wait to see her again. It was especially comforting to know that she trusted him enough to introduce him to her parents—a sign their relationship was getting serious. He had never derived such satisfaction from a romantic relationship. He wondered if it was merely delayed gratification, or something real. He couldn't wait to tell Alan.

Duke Revic's mansion was much smaller and much newer than Angela's—about six thousand square feet by David's estimation. Grayton Hall, as it was named, was constructed in a contemporary, European style—complete with five gables—featuring a wide stone entry and a front courtyard that included a sculptured fountain.

A butler led David through the foyer into the great room. "Dr. David Sholfield," he announced formally as they entered.

David noted the interior. It was also contemporary, including a two-story cathedral ceiling and walls of pastel grey textured plaster with white trim. An off-white carpet with tiny, grey rectangles printed in a symmetrical design covered the entire floor, and a white painted stone fireplace jutted from the left wall. Four seal-colored suede reclining sofas were positioned around a large, lavishly carved java-colored cocktail table. The walls were adorned with fine paintings.

Angela, who was seated with her parents on one of the sofas, smiled and waved.

"It's good to meet you, David," Angela's father said as he stood and extended his hand. "I'm Timothy Stockman, and this is my wife, Gloria."

"Pleased to make your acquaintances," David said, firmly grasping Angela's father's hand. Angela's parents appeared to be in their early sixties.

Timothy was of average height and build, with a cleft chin and down-turned lips. He retained most of his brown hair, which was flecked with grey. He was smartly attired in a black tuxedo with a one-button peak-lapel jacket and a pleated white dress shirt.

Gloria was slim and trim. Her bleached-blonde hair was coiffed in an up-style. She wore a draped, amethyst evening gown with a high choker neckline and a trapeze-style top. Her former beauty had begun to fade with age. David thought it said something about her character that she hadn't used cosmetic surgery even though she could easily afford it.

"I hear you're new to our fair city," Timothy said.

David glanced at Angela again. She looked stunning in her burgundy cocktail dress, featuring textured pleats in a basket-weave design. A loose, flowing knee-length skirt completed the ensemble. Her beautiful, brown eyes were enhanced by the artful use of makeup, her full lips trimmed with red lipstick. Like her mother, her black hair was set in an up-style, revealing the exquisite contours of her cheekbones and ears. "Yes, I like what I've discovered so far," David responded.

"It's a big city, and there's plenty to do and to see," Timothy continued with a friendly smile, ignoring the innuendo. "The Chicago Cultural Center is a great place to start. They have various art exhibitions, as well as theater, music, literary programs, and dance. There are also many outdoor activities on the lake and elsewhere during the summer months."

"Sounds like I need a tour guide," Dave remarked. "I've managed to get lost on several occasions."

"The River North neighborhood is a must-see," Angela said. "It has outstanding restaurants and nightclubs, and it's only a mile from the lake."

"We must invite you for a cruise on our yacht sometime," Gloria said in a gracious tone. "The lake provides the absolute best view of the Chicago skyline."

Just then, the butler appeared. "Mayor Stevens and Mrs. Stevens," he announced officiously.

David noted Mayor Stevens's personable demeanor, which must have served his political career well over the years. Like Timothy, he wore a black tux, a pleated white shirt, and a bow tie. The lovely Mrs. Stevens—strikingly attired in a silver strapless evening gown with a sweetheart top that flowed down in gentle waves toward her ankles—appeared at least ten years younger than her husband.

"Mayor Stevens! How nice to see you again," Timothy said, giving the mayor a firm handshake. "I was just telling our friend David here about our fine city."

"Nice to see you again, Timothy," the mayor said with an affable smile. "And you too, Gloria. I'm glad to hear the dome restoration project is back on schedule."

"We'll have it ready on time, Mayor," Angela's father stated confidently.

"Your company has never let us down," the mayor remarked with an approving smile.

He turned to David and smiled broadly. "David, what's your occupation, if I may ask?"

"I'm a cardiac surgeon at Northwestern Memorial," David said. Although he had attended parties like this in the past—his father had numerous business dealings with Pittsburgh politicians—he felt nervous meeting the mayor. He cleared his throat. "I recently moved here from Cleveland to begin my practice."

"It's always a pleasure to greet a new resident of Chicago," the mayor said. "I suggest that you sample our many attractions. We're currently having our annual "Summer Dance" festival in Grant Park, with free, live concerts, including musical acts and dancers."

David's initial nervousness faded as Angela's father and the mayor continued extolling the city's wares. He was thrilled at the prospect of spending the next few months exploring the city with Angela.

"Thomas Harrison," the butler announced. David's eyebrows lifted in surprise as he turned toward the entrance. Considering his recent breakdown and his tragic loss, Tom was the last person David expected to see at a stuffy, formal affair.

"Thomas, I'm so glad you could come," Angela said with a gracious smile. She turned to David. "I thought it would be nice to include Tom at the dinner party."

"Good to see you again, Tom," David said, taking the young professor's hand in a firm grip. Perhaps inviting him wasn't such a bad idea. The man could certainly use some cheering.

"My pleasure," Thomas responded with a half-smile.

To his surprise, David observed that Tom appeared to have regained his vitality and confidence. "You look like you've been out in the sun," David said, noting the man's dark tan.

"Yes, I have," Tom said, grinning. "I've been playing some golf. On my doctor's recommendation, of course. I'm feeling much better now."

"I'm very glad to hear that," David said.

The butler returned and announced two more couples—the Riningers and the Krausses.

Shortly after the introductions were made, the host presented himself.

"Hello, everyone," the duke began with an accommodating smile. "For those whom I have not had the pleasure of meeting, I am Duke Vojislav Revic of Horvat, of the Kingdom of Slavania, and this is my date, Leona Goebel. I thank all of you for attending my little gathering this evening."

David noted the man's perfect English and gave the aristocrat a probing stare. The duke was tall—standing about six feet two—and wore his shiny black hair combed to the side. He had the features of a model, with high cheekbones and an aquiline nose.

Young, athletic, and handsome, he looked very charismatic in his single-breasted white tuxedo, complete with satin, black-trimmed lapels. The man was virtually brimming over with vitality.

His date was an attractive young blonde, attired in a skimpy black cocktail dress and adorned with a myriad of jewels.

David glanced at Angela, noting that she was staring at the duke with a fascinated expression. He wondered what she was thinking.

"Follow me," the duke said, smiling cordially. "It's time for dinner."

As the guests arrived at the formal dining room, David took in the excellent craftsmanship of the dining table. Constructed from white ash and oak, it was fashioned in the grand European tradition of elegance, with cabriole legs, bracketed feet, and canted and bowed fronts. A rich, russet, burnished finish gave the tabletop an elegant glow. Twelve matching splat side-chairs and two splat armchairs with purple leather-covered backs surrounded the table. A China cabinet and a curio cabinet stood like guardian soldiers against opposing walls.

The butler showed everyone their seats. The duke sat at the head of the table with his date on his right, followed by the Riningers and the Krausses. Mayor Stevens was seated at the opposite end, with his wife on his right. The rest of the guests—the Stockmans, Angela, David, and Thomas—were seated on the duke's left.

Two female servers clad in white uniforms served the first course—a tasty combination of sautéed mushrooms in puff pastry and shrimp cocktail.

When they were finished, the duke raised his glass. "I wish to offer a toast to my good friends and business associates who have helped bring my country into the twenty-first century.

"First, I would like to thank Walter Rininger for his help in providing the raw materials necessary for the modernization of our infrastructure. My thanks also to Timothy Stockman, who lent his expertise in the development of our commercial real estate. I also wish to thank Jack Krauss for his help in modernizing our technology. Last but not least, thank you to Mayor Stevens for bringing together all the talent.

"It's especially fitting to celebrate the anniversary of your country's independence with you," the duke continued with a broad smile. "I am familiar with the struggles your founding fathers went through in gaining their freedom. My country has also recently been through a similar conflict. Thank you all."

"I studied the region during the Bosnian War," Angela said after everyone had finished applauding. "Slavania—originally a republic of Yugoslavia—lies on the Balkan Peninsula bordering the Adriatic Sea. A year after the Communist Party ended its monopoly of political power, your country, along with five other republics, broke away and declared its independence. It's quite appropriate to celebrate your county's freedom with ours."

"Very good, Angela," the duke said with a complimentary nod. "We lived under Communism for many years, its roots planted in the resistance movement against the Germans during World War II. At the time, it seemed necessary protection to band together against them. Unfortunately, after all the republics in the region broke away, the Bosnian conflict ensued. Slavania has seen its share of wars. Because of external threats, the Slavanian government decided to organize into a constitutional monarchy, to provide a more efficient focus of power than is traditionally found in an aristocracy or a democracy."

The duke smiled brightly. "But that's all in the past. We are currently engaged in building a new republic, with all the liberties and modern amenities you enjoy here in the States.

"I have spoken with your father," the duke continued, turning toward David. "Did you know I invited him to my party this evening? I'm sorry to hear about his illness."

"You know my father?" David asked with a look of surprise.

"Of course. Sholfield Oil has constructed several deep-water oil rigs for us in the Adriatic."

"I remember now," David said. "It was one of the places I visited as a youth. Small world, isn't it?"

He glanced at Angela. She was staring at the duke, her lovely lips curved upward in a half-smile. David abruptly stared at his plate, attempting to suppress a sudden flare of jealousy. Was Angie overly impressed by the duke's refined panache? He quickly relaxed, reminding himself that she had asked him here to meet her parents.

As the meal progressed, David's jealousy returned as he noted the rapt attention Angela paid to the handsome aristocrat as he entertained his guests with Slavanian folklore. He mentally chided himself for his immature reaction. He knew she was merely displaying the polite interest appropriate for a guest attending a sophisticated dinner party.

Eventually, after a traditionally American dessert of cake and ice cream, the duke stood from the table and clinked his wineglass with a spoon. "Now, everyone," he said after gaining his guest's attention. "If you please, let us continue our celebration outdoors."

It was near dark as the guests followed the duke out onto the rear deck. Strings of multicolored lights, glowing pastel-colored globes, and a chamber orchestra—performing on a portable stage adjacent to the patio—enhanced the pleasurable ambiance of the gathering. Several cocktail waitresses carrying trays of drinks and finger foods moved deftly among the guests, catering to their every whim. "Make yourselves comfortable, everyone," the duke said engagingly.

"Are you enjoying the party, David?" Angela asked, concluding a conversation with her parents.

"It's okay," David replied nonchalantly. He felt a sudden twinge of guilt, remembering she had given him no reason to distrust her. It wasn't like him to harbor negative feelings.

"I'm sorry to hear about your father," Angela continued in a comforting tone. "What's wrong with him, if you don't mind me asking?"

"I'm afraid it's serious," David replied with a somber expression. "He's got colon cancer. The prognosis is favorable, though. His doctor caught it early and he's responding to treatment."

David paused, then changed the subject. "It was nice of you to invite Tom. He seems to be doing much better."

"I feel so sorry for him," Angela replied with a sigh. "He's sustained a great loss. He was very much in love with Joanne, and I'm hoping the party will help take his mind off of her for a while."

"That's good thinking on your part. I'll go talk to him. We don't want him to feel left out, do we?"

"That would be a nice gesture, honey."

David felt a thrill of delight at her words, abruptly vanquishing any remaining animosity toward the duke. He smiled and took another sip of his martini. It was a joyous celebration, not only of the birth of a great nation but the beginning of a serious relationship with the woman of his dreams. He realized that for the first time in his life, he was falling in love.

"You mentioned that you enjoy golfing, Tom," David remarked with a grin as he approached the young professor.

"It's no big deal, really," Tom replied. "I thought it would take my mind off of things."

David wondered if it was the right time to bring up Joanne's death. Voicing his concern might evoke a negative response from the high-strung young man. On the other hand, Tom might think him callous if he didn't voice his sympathies. "I was really sorry to hear about your girlfriend," he ventured.

David's apprehensions vanished as Tom smiled. "Yeah, I was really in love with her. I met her a year and a half ago at one of Angie's parties. She was a grad student then. After talking to her a few times, I finally got up the nerve to ask her out. She was really beautiful. I didn't think I had a chance, so it was no surprise when she rejected my advances."

David realized that Tom was sharing his feelings openly. He needed someone to talk to and had chosen David—meaning they had become friends. "I'm surprised that you persisted, especially after being rejected like that," David remarked. "Most guys would have given up. If you don't mind me asking, how did you manage to turn her around?"

"Simple persistence," Tom said with a shrug. "A little faith in oneself doesn't hurt either." He continued, "I'm glad to see that things are working out between you and Angela."

"Yeah," David said, grinning. "I'm crazy about her. I wasn't sure if she liked me at first, but after a few dates, she made it clear that she wanted to pursue a relationship."

"It's amazing how love always finds a way," Tom remarked. Tears abruptly began running down his cheeks. He produced a handkerchief. "Sorry about that," he said, dabbing at his tears. "I seem to cry at the smallest things nowadays."

"It's perfectly understandable," David said with a consoling smile.

Just then a waitress approached. "Would you gentlemen care for a cocktail?"

Tom stared at her for a moment, then he abruptly grabbed a drink from her tray and gulped it down. "Do I know you?" they both said in unison.

Tom's face suddenly turned ashen grey. "Th—they're back," he stammered. His hands began shaking. "Excuse me," he said in a wavering voice. "I need to use the restroom."

David watched in bewilderment as Tom stumbled toward the doorway. Then David turned back to the waitress who was awaiting his order. "I'll have a martini, please."

As David accepted the glass, he spotted Angela engaged in a discussion with the duke. When he noted the expression of pleasurable anticipation upon her face, David's jealousy immediately returned—very strong this time, erupting in a fiery, volcanic explosion of anger.

David downed his drink and slowly walked toward Angela; his eyes glued to the smooth, grey, concrete floor. He frantically attempted to calm himself and find the right words.

"Hi, Angela," he said in a soft tone, masking his roiling emotions. "I'm sorry to intrude, but I think something's wrong with Tom."

Angela turned away from the duke and smiled innocently. "I hope it's nothing serious."

"He's acting strange again, but he seems okay, at least physically."

"That's good to hear," the duke said, facing David. He offered a charming smile. "Please let me know if there's anything I can do."

David felt a sensation of power emanating from the man. It wasn't a frightening sensation: On the contrary, it had a soothing effect, calming his raging emotions. The duke possessed a very compelling charisma. No wonder Angela seemed so captivated by him. "It's probably nothing," David said. "I'm sure he'll rejoin the party shortly."

"Why don't we have a nice talk with my parents, David?" Angela suggested. "It's time for everyone to get better acquainted."

David's jealousy dissipated once again. Perhaps Angela's attraction to the duke was nothing more than idle curiosity. Once again, he mentally chided himself for his adolescent reaction, resolving to be more trusting in the future. He took her by the hand and walked her across the porch.

They spent the better part of an hour conversing. Angela's parents seemed sociable enough, and more importantly, they made David feel accepted. Angela appeared very attentive to his words, giving him tantalizing looks now and then. He breathed out a sigh of relief, feeling their relationship was very much on track.

It was just after ten when the lights abruptly switched off. "Now, my American friends," the duke said in the ensuing darkness. "I have a special treat for you." He clapped his hands. "Let the fireworks begin!"

Suddenly, the surrounding darkness was pierced by the brilliant illumination of rockets as they rose into the air, exploding in bright, luminescent patterns of red, blue, orange, green, and white light, accompanied by loud thunderclaps.

David observed the brilliant, colorful display with amusement. "The duke must have gone all out," he remarked to Angela. "It's quite the professional production."

"This is great!" Angela exclaimed between the loud booms. "I love fireworks!"

David noted her lovely features, highlighted by the multicolored pyrotechnics, filled with childlike excitement. She paused for a moment, and then her expression abruptly changed. Becoming serious, she moved closer and kissed him sensuously on the lips. "And I love you too."

Feelings of transcendent joy cascaded through David's entire body as she revealed her innermost feelings. "I love you too, Angela," he softly proclaimed. He had never felt this way about a woman before, and he wanted to shout it out to all the world.

They briefly kissed again. "Meet me at my guesthouse after the party tonight," she said, giving him a naughty look.

The fireworks never looked better as David watched the grand finale. It was when the lights came on that he noticed Tom. The young professor was groveling on the lawn, his body writhing erratically.

"Don't let them in!" the young man shouted. "Please don't let them in!"

He suddenly stood and pointed to the duke. "It's too late!" Tom yelled. "They're getting in!"

He abruptly fell onto the ground and went into convulsions.

"David!" the duke shouted. "Come here and help me hold him down."

Tom squirmed as the men tried to constrain him. As the minutes passed, he gradually calmed until his body became completely motionless.

David realized that Tom was unconscious. "There's a pulse," David said, holding two fingers to Tom's neck. "I'm afraid he's gone into shock, though. It appears he's been badly frightened by something."

He turned to the other guests who were clustered around them, their faces expressing shock and concern. "Would someone call an ambulance, please?"

# CHAPTER FOUR

"Good to see you, Tom," David said cheerfully as he walked into the hospital room. "How are you feeling?"

"A lot better," Tom replied. "I think they're going to transfer me to the psych ward, though."

David noted a slur in Tom's words. Although his friend had obviously been well-medicated, at least he was rational. "I'm sure there's a reasonable explanation for everything," David said. "You've been through a lot lately. Have you been getting many visitors?"

"No. The hospital hasn't allowed visitors until today. You're the first."

"How about your parents? Do they know what happened?"

"Unfortunately, they've been unable to make the trip. They're both suffering from serious health problems. They're in a nursing home in West Virginia."

"I'm sorry to hear that. If you're ready for company, I'm sure Angela would be happy to visit, along with your other colleagues."

"Come closer," Tom said with a frown. "I want to ask a favor of you," he said softly.

"Sure, Tom." There was no hesitation in David's response—he felt nothing but sympathy for the beleaguered professor. "What can I do for you?"

Tom picked up a binder from the bedside table, opened it, and unclipped a sheet of notebook paper. "My parents have a cabin in West Virginia," he said, handing David the paper. "I want you to go there and get something for me. It's a cedar chest. It's very important to me."

"I would be happy to oblige," David said. He glanced at the paper. Tom had sketched a map on it, detailing the directions to the cabin. "I have a few days off this weekend. I can leave on Friday."

Tom's eyes brightened a little. "Thank you so much," he said. "You'll find the chest in the loft on the second floor."

David drove along the country road, admiring the scenic view of the lush, green forested mountains. West Virginia was beautiful this time of year.

He turned down the side road Tom had marked on the map and proceeded slowly along the dirt surface, swerving from side to side to avoid the larger chuckholes and passing a few cabins along the way.

Eventually, the road ended in a clearing with a solitary cabin standing in the middle of it. David noted the unkempt lawn and shrubbery. Unlike the grounds, however, the farmhouse-style retreat appeared to be in good condition. Split-log siding and a balustrade gave the place rustic charm. The angled roof sloped downward in front of the building, creating a covered porch.

David got out of the car, walked to the front door, and found the key Tom had left under the doormat. Then he opened the door and entered the living room, pausing for a moment to admire the interior. The room was quite beautiful, complete with a barn-shaped ceiling with side windows on the top. The walls, floor, and ceiling were all covered in a natural wood finish. A beige cloth-covered couch and three brown leather recliners formed a semicircle facing the front windows. A large stone fireplace dominated the left wall.

Following the instructions on the side notes of the map, David climbed the stairs, opened the first door on the right, and walked into the second-floor loft. It was too dark to see anything. After fumbling around for a few moments, he found the light switch. He inhaled sharply as the lights came on.

He was standing in an attic bedroom with a low, peaked ceiling. The walls had been painted black. The single window was covered by black silk drapery. In front of the window stood a white-painted wooden altar, rising about four feet off the ground—the top covered in red velvet, with two brass candelabras holding black candles placed at either end. A small, wooden table stood behind it. The floor was covered with strange symbols painted in fluorescent red. In the center was the image of a large, upside-down cross, painted white in a textured weave using intricate brushstrokes. The cross was surrounded by a white, circular border, painted in the same manner.

David felt the hairs on the back of his neck rise. Apparently, Tom was involved in witchcraft of some kind. He suddenly felt an overpowering sense of alarm and fear as if he was witnessing an impending, unpreventable disaster. He realized that there was no rational explanation for the feeling—the décor alone, although certainly strange, was insufficient to have induced such a profound emotional reaction.

Shaking off his apprehension, David walked to the first set of closet doors and opened them. There was nothing inside but an empty clothes rack. The next set of doors opened into a small storage area. The cedar chest was sitting on the floor by itself.

Emboldened by curiosity, David tentatively pulled on the lid with his fingers. It was unlocked, so he peered inside and saw two books. One was bound in leather, and the other was a plain notebook. He opened the leather-bound one first. It was a work of about 150 pages, a combination of writings and strange symbols. The script was unfamiliar to him, so he returned it to the chest and opened the notebook. It was about twenty-five pages in length, written on both sides of each page in the same language as the book, but contained no symbols.

Suddenly, David heard a loud, popping sound. He jumped to his feet and scanned the room. There was nothing there. He closed the chest, ran downstairs, and searched all the rooms, afterward breathing out a sigh of relief that everything was secure. Without hesitation, he quickly went back upstairs, retrieved the chest, and left the premises.

"I can't believe you had me meet you here, Alan," David remarked as they seated themselves at the bar of another trendy nightclub. The Ground Under was a disco bar, packed with racially diverse twenty-somethings and two deejays spinning a variety of hip-hop and techno tunes. A spacious dance floor, complete with state-of-the-art disco lighting, occupied at least half of the club's interior. David estimated that at least fifty people were dancing on it.

"Are you kidding?" Alan remarked. "Look at all the ladies. If I can't meet someone here, I guess I never will."

"What happened to that cute gal at Blue Sunday? She seemed quite interested if I remember correctly."

"Yeah, it seemed that way at first. We stayed till closing and then went out to breakfast. I thought it was in the bag. I don't know what happened, but she seemed to cool off during the meal. I must have said something that offended her. Who knows. She took off afterward without giving me her phone number."

"That's strange," David said, giving his friend a perplexed look. "I got the impression that she really wanted to meet you. But don't take it too hard, buddy. Women can be very difficult to read. I've never been able to figure them out either."

David turned toward the bartender, who was patiently awaiting their order. "I'll have a White Russian, please."

"Draft beer for me," Alan said. "Speaking of women, I finally got up the courage to call Becky."

"That's great. Persistence is the key to success with women, I think. At least some of them, anyway. Did she give you the green light?"

"Unfortunately, no," Alan replied with a discouraged look. "She said she had other plans. She didn't blow me off entirely, though. I'll call her again in a couple of weeks. I don't want to seem too eager. Anyway, how are things going between you and Angie?"

"I can't describe the way she makes me feel," David replied with a faraway expression. "She invited me to a party at some European aristocrat's mansion and we played 'meet the parents.' We really connected; you know?"

"I gather that you guys have lots of sex," Alan said, grinning. "I'm happy for you. It sounds like you really fell for each other. It must be getting serious if she invited you to meet her parents. I was right about her liking you, wasn't I?"

"You know, Alan, I wasn't sure how she felt about me at first, but I guess you were right. It must be love, man. I haven't seen her in two weeks—you know how busy I've been at the hospital lately—and it's driving me crazy. I can't stand being away from her."

"You know, our relationship really came together at that aristocrat's party, but something strange happened. You remember Tom Harrison?"

"How can I forget? He was a really weird dude, man. You know he died, right?"

"What!" David exclaimed. "When?"

"Just a few days ago. I heard it from Becky. She said he had a massive heart attack. The nurse found him curled up in a fetal position with his hands clenched together. Apparently, something had frightened him very badly."

"That's terrible," David said with a frown. "I wonder what could have scared him so. Maybe it had to do with something that happened at the party. It was the Fourth of July and the duke put on a firework show—a very professional display. I think he was trying to impress the guests. Anyway, when it was over, Tom freaked out. I mean, he went totally psychotic. Then he went into convulsions and then into shock. We had to call an ambulance."

"That's not all that surprising, considering he just lost the love of his life," Alan commented.

"Yeah, but here's the thing. The next day, I went to the hospital to visit him—as a concerned friend, you know? He didn't act nuts at all. Maybe the drugs calmed him down. Anyway, when I arrived, he gave me a map of his parents' cabin in West Virginia.

He asked me to go there and get something for him—a cedar chest."

"Really!" Alan remarked with a curious expression. "Did you go?"

"Yeah, I did. He was very adamant about it, and I felt sorry for him, so I agreed to go. When I arrived, I went straight up to the loft where he kept the chest. The place was decorated like the Church of Satan. It looked like he was practicing black magic."

"I'll bet that was a shock," Alan said, taking a long pull on his mug of beer. "It makes sense, though, in a wacky sort of way. He was a folklore professor. Maybe he was casting spells he had learned from his studies. Amazing!"

"He was definitely practicing something very nasty. Anyway, there were a couple of books in the chest. I couldn't understand the language they were written in, though. I was going to ask him about it, but now that he's dead, there's no point. What do you think I should do with the books?"

"Keep em," Alan said unequivocally. "He certainly has no need for them, does he?"

"That's true, but they could be worth some money. One of the books—judging from its antique appearance—could be a collector's item."

"You could contact his family and ask if they want them."

"That's problematic. Tom is an only child, and his parents are in a nursing home with serious health problems."

Alan grinned. "In that case, you have become the proud owner of two books of dubious value."

Then Alan's expression abruptly turned serious. "You know, David, you could ask Angie to have them translated. There must be an etymology or a linguistics professor at the college."

"Good idea," David said, finishing his drink. "I need to call her again anyway. We've been playing a lot of phone tag lately." He turned to the bartender. "Another round, please."

The next day, David called Angela. "Hi, sweetheart," he said when she came on the line. "It's good to finally be talking to you. I know it's only been two weeks since the party, but it feels more like two years. How are you?"

"Fine," Angela said indifferently.

David was surprised at her lackluster response. "Are you feeling okay?"

"Yeah, I'm okay," she replied after a longer pause. "Just a bit distracted. Do you remember my parents' invitation to go boating?"

"Yeah, I've been looking forward to it. Your parents are great, by the way. They treated me very well at the party."

"They like you too, David. Anyway, we were wondering if you would like to join us Saturday afternoon?"

"I'm sorry, Angie. I would love to, but I'm on call this weekend. How about a rain check?"

"I'll let them know," Angela replied with a sigh.

There was another pause. David thought quickly. This wasn't going as smoothly as he had anticipated. He wanted to see her before returning to work on Friday, but she sounded unwell. Perhaps she was just tired. "I know it's rather short notice, but how about dinner tomorrow evening?" he ventured.

"I guess that would be okay."

David experienced a profound sense of relief. "I hope you don't mind, but could you choose the restaurant? I haven't had time to familiarize myself with the area yet."

"Well, that's not the most romantic invitation I've ever received, but I suppose I can accommodate your request." She sighed again. "Pick me up at seven and we'll take it from there. I'm sorry, I have to go now."

"I love you," he said. The only thing he heard was a click as she hung up the phone.

On Thursday evening, David handed the keys to the valet and listened to Angela explain her restaurant choice as they walked toward the entrance. Charlie Crocker's, he learned, was the namesake restaurant of a well-known Chicago chef. Located in the Lincoln Park area, it was regarded as one of the finest eateries in the world. The restaurant was the celebrity chef's idea of creative fine dining, featuring French and Belgian cuisine, with prices to match.

As the couple entered, a formally clad host led them into one of the restaurant's four unique dining rooms. The interior was decorated in an elegant but subdued style, with golden wallpaper, red carpeting, and white tablecloths. A small vase of freshly cut flowers decorated each table.

"Charlie's features three wine cellars," Angela remarked as they opened their menus. "I'm sure we can find exactly what we want here."

"I've eaten in fine restaurants before," David remarked, perplexed at the detailed description of the entrées, "but these menu items are quite different from the norm. Do you have any suggestions?"

"Do I have to make all your decisions?" Angela remarked with a look of annoyance. "Where's your spontaneity? Go out on a limb for once and try something different. By the way, no matter what you choose, it will be good for you—all the food is organic."

"I suppose you're right," David replied with a grin, ignoring her reprimand. "I'll try the lamb rack with chanterelles and fermented black garlic."

After their orders were taken and committed to memory by a waiter, a sommelier appeared and helped the couple select the proper wine for each course.

Afterward, David gave Angela an affectionate smile. "Do you realize that this is our first real date?"

"I hadn't really thought about it, but I suppose you're right." She paused for a moment. "Did you hear about Tom?" she asked, changing the subject. "It's such a shame that his life was taken so suddenly."

David paused and stared at his date. Angela looked ravishing in her sheer, champagne-colored evening gown. Her lovely, brown eyes sparkled brightly in the incandescent lighting, her full lips puckering sensuously as she sipped her wine.

"I saw him a few days before he died," David finally responded, looking down at the table with a sad expression. "He asked me to travel to his parents' cabin in West Virginia to pick up a cedar chest for him."

"That's interesting," Angela remarked with a curious expression. "Did you go?"

"Yeah. The chest was stored in a loft on the second floor. The place looked really weird. I think he was practicing black magic. Unfortunately, he died before I had a chance to give him the chest."

"Wow!" Angie exclaimed. "He never told me he was into witchcraft. How interesting." She abruptly pouted. "I wish you would've told me about your little escapade. I would have loved to accompany you." Then she gave him a provocative smile. "We could have had such a nice time together in the mountains."

David felt his heartbeat accelerate, his body responding to her innuendo. "I tried to reach you, but you never returned my call, honey."

"So, what did you find in the chest?" Angela asked eagerly.

David noted once again how quickly her demeanor vacillated between adult maturity and childlike innocence. "Just a couple of books—one of them looked very ancient and valuable, and the other was just a regular notebook. I don't know what's in them . . . I think they're written in a foreign language. I was wondering if you could have one of the language professors at the college translate them."

"I would love to," she said with a smile. "That would make up for your un-chivalrous conduct lately."

"What do you mean, dear?" Once again, David struggled to read her. The continuous changes in her demeanor unsettled him. He wondered if she was still in love with him.

"You know, David," Angela said with a look of exasperation, "you really haven't provided the proper romantic treatment a lady deserves from her beau." As he began to respond, she held up her hand.

"When courting a lady," she continued, "a gentleman must always strive to develop an expectancy—acting in ways that promote passionate feelings of desire and affection within her heart. Unfortunately, you have not been conducting yourself in such a manner."

David felt a keen sense of regret as she spoke. She was reprimanding him for his ungentlemanly behavior, like a schoolteacher scolding a wayward student for his lax study habits. "I feel duly chastened," he said, attempting a smile. "Let me make it up to you."

"I don't know," she responded. Her tone was decidedly unsympathetic. "You must realize that you've been somewhat of a bore lately. You never do anything surprising—I've received neither gifts nor flowers. You haven't even bothered to plan a successful date, and—most troubling thing all—I've received no love letters. Not a single one! How do you expect me to respond when you have utterly failed to demonstrate your ardent desire for the woman you profess to be in love with?"

"I—I really don't know," David replied lamely. Her reproof had caught him completely off guard. He realized that she had a point. He hadn't done anything to demonstrate his love for her. All he had done was say the words, and talk is cheap. He had been taking her love for granted.

"Is that all you can say for yourself?" Angela asked with a look of irritation. "The evening has become quite boring," she said, abruptly standing from the table.

"I'm so sorry," David said, tears welling up in his eyes. "I had no idea you felt that way, but you're right—I've been a total bore. I promise I will change that immediately, okay?"

She turned away without a reply and headed for the exit.

David followed her outside. "At least let me give you a ride home," he said earnestly as they reached the curb.

"That won't be necessary," Angela replied in a firm tone. "I'll catch a cab." She suddenly turned and stared at him. "Tell you what. Give me those books and I'll see about having them translated. Do you have them with you?"

"They're in my car."

"I'll wait for you in the cab," she said as one pulled up to the curb.

"Okay. I'll be right back."

A minute later, David returned with the books.

"I'll call you when I find out something," Angela said in an impersonal tone.

David let out a sigh as the cab pulled away. At that moment, it seemed their relationship was on shaky ground at best. She hadn't blown him off completely, though. It was their first argument, he reasoned, and all couples had them from time to time. He made a silent vow to do everything in his power to make amends.

David walked into his apartment, turned on the lights, and stared at the living room in dismay. The place had been ransacked. Every piece of furniture had been overturned, and the television and stereo had been dismantled.

He ran into the bedroom, finding it in the same state of disarray. The mattress and box spring had been upended and were leaning against the wall. Every item of clothing had been pulled out of the dresser drawers and closets and lay strewn about the floor.

The guest bedroom and kitchen were in the same disheveled state. Nothing had been spared. It was obvious that someone was very intent on finding something. He ran to the phone and called the police.

Fifteen minutes later, he heard a knock on the door. "I'm Detective Scott," the officer said as David opened the door a crack. "Mind if I come in?"

"Please." David opened the door after the detective displayed his badge.

Detective Scott was a large man—standing about six feet three—with a stocky build, brown hair, and hazel eyes. He was dressed in a wrinkled, grey suit, a white shirt, and a blue and white striped necktie.

"Same as the others," he remarked after scanning the living room. "It looks like a professional job. Whoever did this was thorough. Let me see the other rooms."

David led the detective from room to room, watching silently as he made his inspection.

"I'm going to have the place dusted for prints," the detective said after concluding his examination. "I doubt if anything will turn up, though. Is anything missing?"

"Not that I know of," David replied. "Earlier, you mentioned that my apartment is the same as the others. What did you mean by that?"

"There's been a series of break-ins," the detective replied, pulling a notepad out of his jacket pocket. "That's why the captain put me on the case. All of the victims' places were searched in the same manner."

"Can you tell me the names of the other victims?"

"I guess there's no harm in that," the detective replied. "Nothing was stolen from them either. Do you know a man by the name of Brett Leman?"

"I do," David said animatedly. "I think I know who the other victims are."

"I appreciate any further information you might have," the detective said.

"How about Chris Skinner, Ann Chandler, Becky Goodman, or Angela Stockman?"

"Looks like we have a connection," the detective replied. "We received calls from all of them. I take it you're all acquainted."

"Yeah. They're professors at Columbia College. They hang out together on summer breaks. As for me, I'm new in town. I just started my medical practice at Northwestern a couple of months ago. I met Angela at a nightclub, and she introduced me to her friends."

"Someone believes one of you possesses something valuable," the detective said, "but they don't know who, so they searched all of your places. The perp must want something very badly to take that kind of risk. Do you have any idea what he or she might be searching for?"

An image of the cedar chest abruptly flashed into David's mind. He was about to tell the detective but decided against it—and he didn't have the books anyway. "No, I can't think of anything offhand. I never keep valuables lying around my apartment."

"If you think of anything, give me a call," the detective said, handing David his card. "I would advise staying clear of the others for a while—for your safety. You understand?"

"Am I in danger, Detective?"

"Just a precaution," he replied as he walked towards the door. "I'll be in touch."

David disconsolately followed Alan into the nightclub. The Funky Zen was another one of his friend's offbeat nightspot choices, located west of the River North gallery district. Renovated from a defunct factory, it blended in with the surroundings. There was even a rusted iron Buddha mounted on the steel front door.

Once inside, however, David found the interior pleasantly contemporary. The ambiance was distinctly seductive.

The floor space was sectioned off into dens featuring black leather and faux leopard-skin couches, mural-covered walls, lots of candles, and several unique antique fixtures. Alan explained that they had been salvaged from an old church.

A small gathering of yuppies and hipsters swayed and jostled to the hip-hop selections of the deejay on a spacious, well-lit dance floor.

The friends seated themselves on one of the couches and ordered drinks from a scantily-clad waitress. "The service here isn't bad," David remarked.

"I'll say," Alan said, eyeing the waitress appreciatively as she walked away. "Look at that pair of legs."

"Judging from your remarks, I'm guessing that you're still devoid of a girlfriend," David said with a grin.

"I guess it doesn't take a clinical psychologist to analyze that one," Alan responded glumly, his eyes continuing to scan the room. "I'm not giving up just yet, though," he said, smiling. "Check out the hotties on that couch over there. The blonde's giving you the eye."

"You know, Alan, the way I've been feeling lately, I might just take you up on that," David said with a melancholic expression. He glanced at the women and looked back at Alan. "You know, I haven't seen Angie since our dinner date last month. She's driving me crazy."

"Relax, man, and tell your good buddy what happened," Alan said, flashing his well-rehearsed smile at the ladies.

"She took me to this fancy restaurant and we had an argument. She said I wasn't romantic enough, that I was taking her for granted. She was expecting a chivalrous courtship, you know, with flowers, unexpected surprises, love letters—that kind of thing. But I never did any of that. She seemed very disappointed."

"Something about that doesn't quite add up," Alan remarked. "When you first met, did she ever mention that she liked presents? Did she ever hint about desiring special attention?"

"I can't remember her mentioning anything like that. She gave me a copy of the *Kama Sutra*, though. I should have taken that as a hint. She wanted me to romance her, and for some reason, I failed to catch on." His eyes moistened. "She finally resorted to giving me suggestions about how to treat her," he said, his voice wavering. "I really muffed it, Alan. I think I've lost her."

Just then, the waitress arrived with their cocktails. "Keep 'em coming, honey," Alan said, giving her a wink and a ten-dollar tip. The waitress smiled and returned the wink.

"It's okay, man," Alan continued. He took a sip of his martini. "She hasn't broken it off, has she?"

"Not officially, but she won't return any of my phone calls."

"Perhaps that's not so surprising. Think about it—Angie's a beautiful, high-bred intellectual. She's used to being pampered, and when she's not treated in an accustomed manner, her teacher mentality kicks in. She's not breaking up with you, she's instructing you how to court her properly. Otherwise, she would have broken it off by now."

He paused and took another sip. "I don't think she'll answer your calls until you prove yourself," he continued. "My advice is to send her some love letters—really mushy ones, you know? I'll bet she writes you back."

"I've already tried that," David said dejectedly. "She hasn't answered any of them. I've even sent her gifts and flowers, but they were all returned."

"That's downright cold," Alan said. "I guess that blows my theory out of the water. You know, buddy, I hate to say it, but you need to have a face-to-face with her and find out what's going on. She owes you that much."

Alan paused in thought for a few moments. "I have an idea," he said, his expression brightening. "How about this: You show up at her parents' house unannounced and demand an explanation."

"I don't know," David said skeptically. "Don't you think that's a little risky? They could have me thrown off the premises for trespassing."

"Come on, man. What are they going to do—have you arrested and thrown in jail? You need to go over there. I'm not kidding. Otherwise, you'll never know how things might have turned out. And when you see her, lay it on really thick. Put a guilt trip on her by telling how miserable you've been without her. You never know. It might stir up some lingering tender feelings for you. She might agree to date you again. You know—a sympathy date."

"I see your point," David said, downing his drink. "Tell you what. I'll go over there on one condition: that you come with me. That way, if I get thrown in jail, I'll have someone to keep me company."

"What are friends for?" Alan said, laughing. "You know, buddy, I'm no good at all those complicated dating rituals either. I just want a woman who gets down to business—no pretenses." He glanced at the two women at the adjacent table. "I think the ladies over there want to meet us. It's time to check them out."

"I don't think so," David said, managing a wan smile. "I'm still in love, remember? I don't want to blow my chance at salvaging my relationship with Angie, slim as it might be."

"I take your point," Alan said with a shrug. "I guess I can meet up with the ladies later. They don't look like they're going anywhere."

Just then, two young men approached the women. After a brief conversation, they stood up and accompanied the men to the dance floor.

"Looks like I struck out again," Alan said with a disappointed expression.

# CHAPTER FIVE

David strode up to the front door of the Stockman mansion and rang the doorbell. After a few moments, the door opened. "May I help you?" the maid said in a formal tone.

"Is Angela here?" David asked deferentially, attempting to mask his anxiety.

"I'm sorry, she's not, David," the maid replied with a congenial smile. "Try the guesthouse."

"That was easy, now, wasn't it?" Alan said with a grin as she closed the door.

"I must have scored some brownie points with the maid," David replied.

"That means you're still in with her parents. Perhaps they can persuade her to give you another chance."

"Let's walk to the guesthouse, okay?" David said as Alan began walking toward the car. "I could use the exercise."

"Since when do you care about exercise? Wait a second, I get it . . ." Alan said, his eyes narrowing. "You don't want Angie to know we're here. You want to check up on her."

"She's been acting very strange lately," David said, frowning. "Let's see what she's up to."

A few minutes later, they arrived at the bungalow. From his previous visits, David knew there was a bedroom inside the front left corner of the guesthouse. Angela used it as her private reading room.

After silently motioning for Alan to follow, David walked quietly up to the window and peered inside. He inhaled sharply. Angela was seated on the bed with Duke Revic. They were kissing passionately.

As David struggled to maintain his composure, he noted that both the leather-bound book and the notebook were lying on the desk across from the bed. He motioned for Alan to have a look.

Alan looked through the window for a moment, then quickly backed away. "They're leaving!" he said in a frantic whisper.

The two friends ran into the woods, hid behind some trees, and watched as the couple walked arm in arm out of the cabin and entered the brand-new black Mercedes parked in the driveway.

As Angela and the Duke drove away, David turned to Alan with a tear-streaked face. "I can't believe she did this to me," he said in a shaky voice. He fell to his knees and began sobbing.

"I'm really sorry, buddy," Alan said, giving his friend a sympathetic look. "What do you say we head back into town and find a nice little watering hole? The drinks are on me."

"Thanks, Alan, but not just yet," David said firmly, pulling himself together. "I want to go inside. Remember those books I told you about from Tom's cabin?"

"Yeah. What about them?"

"I saw them sitting on the desk in Angela's study. I'm going inside to get them."

Alan's face suddenly turned pale and he began trembling. "I, I don't think that would be a good idea," he stammered.

"What the heck's the matter with you, Alan?" David asked, noting the frightened look on his friend's face.

"That's breaking and entering, man," Alan managed. He grasped David's wrist. "Can we get out of here, please? I don't like the idea of spending time in a jail cell."

David pulled his hand away. "You can leave if you want, but I'm going inside. I want to know what's so important about those books. I think someone's been looking for them, and I want to know why. What have we got to lose? Angela's parents won't turn us in if we get caught."

Alan reluctantly followed David to the front porch. David tried the door handle, but it was locked. "There must be a way inside," he said. "I'm going to check the windows."

"I can't believe you're actually going to break in," Alan said. He was still trembling.

David snapped his fingers. "I remember now. There's a covered patio in the back. Angie told me she keeps a key stashed under the mat. Maybe it's still there. Wait here."

"Hurry," Alan said. "I don't want to be here when Angie comes back."

A minute later, David returned with the key and opened the front door. When they arrived in the study, David said, "I'll get the books and we can split."

As David walked to the desk, Alan lunged at him, knocking his head against the hard, wooden surface. "I told you to leave the books alone!" Alan shouted. He held David's head firmly against the desktop while attempting to retrieve the books with his other hand.

David pushed on the desk as hard as he could, forcing Alan to lose his balance and fall to the floor.

David jumped on him, using all his strength to keep Alan pinned down as he attempted to work his way loose. In a final effort to subdue him, David punched him in the face and neck.

"Okay, okay—I give," Alan managed, rubbing his neck with his hands. He was still choking from David's blow to his neck.

When David released him, Alan remained on the floor. He put a hand to his nose and then glanced at it, checking for blood. "You almost broke my nose, man," he said, pulling out a handkerchief.

"Tell me what's going on, or I'll put you in the hospital, I swear," David said angrily, holding his fist threateningly over Alan's face.

Alan raised his hands into the air and said, "I promise I won't try anything, okay, man?"

"All right," David replied, backing away slowly, "but you had better start talking."

Alan managed to stand up, then he slowly hobbled to the bed and sat down.

"Okay," he said after catching his breath. "I'll level with you. You were set up. Revic paid me to introduce you to Angie."

"You're kidding, right?" David said, giving Alan a look of disbelief. He began pacing back and forth. "I can't believe this. You're saying that you set me up with Angie at Curley's?"

"That's right. We set it up so it would look real—the sexy looks she gave you and everything." An apologetic expression appeared on his face. "I'm sorry, man. I didn't think you would actually fall in love with her."

David grabbed Alan by the shirt. "I should beat the hell out of you right now!" he shouted angrily. Then he dropped his arms. "I thought Angie loved me."

"She's Revic's babe, man. I overheard her talking with him on her cell last month when we were at her parents' house. She was speaking to him very affectionately, calling him her 'sweet duke.' There's something strange about their relationship. It's like he put a spell on her or something."

"It doesn't make sense," David said. "If she's his girlfriend, why did he want you to set me up with her?"

"I can explain that. I met him when you first started working at the hospital. He appeared out of the blue and offered to pay me a lot of money to introduce you to Angie. I refused at first. That is until he explained that a friend of hers had stolen a book that belonged to him."

"And that friend happened to be Tom, right?"

"Yeah. He said that Tom had hidden the book and wouldn't tell Angie where it was. That's where you came in. The duke thought that Tom might confide in you because you're a doctor and he had no other friends besides Angie. Then the duke gave me this look—it was really evil, man. I got scared and agreed to help him."

"I think I understand what happened next," David said with a thoughtful expression. "Once I handed the books over to Angie for translation, she dumped me. She didn't need me anymore. Right, Alan?"

"Yeah, so now that he has what he wants, let's leave the books alone, okay? We don't want to get on Revic's bad side. He'll come after us for sure."

"There's still one question left to be answered, Alan. If Revic got his books back, then why was my place ransacked?"

"Maybe somebody else is after them," Alan mused.

David walked to the desk, picked up the notebook, and began skimming through the pages. "Well, what do you know!" he remarked in surprise. "Angie had it translated. Check this out." He handed it to Alan.

"The last half of the notebook is written in English," Alan remarked after leafing through it. "The title says *The Memoirs of Thomas Harrison*."

David snatched the notebook out of Alan's hands. "I'm taking it."

David woke up late Saturday morning feeling despondent. All he could think about was Angela. She was the first woman he had ever let into his heart, and now she had broken it. He was glad Dr. Lucas had been keeping him busy at the hospital, providing a much-needed distraction. Without his work, he would be a mental case.

David got out of bed and scowled at the piles of clothing scattered about the floor—he still hadn't bothered to clean up the place. He thought about calling Detective Scott but decided against it. If the detective had a suspect, he would have called by now. He decided to spend the day putting his apartment back in order. Perhaps that would keep his mind off of Angie.

Before beginning his chores, David called his parents and learned, to his great relief, that his father was in stable condition. Fortunately, the chemo treatments were keeping cancer at bay.

Then he replayed the message Alan had left on his voicemail. "Hi, David," the message began. "I know you're probably way too mad to talk to me right now, but I wanted to tell you again how very sorry I am. I really want to make this up to you—that is, if you can forgive me. Let's talk, okay?"

David debated whether or not he should return Alan's call. He couldn't blame his friend for Angie's betrayal. On the other hand, there was the matter of trust: Alan hadn't warned him about the duke.

David realized that Revic had boxed Alan into a corner. If Alan had confessed to David that the duke was Angie's girlfriend and that he needed David to gain possession of the chest, there was no doubt in David's mind that the duke would have retaliated against his friend. Alan had no choice but to keep Angie's relationship with the duke a secret from David.

Revic was definitely a manipulative, creepy dude. He wondered how Angie could fall for a guy like that. Maybe he should forget about all of them. He had exchanged niceties with one of the female doctors at the hospital the other day. Her name was Lisa, and she seemed like a nice girl. She would probably go out with him if he asked.

After two hours of deep cleaning, David left the apartment and drove to the mall to do some shopping. As he approached the parking lot, he glanced in his rearview mirror and noted the silver Lincoln directly behind him. It had been following him for the last couple of miles. When he pulled into the parking lot, it continued on its way. Maybe it was nothing.

David spent several hours at the mall, dining, and shopping, continuously scanning the crowd as he walked from store to store. He couldn't shake the feeling that he was being watched but didn't notice anything unusual. As he began the drive back to his apartment, he glanced at his rearview mirror and saw Lincoln again. He abruptly pulled to the side of the road, hoping to get the license plate number, but the car sped away too quickly.

David arrived at his apartment feeling lonely and despondent as thoughts of Angela began drifting through his mind. He walked into the bedroom, sat down on the bed, and stared at the phone on his nightstand. He thought about calling Lisa, but decided against it, realizing that since he was still in love with Angela, it would be wrong to date her, to use her merely as a means of satisfying his cravings for female companionship. He wasn't ready to talk to Alan either. He might lose his temper and say the wrong thing.

He picked up the phone and checked his voicemail, wondering if there was any news about his father. To his surprise, there was a message from Angela.

"Hi, David," the message began. David noted her distraught tone and the hoarseness in her voice as if she had been crying. "If you erase this message, I won't blame you," she continued. "I know I hurt you very badly," she said after a few sobs.

"I'm so sorry. I don't know what I was thinking. Alan told me that you saw me with the duke at the guesthouse last week. I know you probably won't believe this, but I realize how wrong that was. I broke up with him a few days ago. I'm never going to see him again. All I'm asking for is a chance to explain. Please call."

A myriad of emotions swept through David as he put down the phone. His initial reaction was anger, quickly supplanted by feelings of grief and disbelief. She had a lot of nerve, calling him after everything that had happened. Did she think that he could really believe that she cared for him, or that he would give her another chance after seeing her with the duke? She had lost his trust.

David woke up the next morning feeling an urgent desire to call Angela. He wanted to listen to her side of the story. Of course, he had no intention of taking her back, but he needed closure, he needed to ease his mind and his heart.

He steeled himself, picked up the phone, and dialed her number.

"Who's calling, please?" the housekeeper asked.

"It's David. Is Angela there?"

"Just a minute," she replied.

A few moments later, Angela came on the line. "Hi, David," she said. She sounded tired. "I'm so glad you called."

"I want to talk," David said bluntly. "Not on the phone. Meet me at Greenwood Park. It's close to the hospital. One o'clock. Okay?"

"I know where it is," Angela said. "I'll be there."

David showed up ten minutes late. Greenwood Park was a public park with picnic tables, a swimming pool, and a playground. It was a place where parents could take their kids for summer outings. He parked his car in the lot, walked to the nearest group of picnic tables, and spotted Angela seated at the farthest one on the left. She had spread a tablecloth over the table. As he approached, she opened a cooler and produced sandwiches and beverages. "Hi, David," she said, giving him a bright smile.

David noted she wore a pink-striped cotton blouse with a rounded neck, black denim shorts, and white jogging shoes. She looked stunning. "Thanks for the picnic," David said as he sat down.

"It was nothing," Angela said, smiling a little. She handed him a paper plate with a sandwich and potato salad on it. "I imagine that you want an explanation."

David selected a can of root beer from the cooler, pulled the tab, and nodded silently.

Tears began to run down her cheeks. "I'm sorry," she said between sniffles. "This is very hard for me."

"Take your time," David said. Even though she had hurt him terribly, he couldn't deny the tender feelings of compassion that suddenly blossomed in his heart like perennials in the spring sunshine. He stared at her for a moment, attempting to read her. Her remorse seemed genuine.

"I met the duke at one of my father's business dinners last winters," Angela said after regaining her composure. "He had this magnetic, compelling charm about him, and I fell for him. My friends advised me against dating him, but I couldn't resist.

"He was very secretive about his personal life, and that mystery—in addition to his being a European aristocrat—compounded his allure. He spoiled me, taking me to the best shows and restaurants, giving me expensive gifts. He always seemed to know exactly what I wanted."

"Now I understand why you insisted on all the pampering," David said. "The duke had been treating you like royalty. He convinced you that was how a man should show his love and affection."

Angela's face reddened with embarrassment. "That was very selfish of me. I'm very sorry. May I continue?

"At first the duke seemed delightful and sensitive," she said, "but after a while, I suspected that he was not being completely honest with me. He would go away for days at a time, not telling me where he was or why he left. Unfortunately, I didn't see the warning signals at the time. When he was away, I felt miserable—always wondering what he was up to—but when he returned, my suspicions seemed to melt away. I realize now how irrational that was, but at the time, I didn't see it. It was like I was wearing blinders. My friends told me that he had put a spell on me.

"At the beginning of July, I finally confronted him about his disappearances, threatening to break it off if he didn't come clean. I suspected him of cheating. I was very upset. Then he smiled that charming smile of his and told me that he was a sorcerer and that he belonged to a coven of witches.

"I was intrigued. I wanted him to tell me everything—what he did at the coven, what powers he had, and so on. He promised he would teach me about witchcraft, but only if I did something for him in return."

"I think I know what that was," David interjected. "He wanted you to gain my confidence and then introduce me to Tom, hoping that he would eventually reveal where the duke's precious books were hidden, right?"

"He was looking for the Numericon," Angela said, nodding affirmatively. "It's the book of shadows the coven uses to conjure demons and cast spells. The duke claimed that Tom, who was also a member of the coven, had stolen the book. He was very adamant about getting it back."

"Really!" David exclaimed. "Let me get this straight. Tom and Revic were both members of the same coven. Tom had stolen the Numericon for whatever reason, and the duke wanted it back. That's where I came into the picture, correct?"

"Not at first. Being the curious person that I am, I was extremely desirous to learn about the coven, so I acquiesced to the duke's wishes and questioned Tom about the Numericon. Since Tom knew that I was dating the duke, he flatly refused to divulge its location. When that plan failed, the duke came up with another.

"The duke is an emissary to the King of Slavania," she continued, "supervising business matters here in the States, including dealings with your father's oil company. That's how he learned you were residing in Chicago. Since you're a doctor, the duke thought that Tom, who was mentally unstable, might trust you enough to disclose the location, especially under duress. All Vojislav needed was a catalyst. I suspect that the duke administered hallucinogenic drugs to Tom at the Fourth of July party, exacerbating his paranoia."

"That was very clever of the duke," David remarked. "His plan actually worked. I can guess what happened next. Once you gave the Numericon to the duke, your job was complete. You didn't need me anymore. Of course, the duke didn't need you either. We were just pawns in his scheme. After you cut me loose, my guess is that he dumped you, correct?"

"Yes," Angela said dejectedly. "I should have seen it coming, but I was literally under his spell. I didn't come to my senses until it was over between us. That's when I realized that my feelings for you were genuine."

She paused a moment. "I'm so sorry, David," she said, taking his hand in a firm grip, tears running down her cheeks. "If you decide to never see me again, I will understand. But if you can find it in your heart to forgive me, I will be yours forever. I love you, David."

David felt a sudden stirring of passion for the woman that had betrayed him. "I think I understand what happened and why you did what you did," he said, pushing the whirl of emotions aside, "but there's still one question that's bugging me. You said that Revic was after the Numericon, but the cedar chest contained another book—a notebook. After you and the duke left the guesthouse that day, I went inside and took it. Did the duke mention anything to you about it?"

"I met him again the next day," Angela replied, wiping away her tears with a napkin. "That's when we broke up. I saw him take the Numericon, but he made no mention of a notebook."

Her expression abruptly turned apprehensive. "I'm scared of him, David. What if he comes after us?"

"I find it strange that he didn't mention anything about Tom's notebook," Dave mused, "especially after taking the trouble to translate it. By the way, did you have someone at the college do the translation?"

"No. The duke said it was written in an ancient gypsy language that only he was familiar with. He translated it himself."

David managed a smile and grasped Angela's hands. "Don't worry about Revic. I'm certain he's through with you now that he has what he wants. If he wanted to harm you, he would have done it already."

He pressed her hands gently within his. "Thank you for explaining everything to me, Angela. I understand why you acted the way you did, but I still have a lot of feelings to sort through. I need some time. How about if I call you in a few days?"

"That's more than I could hope for," she replied, her eyes pleading for forgiveness.

After helping Angela put everything away, David walked her to her car. Before leaving, she rolled down the window. "Please call soon, David," she said, her face streaked with tears.

David's eyes moistened as he watched her drive away. A few moments later, he dried his tears with a napkin and began walking toward his car.

Hearing the sound of footsteps behind him, he quickly turned and beheld a lady standing about two yards away. She wore a form-fitting, black jumpsuit with a silver pendant dangling from her neck on a thick, gold chain. Her black hair was long and thick, especially for a woman in her early sixties. She looked very fit for her age, and her features were wrinkle-free and beautiful. Her brown eyes had a piercing quality that made him uncomfortable.

"Give me the book," she said. She was not smiling.

"I don't have it," David managed, feeling uneasy. "Have you been following me? Please leave me alone." A feeling of dread enveloped him as she stepped closer, then she suddenly turned and walked away.

"What a creepy lady," he muttered to himself, intently watching her departure.

As he turned back toward his car, he noticed a policeman walking toward him from the opposite end of the parking lot.

"Is everything all right, sir?" the officer asked as he approached.

"Yeah—no problem, Officer," David replied nonchalantly.

David was abruptly awakened out of a sound sleep by someone pounding on the door. He peered at the alarm clock on his nightstand.

"Who could it be at ten o'clock on a Saturday morning?" he muttered. He rolled out of bed, jogged down the small hallway, and opened the door.

"Detective Scott," he said sleepily.

"May I come in?" the detective asked with a serious expression.

"By all means." David closed the door after the detective. "Have a seat."

"Do you have some information about the break-in?" David asked.

"I came here for another reason," the detective replied calmly.

David felt a chill run up his spine. "Is something wrong?"

"I need to ask you a question, and I want you to be completely honest with me. Okay, Dr. Sholfield?"

"Sure, Detective. What do you want to know?"

"Where were you between the hours of eight and eleven p.m. on Thursday night?"

"I was working at the hospital. Is something wrong?"

"I'm sorry to have to tell you this," the detective said with a frown, "but Angela Stockman is dead."

Stunned by the news, David's face turned very pale. As he began to faint, the detective steadied him and waited patiently until the color came back into David's face.

"Are you okay, Dr. Sholfield?"

"I don't know," David replied blankly. "What happened to her?"

"Angela was murdered Thursday night by an unknown assailant."

"Murdered?" David repeated. "Do you have any leads?"

"Not yet. Does she have any enemies that you know of?"

"I don't know anyone who would want her dead. But I do know that she had recently broken up with her boyfriend—a European aristocrat by the name of Duke Revic. Does that name sound familiar to you?"

"Yes. We questioned some of Angela's friends at the college, and they told us she had been dating him. They all think he killed her, but he's not a suspect. He was on a flight to London at the time of the murder."

"I know that he was a member of a coven," David said.

"Could they have something to do with this?"

"Perhaps," the detective replied.

"Look, Dr. Sholfield, I don't usually divulge info about a murder case, but since you're a doctor, I believe I can trust you with this. I'm asking you to keep this confidential, okay?"

"Of course, Detective."

"We found Angela lying naked on the bed in one of the rooms of her guesthouse. It appears to be a bedroom and reading room combination. Do you know which room I'm referring to?"

"Sure."

"We found a cross hanging upside down on the headboard, and black candles on the floor surrounding the bed. It was a ritualistic killing. Her throat was slit and her body was drained of blood. That was the cause of death. Her body was placed upside-down on the bed, with her arms spread out like a cross. From what you just told me; it appears that Vojislav Revic's coven might be involved. Do you know any of the other members?"

"No. Angie wasn't directly involved with them either." Then David snapped his fingers.

"Wait a minute. Do you know who Tom Harrison is?"

"No."

"He was a friend of Angie's. She said that he was a member of the coven. Unfortunately, he died last month."

"Interesting."

"He died in Mercy Hospital under what I believe to be suspicious circumstances."

"I'll check it out." The detective stood from the couch and extended his hand.

"I'm sorry about all of this. I'll call you when I learn something."

"Thank you, Detective Scott."

David let the detective out the door, threw himself down on the couch, and burst into tears.

The days following Angela's death passed very slowly and painfully for David. He attended the funeral on the following Monday, at the request of Angela's family. Although they had treated him kindly, he felt like an outsider.

He spent the rest of the week pulling double shifts at the hospital, using work as a means to fend off his grief and loneliness. Alan and some of Angela's friends made several attempts to contact him, but he avoided them.

It was late Saturday morning. David had awakened early but had lain in bed for several hours, not having any particular reason to get up. He felt depressed and lonely. He was in a strange town, far removed from his family. The few friends he had made were either dead or had deceived him. He had called his mother yesterday and they had talked for a while. Fortunately, his father was still in remission—the only piece of good news he'd received.

David finally got out of bed and checked his messages. There was nothing from the hospital, which was okay. With all the hours he had been putting in lately, he could use the break. Unfortunately, there was still no word from Detective Scott. David had no idea how he was going to fill the day. Everything reminded him of Angie. He decided to stay home and watch college football.

Suddenly the phone rang. "Who is it?" he answered in an irritated tone, not bothering to check his caller ID.

"It's Alan. Please don't hang up."

David paused, considering his options. "What do you want?"

"I just wanted to tell you how sorry I am about Angie."

David waited on the other end of the line, not sure what to say.

"Look, David," Alan continued. "I know you have no reason to trust me, but I thought you might need someone to talk to."

Alan had a point. David had spoken to no one since Angela's death. He could really use a talk, and his former best friend was the only person familiar with his situation. "You know I'm still mad at you, Alan."

"I understand. Please let me make it up to you. I'll never take our friendship for granted again—I promise. All I'm asking for is a chance to earn your trust."

"I guess there's no harm in talking. Besides, I don't want to spend all day cooped up in my lousy apartment. So where do you want to meet?"

"Thank you," Alan replied, sounding relieved. "Meet me at the coffee shop—you know, the one near the hospital."

Alan was already there—seated at a table in the back—when David arrived. As he approached, Alan grinned and raised his cup of coffee. "Thanks for coming, David."

"Someone followed me on the way here," David said as he sat down. He eyed Alan suspiciously. "You wouldn't happen to know anything about that, would you?"

"I guess I can't expect you to trust me," Alan said, "but I honestly have no idea. So how are you doing, anyway?"

"I'm okay, considering the circumstances," David replied, noting the genuine concern on Alan's face.

"I'm glad to hear that." Alan sighed. "I've been very worried about you, Doc."

After they ordered from the waitress, Alan started to speak again. Then he abruptly stopped, his face reddening with embarrassment as he struggled to find the appropriate words.

"Okay—let's hear it," David finally said with an amused grin, observing Alan's obvious discomfort. "Why do you want me to be your friend?"

"I don't know if this will help you understand," Alan replied after taking a deep breath, "but when Revic first asked me to introduce you to Angie, you had just started working at the hospital. I didn't think it was a big deal at the time. I thought you would be pleased—with her looks and everything—you know?"

He sipped on his coffee and continued. "I didn't know Angie was his girlfriend until we went to her parents' house, I swear. He didn't mention anything about that when he asked me to set up the meeting at Curley's."

"I don't understand why you didn't clue me in before I went and fell in love with her, man." David gave Alan a look of annoyance. "You could have told me at the dinner party. What kind of friend would leave his buddy in the dark like that?"

"I know it was wrong not to tell you, but I was afraid of losing your friendship. I felt like a heel when I found out that Revic had set you up. Also, by then, I was afraid of what the duke would do to me if I clued you in on his scheme to get the Numericon from Tom. He's a real nasty character, believe me."

"I understand," David said as feelings of sympathy for his former friend began welling up inside him. "Revic put you in a tough spot. You had already accepted money from him, so you were bound to see the thing through, at least until he got his precious book of shadows back. Have you spoken to him since?"

"No," Alan said, shaking his head decisively. "I had no further contact with him. I'm sorry, David. I didn't want to see you get hurt, but I hope you can understand that I was stuck in the middle of a bad situation."

"I accept your apology," David said. He gave Alan a forgiving grin. "But you owe me big-time."

"Thank you. You're not the only one who needs a friend right now." He paused a moment before his expression turned serious. "I didn't want to bring this up earlier, but I was shocked and deeply saddened by Angie's murder. How are you handling it?"

"I'm not going to lie to you, Alan. I've been really depressed since it happened. I really loved her. Do you know the thing that hurt me the most?"

Alan shook his head.

"She called me the weekend before she was killed, saying that she wanted to talk. We met at Greenwood Park and had a picnic lunch there. She said that she still loved me and that she wanted me back. She wanted me to believe that there was still hope for us."

"How unexpected," Alan remarked with a look of surprise. "All's fair in love and war, I guess. What reason did she give for her sudden change of heart?"

"She said that the duke had used her, that he was into witchcraft and had cast a spell on her."

"Witchcraft?" Alan mused. "Was she into that too?"

"No, but it turns out that Tom and the duke were both members of the same coven. Apparently, Tom had stolen the spell-casting book that Revic had wanted back."

"That sounds really weird," Alan remarked. "How about the other professors she hung out with? Were they members of the coven too?"

"I don't think so. Their places were searched the same as mine. And there's one other thing. When I was at the park, this strange woman dressed in black appeared and demanded that I return the spell-casting book. I'm wondering if she's a witch from Revic's coven, and I also wonder if she's the one who's been following me. If Revic has the book, why would the coven come after me?"

"Revic must have taken it with him to Europe without telling them. He probably lied and told the coven that you had the book in order to deflect their suspicions away from him."

"That makes sense, but there's still one question that remains unanswered: Why would the coven want to kill Angela?"

"Satan worship," Alan replied with a frightened expression. "I don't know much about witchcraft, but the blackest of all magic is human sacrifice. If I were you, I would tell the cops about the witch. If the coven thinks you have their book, you could be in grave danger."

"I hadn't thought of that," David said. His hands began to tremble as he sipped his coffee. "Detective Scott is handling the case. I'll give him a call when I get home."

"Here's another thought," Alan said. "Have you read Tom's memoirs yet?"

"No. I've been way too busy with work and the funeral and everything."

"If I were you, I'd go straight home and read it. I know the guy was crazy, but his book might contain some valuable information."

"I'm glad we talked," David said, standing from the table. He shook Alan's hand. "I'll give you a call, buddy. Soon, okay?"

As David drove back to his apartment, he scanned the road, looking for the silver Lincoln. He breathed out a sigh of relief as he pulled into the parking lot—he had not been followed.

Just as he stepped out of his car, the Lincoln appeared, speeding around the corner of an adjacent building. It pulled up beside him, and a second later, a woman stepped out of the passenger side. David's stomach tightened in fear as he recognized her. It was the witch he had encountered in the park. This time she wore a black silk blouse and matching pants.

"Give me the Numericon," she said sternly.

"I told you, lady, I don't have it," David responded angrily.

She raised her arms and began moving them as if sketching out an invisible pattern in the air while chanting something in an unfamiliar language.

A moment later, David felt a numbing sensation spreading throughout his body. He tried to move his arms and legs, but nothing happened. He was completely paralyzed.

Suddenly, a tall, muscular man with long brown hair appeared at the opposite end of the parking lot and began jogging toward them. At his approach, the witch jumped into her car and drove away.

"You won't be having any more problems with her," the stranger said, smiling at David.

"Who are you?" David asked, giving the stranger an appraising stare as he rubbed the circulation back into his limbs. The man's swarthy features and muscular build reminded him of a lumberjack.

The stranger moved closer and put something in David's hand. "Take the Lyricor," he said. "You will need it very soon."

David stared at the object in his hand. It was a flat, white polished stone about six inches in diameter. "What did you say?" he asked with a puzzled expression. When he looked up, the man was already at the far end of the parking lot.

"Read the notebook!" the stranger shouted. Then he disappeared behind another apartment building.

David walked into his apartment, set the white stone on the cocktail table, and checked his voicemail. There was a message from Detective Scott—he was still tracking down the members of Revic's coven.

David crumpled down onto the couch, depressed and exhausted by the tragic events that had befallen him. Everything had begun falling apart after he had retrieved the cedar chest from Tom's cabin. First, Tom had died a mysterious death, and then, after Angela had dumped him, his apartment had been ransacked. Then he had been followed by a strange woman—most likely a witch from Revic's coven—who believed that he possessed their book of shadows.

He had broken off his friendship with Alan after learning of his friend's deception, but then the worst had happened: Angela, after seeking David's forgiveness, was brutally murdered, dashing his hopes of a reconciliation, sending him into a downward spiral of despair.

Thank God for his work at the hospital. It was the only thing holding him together. Since the police had yet to come up with any substantial leads, he had no choice but to bide his time, hoping that something would turn up. He was glad he had made up with Alan—he couldn't bear the thought of going it alone in a big town like Chicago after losing the woman he so dearly loved.

David sat up abruptly as he recalled the encounter with the witch in the parking lot. Since she was likely a member of Revic's coven, he should report the encounter to the detective. The police would probably stake out the parking lot if she returned, which would provide much-needed peace of mind and security.

After leaving a message on Detective Scott's cell, David picked up the white stone and examined it. There were no markings of any kind, nothing to indicate what it was used for. He had so many questions and no answers. He put it back on the table, recalling the brown-haired man's cryptic remarks. He had called it "the Lyricor" and told David to read Tom's memoirs.

David quickly retrieved the notebook from the bedroom, returned to the couch, and opened the book to the first page.

# CHAPTER SIX

## THE MEMOIRS OF THOMAS HARRISON

They come closer. The demons are lurking in the shadows outside the cabin. My protection spells are becoming increasingly ineffective. I fear for my life. It's only a matter of time until they come for me. Because of the little time I have remaining, I've decided to spend my last few days writing an abbreviated autobiography explaining how I came to this desperate state.

I'm an only child, raised by working-class parents in a small town in West Virginia. My father worked in the coal mine, and my mother was a waitress in the town's solitary restaurant. They worked hard and saved their money so I could get a college education. They treated me well, God bless them. I have no complaints on that score.

After eight long years of study, I received my doctorate in history from West Virginia University. College life suited me well, although I didn't do much socializing. With average looks and an introverted personality, my track record with the ladies was well short of stellar. During my stay, I had only three girlfriends. They all dumped me for better-looking guys within a month or two.

After graduation, I landed a job as a history professor at Columbia College. The salary wasn't much, but it provided ample opportunity to indulge my penchant for offbeat studies. It was through my studies of American and European folklore that I became acquainted with magic and witchcraft.

During the spring of 2005, I began socializing with some of the faculty members. Actually, it was Angela Stockman—the only staff member who actually befriended me—who introduced me to them. One day, she invited me to an outing held at her parents' mansion. I was amazed to learn that she was heiress to the Stockman fortune—acquired through her grandfather's success in real estate development. Since neither of us had siblings, we hit it off pretty well, but I knew from the beginning that our relationship would never develop into anything beyond friendship.

It was at the party that I met Joanne Bresker. She was a graduate student majoring in art education. She was blonde-haired and blue-eyed, with distinctive features like those of a model. It was not just her beauty that attracted me. She was a talented artist as well. I had seen some of her work on display at the university. She was really good.

After Angela introduced us, we conversed a little, but it was evident that she held no personal interest. I asked if she wanted to have dinner the following weekend, but she declined, saying that she had a boyfriend. I subsequently learned from Angela that the story was a fabrication, that she had recently broken up with the jerk after being abused by him. I rationalized her rejection, convincing myself that her abusive relationship was the cause, that she simply needed some healing time before re-entering the dating arena.

I saw Joanne again a few weeks later. It was the beginning of June, the summer recess, and Angela had invited her faculty friends to a beach party. I still remember how fabulous Joanne looked in her bikini. I was completely enthralled as I watched her laugh and cavort about with her friends on the beach. By the end of the day, I had fallen in love with her. After mustering all of my courage, I asked her out again, hoping that she might be ready to start dating—but she respectfully declined.

I saw her the next weekend at a dinner party at Angela's and tried one more time, but she told me in no uncertain terms that I had no chance, and furthermore, that I should stop pestering her. This time there was no mistaking it—she wanted nothing to do with me.

It was not the first time I had experienced rejection. In the past, I had always managed to survive the pain and move on with my life, but this time was different. I was totally in love and couldn't get her out of my mind no matter how hard I tried.

By then I had a theoretical knowledge of white magic, acquired through my study of folklore. I had never given the subject any credence, other than from a scholarly viewpoint, but now I had an all-encompassing reason to put my knowledge into practice—my undying love for Joanne!

My mother owned a cabin in West Virginia that she had inherited from her father. It was the perfect place to cast a spell. My parents never used it, and there were no neighbors.

Upon arrival, I went directly upstairs to the second-floor loft and cast the spell, using a combination of natural, talismanic, and Thelemic magic, hoping that the combination of all three elements would increase its potency. For the natural element, I used heart-shaped violet leaves. For the talisman, I used an amulet, previously purchased at a jewelry store. The Thelemic part of the spell was easy. I focused my all-consuming desire for Joanne into the spell, hoping that it would magically transform her into my one-and-only true love forever. For the sake of brevity, I will not describe the details of the spell, but I will state that I performed a ritual at the cabin using the elements I'd collected.

I had a chance to test the effectiveness of my spell a week later at another one of Angela's gatherings. I spotted Joanne immediately when I arrived. She was playing volleyball. I admired the graceful movements of her body, the lovely curves of her suntanned legs, as she ran around the field in her shorts. At the conclusion of the game, everyone assembled for an outdoor lunch. I sat at an adjacent table, observing her from a distance, not speaking to her, knowing that if the spell had taken effect, she would come to me. Unfortunately, she completely ignored me. Not having the fortitude to withstand another rejection and the nasty scene that would most likely ensue, I left the party early, disillusioned by my failure.

Upon further study, I learned that white magic love spells were primarily used to enhance existing relationships, not to begin new ones. My theory—combining several elements of white magic to enhance the spell's potency—had been proven incorrect. Realizing that a more powerful brand of magic was needed, I knew I had reached the point where I was willing to do anything to gain Joanne's love.

Having spent the entire summer socializing with Angela and her friends, she and I had become close to the point that I confided in her, revealing my love for Joanne. Because of our evolving friendship and mutual trust, Angela confided in me as well, informing me that she had begun dating a European aristocrat by the name of Duke Revic and had fallen for him.

Learning of my quandary from Angela, the duke met with me shortly thereafter, informing me that he was a sorcerer and a member of a local witches' coven. He explained that my timing was perfect: They were looking for a thirteenth member, and my well-rounded knowledge of witchcraft made me an excellent recruit. He explained that as a member, I would have direct access to the book of shadows and the powerful spells contained therein. I jumped at the chance, hoping to gain access to a love spell powerful enough to produce the results I so ardently desired.

The duke explained that before I could join the coven, I would need an interview with Claire Shuman, the high priestess. According to tradition, my initiation would normally commence a year and a day from the interview, but because of my theoretical knowledge of witchcraft and their desire to fill the membership gap, I would not have to wait that long. Assuming a satisfactory interview, my initiation would commence on the afternoon of September 22—the autumnal equinox. The duke gave me several texts to study in the meantime.

It was the second week of August when the duke introduced me to Claire. We met in the dining room of her mansion, which was built in a contemporary, chateauesque style. It was a lovely home, with a steeply pitched roof, a heavily ornamented cut-stone exterior, and a massive turret-style bay. I felt honored to be in the company of such wealthy and influential people.

The interview—held at Claire's kitchen table—lasted about an hour. After testing my knowledge of witchcraft, she concluded with a single question: "Why do you want to join our coven?"

Uncomfortable with the question—I thought my reason for joining was not a particularly noble one—I paused for a full minute, running several plausible-sounding explanations through my mind. I eventually decided upon honesty since she would eventually discover the real reason anyway.

I took a deep breath, looked her in the eye, and replied that I was in love with a certain woman who did not reciprocate my feelings and that I wanted to cast a love spell on her so we could be together forever.

Claire stared at me for a moment, her face expressionless. I thought she was going to dismiss me outright. Then, to my surprise, she smiled and said that she thought my reason was an excellent one. Most initiates, she said, had only superficial reasons for joining, or even worse, wished to harm someone. One should join a coven only if they were at peace with the world and knew exactly what they wanted.

Then she squeezed my hand affectionately and said that I would be initiated into the coven on the autumnal equinox, on the condition that I would spend the next month at her home learning the necessary rituals. She further explained that the other members of the coven were female, except the duke, who was the high priest. I would be next in line for the position if I desired it, as he was planning on returning to his native country the following summer. If I accepted the leadership position, further instruction would be necessary—the second-and third-degree initiations into the Craft.

Anxious to begin my training, I eagerly agreed to the proposal, explaining that I needed to return to the university and request a sabbatical. I assured Claire that it would pose no problem because I had already met the university's six-year requirement.

After putting my affairs in order, I returned to Claire's home a week later and commenced my training in earnest. I spent most of my time in one of the comfortably appointed guest rooms, studying by day and sleeping at night. Although there were no restrictions—I could come and go as I pleased—I chose to stay in my room and immerse myself in my studies. Meals were provided by the kitchen staff on a regular basis. I didn't see much of Claire, except at mealtimes and when rituals were to be performed.

I gradually became acquainted with the other members of the coven. Most of the women were promiscuous, and several offered sexual favors. Although I was flattered—they were young and beautiful—I declined their enticements. I guess one could call me a romantic. I was saving myself for Joanne.

Although Claire had no official partner, I ascertained that she was having sex with some of the other women, as well as with the duke. She never spoke of personal matters, only about the Craft. She constantly tested my growing knowledge, providing hands-on demonstrations of the rituals as well as overseeing those performed by the coven.

On the afternoon of September 22, the coven assembled in Claire's basement. and together we performed my initiation ritual. For the sake of the reader's understanding, I will briefly provide some background information before describing the details.

The coven was organized in the traditional manner of Wicca—a pagan, nature-based religion—worshipping both a god and a goddess. The deities are defined as personifications of the underlying life force found in nature. Wicca has three degrees of initiation: The first degree is required to gain membership. The second and third degrees are required to attain the offices of the high priest and high priestess.

The initiation was fairly straightforward. Instead of describing every detail—the actual workings of the coven are a closely guarded secret—I will provide a general description as follows:

The coven assembled sky-clad (naked) inside a magic circle that had been consecrated and purified. In the center of the circle was a wooden altar containing the book of shadows, an athame (a magic sword), a candle, a scourge, a bell, and three pentacles.

After everyone was purified, the high priest left the circle, pointed the athame at my breast, and chanted some verses. Then he blindfolded me and led me into the circle. He took pieces of cord from the altar and tied my hands together behind my back, pulled them up, and then tied the opposite ends around my neck. The loose end is called a cable tow. He led me around the circle by the cable tow, stopping at each point of the compass—north, south, east, and west—while chanting more verses.

He bade me kneel before the altar, then struck a bell and asked me questions concerning the sincerity of my intentions. Next, he took a scourge from the altar and lightly stroked me across the buttocks. After swearing me to secrecy, he unbound my hands and removed the cable tow. Finally, he presented the athame to me, along with various other tools used in performing the rituals, and closed the ceremony with more chanting. To my utter delight, I was now officially a member of the coven.

Since the equinox had fallen on a Thursday, the coven decided to remain at Claire's for the weekend and engage in more spell-castings. To my great joy and delight, a love spell for Joanne was on the agenda.

After the coven had concluded all the pertinent rituals, including the love spell, Claire was generous enough to give me a few weeks of leave to pursue my love interest, and I returned to my apartment with expectations running high.

I was optimistic that the power of the coven had rendered the spell effectual, and although I couldn't force Joanne to do anything against her will, I felt confident that her heart would be open to my advances. Upon my return, I contacted Angela and asked her to throw a party at her parents' mansion and invite Joanne. I felt uncomfortable asking Joanne on a date directly for obvious reasons, even with the love spell in play.

Angela happily agreed to my request and scheduled the dinner party for the next Saturday evening. It being an especially warm evening, Angela decided to entertain her guests outdoors on the spacious porch. Although she'd changed the location of the party from indoors to outdoors, the catering company was able to set up a stage for the live band and a portable dance floor in front of it, complete with disco lighting and a wet bar.

It was fortuitous that I didn't see Joanne when I first arrived because I was extremely nervous. All my previous relationships had ended in failure, and even the witches' sexual advances at the coven had not cured my perpetual introversion.

After conversing with several of Angela's friends, I returned to the wet bar for another drink. It was then that I saw Joanne. She looked sensational, dressed in a fiery red, tight-fitting party dress with a halter top that revealed her cleavage. I noted the stylish drop waist, which allowed the dress to drape in the midsection, and the skirt—cut to a mini-length—which showcased her fabulous legs. She looked even more beautiful than I remembered.

I braced myself, took a sip of my martini, and gave her my friendliest smile. "Nice to see you again, Joanne," I said in what I hoped was a casual tone.

I stood there for several seconds, waiting in a perfect agony as she gave me a probing stare. My fears quickly subsided when she suddenly returned my smile. "Yes," she replied. "It's very nice to see you again, Tom."

It was remarkable how completely her attitude had changed. She no longer held me in disdain. On the contrary, she treated me warmly, like a good friend she hadn't seen in a while.

On a chivalrous impulse, I asked her what she wanted to drink and quickly fetched it, along with a double whiskey for myself. I wanted to be well-insulated in case things went awry.

"You know," she said, sipping on her mint julep, "I was very rude to you last summer. I'm very sorry about the way I treated you. You were just trying to be nice."

"I'm glad you feel that way," I responded, breathing a sigh of relief. Her apology seemed sincere. "And I must mention how nice you look this evening." I knew it was a pretty inept line, but it was a start.

"Thank you," she responded with a smile. "And you look very nice as well."

It was incredible. She had actually given me a compliment, the first I had received in a very long time. Her kind words and demeanor instantly filled me with a newfound sense of confidence. Yes, the love spell had opened the door to her heart. I knew that if I behaved in a personable manner—a difficult challenge for an introvert—everything would work out and she would be mine.

We spent the remainder of the evening dancing and chatting. Everything went smoothly. She was every bit as interesting as I had hoped, and everything I said seemed to please her. At the conclusion of the party, I asked her to have dinner with me the following Friday. My heart leapt for joy when she accepted.

The following October was the happiest time of my life. I was deliriously, blissfully in love. I dated Joanne on a regular basis, taking her to theaters, restaurants, the beach, and parks. By the end of the month, she was as much in love with me as I was with her.

I checked in with Claire every week, excitedly detailing my progress. She was delighted with the results of the love spell and happy that things were working out.

When she requested that I spend a few more weekends with the coven to prepare for my second-degree initiation, I cheerfully agreed. I withheld my coven membership from Joanne, saying that I was spending my sabbatical researching the field of witchcraft and that I needed to interview the coven on the weekends. Although we missed each other terribly, my absences served to increase the intensity of our love.

I spent the entire month of November driving back and forth between Claire's place and mine. On Sunday evenings, when I returned to my apartment, Joanne was always waiting with a dinner prepared from scratch, which I readily enjoyed. Her cooking was excellent.

By the end of the month, I had completed my second-degree initiation, and Joanne agreed to move in with me on the condition that after her graduation, which was at the end of the year, we would get married and move into our own house. Since several job opportunities awaited her, we wouldn't have to move to another city.

Unfortunately, our happiness didn't last. It was the beginning of December when Joanne discovered the lump in her left breast. After consulting with her physician, and several mammograms later, we learned that she had breast cancer. Fortunately, the prognosis was good. It was still in the early stages, and the doctor assured us that with the proper treatment and surgery, she would be fine.

Joanne was upset by the news. I tried to console her, but she insisted that her scarred, post-surgery body would be unappealing and I would be better off with someone else. She ignored all of my pleadings and supplications and moved out of the apartment.

I was completely devastated. We were so much in love that it had never occurred to me that she would actually leave me. I began wondering if the love spell had worn off.

In desperation, I called Claire. After listening to my tearful explanation, she told me not to worry, that the coven would cast a healing spell as well as a new love spell. In an attempt to placate my distress, she explained that once the spells were cast, Joanne would come to her senses and we would be reunited.

The coven assembled in Claire's basement a few days later and performed the healing ritual and a new love spell.

After rejecting the sexual advances of two of the witches who wished to console me in my grief, I returned straightaway to my apartment, called Joanne, and asked to accompany her to her next checkup. She agreed, and a few days later, her doctor informed us of the test results. We learned that not only was cancer still present but also that it had metastasized to her bones and liver. The doctor was surprised by the rapid acceleration of the disease and said, in his opinion, that she only had nine or ten months to live.

The doctor's prognosis filled me with despair. The coven, with all its power and experience, had been unable to save her. I called Claire and tearfully explained the situation. To my surprise, she said that there was another option, but she didn't want to discuss it over the phone.

The next day I met with both Claire and the duke in her great room. She gave me a stiff drink and said that there was another way to cure Joanne. Her declaration gave me no optimism. On the contrary, I was filled with doubt and suspicion—because the previous spell had failed and possibly backfired.

The duke asked if I had ever heard of necromancy. I shivered when I saw the malevolent expression on his face. Gathering my composure, I replied that during my studies at the university, I had learned that before the Renaissance, the term referred to a form of divination used to summon spirits in order to provide protection and wisdom. In the modern era, however, the meaning of the word had metamorphosed into the evil practice of demon summoning and its corollary, the resurrection of the dead.

The duke explained that the Wiccan form of witchcraft practiced by the coven was too weak to heal Joanne. Only the use of necromancy, wielded by an authorized servant, would suffice. As he spoke, I was immediately overcome by feelings of dread and terror at the words 'authorized servant.' From my folklore studies, I knew that only someone anointed to the priesthood of Satan could actually summon demons and have them do his bidding. In other words, one must become an active Satan worshipper.

Noting the stricken look on my face, Claire repeated her point that the art of necromancy provided the only possibility of healing Joanne. Then, after swearing me to secrecy, she divulged her terrible secret: that she and the duke had both made pacts with Satan, giving them the proper authority to minister in the black arts. She explained, to my chagrin, that if I wanted their help, I would have to give my allegiance as well.

I remarked that I thought it strange that a demon could have the power to heal, but Claire said that Satan was all-powerful and could do many wondrous works.

It was at that moment that I entered the forbidden path of darkness, the path from which one can never return. I was willing to do anything to save Joanne, even forfeit my own soul in the process. I accepted their offer to become a servant of the Lord of Darkness.

Claire explained that in order to gain the necessary power to summon demons, I would need to be ordained into one of Satan's priesthoods. Although it was a preparatory priesthood, it would provide the requisite authority.

Additionally, a knowledge of the appropriate symbols, names, and signs was required, as well as the exact details of the rituals, including the protection spells necessary for my own survival in case the demon turned against me.

Claire explained that my training must begin immediately if we were to save Joanne. Fortunately, I was still on sabbatical. I would spend every waking moment preparing.

I exerted myself to the utmost during the next several weeks, gaining a working knowledge of the language of the Numericon, which was written in an ancient gypsy language. After a few more weeks, I had learned the necessary rituals and was ready to proceed. I will not disclose the exact nature of the anointing and the rituals for fear of my life, but I will give an account of what happened afterward.

I decided to conjure Astaroth, a demon of the first hierarchy. Demons are classified into three main hierarchies, but I was only interested in the first. According to the Numericon, Astaroth was summoned to produce vanity and laziness in the necromancer's victims, but he also had a lighter side—he could heal. I learned that I couldn't command him, but I could attempt to persuade him, offering my worship and obedience in return for his help.

Having mastered the requisite rituals and spells detailed in the Numericon, I was ready to conjure the demon. I will now describe the ritual in a general sense, omitting significant details so that no one reading this will try and use the forbidden knowledge without the proper authorization and training, which would lead to certain death.

I decided to perform the invocation at the demon hour on Christmas morning. I thought the demon might be pleased with my choice since that was the day the Christians celebrated the birth of Christ. Also, the demon hour is the hour between three and four in the morning, the optimal window for the occurrence of demonic activity. As for the location, I selected a woodland meadow in the back of Claire's property since demons don't appear inside human habitations.

At two a.m. on Christmas morning, I, along with Duke Revic—my mentor and associate in the venture—repaired to the meadow, dressed in our priestly attire. The sky was clear and the moon was shining, providing adequate lighting.

We inscribed magic circles—named the Circles of Power—on the ground with white spray paint. The painted area consisted of a large square with two concentric circles inside. The spaces between them were filled with triangles and crosses. Within the second circle was another square, delineating the area where I and the duke would stand.

After the paint dried, we purified the area with holy water and protection spells, using the holy names of God and the Saints to prevent the demon from entering the circles.

At exactly three a.m., I walked inside the inner square and chanted the proper verses, holding a Hebrew Bible in one hand and a wand in the other.

A few minutes later, while breathlessly awaiting the appearance of the demon, the snapping of a twig broke the profound stillness of the woods. I peered in the direction of the sound and beheld movement in the shadows of the trees just beyond the moonlit clearing.

A moment later, I heard a voice say, "Show me the symbol." It wasn't a voice, really, but more like a thought inside my brain, like a gravelly whisper. I handed the Bible and the wand to the duke removed the paper with the symbol drawn on it from my robe, unfolded it, and held it at arm's length with both hands, displaying it in the direction of the movement.

"Does it have a name?" the demon asked in my mind. I replied yes, and spoke the name in a loud voice.

"Show me the sign," he said.

After giving him the proper sign, the demon said, "What is thy desire?"

I breathed out a sigh of relief—I had passed the first test. I showed him a picture of Joanne and respectfully requested that he heal her.

I felt his amusement, which he projected into my mind somehow. "I know your thoughts," came the reply.

"I will grant your request if you will worship me."

I knelt to the ground and told him that he was my god and that I would do anything he asked.

"You must prove your obedience," the demon said. "I know your fondness for your parents. They must die by the beginning of the new year. I will know if you are successful. Only after the deed is accomplished will I grant your request."

I took the Bible and the wand from the duke and chanted a few more verses, dismissing the demon. A moment later, I felt a strong gust of wind as it departed to the underworld.

To ensure our safety, the duke and I spent another half-hour casting protection spells before stepping outside the circles.

Although the conjuration had been a success, I was overwhelmed with feelings of disappointment and sadness at the demon's request. During the course of my preparations, I had learned that the demon would test my obedience with a task, never imagining that it would be something so horrific.

I realized that there were no other options at this late stage—Joanne was dying, and I only had a week to comply with the demon's request.

It was at that moment that I began to rationalize the terrible deed, telling myself that Joanne had her whole life ahead of her and that my parents' best years were already spent.

Pushing aside all thoughts and emotions to the contrary, I left immediately for West Virginia. If I hurried, I would arrive in time for a late Christmas dinner.

I felt no joy in celebrating Christmas that night at my parents' home. I gazed across the dining room table at them, attempting to quell the guilt and disgust I felt at my duplicity. During the drive to their home, I had concocted a simple plan: I would shoot them in the head with my father's hunting rifle while they were sleeping. Since nothing was stolen, and my parents were suffering from dementia, it would look like a double suicide.

I decided to stay the night and wait in my old bedroom. As I waited for them to fall asleep, my mind continually harrowed up images of my parents lying in their bed with their blood and brains scattered all over it, or looking up at me with hateful expressions from their coffins during the funeral service. After about an hour, I knew I didn't have the necessary fortitude to kill them. The next morning, in desperation, I called the duke and asked for his advice.

He explained that, under special circumstances, a necromancer could enter into a compromise with a demon—in my case, offering something of greater benefit than the death of my parents. The duke explained that all demons desired to possess an earthly body since that blessing had been denied them forever when God cast them out of heaven before he created the earth. If I offered the demon a human body to possess, he would most likely accept the offering and consent to my wishes.

I ended the conversation feeling a mix of hope and reassurance. The duke had given me a viable alternative to the heinous and unthinkable act of murdering my parents. That night, I crafted a new plan.

I returned to Chicago on January 1st and was thrilled to read in the letter my beloved sent me that she realized how much she still loved me and that she wanted to make up. Unfortunately, her cancer had slowly continued to metastasize and she had been moved to the cancer ward at the University of Chicago Medical Center. Her precarious state of health, coupled with her newly professed love, provided a powerful inducement to put my plan into action.

After spending two glorious days together, I informed Joanne that I must leave on an errand but would return in a week or so. After a tearful goodbye, I promptly initiated the first phase of my plan, committing myself to the mental ward of a nearby hospital, claiming a nervous breakdown, and citing my fiancée's impending death as the reason. I quickly befriended a patient named Isabella Tristoy—an attractive brunette in her mid-thirties who was suffering from a similar malady caused by an abusive boyfriend.

Convinced that Isabella would make the perfect subject, I primed her with a love spell and spent the next few days successfully gaining her trust. Her condition improved markedly, and several days later the doctor approved her release and mine, advising her to leave town for a few weeks in order to continue the healing process in a stress-free environment.

After gaining Claire's permission, I asked Isabella to accompany me to the witch's estate, explaining that she could stay in the country mansion as long as she pleased and that we would provide protection from her angry boyfriend. She jumped at the chance, saying that I was the first man who had ever shown her any kindness and respect. It was all too easy.

When we arrived, Claire was very hospitable to Isabella, accommodating her in one of the upstairs guest rooms.

I spent the next few days with Isabella, watching movies and entertaining her with stories of American and European folklore. The more time I spent with her, the worse I felt. It was evident that she was falling in love with me. I began to reconsider my plan but quickly regained my resolve after learning that Joanne's condition was still deteriorating.

The duke arrived two days later, and we immediately made the necessary preparations. First, we drugged Isabella into a semi-comatose state.

Then we carried her to the meadow of our previous conjuration and redrew and purified the Circles of Power.

When the duke and I took our places, the duke had to support Isabella, keeping his shoulder under her arm to prevent her from falling outside the boundaries of the inner rectangle.

I performed the ritual and the demon appeared as before, lurking in the shadows of the trees and asking the same questions.

After receiving the appropriate responses, it spoke to me in my mind, saying that it knew why I had summoned it and that it would accept my gift and heal Joanne.

Without hesitation, I pushed Isabella out of the circle and nervously awaited the outcome. A few moments later, she began wailing and thrashing about, attempting to fight off the demon.

After struggling for about a half-hour, Isabella's body went limp. She had finally submitted to the possession. A few moments later, she stood up very slowly and pointed to her chest.

"My thanks unto thee for this gift," the demon said. It seemed strange hearing it speak in Isabella's voice. It laughed diabolically. "I cannot heal Joanne. Satan revoked my power several hundred years ago."

I watched with morbid interest as Isabella's body turned around, her body jerking to and fro as the demon attempted to gain control of her legs. Then it abruptly turned and faced me.

After causing Isabella's lips to move upward in a stiff grin, it said, "Because of your generous gift, I will give thee a hint. Find the one possessing the sorcerer's stone. It can heal your friend. The Master knows where to find him."

Then it ran off into the woods, laughing hysterically.

After casting a number of protection spells, the duke and I returned to the manor house. I felt totally dejected. Not only was my soul damned to hell, but also I was an accomplice to the demonic possession of an innocent soul. Further, Joanne remained at the mercy of cancer that was eating the life out of her body.

Two days later, the coven gathered for our usual weekend spell castings. Afterward, I had a private meeting with the duke and Claire, broaching the subject of the sorcerer's stone, explaining that after conducting some research, I had learned that it was referred to in certain works of antiquity by another name—the lapis philosophorum, or the philosopher's stone. It was made of an unknown substance that allegedly could turn base metals into gold and also could rejuvenate the body.

I told them that I wanted to bring its healing power to bear on Joanne. I didn't mention the fact that its rejuvenating power could prolong our blissful existence together for all eternity.

I did tell them that the demon had hinted at the possibility of the stone's existence and that Satan knew who possessed it. Through my research, I learned that a thirteenth-century philosopher by the name of Albertus Magnus had received it and had passed it along to his star pupil, Thomas Aquinas. Perhaps they were still alive, kept forever young by the stone's power.

When I informed Claire and the duke of my intention to conjure Lucifer himself, they upbraided me, saying that it was utter foolishness. Satan could not be conjured, they told me, and anyone who tried would suffer a horrible death. Even if he appeared, I had nothing of value to offer him, except my soul.

They ended the meeting abruptly, with Claire warning me in no uncertain terms that she would excommunicate me from the coven if I ever mentioned it again.

I returned to my room and ruminated upon what I had learned, eventually deciding that I would do anything, even to the point of delivering my soul to Satan, to save Joanne and be with her forever. Since Claire and the duke were vehemently opposed to my plan, I would have to steal the Numericon and then strike out on my own, performing the necessary rituals in absolute seclusion.

I knew that I would be banished from the coven, but I didn't care. I had nothing else to lose because my soul was already damned forever. I thought that my parents' cabin would make the perfect sanctuary. The coven had no knowledge of it, and I could perform the rituals in perfect solitude.

That night, after everyone was asleep, I crept into the basement, unlocked the safe, and made off with the Numericon. Claire had given me the combination to the lock after my anointing to the higher Satanic priesthood.

Before proceeding to the cabin, I returned to my parents' home and was shocked to learn that they had been transferred to a nursing home. The doctor explained that they had both been stricken with Alzheimer's disease and could no longer care for themselves. In particular, the simultaneous onset of the disease was very puzzling to the doctor. I suspected that Claire and the duke had used their necromancy to unleash a horde of demons upon my parents in reprisal for stealing the coven's book of shadows.

Fearing for my safety, I immediately drove to my parents' cabin and spent the entire day casting protection spells upon the property and myself. Then I commenced my study of the Numericon in earnest.

I learned, to my surprise, that unlike his demons, Satan didn't require a conjuration. However, in order to invoke his presence, a temple had to be constructed and consecrated with the blood offering of a sacrificial animal. Without it, he would not manifest himself.

The invocation was a simple ritual called the Black Mass. Since Claire and the duke had previously initiated me into two of Satan's priesthoods, I held the requisite authority to perform it.

Before performing the ritual, I had to ingest certain drugs—a combination of hallucinogens and barbiturates—so that my mind would be pliable and open to suggestions. Additionally, I must be prepared to offer up both body and soul if the Master required it.

After spending the next two weeks converting the second-floor loft into a temple of Satan, I consecrated it, ingested the drugs, and performed a Black Mass, the details of which I will omit for obvious reasons.

After finishing my final invocation, I prostrated myself on the floor and waited. A few minutes later, the room gradually began to brighten, the light increasing in intensity until the room became as bright as day. Then I heard a voice inside my mind say, "Behold your Master."

I find it most difficult to describe my feelings as I perceived the voice. The words, including the emotional content, were projected into my mind telepathically. It was very surreal. Although I was high from the drugs, I could discern Satan's pleasure in my diligent preparations. Nevertheless, my limbs quaked with terror. I paused for a moment, summoned all my courage, and then lifted my head and beheld my Master.

He looked like an angel, floating in the air above me. Although his head was covered by a hood, I could discern his handsome and refined features. His eyes were brown and piercing. He wore a long, white, silken robe that hung down to his ankles. A purple sash with red emblems embossed into the fabric was tied about his waist. His feet were shod with black sandals studded with brilliant gemstones, and he held a scepter in his left hand. I noted that the bright light illuminating the room emanated from his personage, radiating outward in waves of power.

I summoned all of my courage and asked him about the sash. He smiled and replied that the emblems on it symbolized his priesthoods. Then he consoled me, saying that there was nothing to fear, that he had no wish to harm me. He explained that the world had everything backward, that it was God who made his people suffer, and that it was Lucifer who wanted to redeem them from their pain. He did not desire the destruction of mankind as the Christians believed. He said that it was my mission as his disciple to help dispel this evil myth and bring more worshippers to him.

I felt immensely relieved upon learning that he would not harm me. I gathered myself once more and asked him the question that had kept me awake for so many nights: "Master: Where is the philosopher's stone located?"

He smiled benevolently and replied that it was his will that I procure it, that much good would come from its use, as long as I wielded its great power in accordance with his wishes. He explained that, although the precise location of the stone was unknown, it was held by a servant of God. However, there was another stone—the Lyricor—that would provide the general location.

He explained that a certain nomadic tribe of Bedouins, located in the Sahara Desert, possessed the Lyricor. Unfortunately, they would not release it of their own free will. As such, he said I must conjure the demon of death—Azazel—and command it to kill them. Once the Lyricor was safely in my possession, it would provide the general location of the philosopher's stone. Then I must find a cross within the area circumscribed by the Lyricor, which would lead me directly to the servant who possessed the stone.

He said I would also need the Lyricor to access the stone once I obtained it. Before I could ask him any more questions, he abruptly vanished, leaving the loft in darkness.

I returned to the hospital and spent a few tense days with Joanne. The doctor's prognosis was grave—she had, at best, six months of life remaining. Although initially happy at my return, she became despondent when I explained my impending journey to Africa. She tearfully entreated me not to go, and I almost relented. Leaving her was the hardest thing I had ever done. Although my heart was torn with sadness, I was absolutely determined to see the thing through. I reassured her, saying that our separation was only temporary, that when I returned, we would be together forever.

After procuring the necessary papers, I boarded a flight for New York City. From there, I flew to London, then on to Algeria—which, according to my research, was the most likely place to begin. Then after landing in Algiers, the capital city, I consulted with several guides, eventually finding one that claimed to know the approximate location of the al-Mutairi tribe—the last known nomadic tribe still residing in the southernmost part of the country.

My guide, Kris, informed me that our best hope was locating the oasis frequented by the tribe. From Algiers, we flew to the city of Tamanrasset, a squalid little town located about twenty miles away from the Ahaggar Mountains, where the tribe was known to roam.

It was morning when we landed at the Tamanrasset Airport, a single airstrip on the outskirts of town. As we headed into the city, my guide explained that since the oasis was nearby, there was no need to carry many provisions.

An hour later, after renting two camels and donning our burnooses—the loose-fitting, hooded cloaks that would shelter us from the desert heat—we proceeded north to the mountain range. As we traveled, I was moved by the amazingly beautiful landscape, gradually changing from savanna to sand dunes to mountains. We struck camp at sundown and slept under the stars, lying on mats placed over the sand. The nights were warm and dry in the Sahara, so we didn't need tents.

We awakened at sunrise and continued our journey into the mountains, heading toward the nearest several oases located there. My guide had no trouble finding one. It was a large oasis surrounded by a small village. Kris doubted that we would find the tribe there, explaining that they preferred the less populated areas. After searching the village to no avail, we spent another night sleeping outdoors and then broke camp just after dawn.

Early that afternoon we found a small oasis, which was nothing more than a pond of water surrounded by several palm trees and bushes. To my disappointment, no one was there. The guide explained that the tribe was in transit to another oasis.

I became impatient and angry because I had wasted another week of precious time on a journey that had failed to produce the desired results. I thought about casting a nausea spell on my ineffectual guide but decided against it. It wasn't really his fault since he had done everything I had asked. Realizing that I had reached the point at which no mere mortal could help, I decided to conjure the demon Azazel and ask him where the tribe was located.

I waited until sunset to begin my preparations. As I began drawing the circles of protection, my guide stared at me with a puzzled expression and asked what I was doing. When I replied that I was preparing to conjure a demon, he became frightened and departed on his camel.

That night I performed the ritual and successfully conjured the demon. Not only did it reveal the location of the tribe, which was granted to me in a vision, but also it promised to help me obtain the Lyricor as well.

It even conferred upon me the gift of tongues, enabling me to speak and understand the Arabic language. Upon asking the demon what it wanted in return, it replied cryptically that it would let me know at a later time.

The next morning, I traveled into the desert, following the directions given by the demon. A few hours later, I found the tribe—a small group of approximately twenty people, including men, women, and children camped by a small oasis. Their possessions were scanty. I counted ten tents, five camels, and a small flock of sheep. The tribesmen were attired in long, hooded robes called djellabas. The men wore headgear made from rufiyaa cloth and agal-rope. The married women wrapped black cloths—called Asabas—around their foreheads in addition to the headgear. The people were friendly enough—it didn't hurt that I spoke Arabic—and the sheikh offered me to stay the night and enjoy his hospitality.

I was surprised to find a small group of Christian missionaries, who had journeyed all the way from England, staying with them. After introducing me to the missionaries, the sheikh explained that his tribe was incomplete, that only a few families remained in the desert. The main group had renounced their nomadic lifestyles and moved into the cities several years ago. He further explained that the missionaries were his guests and that he was interested in their teachings.

That evening, after partaking of a simple meal of mutton and dates washed down with copious amounts of cardamom-spiced coffee, I walked into the desert and conjured Azazel for the second time. The demon explained that, contrary to the Master's wishes, several nomads had been converted to the Christian faith. Because the newly converted would spread their newfound religion into the nearby cities through their strong family ties, it was necessary to execute the entire tribe, including the missionaries. The demon stated that their death was my responsibility. It was the payment required of me.

I dismissed the demon and returned to the camp, feeling strangely buoyant. The previous conjurations had increased the power of my sorcery. It would be a simple matter to cast a spell on the oasis and poison the water. After the tribesmen were dead, I would possess the Lyricor and be one important step closer to saving my beloved.

After enjoying an evening of Bedouin entertainment, consisting of music, poetry, and dance, I fell asleep in one of the tents. Early the next morning, I awakened to an eerie silence. I rushed outside, surveyed the campsite, and found no one around. I quickly discovered the reason when

I looked inside the tents. Everyone, including the missionaries, was dead, apparently from asphyxiation.

I became extremely frightened when I realized that the demon was responsible for their deaths, perhaps with the aid of an untold number of other hellish ghouls. That meant that my banishing spell had failed—and the demon had not retreated into the underworld. Apparently, my conjuring had served to increase the demon's power as well as my own.

Realizing that it could have murdered me as easily as the others, I spent the next two hours casting the most powerful protection spells I knew, hoping they were adequate to ensure my safety. Then I embarked upon a frantic search for the Lyricor, rummaging through everyone's belongings, eventually realizing, with a sinking feeling of despair, that either the tribe did not possess it or they had hidden it somewhere. Since they were all dead, I would never be able to find it.

I fell to the ground and cried my heart out, wracked with agony, the intensity of which I had never before experienced. Satan had lied to me, sending me on a wild-goose chase to Algeria, knowing all along that I would never find the Lyricor. I had become his unwitting pawn. He had used me for the sole purpose of ending the Christian missionary effort in the Sahara.

I made my way back to Tamanrasset, completely miserable and devoid of all hope, knowing that without the philosopher's stone I could not save Joanne.

It was the beginning of March when I finally returned to Chicago. As expected, Joanne's condition had worsened. I spent every waking hour by her side, attempting to console and comfort her. The next two months passed very slowly as I sat there helplessly, watching her body waste away.

My protection spells had become increasingly ineffective against the demons and their legion of underlings, who began hounding me day and night, attempting to break through the virtual doorway I had unwittingly created through my sorcery. Out of necessity, I drew protection circles around my bed, dousing them with holy water every night to keep the demons from possessing my soul while I slept.

It is now May of 2006, and I bring my writings to a close. I have decided to secure my memoirs and the Numericon, storing them in a cedar chest in the loft of my parents' cabin where Duke Revic won't be able to find them. Then I will return to Chicago and spend Joanne's final hours with her.

In closing, I leave a solemn warning to anyone who reads these memoirs. Do not attempt to travel down the dark path I have trodden, no matter how desperate your circumstances may seem. Do not, for any reason, ever attempt any of the spells described in this book, even if you think you have sufficient knowledge and protection. The black arts, when pursued to the extreme, lead only to pain, terror, and death.

God have mercy upon my soul.

Signed,
Thomas Harrison

# CHAPTER SEVEN

David put down the notebook and fell back onto the sofa with a sigh. It was impossible to have known just how far Tom had immersed himself in the dark side—conjuring demons and even striking a deal with Satan himself. Was the man completely delusional? No one in their right mind would do such a thing.

On the other hand, he understood the underlying motive behind Tom's radical behavior. His own deep and abiding love for Angela provided some insight. He wondered, if faced with the same knowledge of her impending death, just how far he would have gone to save her.

David sat up with a jolt, recalling that the device Tom had risked his life searching for was real and that it was in David's possession. He had assumed that Tom's writings were merely the distorted ramblings of a madman, but the existence of the Lyricor validated at least a portion of them. His mind, filled with questions. Did the philosopher's stone actually exist? Did demons exist, and was it possible to conjure them? He shuddered at the thought. He glanced at the clock. Surprised at how late it was, he went straight to bed.

David was awakened early the next morning by the telephone on his nightstand. It was his mother. "I'm sorry to tell you this, David," she said in a distraught tone. "It's your father. He's taken a turn for the worse."

"What's wrong with Dad?" David asked, feeling a chill run through his body.

"The tests came back positive," she said, breaking into sobs. "I'm afraid he has pancreatic cancer."

"I'll take the next flight home," David said. "Is Dottie there yet?"

"Yes, she has just arrived. I'll have her pick you up at the airport."

David prepared for his journey in haste, making the necessary flight arrangements, throwing a few clothes into his suitcase, and making a call to Dr. Lucas. Fortunately, the surgeon agreed to his request for personal leave.

He drove to the airport, reflecting upon the previous month's unsettling and tragic events. First, there was the conspiracy surrounding his beloved Angela, followed by her tragic death. Unfortunately, there was no solace from his grief and pain. There was no closure because her killer had not been apprehended.

Now, facing the death of his father, he felt even more depressed. How could he continue his medical practice after all that had happened? He knew it was unwise to throw away a promising career, especially one that he had worked so exceedingly hard for, but he didn't know if he could live in Chicago anymore. The memories there were too painful. He needed time to come to grips with the new, harsh reality that had so rapidly and utterly sapped all the joy from his life.

David burst into tears and pulled the car to the side of the road. Though still crying, he resumed driving a few minutes later so as not to miss his flight. As he pulled into the parking lot of O'Hare, he realized that he shouldn't be making snap decisions. He needed time to view things from their proper perspective. Fortunately, Dr. Lucas had given him an indefinite leave of absence, allowing him the time he needed to consider and weigh his options.

David's sister, Dottie, was waiting when David walked out of the arrival gate at the Pittsburgh International Airport. "I'm so sorry," she said, hugging him tearfully. With dark hair, blue eyes, and high cheekbones, Dottie bore a striking resemblance to her younger brother.

"How's Mom holding up?" David asked with a look of concern as they proceeded to the baggage claim area.

"Not very well, I'm afraid. She's been spending all her time at the hospital with Dad and hasn't been getting much sleep. I've spoken to her about it, but she won't listen. Maybe you can talk to her."

"Where's Frank?" David asked.

"He had to stay home and take care of the children. We decided it would be better not to pull them out of school. Our father still has several months to live, according to the doctors."

"That's a reassuring thought," David said sarcastically. He immediately regretted the comment, noting the tears that moistened his sister's eyes. "Hey sis, I'm sorry. I didn't mean to come off sounding like a jerk."

"We're both going through a rough time right now," Dottie replied, managing a smile. "Let's just forget it, okay?"

David drove home recalling the joyous times spent with his father. Although away on business most of the time, his father had always made time for them when he was home—playing baseball, swimming, taking them to ball games, and doing all the things good fathers do with their children.

When David was fourteen, his father had taken him overseas to begin his training in the oil business. When they toured the drilling rigs, his father had the engineers explain how they were designed. He spent many hours with David that summer, as well as the next four summers, explaining the inner workings of the business. Those were the happiest days of David's life.

Although David's father was wealthy, he always treated everyone with respect, right down to the housekeeping staff and gardener. To keep David grounded, his father had kept him in public school, even though all the other wealthy parents in their neighborhood had sent their children to private boarding schools.

David was glad his father hadn't given him special treatment. Although drug usage was rampant in his high school, he had stayed clear of it and had taken his studies seriously, assuming that he would work in his father's company after graduating from college. Unfortunately, in his junior year, his best friend died from an accidental drug overdose. It was then that he decided to become a doctor.

His sister had gone on to college as well, becoming a high school English teacher. She had met her fiancé, Frank Landsburg—a math teacher—at the same school. They married a year later and had three children—Samantha, Frank Jr., and Brian.

"It's nice to be home again," David remarked as they drove through the main gate. The family mansion, constructed in the Tudor Revival style and built in 1934 by his grandfather, sat fat and happy upon approximately one hundred acres of land. The walls were made of white stucco, set off by dark brown half-timbering. The mansion featured five prominent cross gables, complete with tall, narrow lattice windows. The roof was steeply pitched and featured three massive chimneys topped with decorative pots and rounded parapets.

The siblings met their mother in the small dining room, which was pleasantly decorated in a mid-twentieth-century design. A blue glass table with light blue and white table settings nestled under a shimmering, capiz-shell chandelier, lending the room a contemporary ambiance despite the prominent Victorian features, including a curved, front wall with three large windows, a ten-foot-high cove ceiling, and built-in walnut cabinets.

A female server wearing a white lace apron over a blue blouse and skirt promptly appeared with beverages and appetizers. "I thought you could use some nourishment before we go see your father," his mother said, managing a wan smile.

Her tall, thin figure was accentuated by a tailored plaid jacket and skirt ensemble. A pair of lovely brown eyes framed by curly, highlighted brown hair enhanced her otherwise plain features. David noted her exhausted appearance.

"I'm sorry to hear about Dad," he said, tears watering his eyes. He wiped them away with a napkin. "I know about pancreatic cancer. I'll be honest with you, Mom. There's no cure."

His mother burst into tears. Dottie sat by her side and consoled her, and David put his arm around her as she continued to weep. He mentally chastised himself for being so tactless.

"I'm sorry," David's mother said after regaining her composure. "I know there's no cure. The doctors have told me to prepare for the worst. They're giving him six months."

They sat in silence for a few moments, unsure of what to say. "So, tell me about Chicago, David," his mother said, changing the subject.

David hesitated for a moment. It wasn't the right time to bring up Angela, he decided. "I've been keeping busy at the hospital," he said, managing a grin. "Dr. Lucas is a great doctor. It's a privilege working with his team."

"I always knew you would do well for yourself," his mother said proudly, giving him an approving smile. "Your heart is in it. I can see that."

After a simple lunch of beefeater salad and wine, they were chauffeured to the hospital in the company limo. David put on a brave smile as he entered his father's room. "Good to see you again, Dad."

His father was sitting up in the hospital bed, appearing slightly jaundiced. Though obviously unwell, he retained his handsome appearance—the blue eyes and high cheekbones that characterized the Sholfield line. "I'm glad you're here, son," he said with a bright smile. "I'm anxious to hear about Chicago."

They exchanged amenities for a few minutes, then David's father turned to his wife. "If you and Dottie will excuse us, there's a business matter I need to discuss with David."

After they departed, he gave his son a wistful smile. "You know that I don't have long to live, don't you, son?"

Tears began to roll down David's cheeks. He stood and moved to the bedside, then patted his father's shoulder. "I know, Dad. I'm here for you, okay?"

"I know you are, son. I'm glad you could get away from your practice for a bit. There's something I need to discuss with you. After the doctors discovered my condition, I called a board meeting and made them aware of my situation. I told them that it was my intention to leave the company to you."

Feeling his knees grow weak, David sat down on the side of the bed. "I don't know what to say," he said, a myriad of thoughts running through his mind.

"As you know, Sholfield Oil is a private company," his father continued, "and I hold the controlling interest. I have given instructions to my second in command—Jack Murphy—to have the papers ready for your signature Monday morning. I'm turning over the controlling interest to you."

As David began to reply, his father held up his hand. "I know you've chosen to be a doctor, son, but your sister is busy raising her children and she doesn't have the background in company matters like you do. All I ask," he continued, "is that you honor your dying father's wishes and keep the company in the family. You can run it yourself, or you can put someone else in charge. I suggest you use Jack. He's been my right-hand man for the last thirty years, and I trust him like family. In either case, you will be the chairman of the board. As such, you must attend the annual shareholders meeting and an occasional quarterly board meeting."

David thought about refusing. He had no interest in running the company. However, his father had given him the option of putting someone else in charge. He could continue his medical practice with little interruption, though he would need to keep an eye on things. In any case, he had no desire to defy his father's last wishes.

David nodded his head. "Thanks for placing your trust and confidence in me," he said with a smile of gratitude. "I will honor your wishes."

That night, after spending a couple of hours chatting with his sister and mother during supper, David retired to his bedroom. He smiled wistfully as he gazed upon the room. His mother had kept it exactly the same as it was when he had left for college.

He unpacked his suitcase and dutifully hung up his clothes, saving the housekeeper the trouble. He had always liked keeping his room neat and tidy. He walked back to the suitcase, opened it, and peered inside, noting the Lyricor. He recalled Tom's memoirs, the depressing account of his failure to find the locating device, and the death of both his girlfriend and himself.

David wondered why the brown-haired stranger had given the Lyricor to him. The thought occurred to David that perhaps God was somehow involved in this, perhaps giving him a way to save his father.

As David picked up the Lyricor, it began glowing with a soft, golden light. A series of numbers abruptly appeared on its surface in red, Arabic numerals. Surprised by the sudden change in its appearance, he dropped the stone onto the floor.

He hesitated for a moment, wondering if it was safe to hold it. Then, after steeling himself, he picked it up again, carried it to his desk, and breathed out a sigh of relief. So far, so good.

He opened the top drawer, located a pad and pen, and copied down the numerals. After a few moments, the stone stopped glowing and the numbers disappeared from its surface. Suddenly feeling very tired, David returned the Lyricor to his suitcase and went to bed.

"Go right on in, Mr. Sholfield," the secretary said with a friendly smile as David walked into the reception room. "Mr. Murphy is expecting you."

David took a deep breath, steadied himself, and stepped through the door of Jack's office. He was surprised at the office's ordinary appearance, considering the man's position as a top-level business executive. Several pictures of modern art hung from plain, white walls. There were four potted palms—one in each corner—and a large window providing an excellent view of downtown Pittsburgh. The furniture was minimal, consisting of a rather ordinary-looking scratched walnut desk with four chairs surrounding it. It appeared that Jack didn't use his office very often.

Jack stood up from his desk, smiled affably, and extended his hand. "How nice to meet you, David," he said in a deep voice.

Jack appeared in his early fifties; his brown hair flecked with grey. He stood about five feet ten with a stocky build, brown eyes, and average features. David noted his suit was as modest as his office—definitely not a designer brand. "Good to meet you, sir," he responded, shaking the man's hand.

"I've had the pleasure of working with your father for over thirty years now," Jack said with an accommodating smile. "I want you to know that you can come to me for anything. Okay, David?"

"Thank you, Mr. Murphy. My main concern is that the company remains in safe hands. I don't know if my father told you, but I'm a cardiac surgeon. I have no intention of leaving my practice, which requires most of my time and energy. I will not be running the company. My father suggested that after I become the majority stockholder, I should put you in charge. He said that you can be trusted. Is that agreeable to you?"

The executive sat down at his desk, opened a drawer, and produced a stack of papers. "It's all here in writing, son. I suggest you read all the documents and have them checked over by your attorney. I assure you; everything is in order. Once you sign the documents, the process of turning your father's company over to you will proceed quickly and smoothly. As I mentioned, you can contact me personally anytime you need further information. You can call me Jack, by the way."

"That's reassuring to know, Jack," David said with a relieved expression. "I feel good about this. I want you to know that when I take control of the company, you may run it as you see fit. You have my promise that I will not second-guess any of your decisions."

David spent the next two hours in Jack's office as the executive explained the various terms and conditions contained in the documents, closing with a brief update of current company projects.

As he was leaving, David handed Jack a slip of paper. "I know this is off the subject," he said, "but do you have any idea what these numbers might refer to?"

Jack glanced at the paper, his eyes instantly brightening in recognition. "I sure do. Those are latitudes and longitudes. We use them all the time."

David spent the rest of the week shuttling back and forth between the hospital and the corporate office building, speaking with his father, Jack, and the management team, learning all he could about the company.

The following Monday, David returned to Jack's office and signed the documents in the presence of a notary, with two other company officers witnessing the act. Then he met with the board members and was formally announced as chairman of the board, with Jack Murphy as CEO.

Exhausted from the seemingly endless days of business meetings, David drove straight home and retired to his room. He lay down on the bed thinking it ironic that his sad and lonely feelings were the exact opposite of the elation he had always thought he would feel when he inherited his father's company.

Thoughts and images of Angela abruptly came into his mind. The only woman he had ever loved was dead. He had spoken with Detective Scott on Wednesday, but the detective still had no leads—the coven's cloak of secrecy had served them well. Since there was no evidence directly linking Duke Revic to the crime, he couldn't be extradited back to Chicago for questioning, and Tom had left no clues in his memoirs about the coven members' identities or locations.

Now David's father was dying, his body infected with a virulent, incurable form of cancer. It had become increasingly difficult visiting him in the hospital, watching him wither away, unable to offer any help as a doctor, or as a son.

Suddenly, David sat up and pulled the slip of paper out of his pocket. Perhaps there was something he could do after all. It was a long shot, though. Jack had stated that the numbers from the Lyricor were coordinates. Had it revealed the location of the philosopher's stone? The whole thing seemed preposterous, but it was his only remaining hope. He had heard stories of people embarking upon wild adventures in search of offbeat cures for their loved ones. If they were willing to go to such extreme lengths to save their loved one's lives, why shouldn't he?

The next morning, David drove to the corporate office building and spoke with a company geologist. Using the coordinates David gave him, the man was able to plot the location on a map.

David returned home feeling relaxed and free of worry for the first time in months. His decision to find a cure for his father had completely changed his attitude.

"I need to talk to you about something, Mom," David said as he met his mother and sister in the small dining room that afternoon.

"Of course, dear," she said. "What's on your mind?"

He paused for a moment before replying, strengthening his resolve as he noted the comfort his presence gave her. He realized how much she needed his support. "I'm leaving for Nova Scotia as soon as I get my travel papers in order," he said bluntly.

She set down her cup of coffee and gave him a look of concern. "Does this have something to do with the company, David?"

He had to give her credit—she was taking it well. "No, Mom," he replied. "It's about Dad. I know this sounds strange, but I've come across some valuable information regarding a cure."

"That sounds very strange coming from you," Dottie remarked. "You sound like one of those weak-minded individuals who latch onto any crackpot idea out of desperation. You're a doctor. You must certainly know how many quacks there are out there, offering false hope to their poor victims. It's really very sad, you know."

"I know it sounds bad, sis," David said, his face brightening a little, "but if there's any chance of finding a cure, no matter how slim, I must take it. I promise I won't get my hopes up, okay?"

"Please don't be away too long, dear," his mother said with pleading eyes. "I will need you with us before your father's disease gets the better of him."

Ten days later, David arrived in Louisbourg, Nova Scotia, and checked into a bed-and-breakfast in nearby Cape Breton. Although tired from the two-hundred-kilometer drive from the Halifax Stanfield International Airport, he decided to press onward to the Fortress of Louisbourg, the general location of the coordinates.

When planning his trip, David had learned that the fortress was a national park, the largest historical reconstruction in Canada. Originally built to protect France's interests in the new world, it was renovated in the 1960s as a tourist destination. As such, it offered a unique window into the past, in particular, Canada's eighteenth-century colonial history. But he was not there for the history.

David quickly passed through the visitor's center and embarked upon a tour of the fortress. He watched with amusement the re-enactment of life in the 1700s—streets lined with quaint shops and soldiers dressed in period costumes.

The fortress itself was quite large, covering a twelve-acre area with over fifty buildings. He spent the entire day searching through half of the buildings, not knowing what he was looking for. At five p.m. the park closed, and he left feeling disappointed, having found no clues to the location of the mythical philosopher's stone.

David returned to the bed-and-breakfast, ate a light supper at a nearby seafood restaurant, then retired to his room. It was small but clean, with a hardwood floor, a queen-sized bed, a recliner, a rocking chair, a coffee table, a small television, and an antique wooden dresser.

Melancholia filled him as he lay on the quilted bedspread, thoughts of Angela resurfacing once again. He knew it was unhealthy to dwell on her memory. He needed to find closure and move on. Perhaps talking to a friend would help. He decided to call Alan.

"Well, what do you know," Alan said in a surprised tone. "How are you, my good friend?"

"It's really good to hear your voice, Alan," David said. "You won't believe this, but I'm in Nova Scotia."

"What the heck are you doing in Nova Scotia, buddy?"

"Do you remember the notebook I took from Angie's guesthouse?"

"Tom's memoirs. Did you finally read them?"

"Oh yeah. It turns out that Tom was into some very heavy witchcraft."

"I guess that explains his psychotic behavior. So, what did you find out?"

"He was looking for an object called the Lyricor. Apparently, it's a device used to reveal the location of something called the philosopher's stone."

"The philosopher's stone. I vaguely remember the term. I did a little research on it in college. It was used in medieval times by sorcerers to turn base metals into gold. It was also reputed to have healing properties. Sounds like folklore, man."

"I thought so too at first, but it turns out that the Lyricor is real."

"Really! How do you know that?"

"You won't believe this, but a stranger appeared out of the blue and gave it to me. I swear it's true, and it even gave me a set of coordinates. That's why I'm in Nova Scotia."

"I get it. You want to find the philosopher's stone to heal your father. But how do you know it even exists, or that the Lyricor is real, for that matter? Tom was a mental case."

"Yeah, I know. I spent the entire day looking for clues but came up empty. I don't even know what I'm looking for."

"Did Tom say anything in his writings about who possessed the philosopher's stone in the past?"

"As a matter of fact, he did," David said, recalling Tom's account. "According to the folklore, the last known person who supposedly had it was Thomas Aquinas."

"I remember studying him in my philosophy class," Alan said. "He was a Catholic priest in the Dominican Order, a philosopher, and a theologian as well. He was a very smart cookie. I think you're looking for an Anglican monk. Friars used to be part of the Dominican Order, but they've recently merged with the Anglicans. Did Tom mention anything else about the stone?"

"Yeah. He said that the Lyricor would give the general location, and a cross would point to the person possessing the philosopher's stone. Someone who is a servant of God."

"Well, that narrows it down somewhat. In my opinion, you're looking for a monk with a large cross. If I remember correctly, St. Thomas was a big guy with a large head and a receding hairline. He should be easy to spot in a crowd, especially dressed in a monk's robe."

"Thank you so much, Alan," David said gratefully. "Now I know who I'm looking for."

"Anytime, my friend. Good luck with your quest. Don't forget to keep in touch and let me know how you're doing, okay?"

Early the next morning, David returned to the fortress. After a short walk, he came upon a chapel named the Chapelle St. Louis. He entered the building and thoroughly scanned the interior. The small chapel featured a vaulted plaster ceiling and a few stained-glass windows. He noted the large cross hanging on the wall behind the pulpit. Thinking that the monk might make an appearance, he walked outside and stood near the entrance, watching everyone that entered.

Two hours later, David's patience was rewarded as a large, bald man attired in a brown monk's habit entered the chapel. He waited outside, and when the monk reappeared several minutes later, David followed. After walking two blocks, the monk entered a flower shop. David cautiously approached, then stopped half a block away, keeping his eyes firmly focused on the entrance.

When the monk failed to reappear, he entered the shop and searched the premises. He felt a sting of disappointment after questioning the florist, who had been preoccupied with a flower arrangement and had seen nothing.

After spending the rest of the day searching, David returned to his room and lay down on the bed, once again experiencing the familiar emotions of disappointment and loneliness. He had found a cross but had lost the monk. Could the man really be the fabled Thomas Aquinas, kept alive through the centuries by the supernatural properties of the philosopher's stone? It all seemed so far-fetched.

He began to doubt his mission, recalling Tom's psychotic outburst at Duke Revic's Fourth of July party. Now here he was, far away from his family during a time of crisis, chasing down clues buried in the writings of a madman. Maybe he was just as crazy as Tom.

Feeling hungry, David returned to the seafood restaurant. After being seated, he noted two women—a blonde and a brunette—seated at a table opposite him. Both women were young and attractive, dressed in casual attire.

"Would you care to join us?" the blonde asked unabashedly, giving David an inviting smile.

David hesitated before responding, wondering if he was fit for the company. The women were obviously American. Perhaps their companionship would cheer him up a little. "That would be fine," he replied with a polite smile.

"I see you're from the States," the blonde remarked as he sat down next to her.

"I'm David. David Sholfield," he said, shaking her hand gently. "And you are?"

"I'm Jamie and this is Holly," she replied, nodding to the brunette. "We're on vacation, visiting Holly's family." She smiled alluringly. "And you?"

"I'm taking a break too," David replied, his mind awhirl. Unfortunately, he hadn't bothered to prepare a cover story. They would deem him crazy if he revealed the truth. "When I was in Toronto, I heard about the fortress," he decided upon, "so I extended my trip to include it." He was definitely attracted to Jamie, with her blonde hair, blue eyes, and a cute nose.

"It's really something, isn't it?" Holly said, giving him a charming smile. "The way they recreated everything. It's like we hopped into a time machine and traveled back to the eighteenth century."

David had the distinct impression that Holly was attracted to him as well. "It's remarkable that they were able to recreate everything so authentically," he remarked nonchalantly.

The women continued their light conversation throughout the meal, giving David an enthusiastic recap of the latest US sporting events. He realized that it was the first evening since Angela's death that he hadn't felt lonely. He thought about asking the ladies out to a nightclub afterward but decided against it, mentally chiding himself. He wasn't here for a romantic getaway.

After dinner, Jamie gave him a provocative grin. "We were thinking of taking in a little nightlife. Would you care to join us?"

"Thanks for the offer," David replied impassively, noting the disappointed look on her face. "It sounds like a nice idea, but I need to get some sleep. I'm returning to the fortress first thing in the morning."

Holly produced a slip of paper and a pen from her purse and jotted down her phone number. "If you change your mind, give us a call," she said, handing him the slip of paper. As he stood up to leave, she gave him a wink.

David spent the next day standing in front of the chapel, scanning the crowd and hoping that the monk would reappear. As closing time approached, he made a thorough search of the surrounding area but found nothing of interest.

David returned to the restaurant feeling morose, wondering once again if he had been sent on a wild-goose chase by a madman. He began to question the authenticity of the Lyricor—although the numbers that had mysteriously appeared on its surface were actual coordinates, they had failed to lead him to the philosopher's stone. Was he being scammed for some reason? He had recently come into wealth, inheriting his father's company. Perhaps the brown-haired stranger who had given him the white stone was setting him up, preying upon his desire to find a cure for his father.

David looked around the dining area as he followed the hostess to his table. Annoyed by his disappointment at not seeing Holly and Jamie, he reprimanded himself. It was foolish to be concerned about two strange women he knew nothing about. Why should he care whether he saw them again? On the other hand, it was only natural to feel lonely, considering everything that had happened. Perhaps he shouldn't be so hard on himself.

When the waitress appeared, David decided to comfort himself with a hearty dinner, ordering steak, fresh lobster, and crab legs. He took his time eating the savory meal, recalling what he had learned about the philosopher's stone. If the Lyricor was real, the fortress must be the correct location. But how could he discover, among the thousands of tourists passing through, which one possessed the stone?

Tom had stated in his memoirs that a cross would point to the person in question and that he was a servant of God. That narrowed his search down somewhat. He had found a large cross in the fortress chapel, and a monk resembling the description of Thomas Aquinas. Unfortunately, the monk had failed to reappear. Perhaps persistence was the key.

By the time David finished his meal, his melancholia had returned. The thought of returning to the lonely hotel room was untenable. Recalling that Holly had given him her phone number, he retrieved the slip of paper from his jacket pocket and entered the number into his cell phone. Perhaps a little female companionship would take the edge off.

After a few rings, she answered. "Hello, David!" she replied cheerfully. "I'm so glad you called. We were just getting ready to head down to the lounge. We're staying at the Fortress Inn. Would you care to join us for a drink?"

David felt a surge of excitement at her request, immediately dispelling his despondency. The idea of spending the evening in the company of lovely young women was very compelling. "I'll meet you there," he replied.

A half-hour later, David arrived at Jake's Restaurant and Lounge, located inside the Fortress Inn. It featured a nice stand-up bar draped in a variety of flags from all over the world, a big-screen satellite TV, two pool tables, a pair of dartboards, and four video poker machines. The young women were at the far end, gleefully engaged in a game of darts.

"Not bad," David remarked as Jamie hit the center of the target.

"Just a lucky toss, I guess," she said.

A seductive expression appeared on her face. "How nice you look this evening, David."

"Thanks for the compliment," David said. "You and Holly look nice as well." He thought that they looked appealing, dressed in their low-cut, tight-fitting party dresses and their mutual attraction to David was unmistakable.

"Let's go to the bar and order drinks," Jamie said after throwing her last dart. "My wrists are getting sore from playing this silly game."

"Are you enjoying your stay?" Holly asked after they had ordered drinks from the bartender.

"I guess," David replied.

"You don't sound very enthused," Jamie said. "I love the history of this place."

"I'm afraid I haven't done my homework," David said, breaking into a smile. "Perhaps you can give me a briefing."

Jamie threw her head back and laughed in an uninhibited manner. David thought she looked very sexy when she did that. "I guess I can accommodate your request. The fortress was originally built by the French in order to protect their interests. It was meant to be the first line of defense in France's eighteenth-century struggle against England's quest for supremacy of North America."

"That sounds typical," David remarked. "A bunch of politicians squabbling over territory and riches."

"That's an original way to put it," Jamie said, grinning. "Anyway, the English managed to capture the fortress in a six-week siege back in 1745. Three years later, it was returned to France. Then it fell to the British again in another siege in 1758. Then, around 1761, the idiots blew it to pieces, where it remained in a state of shambles until the Canadians reconstructed it two centuries later."

"I read somewhere that the Canadian government rebuilt it from scratch," David remarked. "That must have been a considerable undertaking." He ordered another round of drinks. He was beginning to enjoy himself.

After finishing their drinks, the threesome decided to try their luck at video poker. "I'm not very good at video games," David remarked as they sat down in front of the machines.

"Video poker is the coolest game you can play," Holly said with an enthusiastic grin. "I'll show you how it's done."

After several rounds of drinks and over an hour at the machines, David was ready to leave. He glanced at his watch. "It's getting late, ladies," he said. "I need to get back to the hotel."

"But we were having such an enjoyable time," Jamie said, giving him a sultry smile. "How about joining us for a nightcap? Our room is just upstairs."

David glanced appreciatively at Jamie's near-perfect figure, showcased by the tailored cut of her party dress. Not only was she a charming conversationalist, but she was also very charismatic. "I guess that would be okay," he replied.

David appraised the ladies' second-floor hotel room as he entered. With two double beds, a bathroom, cable TV, a telephone, a desk-credenza combination, a small refrigerator, and an alarm clock radio, it was unremarkable. Three of the walls were painted white, and the separating wall between the bedroom and bathroom was covered in satiny, blue-and-mauve striped wallpaper.

Jamie produced a bottle of champagne from the refrigerator while Holly retrieved three glasses from the bathroom. After pouring the champagne, Jamie lifted her glass in a toast. "Here's to our new friend, David. May your journey be a joyous and an interesting one."

After the toast, Holly moved in close and unabashedly French-kissed David. "How's that for interesting?" she said, smiling sensuously.

David watched in fascination as Holly began a striptease, taking off her clothes one piece at a time while dancing around the room and wiggling her hips. Then Jamie gently pushed him down on the bed. "I would like a little of that if you don't mind."

As David attempted to kiss her, his vision suddenly blurred. "I'm not feeling very well," he said. His tongue felt thick and heavy, and he realized that he was slurring his words. The last thing he heard was Jamie saying, "You gave him too much, Holly. He's going under too fast. We can't even have sex with him."

David awakened feeling very groggy. He rolled over and glanced at the clock: a few minutes after eleven. He sat up with a start, realizing that he was still in Holly and Jamie's room. He wondered if they had drugged him. He quickly checked his trousers and breathed out a sigh of relief. His wallet was intact, along with his credit cards and cash. After quickly searching the room and finding no sign of the women or their belongings, he showered, put on his clothes, and walked to the front desk. "Do you know what happened to the women staying in room 105?" he asked the desk clerk.

"They checked out this morning," the man replied. When he saw the puzzled look on David's face, the clerk gave him a sympathetic grin. "Sorry, bud. Looks like you got stood up."

David drove back to the bed-and-breakfast, ran to his room, and hurriedly rummaged through his belongings. Moments later, his worst fears were confirmed: The Lyricor was missing. He forced himself to sit down and relax. Eventually, he calmed down and began pondering the events, theorizing that Holly and Jamie were witches sent from Revic's coven.

It was a stretch, though. How had they known about the Lyricor? The duke, who knew of its existence, must have been keeping tabs on him. Perhaps his sudden departure for Nova Scotia was a red flag, informing the duke that he had obtained the locating device. Now, through his negligence, it was lost. The philosopher's stone was still within reach, however he pulled himself together and returned to the fortress.

Upon arrival, David walked directly to the chapel, where he spent the rest of the day standing watch. Unfortunately, the monk did not reappear. He remained there until closing and made a final search, once again in vain. David wondered if the monk had been to the chapel that morning while he was still at the hotel sleeping off the effects of the knockout drug.

David returned to the bed-and-breakfast feeling totally dejected, desiring to forget all about the crazy scheme. He would return home and spend the remaining time with his dying father.

As he entered his room, he was shocked and frightened by what he saw. Holly and Jamie stood alongside the bed, wearing black cloaks with hoods drawn over their heads. "What are you two doing here?" he asked in a shaky voice.

Suddenly Holly grabbed him by the shoulders and pushed him down onto the bed. Then she held him there as Jamie put a knife to his throat. It wasn't actually a knife, he thought, but a small, ceremonial sword of some kind.

"It's called an athame," Jamie said in a brusque tone, noting his stare.

"We can't figure out how to activate the Lyricor," she continued with a snarl. "If you don't want to get hurt, you will show us now."

She nodded at Holly. "Bring it here."

Holly released her hold on David's shoulders and then produced the white stone from her handbag.

Just then, the door opened, and a man strode into the room. He had long brown hair and a husky build and was dressed in work overalls. David recognized him as the same man who had given him the Lyricor. The man raised his arms into the air. "In the name of the Almighty," he said in a firm voice, "I command you creatures from hell to depart."

A white-faced Jamie dropped the athame, and after giving the man a look of pure hatred, she skulked out the door alongside Holly.

"They won't be bothering you anymore," he said in a calm tone.

"Thanks," David responded, still shaken by the events that had just occurred. "What's your name?"

"I am Everet," the stranger replied with a serious expression. "You must be careful from now on. As you have witnessed, there are wicked people who desire the Lyricor. They aim to possess the philosopher's stone and use it to further their evil designs. You must not let that happen. One other thing: The Lyricor will not function if taken by force. It must be freely given."

"I get it. The witches came back because they need me to access it." David glanced down at the Lyricor, which Holly had dropped on the floor in her hasty retreat. To his surprise, it was glowing again. He picked it up and peered at the red numbers appearing on its smooth, white surface. "New coordinates," he mused, turning back to Everet, but the man had already left the room.

# Chapter Eight

David glanced at the map the company geologist had faxed to the bed-and-breakfast. "The Democratic Republic of Congo," he muttered under his breath. Wasting no time, he immediately checked out and drove to the Halifax airport. Arriving two hours later, he was pleased to learn that there was a direct flight to Kinshasa, the capital city of the DRC.

David slept through most of the fifteen-hour flight, awakening late the next morning as the plane landed. After proceeding through customs and the baggage claim without incident, David met his guide, entered his car, and drove into town.

The once-modern town of Kinshasa was suffering from the stagnation and decay of war explained Larry, David's guide, as they drove along. Ten minutes later, they arrived at the US embassy. After speaking to the clerk at the information desk, David took the elevator to the American Citizens Services Office, located on the second floor. A young, portly, dark-haired American greeted him with a friendly smile as he entered the cluttered office. "Hi. I'm Ben Sharp," the man said. "How can I help you today?"

"Hi, Ben. I'm Dr. David Sholfield," David responded, extending his hand. "Good to meet you. I'm looking to find the quickest way to Dembambo. It's a mission about fifty miles south of Lisala."

Ben typed a few keystrokes into his computer. "Yeah. There's a transport chopper that airlifts supplies into the villages once a month." He gave David a quizzical grin. "For your info, it's in the heart of one of the thickest tropical rainforests in the world. I can get you on the next supply run, although I don't recommend it. Going there, is risky for Americans. There's been trouble with the military."

"I want to go anyway," David answered firmly. "When does the helicopter leave?"

"In two days. I'll get you the necessary papers. When you get to your hotel, call me and I'll give you the details." He frowned as he pressed his business card into David's palm. "Please be careful, Doctor."

After spending two boring days touring the city, David boarded a UN cargo helicopter bound for the northern villages. He stared out the window admiring the magnificent view—the cerulean-colored waters of the Congo River contrasted brilliantly in the bright sunlight with the verdant rainforest canopy as it snaked its way through the jungle.

After refueling in Kisangani, they flew directly to the Dembambo mission. According to the pilot, it was a small village with a population of about two hundred people.

The helicopter landed, and David stepped onto the dirt clearing and scanned the area. A church, a hospital, and a school stood about a hundred meters away on the opposite side, surrounded by palm trees. There were a few other buildings as well—the living quarters of the staff, along with a supply shed and a natural gas-fueled power plant. Behind the buildings were many rows of mud-brick huts with thatched roofs and the fields the villagers used to grow their crops.

Two staff members and five villagers approached—David suspected they had been enlisted to unload the supplies.

"I'm Dr. Michael Hayden, and this is my wife, Nancy," the doctor said, extending his hand.

"Good to meet you both," David responded as he shook the doctor's hand. "I'm glad you speak English."

Dr. Hayden was a young man in his early thirties with blond hair, blue eyes, and a dimpled smile. He was dressed in khakis. His wife, a pretty brunette approximately the same age, was dressed in similar apparel. David thought they made an attractive couple.

"Are you going to be staying with us?" Nancy asked.

"Just until the next supply run. If that's okay," David said. "I can pay for my food and lodgings."

"You are most certainly welcome," the doctor said. "There haven't been any Americans around here lately—besides the helicopter pilot, that is. We could use the extra help."

The doctor turned to the villagers standing beside him and said something in Swahili. As they began unloading the supplies, Nancy said, "Please join us in our humble abode for a bite to eat."

David followed the doctor and his wife to a modest, beige, one-story vinyl-sided home. From the outside, it appeared purely functional, but as he walked through the living area into the informal dining room, he noted that the adjacent kitchen was equipped with all the modern conveniences. "Everything looks new," he remarked, taking a seat at the table across from Dr. Hayden and his wife.

"The mission was recently built," the doctor replied with a grin. "We've only been here for a year and a half. We're sponsored by the Baptists and the US government. They want us to be as comfortable as possible as we embark upon this important work."

"When I began my journey, I was told to be careful," David said. "Is it safe here?"

"That's a reasonable question," the doctor replied, his expression turning serious. "Let me fill you in on a little recent history. The Congo has been a war-torn country for many years. The current president—his name is Joseph Kabila—took over the government in 2001. He succeeded his father, who was sharing power with rebel groups from Uganda and Rwanda at the time. After his father's assassination in 2004, an insurgency erupted, caused by various rebel factions supported by the Rwandan government. By the end of the year, the death toll had reached almost four million."

"Wow!" David exclaimed. "That's a lot of death."

"Yes, it was very bad," Michael continued. "But since then, political progress has been made. A new constitution was ratified in January of this year. On July 30 we had our first democratic election, and Kabila was declared president. That happened just last week, so you should be safe. There's been a cease-fire."

"I guess my timing is pretty good then," David remarked with a relieved expression.

"David, this is Reverend Earl Curry and his wife, Janice," the doctor said as the minister and his wife entered the dining room.

"Hi," David said, extending his hand to Earl with a smile. "Good to meet both of you."

"Glad to meet you too, David," Earl said, shaking David's hand.

As they sat down, David noted the man's black shirt and white cleric's collar. The minister, who appeared to be quite young—perhaps in his mid-twenties—was short and pudgy in stature with slicked-back brown hair and squinty brown eyes. His wife was a brunette and overweight as well, with a round face and a double chin.

"So, what brings you to this remote region of the world?" Janice asked with a courteous smile.

"Curiosity," David replied vaguely, deciding against mentioning his medical qualifications. "I wanted to do a little exploring. You know, to experience the tropical rainforest firsthand."

"You picked the right place then," Earl said. "There's plenty to see just outside our little village. I assume you will attend our church service on Sunday morning?"

"I wouldn't miss it," David said, smiling. He glanced down at his plate, wondering if the pastor possessed the philosopher's stone since his appearance was quite vibrant. Perhaps he was using its power to maintain his youth. David would definitely attend the church service on Sunday.

"You're welcome to stay as long as you like," Janice said. "I'll have the men set up a tent for you."

"That's most accommodating," David responded gratefully. "I would be happy to pay for my accommodations during my stay."

"We don't have any need for money around here," the doctor said with a chuckle. "Everything's paid for in advance and shipped in by a transport chopper."

"I understand, but if you need help with anything, feel free to ask. I suppose all of you have plenty to do in maintaining a mission like this," David continued, glancing at the housemaid as she began serving lunch. "Are the villagers helpful?"

"When they're well," Michael replied. "They're called the Bantus. They've been living in the jungle for generations, relying on its natural resources. One of the goals of our mission has been to teach them how to cultivate the land. Unfortunately, the rainforest soil is poor for growing crops, resulting in low productivity. Because the land can only support a low population density, the villagers must hunt as well."

"It looks like you've succeeded in helping the people so far," David said. "I don't see anyone starving."

"So far, so good," Michael said with a sigh. "But these people are living on borrowed time."

"Charlie and Carol Fleischer are the schoolteachers," the doctor continued. "They're a husband-and-wife team. He teaches up to the eighth-grade level, and she teaches the young children. The villagers can't get a high school education here. We counsel them to leave the village and take up residence in Kinshasa for that, which is difficult for a number of reasons. We're also dealing with recurring health problems—such as the recent outbreak of malaria. As a matter of fact, I need to get back to the hospital. Will you excuse me?"

The doctor stood from the table and gave David a smile. "Stop by the hospital tomorrow morning after you've rested. I'm sure I can find something for you to do unless you have other plans."

David remained at the table for another hour, chatting with the pastor and his wife about their mission experiences. Although burning with curiosity, he felt uneasy about broaching the subject of the philosopher's stone. He would need to be patient and wait for the right opportunity to arise.

As they stood from the table, two villagers entered the dining room. To David's surprise, one of them spoke to Earl in French. The minister turned to David and smiled. "Your tent is ready."

"Thank you so much, Earl," David said with a grateful smile. "I appreciate your hospitality."

David and the minister followed the villagers to the tent, which had been erected behind the hospital. It was made from thick, brown canvass and was quite large.

David walked inside. There was a portable double bed standing about three feet off the ground, its long, metal legs submerged in plastic pails filled with water.

"The bed's raised to keep the bugs and snakes from getting at you while you're sleeping," Earl said with a chuckle.

"I appreciate that," David responded. "I see you've included a dresser and a nightstand with a reading lamp. It's perfect."

"I know it's not exactly the Ritz-Carlton," the minister said with a shrug, "but I hope your accommodations will be satisfactory for the time being. If you get hungry, you can always find something to eat in the commissary inside the hospital. There's a locker room and a bathroom with a shower as well. And now, I leave you to your rest."

David arose early the next morning and walked directly to the hospital. "It's pretty small," Dr. Hayden remarked, meeting David at the front door. As they stepped inside, the doctor said, "As you can see, the triage room is equipped only with the basics. Down this way we have the patients' quarters," Michael continued as they entered the central treatment area. He lifted his hands into the air in a dramatic gesture. "The patients all reside in this one room—fifty beds in total. We don't do surgery here, though. The serious cases are airlifted to Kinshasa."

"It looks almost full," David observed.

"Unfortunately, yes. As I mentioned earlier, we're dealing with an outbreak."

David noted the sickly faces of the young children who occupied the majority of the beds. "I have some medical training," he blurted, feeling an abrupt surge of compassion.

"I'm happy to hear that," Michael responded with an approving smile. "We could use your help. I only have one nurse and four assistants from the village to handle the entire epidemic."

David glanced at the nurse standing in the far-left corner of the room. She was young and pretty, with jet-black hair tucked under her nurse's cap. Her skin was a creamy, light brown color. She had blue eyes and a thin nose. Her full lips, together with her skin color, signaled a mixed heritage. He paused for a moment, watching her treat a young boy, then turned to Michael. "I would be glad to help."

"I see you approve of Aaliyah," Michael said with a perceptive smile. "Have you eaten this morning?" he asked, changing the subject.

"Not yet."

"You must be hungry. There's a commissary just down the hall. Why don't you grab a bite to eat and join me afterward?"

The commissary was self-service, consisting of one cafeteria table, six folding metal chairs—three on each side—and two counters, one of which was cluttered with several functional items, including a toaster, a coffee pot, a microwave oven, plastic utensils, paper plates, cups, bowls, and plastic containers of butter and peanut butter. A few food items were scattered about on the other counter—several boxes of cereal, a round plastic container full of English muffins, and another container of donuts. Beneath the counters were two small refrigerators and a freezer. Boxes of foodstuffs were stacked on plastic shelving along the opposite wall.

David helped himself to a bowl of cereal, two donuts, and a cup of coffee. He found milk and cream in one of the refrigerators.

A half-hour later, Michael led David down the hallway into a well-stocked lab equipped with scales, glassware, microscopes, and various chemicals used for medical testing.

"I had Aaliyah take blood samples from all the patients," the doctor said, handing David a folder. "Then I took blood smears. They all tested positive for one of the malaria parasites. Are you familiar with the treatment for malaria patients?"

David scanned the test results. "Yes," he replied. "The prescribed medication is dependent upon the degree of infection and the specific type of parasite. Unfortunately, I see from your tests that you're dealing with *Plasmodium falciparum.* Life-threatening complications can occur from this type of parasite, such as brain infections, fluid in the lungs, kidney failure, and fever. In the most severe cases, the quickest way to remove the parasite is through blood transfusions, along with quinidine gluconate injections."

"That's correct," Michael said. "This parasite is resistant to chloroquine, so I'm treating them with quinine sulfate and pyrimethamine-sulfadoxine. Fortunately, most of the patients are responding to the treatment. I'm swamped, though," the doctor continued. "I absolutely must start the blood transfusions immediately on the worst cases, and to do that, I need donors from the village. All the donors must be tested, as well as the patients."

"I can do the blood tests," David ventured. "That will free you up to do the transfusions."

"That would be great," Michael said with an appreciative smile. Then he gave David a quizzical look. "I don't mean to pry, but you're a doctor, aren't you?"

"Let's just say that I have some medical expertise," David replied.

"Then we'll leave it at that," Michael said with a grin. "I'll have Aaliyah take a round of blood samples and bring them to the lab."

David spent the next half-hour preparing the lab for blood testing. Just as he was finishing, Aaliyah entered with a tray of samples.

"I'm so glad you're here," the nurse said, giving David a friendly smile. "We're having trouble keeping up with the pace of the epidemic. I was afraid we were going to lose some of our patients. That is, until you came along."

"Glad to be of help," David said, taking the tray from her. "I'm David, by the way."

"Yes. Michael told me. I'm Aaliyah."

David felt his heart flutter as he noted her attractive features. There was a sensual quality about her smile, he realized. He definitely wanted to get better acquainted, but he didn't want to seem too forward. "I realize that time is of the essence," he decided upon. "I'll have the results ready as soon as possible."

David spent the rest of the day testing blood samples. Just as he was preparing to leave, Michael entered the lab. "Good work, David," he said with an approving smile. "It's after dinnertime already. Would you care to join us for a meal?"

David wiped the sweat from his brow and glanced at the thermostat, realizing that the air conditioner wasn't keeping up with the tropical climate. The temperature in the lab was almost eighty degrees. "Thanks," he replied. "I seem to have worked up an appetite."

It was early Saturday evening when David finished his work at the hospital. He ate a quick meal at the commissary and decided to go for a walk. After five straight days of grey clouds and heavy rainfall, it felt great to finally be able to go outside and stare into a blue sky and feel the heat of the bright sunshine.

He decided to head down the solitary logging road leading into the jungle. As he entered the rainforest, he stopped for a moment, amazed at the variety of sights and sounds. Huge trees jutted into the air, 150 feet above his head. He noted the second layer of smaller trees, rising to a lesser height, and finally, the third layer of lianas, bushes, and ferns of incredible diversity.

Several monkeys were playing in a nearby tree, adding to the rich panoply of sound created by the dense population of indigenous wildlife. He could sense the living energy of the rainforest—like a palpable force.

As David walked, his mind began to wander through the events of the past few months. So much had happened: The murder of his girlfriend, the terrifying ordeal with the witches in Nova Scotia, and now here he was in the Congo, continuing his quest for the philosopher's stone. Everything seemed so strange and unfamiliar as if he had been thrust into a new world where the rules of reality no longer applied.

He wondered what part the beautiful and mysterious Aaliyah would play in his quest if any. She had been on his mind since they had met. Was it mere infatuation, or something more? He had thought about asking her out but decided against it. There really wasn't anywhere to take her—no nightclubs, no movie theaters, no restaurants.

And of course, they were working together. Although she had participated in light conversation during their infrequent lunches together in the commissary, the nurse's demeanor had remained strictly professional. He had maintained a competent veneer as well, desiring not to complicate their working relationship.

After walking for about ten minutes, dodging numerous, water-filled potholes along the way, David came upon a large clearing on the left side of the road. Several moss-covered boulders and loose stones lay strewn about a patchwork of dirt and grass. A tree-covered hill rose fifty feet into the air behind it.

To his surprise, Aaliyah was sitting on a flat log near the center of the clearing, her back turned toward him. She was sitting very still, so he hesitated before speaking—hoping he wouldn't be intruding upon a private moment.

Realizing that it was the perfect opportunity to meet her in a personal setting and that he probably wouldn't get another chance, David decided to greet her.

"Hi, Aaliyah," he said cheerfully. "I didn't expect to see you here." To his dismay, when she turned to face him, her eyes were red, her face streaked with tears. Something had obviously upset her.

"I'm so sorry," he said, giving her a concerned look. "I didn't mean to interrupt. Are you okay?"

Aaliyah pulled a napkin out of her jeans pocket, wiped away her tears, and cleared her throat. "It's nothing." She looked away. "I'd better be getting back now."

David watched in silence as she rose to her feet, returned to the trail, and began jogging toward the village. Then he seated himself on the same log, wondering what had caused such sadness and if his intrusion had irritated her. She seemed so happy at the hospital. It was obvious that she enjoyed her work, so it must be something personal.

It occurred to him that this was an opportunity in disguise. She probably needed someone to talk to. He would present himself as a concerned friend, which at this point he was, with the hope that she would respond favorably. He wondered if it was too soon to begin a new relationship, reminding himself that if anything did develop, it would only be temporary. After all, he would be returning home on the next supply run.

David entered the church the following morning, noting the chapel pews filled with villagers and mission staff members. Aaliyah was sitting with some of the village women in the back, appearing especially comely in her lilac-flowered church dress. He found the service boring in the extreme since the minister spoke entirely in French.

Just as David was leaving, the pastor approached. "I hope you don't have any plans this afternoon," he said with a benevolent smile. "Are you free to have an early dinner with my wife and me?"

"I would be happy to accept your kind invitation, Earl," David replied brightly. He was thrilled at the prospect. The opportunity to question the minister had finally presented itself.

Early that afternoon, David arrived at the pastor's home—a small bungalow located directly behind the church. When he knocked on the door, Earl greeted him and then showed him into a tiny dining room with pastel green walls. The décor was plain and simple, including a wooden table seating six people, and a small chandelier dangling from the plaster ceiling. A wood-framed picture of Jesus was mounted on one of the walls.

David enjoyed the home-cooked food and conversation as they dined, the couple sharing anecdotes from their mission. Afterward, David accompanied Earl to his study, located in the smaller bedroom. It was amply furnished—considering the room's size—with two desks and chairs, two filing cabinets, a computer, a copy machine, and a fax machine. Bookshelves filled with a variety of reference books and classic literature lined the walls. David felt his pulse accelerate as he noted the large cross hanging on the wall behind the larger of the two desks. It appeared to be made of marble, featuring a gilded olive-leaf design on its vertical bar.

"Have a seat," Earl said, motioning to the chair in front of the smaller desk. The reverend sat down at the larger desk, opened a drawer, and produced a bottle of bourbon and two glasses.

After pouring the whiskey, he handed a glass to David. "So, tell me the real reason you're here, David," he said evenly.

David looked away and took a sip of bourbon as he attempted to formulate a credible response. He wondered if the minister suspected the reason behind his trip. He knew it was foolhardy to question the pastor directly about the philosopher's stone. He decided to bend the truth a little.

"You might have guessed from my work at the hospital that I'm a doctor. Unfortunately, my father's dying of pancreatic cancer. While researching the disease, I came across a paper written by a renowned biologist who claimed to have found a cure: an extract made from one of the plant species indigenous to this particular rainforest. My goal is to procure a sample and bring it home. I know it sounds like a fool's errand, but you must understand I'm desperate."

"I'm sorry to hear about your father," the minister responded, giving David a concerned look. "I hope you find what you're looking for."

"That's a beautiful cross," David said, changing the subject. "Have you had it for a while?"

Earl rose from his chair and took it down from the wall. "It's been in my family for generations," he said, placing it on the desk. When he grasped the cross firmly by the center and pulled on it, the top opened, displaying a shiny red crystal inside.

David gasped when he saw the crystal. There it was, the philosopher's stone, right there in plain sight. Either the minister had no knowledge of its capabilities, or he assumed David didn't know what it was. "That's a beautiful stone," David remarked.

"Yes, it certainly is," the minister said. "I don't know what gem it's made from, though. It's actually a locket. I keep my mother's picture inside."

David's mind filled with questions as Earl closed the cross and put it back on the wall. The man couldn't be aware of the stone's value; otherwise, he would have kept it hidden away from prying eyes. The thought came to David that if he made Earl a reasonable offer for the cross, the pastor might agree to sell it.

The next morning, David returned to the hospital. When Aaliyah entered the lab, she didn't look at him directly as she handed him the fresh blood samples. David surmised that she felt uncomfortable after their chance encounter in the rainforest. He shrugged off the desire to question her. It wasn't the proper time to bring up personal matters. "Thanks," he said in a neutral tone and immediately returned to his work.

That evening, David went to the commissary and ate his supper as usual. Upon leaving, he came upon Aaliyah and Michael, who were standing in the hallway. The doctor abruptly turned and smiled. "I appreciate your help again today, David. Thank you."

"My pleasure," David responded with a grin.

"See you two bright and early tomorrow," the doctor said.

As Michael walked away, David mustered his courage and asked Aaliyah, "How about joining me for a walk in the forest? I could use the exercise after being cooped up in the lab all day."

To his surprise, the nurse returned his smile. "I'd like that," she said. "Just give me a few minutes to change into something comfortable, okay?"

A half-hour later, they met at the logging road. David noted that Aaliyah's casual attire—her tight jeans and flowery, form-fitting blouse—served to enhance her beauty. As they began walking, Aaliyah pointed at the canopy. "See those large trees on the right?"

David stared upward. The trees in question were very tall—rising approximately 150 feet into the air—their cylindrical boles covered in hard, tough, silvery grey fibrous bark, their branches ending in long, narrow leaves. "Those are some big trees," he remarked in wonder.

"They're called *Brachystegia laurentii*," she explained. "They like lots of water. And those are African teak," she continued, pointing to another stand on the opposite side of the trail.

As they continued walking, she identified several more species, including mahogany, zebrawood, and some obeche trees.

"It's amazing you know all that," David remarked. "Where did you learn so much about trees?"

"I had some free time when I first arrived," Aaliyah replied, "so I did a study of the rainforest. It exhibits great biological diversity, including a variety of interesting animals, such as peacocks, gorillas, monkeys, chimpanzees, elephants, buffalo, shrews, and bongos, just to name a few. Over four hundred species of birds and over one hundred species of mammals reside here."

"What's a bongo?"

"It looks like a deer with spiked horns and white stripes."

"That sounds very exotic."

"It's a beautiful animal. There are plenty of reptiles as well, including alligators, geckos, and frogs."

"Have you ever seen a gorilla?"

"Certainly. They inhabit an area of the jungle about three miles from here."

David was startled by a sudden, loud noise. He glanced in the direction of the sound and saw what looked like a giant, scaly anteater scurrying along the forest floor. "What the heck is that thing?" he asked in an anxious tone.

"You have just witnessed one of the most unusual animal species of the forest," replied Aaliyah, laughing. "It's called a giant pangolin. Don't worry. It hunts termites and ants, not people."

David suddenly felt tired. "Would it be okay if we head back now? It's been a long day."

"Sure," Aaliyah replied with a smile. "We could both use some rest."

Suddenly aware of Aaliyah's exotic beauty, David resisted the urge to kiss her full, sensual lips. Recalling her tear-streaked face the day before, he decided to take it slow. He gleaned from her mannerisms—her ready smile and relaxed tone of voice—that she enjoyed his company. If he was patient, perhaps he would succeed in gaining her confidence.

"I enjoyed the hike," David remarked as they arrived at the mission. "Would you like to do this again tomorrow?" he ventured.

"We'll see," the nurse replied.

When Aaliyah walked into the lab with a tray of blood samples the following afternoon, instead of leaving, she sat down on a chair beside David. "I had a nice time yesterday," she said.

David looked up from his microscope. "That big jungle out there is amazing. And so are you! I can't believe you know so much about it." He felt his heartbeat accelerate as she gave him an approving grin. "Would you like to hike again this evening?"

They met at the logging road two hours later. "Please tell me about yourself, Aaliyah," David said as they walked into the jungle. "What made you decide to travel all the way to the Congo?"

"You seem very curious," the nurse replied, laughing. "I guess I can indulge you. My father is an MD. His practice is in Topeka, Kansas. That's where I grew up."

"That's the capital city, correct?"

"Yeah. It's not much to write home about, though. The largest manufacturer is Goodyear. Topeka has a large health care and social services industry. I grew up wanting to be a doctor like my father. When I graduated, I decided to try nursing school first, to see how I felt about working in the medical field before plunging into the vast amount of debt and training required to become a licensed MD.

"Shortly after I started working at St. Francis Health Center, I heard about the Baptist mission program in Africa. It sounded interesting—I had always been attracted to foreign cultures, and I thought it would be nice to do a little traveling while I was still young. When I read about the plight of the impoverished people here in the Congo, I felt a strong desire to help. So here I am." She turned to David with a curious expression. "What about you, David? Why are you here?"

"For much the same reasons," David said, feeling uncomfortable with the question. He mentally chastised himself for not having a clever story prepared in advance. He had always hated lying. "I like to travel, and I was in the area, so I stopped by the mission to lend a hand." He knew it sounded lame, but he couldn't reveal the real reason. Aaliyah would dismiss him as a lunatic.

"I know this is a little abrupt," he continued, changing the subject, "but can I ask you why you were crying the other day?"

Aaliyah pointed to a large log lying on the ground next to the road. "Let's take a break for a minute, okay? I had a boyfriend back in Topeka," she began after they sat down on the log. "We met in high school and continued dating until I left for Africa. He asked me to marry him a few months before I left. I refused, explaining that I needed to fulfill my dream of serving in a mission first. He wasn't very happy about it, but he loved me enough to let me go. He said that he would wait for me, that he wanted me to be happy, that he didn't want to stand in the way of my dream."

"It sounds like you found yourself a good guy," David remarked.

"I thought so too, until I received a letter from him the day you arrived. He said he was sorry, but he was breaking it off because he had fallen in love with another woman."

David watched helplessly as the beautiful young woman burst into tears

"It's okay," she managed between sobs, noting his concerned expression. "I didn't expect that coming from him, but I'm glad that I found out what kind of person he really is before I went and married him."

David felt uncomfortable, not knowing exactly how to console her. "It's hard to understand people sometimes," he offered. "I know how you feel, actually. I lost my girlfriend a couple of months ago."

"I'm so sorry," Aaliyah said, giving him a compassionate look. "I guess I shouldn't be feeling sorry for myself, should I? Do you want to talk about it?"

David's mind churned as he attempted to formulate a response. He didn't know how Aaliyah would react if she learned that Angela had been murdered. He doubted it would engender the trust he was seeking from the beautiful nurse. "I really don't feel like talking about it right now, if that's okay," he replied.

David felt a strong, passionate response as he noted the concern in her lovely, blue eyes. His gaze moved down to her lips before he quickly remembered his manners. Now wasn't the right moment to kiss her. "It's getting late, Aaliyah," he said, standing from the log. "Shall we go back?"

The following afternoon, Aaliyah entered the lab, put down her tray, and sat next to David. "I enjoyed our talk yesterday," she said with an appreciative smile.

David glanced at the clock. It was four-thirty already, and he was exhausted after putting in another long day at the lab. Although he wanted to see Aaliyah again, at that moment, all he wanted was to grab a bite to eat, return to his tent, and get some sleep. "I did too, Aaliyah," he responded. "I hope you don't mind, but I'm really beat. Maybe we could talk some more tomorrow. Would that be okay?"

David was surprised to see the look of disappointment on her face. "I guess so," she said, pouting. "I have a surprise for you. I guess it can wait."

"A surprise?" he said, his face brightening. "I suppose I could put off my beauty sleep for a little while. Give me an hour to freshen up, okay?"

"Meet me at the road when you're ready," Aaliyah said, giving him an irresistible smile. "I have something to show you."

As David accompanied Aaliyah along the logging road that evening, he realized that his fatigue had completely vanished. "I'm very curious about your surprise," he said, grinning. "Can you give me a hint?"

"No way, buddy," she replied, laughing.

David noted that she had undone her hair, which was straight and black and full. He watched admiringly as it swung to and fro in the gentle breeze, glimmering amid patches of sunlight. He looked away as she glanced at him.

"Is everything okay?" she asked.

"Everything's great."

She stopped walking and pointed to her right. "See that foot trail?"

David could barely discern a narrow trail leading into the jungle. "I didn't notice that before," he said.

"Follow me," Aaliyah said, breaking into a jog.

After a few minutes of running through the knee-high grass, David ran out of breath and had to stop. "Hold on," he said, bending over, gasping for air. "I'm not used to this."

"I guess not," Aaliyah said with a playful grin. She walked back to his side and took him by the hand. "Come on—we're almost there."

A minute later, they arrived at a spacious, grassy clearing. David glanced up at the sky and noted the sun shining through the palm trees surrounding the meadow, creating alternate patterns of shadow and light, rippling across the grassy surface in the breeze. Fifty yards on the other side of the meadow was a steep cliff, rising high up into the air. A dense thicket of liana-covered trees and bushes grew over most of it, except the bare portion facing them, exposing layers of grey rock and brown soil to their view. A torrent of water gushed out of the hilltop, racing down the side of the cliff in white streams, splashing into a pool below.

"What a beautiful waterfall!" David exclaimed. He stared at it for a few moments, feeling as though he was in paradise. "How did you find this wondrous place?"

"One of the women from the village told me about it the other day when she noticed how sad I was. She said it would cheer me up. This is only the second time I've been here."

They walked to the edge of the pool and sat down on a large, flat rock. "I immediately felt better when I came here," she continued, giving him a bright smile. "When you told me about losing your girlfriend, I wanted you to see it. I thought it might cheer you up too."

David gazed into her lovely blue eyes and said, "You don't know how much I appreciate this." He paused for a moment and then moved closer.

In response, she gently put her arms around his shoulders and began kissing him passionately.

After finishing work the next afternoon, David walked into the commissary for a quick meal. He sat at the counter, eating a simple meal of hot dogs and beans, recalling Aaliyah's demeanor when she brought the blood samples into the lab that morning. She had acted totally professional, giving no hint of their passionate lovemaking at the waterfall the evening before.

David had difficulty concentrating on his work, wondering if she hated him, wondering if she thought that he had taken advantage of her while grieving the loss of her boyfriend. He felt confused, plagued by powerful, conflicting emotions of guilt and desire. He desperately wanted to see her again, but it was probably the wrong thing to do, even if she was willing. And he couldn't afford to lose focus.

She was in the process of fulfilling her goal—to serve in an African mission—and the last thing he wanted was to ruin it for both of them. What had begun as a simple friendship had suddenly metamorphosed into an all-consuming romance. He realized that he had no idea how she really felt about him.

He broke out of his reverie and glanced upward. Aaliyah was standing in front of him, patiently awaiting his reply, looking very appealing in her nurse's uniform.

"Please, sit down," he said with a smile.

Aaliyah sat in the adjacent chair and gave him an affectionate look. "About yesterday. I want you to know how wonderful it was for me."

As he began to reply, she put a finger to his lips and said, "It's okay, David. I know you didn't come here to pursue a romantic relationship. I don't want you to feel bad about what happened between us. You didn't take advantage of me. I was completely willing. We both needed some cheering, and what happened was the natural outcome. I want very much to continue seeing you if that is your wish. No strings, I promise. I completely understand your situation."

David felt a sense of relief wash over him as if someone had just poured a bucket of cold water over his hot, perspiring body. "Thank you for understanding. The last thing I want is to take advantage of you. Personally, I'm still a bit confused by what happened, though. All I'm asking is a day or two to sort out my feelings. Is that okay?"

Aaliyah stood from the table and gave him a gracious look. "That's fine, David. No matter what you decide, I still want to be friends, okay?"

The next morning, as David began his daily round of blood tests, Michael ran into the lab. "Come quick, David! There are soldiers outside!"

# Chapter Nine

David followed the doctor as he ran out of the hospital, then attempted to quell the intense fear and trepidation triggered by what he saw.

Parked in front of the school were seven military vehicles: two troop carriers, two cargo trucks, and three tactical vehicles mounted with 50-caliber machine guns. Twenty soldiers surrounded the schoolchildren, who had been gathered together into a group in front of the school. Twenty more soldiers remained in their trucks, awaiting orders from their commander, who was standing between the school and his men, deep in conversation with Earl and the schoolmaster.

As David and Michael walked toward the soldiers, several villagers began to appear. When the commander spotted the doctors, he waved for them to approach and spoke a few sentences in Swahili.

Michael translated for David. "That is Corporal Lusala of the Democratic Congolian Republic Resistance Army. He says he will kill the children if we don't give him the supplies he requires."

David looked to his right and saw more villagers running toward them, brandishing farm tools and angrily shouting unintelligible phrases at the top of their lungs. He felt terrified, realizing that the situation was ready to spiral out of control.

"Earl told the corporal that this is a Christian mission and that we will gladly give them whatever supplies they need," Michael said, translating the minister's words.

The commander gestured to the throng of angry villagers and spoke in a stern voice. "The corporal says he will shoot the children if the villagers don't put down their weapons," Michael continued.

The minister turned to the villagers and motioned for the one standing foremost to approach. They spoke together for a minute. "Earl just told the village leader what the corporal said," Michael said.

The African spat on the ground and made an angry reply. "He said that the villagers will fight the soldiers if they harm the children," Michael said.

In response, the corporal raised his weapon into the air and fired off a few rounds. Although the sound of the gunshots silenced the villagers, they kept their weapons raised, preparing to strike the soldiers at the command of their leader.

"I have an idea," David said to Michael. "I recall you telling me that there's a cease-fire between the rebel factions and the government."

"That's correct," Michael said with a perceptive nod. "They should observe the peace treaty." He turned to the corporal and spoke a few sentences. The commander smiled and spoke again. "The corporal will order his men to desist if the villagers put down their weapons," Michael said. He turned to the village leader and spoke in an earnest tone.

The man abruptly threw down his pitchfork, turned to the villagers, and shouted a few words. In response, they dropped their farm tools onto the ground.

The corporal shouted orders to his men, who then lowered their weapons. Earl and Charlie quickly ushered the children back into the schoolhouse. Michael spoke to the corporal again, then motioned to David. "The corporal wants us to take his men to the supply shed."

After the supplies were safely loaded into the cargo trucks, the soldiers drove off into the rainforest.

"That was a close call," Michael said as he and David sat down in the commissary, cold beers in hand. "If not for your quick thinking, we might have all been killed."

"It was nothing," David said modestly. "Just a self-preservation tactic."

"Unfortunately, we're going to be rationing what little supplies the soldiers left behind," Michael said with a sigh. "I'm glad another shipment will be arriving soon. At least we still have most of our antibiotics."

Michael grinned before changing the subject. "So, tell me, David. How do you like serving in our little mission?"

David returned the grin. "It's quite amazing, actually. So much has happened in the two weeks I've been here."

"There's been a lot going on—dealing with the epidemic and everything," the doctor said. "And you've been an absolute godsend. I could never have managed the blood testing and the transfusions by myself."

Michael paused for a moment and gave David a perceptive look. "Don't think I haven't noticed what's been going on between you and Aaliyah. If you don't mind me asking, are you planning on staying on for a while?"

"That's the million-dollar question, isn't it? You're right—we've become quite fond of each other, and I like working here at the mission as well."

"I have another problem, though," David said, his eyes moistening with tears. I don't really like talking about it, but I think you should know about my father."

"Is something wrong?" Michael asked, giving David a concerned look.

"Unfortunately, my father has pancreatic cancer. He's nearing the final stage of the disease. The doctors are only giving him a few months. I'm torn between staying and going back home to spend time with him before he passes."

"That's a tough decision," Michael said. "I'm afraid I can't give you any advice, but you're welcome to stay as long as you like. Either way, I hope things work out between you and Aaliyah. She needs a good man in her life."

It was late Saturday afternoon when David finished his work. It had been raining all day. As he walked into the commissary for his evening meal, Aaliyah was there, waiting for him. "I heard you saved the day when those rebel soldiers arrived," she said with an approving smile.

David shrugged. "It was nothing more than my survival instinct kicking in."

She stood up and kissed him lightly on the cheek. "That deserves a kiss from a very grateful lady."

In response, David grabbed her around the waist and began kissing her fervently. A minute later, he broke their embrace. "You're all I've been thinking about, you know."

She laughed and took him by the hand. "Let me feed you dinner tonight."

Aaliyah resided in a small, prefabricated, single-story bungalow. He followed her into the tiny kitchen that also served as the dining room, noting that the chairs and table were all molded from the same inexpensive beige plastic material.

"I know it's not very homey, but I'm used to it," she said. "Please make yourself comfortable."

As Aaliyah busied herself preparing a simple meal of pork chops and salad, she spoke of the political struggles of the DRC. Then, after setting out the serving bowls, plates, utensils, and glasses, she produced a bottle of wine from the refrigerator and sat down opposite him. "Dinner is served," she said with a grin. "I hope you don't mind a simple meal."

"Those are the best kind," David said. "It's been a while since I've had home cooking."

As they ate, they conversed about the condition and treatment of the patients, refraining from discussing personal matters. When they finished the meal, Aaliyah gave David an alluring smile. "I see you've decided to continue our romance."

"I guess that's one way of putting it," David said. Then his expression turned serious. "I've been thinking about everything that's happened between us, Aaliyah. I want to continue seeing you, so I've decided to stay on for another month. That is if you want me to."

"Are you sure that's what you really want?"

"There's no doubt in my mind."

"I meant what I said," Aaliyah replied tenderly. "There aren't any strings. You can leave whenever you want. I have my work here, and it's enough for me."

She stood from the table, walked behind David, and gently put her arms around his shoulders. "It's still raining outside. Why don't you stay the night?"

The next morning, David attended church service with Aaliyah. Afterward, at Earl's request, he accompanied the minister to his home.

"You did very well with the soldiers, David," Earl said, pouring two drinks after they were comfortably seated in his office. "I commend you on your wise thinking."

David accepted the proffered glass of brandy and took a sip. "It was really nothing, Earl. Everybody is making a big deal out of it."

"We're very fortunate to have you as our guest. Have you thought of staying on for a while?"

"I have," David replied with a smile. "I feel very welcome here."

"I noticed that you and Aaliyah were sitting together in church this morning," the minister remarked. He paused before chuckling. "Is she the reason you're staying?"

Before David could reply, Earl held up his hand. "No explanations necessary, my friend. However, as your minister, I must counsel you to take heed. I know this might seem a little abrupt, but if you really love her, you should consider making things right with the Lord and marry her. Nothing would give me greater pleasure than to see her marry a nice young man like yourself."

"That's a little sudden if you don't mind me saying so, Earl. But I will consider your advice."

David glanced at the pastor's cross hanging on the wall. Through all the recent events, he had not forgotten the real reason he was here.

He took a deep breath. "That is certainly a unique cross, Earl. I've never seen one quite like it."

"Yes, it's quite beautiful, isn't it? As I mentioned the last time you were here, it's a family heirloom. I'm glad you like it."

"I more than like it," David said. "You see, I collect mementos from my travels, and your cross would make a superb addition to my collection."

Earl gave David a suspicious look. "I'm not sure what you mean."

"What I mean is, I'm aware of its special meaning to you, so I'm willing to pay top dollar. Would ten thousand dollars be an adequate sum?"

Earl appeared perplexed. "I can't believe you just said that."

"I hope you're not offended, Earl. It's just that I desire it for my collection. If you feel that my offer is not a fair one, you can name your price."

To David's dismay, the minister's face reddened with anger. He stood from his chair and shouted, "Don't ever bring this up again! I think you had better leave now."

David continued his torrid love affair during the next three days, spending his nights at Aaliyah's, all the while knowing that their fragile relationship could end at any moment.

Thoughts of the philosopher's stone and his sick father haunted him as well, keying his emotions to an even higher pitch. He knew that time was running out. Perhaps if he explained about his father, Earl might let him use the stone out of sympathy. Of course, the minister would need assurances that it would be safely returned afterward.

He suddenly realized that he had nothing of value to offer the pastor besides money. Nevertheless, he would strengthen his resolve against the looming probability of failure and remain at the mission as long as possible, hoping for a solution to present itself.

It was Thursday afternoon, and David was working in the lab as usual. Hearing footsteps, he looked up from his computer and felt a surge of adrenaline as he saw Aaliyah standing with two ladies on either side. They wore tight black jumpsuits with hoods drawn over their faces. He gasped in recognition as they threw back their hoods.

"We meet again," Jamie said with a terrifying cackle.

"He looks scared," Holly said in a mocking tone.

"How did you find me?" David felt his hands begin to shake.

"It wasn't very difficult," Jamie replied with a condescending smile. "Ben Sharp was very cooperative after we had sex with him. He even lined up our transportation. Our private helicopter is waiting outside."

As the witch pushed Aaliyah forward, David noted the handgun pointed at the nurse's back. "Give us the Lyricor," Jamie said brusquely, "or the nurse dies."

The last thing David wanted was for Aaliyah to get hurt. Just as he was about to agree, he realized that he had a bargaining chip. "I can offer you something much better than the Lyricor," he said. "You can't use it without me anyway, remember?"

"That's why you're coming with us," Holly stated unequivocally.

"Do you know the Lyricor's purpose?" he queried.

"Of course. It reveals the location of the philosopher's stone," Jamie replied.

David smiled. "The Lyricor has already given me the location of the stone. It's right here in this village—inside the cross hanging on the wall of the minister's study."

"That makes sense," Holly said. "The high priest said that a servant of God has the stone and a cross, points to the servant."

"I don't know," Jamie said skeptically. "How do we know if it's genuine?"

David thought quickly. It was a good question. "I'm afraid I can't answer that for you because I don't actually know how it operates. No doubt your high priest will know what to do."

Jamie and Holly exchanged doubtful glances. "We can't get a cell phone signal this far out," Holly said. "We'll take the stone with us." She gave David a menacing look. "And we'll bring you along for insurance."

Jamie pushed the gun further into Aaliyah's back. "Bring us the minister's cross, and be quick about it, or we'll kill the nurse."

David ran to the minister's bungalow and frantically knocked on the door. As he suspected, no one was home.

He ran around to the side and tried the window of Earl's study, but it was locked. Without hesitation, he picked up a large stone from the ground and threw it into the window, causing glass shards to fall inward into the room. He kicked in the remaining shards, carefully crawled through the window, and took the cross off the wall. Then he crawled out of the window and ran back to the hospital, staying behind the buildings and re-entering the hospital through the back door.

He walked into the lab and breathed out a sigh of relief when he saw that Aaliyah was unharmed.

"That was quick," Holly said with a chuckle. "Now let's see the stone."

"Pull off the centerpiece," David said, handing Jamie the cross.

Jamie opened it and peered at the red crystal inside. "It sure looks real enough," she remarked with a smile. "Let's split before someone catches us," she said with a furtive glance toward the door.

"We'd better leave David here," Jamie continued. "If we take him with us, they'll know we stole the cross and the police will be looking for us at the airport."

"Good thinking," Holly said. "They could arrest us for kidnapping as well, but if we leave David here, they'll blame him for the theft. The high priest will know what to do with the stone."

"See you in hell, babe," Holly said to David with a grin. Then she shoved Aaliyah into a nearby table, causing a crashing sound as glassware toppled to the floor.

As the witches ran out the door, David rushed to Aaliyah's side and appraised her condition. She was shivering with fright.

"Did they hurt you?"

"I'm unharmed physically," Aaliyah replied in a shaky voice. "But I feel violated and scared out of my mind. I think I need to sit down." She sat on a nearby chair and looked at him perplexedly. "Who were those creepy women?" she asked after a few minutes of silence.

"It's a long story," David replied. "Let's get out of here."

They returned to Aaliyah's bungalow, and after much prodding on her part, David reluctantly related the details of his quest.

"I can't believe you traveled all the way to the Congo on such a wild-goose chase," Aaliyah remarked after he had finished his tale. Then, after a pause, she smiled. "I'm really happy you showed up, though."

"It may very well be a wild-goose chase," David said, "but I have to know if the sorcerer's stone is real." He hung his head dejectedly. "I guess I'll never know now that the witches have stolen it."

Aaliyah took his hand in a gentle grip. "Thank you for saving me," she said earnestly. "I promise I won't tell anyone what happened. And I'll be your alibi. I'll tell the minister you were working at the hospital all day."

"Thanks, honey," David said, standing up. He encircled her in a loving embrace and kissed her.

The next four days passed quickly for David—working at the hospital by day and spending his nights at Aaliyah's. When the minister questioned him about the missing cross, Aaliyah stood by her story. Although Earl suspected David of stealing it, the minister could not prosecute him. There was no evidence linking him to the crime.

It was on a Tuesday afternoon—the fourth week of David's stay—when he and Aaliyah returned to the waterfall. Although the weather was calm and sunny, it was oppressively hot.

"The helicopter arrives tomorrow," David said as they sat down by the edge of the pool. He became aware of the joyful chorus of birds singing in the surrounding rainforest, and he thought it ironic that the birds sounded so cheerful while he felt so gloomy.

"Whatever you decide is okay with me," Aaliyah said, staring into the waterfall.

He kissed her gently on the cheek. "I really want to stay."

Aaliyah stood up and ran to the grassy edge of the pool. Then she stripped off her clothes and dove into the water. She resurfaced a moment later, laughing. "Come on in, my love," she said, beckoning to him. "The water will cool you off."

Echoing her laughter, David removed his clothing and jumped into the pool. They frolicked about until they tired, then they lay down on the stone together to dry themselves off in the hot sun. "I could get used to this," he remarked with a smile.

They lay silently for some time. "I have to go back to Pittsburgh and see my father before he dies," David said sadly. "Would you consider coming with me?"

Aaliyah's eyes moistened with tears. "You know I can't do that. I still have another year left."

"I can return when it's over. That is, if you want me to."

To David's consternation, Aaliyah burst into tears. "Oh, you silly man," she sobbed. "Go back to your tent and leave me alone. I don't want to see you anymore. Not until you decide what you're going to do." She stood up, ignoring his gentle touch to her arm, walked to her pile of clothes, and began to dress. "I mean it," she said, sniffling. "Put your clothes on and go."

When David arrived at his tent, he lay down on the bed and pondered the situation, his mind churning with indecision. He could stay on for another month, but what good would it do? He knew that he had to return to Pittsburgh soon.

He had spoken to his father the previous day via the mission's satellite telephone after explaining his situation to Michael. As expected, his father's condition was still deteriorating. He had also learned, after speaking to Dr. Lucas, that his job was in serious jeopardy as well.

He had swept aside everything that mattered in his frantic and futile search for the fabled philosopher's stone. As he lay there racking his brain for answers, he noticed a soft, golden glow emanating from his suitcase.

"The Lyricor," he muttered. He climbed out of bed and lifted it from the suitcase. A new series of coordinates had appeared upon its shiny surface.

The helicopter arrived on time the next afternoon, and after the villagers had unloaded the supplies, it was time for David to leave. When he had spoken to Aaliyah that morning, informing her of his decision, she reacted bravely—masking her pain and telling him that she understood.

As David boarded the helicopter, he saw her standing in the clearing with a lovely smile upon her lips. "I'll come back for you!" he shouted as the blades began to spin.

"Goodbye, David!" Aaliyah said, maintaining her smile.

As the helicopter rose into the air, David saw Aaliyah burst into tears and run back into the hospital.

# Chapter Ten

David walked into the hotel room and sighed—another day, another town. Although built in a foreign country, the room's interior was designed in a Holiday Inn–style décor, complete with a queen-size bed, walnut headboard, and matching nightstands. The beige-and-purple sunflower patterned wallpaper complemented the black-and-white striped curtains perfectly. A coffee maker, a minibar, and a cable TV completed the amenities.

David plopped down on the bed and recalled the events of the past few days. On his return to Kinshasa, a company geologist had faxed him a map of the new coordinates—an area lying on the outskirts of Santa Fe, Argentina. He had taken a flight from Kinshasa to Buenos Aires, with layovers in Nairobi, Johannesburg, and São Paulo. From there he rented a car and drove to Santa Fe, a medium-size town of approximately half a million people, located at the junction of the Paraná and Salado rivers. He was relieved to learn that the climate was subtropical—not as extreme as the Congo. Tomorrow he would meet his guide and drive to the exact location of the coordinates, about twenty miles outside the city limits.

Although fatigued from all the traveling, David had trouble falling asleep. Thoughts of Aaliyah kept swirling through his mind. He mentally chided himself, thinking that he shouldn't have allowed himself to develop such a serious attachment to her. He was on a quest, after all, and couldn't afford distractions like that.

It wasn't fair to her either. The reality of the situation was that he had taken advantage of a lonely, brokenhearted woman who had just lost her fiancé. But his aching heart testified that this was no mere infatuation, that he had truly fallen in love. The pain of separation was almost unbearable, but if he remained focused on his objective, he would survive. It was comforting to know that when she completed her mission, they could be together again.

David met his guide the next morning during breakfast in the hotel dining room. Mark was an affable man of Spanish descent, with handsome features and a bright smile. Dressed in business attire, he looked more like a business entrepreneur than a guide. After breakfast, Mark drove him directly to the location he had marked on his map the night before.

"Pull in there," David said as they drove past a cathedral. "What's the name of the church?" he asked as they pulled into the parking lot.

"St. Mary's," Mark replied.

David noted the picturesque appearance of the cathedral—its golden-brown stone walls surrounded by dark-green, tropical vegetation. Twin bell towers jutted high into the air on either side of the main structure, which featured a large stained-glass window located just above the arched entrance. "Wait here," he said to his guide.

David walked into the cathedral, passed through a spacious foyer, and entered the chapel. It was a beautiful church. He paused for a moment, noting the thirty-foot high vaulted ceiling and the white, stucco walls with arched openings. Rows of stained-glass windows lined the top of the walls, splashing patterns of colored sunlight upon the pews and the cream-colored tile floor. There were several rows of pews on either side of a center aisle. The pulpit was surrounded by an elaborate grillwork of brass. David was surprised that no cross hung on the wall behind the pulpit. He decided to sit down in one of the back pews and wait.

About two hours later, a priest walked into the chapel. David ran back to the car and returned with Mark, who helped him translate questions to the priest. Unfortunately, the priest didn't know of any monk matching the description of Thomas Aquinas.

David rode back to the hotel that afternoon feeling disappointed—another day wasted.

The next morning, David had his guide drive around the area surrounding St. Mary's. After learning that it was the only church in the neighborhood, he returned to the cathedral, sat down on one of the back pews, and waited yet again. An hour passed and no one appeared.

Just as he was about to leave, a man wearing a brown broadcloth habit entered the chapel. Although the monk was small in stature, David noted the large white cross hanging from a thick pewter chain around his neck. David watched intently as the monk walked to the altar and knelt in prayer.

A few minutes later, the monk finished his prayers and walked out the front entrance. David waited a few moments before following, then cautiously opened the front door and peered outside. To his surprise, he saw the monk entering a black Cadillac. "I want you to follow that Caddy, Mark," he said.

They followed the black sedan into the city, his guide keeping a comfortable distance between them. A few minutes later, Mark pulled over to the curb as the Cadillac stopped and let the monk out in front of a restaurant. "Wait here," David said and stepped out of the car.

Juanita's was a small outdoor restaurant featuring a large overhead structure of dark wooden timbers, providing the customers welcome shade from the hot sun. Bunches of green and red chilies hung from the rafters, presumably to whet the patrons' appetites. White laminate-covered tables surrounded by tan cloth-backed chairs gave the place a clean and comfortable appearance. The monk was seated at one of the smaller tables.

David slowly approached and gave him a friendly smile. "Do you speak English?"

"I do," the monk replied. "You're an American, yes?"

"How did you guess?" David replied, his smile widening. He noted the monk's excellent English. "Do you mind if I sit and chat with you for a while?"

"That would be nice," the monk replied affably. "I'm Father Justin."

"I'm David Sholfield," David said, seating himself directly across from the monk. "I'm a doctor from Chicago."

"Are you on vacation?"

"I'm on hiatus at the moment. I thought it would be nice to do a little traveling."

"Shall I order for you?" the monk asked as the waiter approached.

"I'll have a beer, please. You go right ahead and order whatever you like. I'm buying."

"Thank you," the monk said politely. After placing their orders, he turned to David and smiled. "It's been a while since I've been Stateside. I served in a monastery in Pennsylvania several years ago."

"That's a nice cross," David observed, changing the subject. "Have you had it for a while?"

"It was a gift from a dear friend," the monk replied casually. "I wear it always."

There was a pause in the conversation. David was running out of ideas. He couldn't just come out and ask the man to hand it over. Perhaps he could make him an offer. "I collect crosses," David said with an innocent smile. "Would you consider selling it?"

"I haven't had any use for money since I took the oath of poverty," the monk replied, smiling good-naturedly. "But I might consider giving it to you under the right circumstances."

"Interesting," David remarked. "And what circumstances might those be?"

"There's an estancia just outside of town. The owner is a friend of mine. He's been sick lately and he's very lonely. I was thinking that you could visit him—you know, cheer him up a little."

"Why me? I'm a total stranger."

The monk laughed, pointed to his ear, and made a circling motion with his finger. "He's not all there if you know what I mean. He doesn't remember things too well anymore, and he trusts no one. If I tell him you're a doctor, he'll trust you. His English is passable, so you won't need a translator."

"But I'm not staying very long," David protested with a frown. "Do you think I could do him any good?"

"I'm certain you could," the monk said, grinning. "You could visit him in the afternoons. It would only be for a few days."

David thought quickly. If he turned down the monk, he would never learn if the man had the philosopher's stone. Perhaps the monk wanted to test his worthiness before passing it on.

"Okay, Father Justin. I'll give it a try," David said. "Where is this place?"

"I need to speak to Mr. Lorente first. Meet me at St. Mary's tomorrow at one p.m."

David stood from the table and extended his hand. "It was nice meeting you, Father Justin. I'll see you tomorrow."

Sleep eluded David once again as he lay in the hotel bed, thoughts of Aaliyah wandering through his mind like the lingering scent of fresh-cut flowers. How he missed her! Recalling that they had promised to keep in touch, he turned on the light, sat down at the desk, and removed the pad of stationery from the top drawer.

David returned to the cathedral at the appointed time the next afternoon. To his relief, Father Justin was waiting at the entrance. "Good to see you, Father," David said with an exuberant smile.

"And you, David," the monk responded politely. "I have spoken to Mr. Lorente, and he is looking forward to your visit. We can leave now, if that is suitable."

They entered the car with the monk sitting in the back, giving directions as they drove. Half an hour later, they arrived at the estancia.

"As you can see, the Estancia Monte Cordero is not built in the Spanish style as you would expect," the monk explained as they pulled up to the main entrance. "It was built in the English style back in 1858. The estate has over fourteen hectares of lawn, which are primarily devoted to livestock production."

As Father Justin and David approached the front porch, they were greeted by a young housemaid who led them through an extravagantly furnished great room and down a hallway into a spacious bedroom. Like the rest of the ranch, the bedroom walls were done in beige stucco, featuring dark-brown chair rails and wrought-iron lamp fixtures. A king-size bed resided in its own alcove, ornamented with red-and-green floral-patterned wallpaper. Beneath the recessed window was a dark-brown wooden built-in cabinet. A white-haired old man was sitting up in the bed, staring at them nearsightedly with a confused look on his wrinkled face.

"He's not used to guests," the monk said. He motioned David to approach the bed. "David, meet Mr. Prudencio Lorente."

Suddenly a stranger burst into the room. The man was short—standing about five feet five—with black hair, obviously of Spanish descent. He was attired in a traditional gaucho outfit, consisting of a brown poncho, loose-fitting green trousers, and a black hat with a round brim.

The gaucho grabbed Father Justin from behind, produced a large knife, and pressed the long blade lightly into his neck. "You know what I want," he said gruffly to David in barely passable English.

"I'm not sure what you mean," David said, feeling both fear and confusion.

"Give me the Lyricor, and I'll be on my way."

"I don't have it with me," David said, stalling.

Then Mr. Lorente screamed something in Spanish, his gaunt face pale with fear.

Startled by the outburst, the gaucho dropped his knife. Seizing the opportunity, David lunged at the man, knocking him to the ground. They tussled on the floor for a few moments until a few staff members, roused by the commotion, ran into the room.

The gaucho, realizing that he couldn't fight them all off, jumped to his feet and ran through their midst, knocking one of the maids to the floor in his hasty exit.

David and the monk pursued, but by the time they reached the front entrance, the intruder was nowhere in sight.

"Who in the heck was that guy?" David asked, gasping for breath.

"I don't know," the monk replied, shaking his head. "Thank you for helping me."

"It was nothing," David said. "I'm just glad you're okay."

The monk conversed with the staff in Spanish for a few minutes, then smiled at David. "They're glad we're okay too. They asked if we would like something to eat."

During supper, David questioned the monk about his cross, but the man refused to talk about it. "You have not completed your task yet," he said, smiling mysteriously. "Then we shall see."

Afterward, David dropped the monk off at another cathedral in town. Our Lady of Guadalupe Basilica was a large edifice with a high bell tower and rows of arches carved into its white-painted granite walls on both the first and second stories.

"Meet me here tomorrow afternoon at one o'clock," Father Justin said, "and we'll visit Mr. Lorente again."

That evening, David lay in his hotel bed, his mind whirling with unanswered questions. Did the monk actually possess the philosopher's stone? According to Everet, the stone could only be passed down to the next person chosen to receive it. No one else could access it. Was God the sole purveyor and arbiter of those rules? If so, they couldn't be broken, and it stood to reason that the monk—if he actually possessed the stone—would confer it only at the proper time.

Then there was the anonymous party who had gone to the trouble of hiring two witches to procure it by force. The witches—most likely members of Revic's coven—had followed him from Nova Scotia to the Congo. He doubted that Claire had anything to do with sending them since she didn't have access to Tom's journal. Of course, the duke could have informed her, but it was unlikely that Revic would share information concerning the philosopher's stone with anyone. Then today, a new player had entered the arena. Was the gaucho on Revic's payroll as well?

The next afternoon, David and Mark arrived at the basilica. After waiting a few minutes for Father Justin, he entered the church and sat down on one of the pews. He waited for another hour, then decided to return to the estancia, wondering if the monk had forgotten about the appointment. Upon arrival, he was greeted by the same housemaid. "Father Justin has not returned," Mark informed him, translating her reply.

"That's very strange," David said to his guide, feeling disappointed and perplexed. Something was wrong. "Drive me back to St. Mary's," he told his guide. "Perhaps he'll turn up there."

He waited in the chapel till dark before returning to his hotel room.

David spent the entire next day searching for Father Justin, visiting all the known locations—the restaurant where they had first met, St. Mary's, the basilica, and the estancia—questioning everyone he met along the way to no avail. He returned to his hotel, dined in the restaurant there, and went to bed early, feeling discouraged.

Suddenly awakened by a noise, David sat up and turned the switch on the bedside lamp—but the lamp remained dark. "The bulb must have burned out," he muttered. In the dim light filtering through the curtains, he discerned movement among the shadows in the left-hand corner of the room. "Is someone there?" he asked.

David became frightened as he heard the noise again, which sounded like several people laughing somewhere off in the distance.

There was more movement. He stared into the shadows, and as his eyes adjusted to the darkness, several indistinguishable shapes became visible, appearing like charcoal-grey blotches lined up against the opposing wall. He heard the laughter again and realized it was coming from the blurry silhouettes.

David was seized with terror as a small lump in the carpet began moving toward him. He sat motionless, paralyzed with fear as the black shape, growing larger by the second, crept closer to the bed. Seconds later, it loomed over him, its height reaching to the ceiling. He realized that the voices were not physical sounds but were present in his mind.

"Give me the Lyricor," the apparition commanded in a loud, deep voice, resonating in his skull.

David snapped awake and then sat up in bed with a deep sigh. He realized that he had been dreaming.

He tentatively tried the lamp switch. To his relief, the light came on. He climbed out of bed and inspected the entire room, scanning every inch of the walls, ceiling, and floor. Nothing appeared out of place. He shivered, recalling the nightmare. When he looked down at his pajamas, he saw they were drenched in sweat.

The next morning, David returned to St. Mary's. After three hours of waiting for Father Justin, he decided to visit some of the other churches in town, hoping to find someone who had seen the monk.

It was late afternoon when David arrived at the Metropolitan Cathedral. The ancient structure was constructed of white stone, with three large archways in the front. Like St. Mary's, twin bell towers jutted upward on opposite sides.

As he approached the building, two nuns emerged from the center arch.

"Ask the nuns if they know Father Justin," David said to his guide.

"They don't know him," Mark said after speaking with the nuns, "but they said there are two monks living in a rectory behind the Guadalupe Basilica. Perhaps they might know him."

The rectory was a small, brownstone cottage with two gables, each with its own chimney. David found a monk tending the garden on the right side of the house.

"Let's go talk to him," David said to his guide.

As they approached, the monk looked up, smiled, and shook David's hand. The man was short and squat, with a bulbous nose and narrow brown eyes.

"I'm Father Renaldo," he said in passable English. "What can I do for you today?"

"I'm Dr. David Sholfield," David replied. "I'm looking for a Franciscan monk named Father Justin. Do you know him?"

The man brought his hand up to his nose and rubbed it as he pondered the question. Then he shook his head. "Father Justin, eh? No, I don't recall hearing that name. He doesn't reside here. Perhaps he's passing through town."

Seeing the disappointed look on David's face, he said, "I'll make some inquiries if you like. Perhaps he's cloistered in the monastery in Buenos Aires."

"Thanks for your help," David said. He produced a card from his jacket pocket and handed it to the monk. "Here's the hotel where I'm staying. Please call me if you hear anything."

David awakened the next morning after a peaceful, incident-free sleep and decided to return to St. Mary's. When he walked into the chapel, to his surprise, Father Justin was kneeling at the altar in prayer. Not wishing to disturb the monk, he seated himself in one of the rear pews and waited.

A few minutes later, the monk stood up and walked toward him. "Good to see you again, my friend," he said with a smile. "How are you?"

"Much better now, I assure you," David replied. "I've been looking for you. Do you still want me to visit Mr. Lorente?"

"That won't be necessary. You will get your cross, but there is one last thing I would ask." Father Justin paused for a moment, grinning enigmatically.

David was consumed with curiosity. Father Justin had just promised him the cross, but apparently, the monk would try his patience one more time.

"It's nothing special," Father Justin said with a chuckle, noting the bewildered look on David's face. "Meet me at Cordiality Fountain at dusk."

As David began to speak, the monk held up his hand. "No questions. Now, if you please, you can give me a ride into town."

David dropped off Father Justin at the basilica, returned to his hotel room, and called his mother. To his dismay, his father's condition had deteriorated even further. The doctor had put him on pain medication and had transferred him to a hospice. In an attempt to assuage his distress, David decided to write another letter to Aaliyah.

It was just before sunset when David arrived at Cordiality Fountain—a work of plumbed concrete statuary standing about ten feet high, featuring three ornamented catch basins supported by a column of concrete flowers and glyphs. A large sculpted seagull graced the top of the fountain, its wings spread as if poised for flight.

David relaxed a little as he watched the water stream out of the top basin, travel down the column into the middle basin, and finally cascade into the large basin at the base, making soothing, splashing sounds.

It was just after dusk when Father Justin appeared. "We don't have much time," the monk said brusquely. "Let's take your car, shall we?"

Following the directions Father Justin gave David's guide, they arrived twenty minutes later at an old abandoned theater on the outskirts of town.

"Leave your guide here and follow me," the monk said.

"What's going on, Father?" David asked as they entered the theater. He scanned the surroundings apprehensively. The inside had been gutted, leaving a large, open space scattered with construction debris. Several safety lights hung from the rafters, casting eerie shadows on the battered walls.

Suddenly four men appeared, all of them dressed in monk habits similar to Father Justin's.

David felt a surge of adrenaline as they encircled him, brandishing small, ceremonial swords. He remembered that Holly had held a similar one to his neck. Jamie had called it an athame.

He cringed in fear as they began chanting in an unfamiliar language.

"Not what you expected—eh, David?" Father Justin said. "You thought I was going to give you the philosopher's stone, didn't you?" He laughed diabolically. "It turns out that you are going to give it to me instead. I know you have the Lyricor. Give it to me now, or you will not live to see the light of day."

"You're not a monk at all!" David shouted, his anger surmounting his fear. "That's why none of the priests in Santa Fe ever heard of you."

As the chanting grew louder, David's chest constricted, making it difficult to breathe.

"Give me the Lyricor, David," the monk said.

"I don't have it with me," David managed, choking out the words in a strangled whisper.

Just as David began to faint, Everet appeared. "What audacity you have, dressing like holy men when you are so unholy," he said, addressing his remarks to Father Justin.

Before the monk could reply, Everet struck him in the neck with both fists. "Now we'll see who can't breathe," he said as the monk fell to the ground, holding his neck and choking. Then the other men charged Everet, slashing at him with their knives.

Everet reacted instantly, twirling in the air acrobatically, dodging the thrusts of their knife blades, kicking them in their chests, and striking their faces with his hands.

Fifteen seconds later, the imposters were all lying prostrate on the ground, knocked unconscious by Everet's strong, sharp blows.

Everet turned to David. "The demon will stop at nothing to acquire the philosopher's stone now that the Lyricor has resurfaced. You should be on your way now."

"Who are you?" David asked in dismay. "Why are you helping me?"

David watched helplessly as Everet turned away without a reply and strode out of the theater.

When David arrived at his hotel room, the first thing he did was open his suitcase. He breathed out a sigh of relief to find the Lyricor safe. It was glowing again, with new coordinates appearing upon its surface.

# Chapter Eleven

The next morning, David caught a direct flight from Buenos Aires to Quito, the capital city of Ecuador. After landing at the Mariscal Sucre International Airport, he was promptly greeted at the gate by his guide, Ted. He noted the man's unique features, recalling from his reading that his guide was of mestizo descent—a mix of American Indian and Caucasian ancestry. Dressed in a dark-blue business suit with a white dress shirt and a red-and-white striped tie, Ted appeared very sharp.

"Quito lies 9,300 feet above sea level on an Andean plateau, with a population of approximately 1.5 million," Ted said in solid English as he drove David to his hotel in a brand-new SUV. "The city has many modern buildings, as well as historic plazas, old churches, and monasteries. They were constructed by the Spaniards when they ruled Ecuador from 1534 to 1830. The city is graced by many palm trees and other tropical vegetation. Farms in the highlands on the outskirts of the city produce beans, corn, potatoes, and wheat. Because of the high elevation, the average temperature is 66 degrees by day, and 50 degrees at night. Because of our proximity to the equator, the temperature never varies. Just to the west lies Pichincha—our one and the only active volcano."

Ted pointed to a large hill located near the center of the city. "On the top of that hill stands a monument to the Virgin Mary. The most interesting feature of the statue is its wings."

"It is certainly unique," David remarked, glancing at the statue. "Ted, I want you to show me the churches and monasteries. I want to learn about the city's history and culture."

"I can be of service in that regard, sir," the guide responded. "The city is very ancient, its origins dating back to the first millennium when the Quitu tribe first resided here. They were eventually conquered by the Caras tribe, who were, in turn, conquered by the Incas in 1462. In 1534, the Spanish invaded, conquering the Incas and establishing the Catholic religion." Ted continued his monologue during the remainder of the twenty-minute drive, recounting the recent history of Quito.

"Thanks for the history lesson," David said as his guide parked the car in front of the hotel lobby. "Tomorrow morning, I want you to take me north, towards the equator. Do you know of any churches or monasteries in the vicinity?"

"Oh yes," Ted replied with a proud smile. "You will be pleased to learn that your hotel is located just a few blocks away from the historic center. There are more than forty restored churches and convents in the area."

David felt his optimism fading. It would be almost impossible to find the holy man amid so many churches, especially within the limited time his father had remaining.

"Meet me in the lobby at six a.m. sharp, Ted," he said as he stepped out of the car. "I want to get an early start."

The Royal Quito Hotel was a contemporary, twelve-story structure of concrete, brick, and glass, complete with a business center, restaurants, and conference rooms. After vigorously consuming an early dinner in the hotel restaurant, David retired to his room, desiring a good night's rest.

The room appeared more like a large bedroom than the typical hotel rooms he had been staying in lately, with golden painted walls, a large gold-and-white draped window, cherry molding, beige carpeting, a king-size bed, and two cherry end tables. The furniture included a tan and burgundy sofa with a wood and glass cocktail table, a full-size dresser, an expensive hickory dining table with purple silk-backed chairs, and a desk. The room had all the usual modern amenities as well.

In an attempt to ward off his recurring feelings of loneliness and melancholy, David decided to call Alan. He missed talking to his friend, and it had been several weeks.

"Hello there, David," Alan said, reading his caller ID. "I haven't heard from you lately. How's your father doing?"

"Not well, unfortunately. He's been transferred to a hospice. He only has a couple of months left, at best."

"That's very bad," Alan said. "I'm sorry to hear that. How are you doing?"

"I'm okay. Just a little stressed, though. I've been doing a lot of traveling. I'm anxious to return to Chicago and get back to work at the hospital."

"So, you're still on that wild-goose chase. I thought you would have called it quits by now."

"I thought about it, but there are some people after me. I think they're witches from Revic's coven."

"That sounds really weird, man. Apparently, they're suffering from the same delusions you are. Seriously, though, I hope you're safe, wherever you are."

David laughed. "Yeah, I'm okay—at least so far. I'm in Quito, Ecuador."

"I envy you, man, being on an exciting adventure like that, traveling the world. I want you to fill me in on all the details when you get back. Okay, buddy?"

"I will."

"Before I forget, Dr. Lucas has been asking about you. I told him you were looking after your father, but he needs to hear from you. It's been a couple of months, you know?"

"Yeah, with all that's happened, I haven't had time to check-in. I'll give him a call for sure. Talk to you soon, Alan. And keep away from those bad girls, okay?"

"Oh yeah, I almost forgot. I have a new girlfriend."

"That's great!" David exclaimed. "I want to meet her when I get back."

"I don't know, David. You're a pretty sharp guy. I don't want her ditching me and hooking up with you, now that you're single and unattached."

"You don't have to worry about that, Alan. I'm in love with a woman I met in Africa."

Alan laughed. "I can't believe you just said that, man. You're the only one I know who could manage pulling off something like that. How can you possibly be serious about some strange gal you just met on the road? Somehow, it doesn't surprise me. Call me again soon."

"Okay, Alan." David hung up feeling very tired. The jet lag had caught up with him again.

David approached the Metropolitan Cathedral, weighed down by discouragement. He had spent the last two days visiting twelve churches and cathedrals in the historic district with zero results. According to his guide, the Metropolitan Cathedral was considered one of the most important religious and spiritual symbols in Ecuador. Several presidents of the republic were buried in its catacombs, as well as many bishops and priests.

He paused for a moment, admiring the cathedral's massive white-painted brick façade. Built in the orthodox neoclassical Spanish style, it gave the impression of solidity and enduring beauty.

David entered the cathedral at the La Plaza Grande entrance and joined a small group of tourists who were gathered there for a tour. The interior was as beautiful as the exterior, the sculpted walls adorned with artwork painted by artists trained at the Quito School of Art. The main altar, in contrast to the Spanish exterior, was designed in the Baroque style.

Just as his group began their tour, David noted a monk entering the nave. He was tall in stature, with a large head and receding hairline, dressed in the traditional black habit of the Benedictine order.

David broke away from the tour and followed the monk as he left the premises, staying well behind him and stopping when the man entered a monastery.

The Carmen Monastery was very beautiful, built in the classic, colonial Spanish style, fronted with rows of cornflower-blue pillars supporting an overhang of white-trimmed arches. David walked to the mahogany double doors of the front entrance, located just inside the middle arch, and knocked.

A few moments later, a monk opened the door. He was of average height and build, with a shaved head, appearing to be in his mid-forties.

"State your business," the monk said sternly in Spanish.

After receiving the translation from Ted, David paused for a moment and gathered his thoughts. "Tell him that I'm looking for a monk. I don't know his name, but he's a big man with a receding hairline."

"Sorry," Ted said, translating the reply. "I don't know anyone matching that description."

"Can I see the abbot?" David asked as the monk began closing the door. "He might know the monk I'm looking for."

"I'm afraid you must have an appointment to see the abbot," the monk replied with a dour expression. Before David could respond, the monk closed the door firmly in his face.

David returned to his hotel room, lay down on the bed, and pondered the gravity of his situation. Quito was the fourth location given him by the Lyricor, and time was running out. His father was under hospice care, with only a month or so left to live. It was absolutely necessary that he locate the philosopher's stone at once, but his only lead was a monk whose appearance matched a vague description of Thomas Aquinas—the last person in recorded history to have allegedly possessed the mythical object. It wasn't much to go on. Tomorrow, he would make an appointment with the abbot at the Carmen Monastery and question him about the monk.

David's thoughts turned once again to Aaliyah. How he missed her radiant smile, the adoring way she looked at him with her lovely, blue eyes. He decided to write her another letter and tell her how much he loved and missed her; how much he was looking forward to seeing her again when she returned to the States.

He thought of asking her to marry him, but that seemed inappropriate in a letter. He would definitely pop the question when they were reunited, though. He didn't care if she wanted to stay in Topeka. It no longer mattered where he ended up living, so long as she was happy.

The next morning, David called the monastery and spoke to the abbot's secretary. The man told him bluntly that the abbot would not see him, that monastery policy strictly forbade divulging any personal information concerning the monks who resided there.

David hung up the phone feeling exasperated and defeated. He was running out of options. In desperation, he asked Ted to drive him back to the monastery.

When he reached the entrance, he paced back and forth for a full minute, racking his brain for any possible way to gain admittance. Suddenly, he snapped his fingers. "I have an idea, Ted. Knock on the door, please."

The door opened after Ted knocked, revealing the same monk they had encountered the day before.

"Have him tell the abbot that I want to donate five thousand dollars to the monastery and that I need to see him immediately."

"Are you sure you want me to tell him that?" Ted asked, a surprised look on his face.

"I am," David replied firmly.

In response, his guide shrugged, turned to the monk, and began a spirited two-way conversation. "He said to wait here," Ted said as the monk closed the door.

A few moments later, it opened, and after speaking a few words to Ted, the monk motioned them inside. The guide turned to David and grinned. "Abbot Morales will see you immediately. He wants you to know that the monastery accepts all major credit cards."

Abbot Morales's office was surprisingly contemporary, outfitted with computers and copy machines. The furniture was constructed of hardwood solids and veneers, including a spacious executive desk, a computer credenza, a storage hutch, and a large bookcase. David thought it ironic how well the monks lived considering the oath of poverty they had taken.

The abbot's secretary took David's credit card as they entered.

Ted shook the abbot's hand, and after a short conversation in Spanish, turned to David and said, "I have made the necessary introductions. The abbot wishes to know who you are looking for."

David grinned. It was so predictable how it always came down to money when one needed to accomplish something. "Tell the abbot I'm looking for a large, Benedictine monk, standing about six feet five, with a sizeable head and a receding hairline. I believe he is very well educated, perhaps a scholar of history and literature, and he may possess a large cross."

After receiving Ted's translation, the abbot nodded and replied in Spanish.

"He knows the man," Ted said, translating the abbot's reply. "His name is Father Nasiqua. He was passing through town and left this morning. He's headed for another monastery in England."

"That's too bad," David said with a frown. "Can the abbot give me the name of the monastery?"

At Ted's request, the abbot opened a drawer and produced a folder. After scanning its contents, he wrote something on a slip of paper.

"I have written down the information," Ted translated. "He's headed for the Andover Priory, which is located in Andover, Hampshire."

"Thank you, Abbot Morales," David said, extending his hand. The abbot shook it, handed him the slip of paper, and said a few more words.

"We are grateful for your donation," Ted said, translating the abbot's remarks. "If you need additional information, please feel free to call upon me at any time."

Just then, the secretary returned with David's credit card.

David accompanied his guide to the car, feeling extremely morose after another day of disappointments. He decided against traveling to England since he was already at the proper location according to the coordinates. He realized that his only remaining hope was to return to the Metropolitan Cathedral and make a final search.

Upon arrival, David sat down on a bench facing the cathedral and began watching the people as they walked in and out. After a few minutes, he took the slip of paper out of his pocket that the abbot had given him and stared at it. Father Nasiqua. There was something familiar about that name. A sudden jolt of excitement catapulted him out of his seat as he realized that the name was an anagram—when the letters were sorted, they spelled *Aquinas*.

"I heard that you were looking for me."

David spun around and beheld a tall Benedictine monk. It was uncanny how closely his features matched the description of St. Thomas. "Are you really Thomas Aquinas?" he said, a look of wonder on his face.

"Let's not talk here," the monk replied, giving David a benevolent smile. "There's a nice little restaurant not far from here. Walk with me."

Within minutes, they arrived at El Risotto. As they entered, David noted the romantic ambiance of the Italian restaurant. Red roses adorned the white cloth-covered tables, with colorful prints of northern Italy gracing the tan stucco walls.

After being seated by the hostess, David repeated his question.

"Yes, I am, actually," the monk replied unassumingly. He scanned the dining area, verifying that no one was within earshot. Then he turned back to David.

"I've been waiting for the proper opportunity to meet you," he said in an undertone. "I have to be careful that no one discovers my true identity, you see."

"It is a great honor to be in the company of a saint," David said respectfully. "There are so many questions I want to ask, but you must know what's central on my mind."

"I do," the monk responded. "But first, let me explain a little about myself. I was born in 1225 in a castle in central Italy."

A waitress appeared and took their orders, then the monk continued his discourse, giving David a brief account of his life.

"That's incredible," David said after the waitress had served their meals. "You must have learned so much, living through so many ages."

"Yes, I have. I've also learned that history has a habit of repeating itself. Mankind always finds a way to make the same mistakes, regardless of technology. I've spent my life studying philosophy and theology, but I won't bore you with all of that right now. I wish to speak to you concerning the stone."

David sat up in his chair and stared at the monk with rapt attention. After all of his searching and traveling, he was on the verge of success.

"I received the stone from my mentor, Albertus Magnus," the monk continued. "He was a Dominican friar and the greatest German philosopher of the Middle Ages. History dates his birth between 1193 and 1206, but he was actually born two centuries earlier, kept alive by the stone's glorious regenerative properties.

"It was presented to him as a gift by an unnamed alchemist for saving the life of the man's daughter. Albertus never divulged the name of the alchemist, or how the man had acquired the stone. That remains a great mystery, but I have no doubt that God and his angels know the truth of it. The stone was given to me at the request of Uriel, one of the seven archangels—the very same angel who stood guard at the gates of the Garden of Eden, wrestled Jacob at Peniel, and led Abraham to the west, to name a few of his many wonderful deeds. His many responsibilities include guarding the stone and holding the key to the Great Pit during the end-times."

"You said that Uriel guards the stone," David said. "Is that why the Lyricor guided me here?"

"Uriel has chosen you to be the next Keeper of the Stone."

David almost choked on his pasta as he attempted to grasp the enormity of what the monk had just said. "I think I understand some of it," he said after calming himself. "You're a saint, so you can converse with angels. But why is Uriel interested in me? I'm certainly a far cry from a saint."

St. Thomas shook his head slowly and gave David a sad look. "Unfortunately, there are no longer any living saints prepared to take on the great responsibility of being the Keeper of the Stone. The world has become far too wicked and complex. Satan has left his mark in every stratum of society, and his servants abound everywhere. Nevertheless, Uriel has designated you to become the next Keeper because of your honest, unassuming nature, and for other reasons known only to God. Our Lord sees into the hearts of all his creatures, so there can be no mistake in this. I have been called to pass the stone on to you."

"May I ask when, where, and how this is to take place?"

"There is no time to waste," St. Thomas replied earnestly. "Satan wishes to thwart our plans. We will meet tonight. You must bring the Lyricor with you to successfully activate the transfer."

David squirmed in his chair at the mention of the Lyricor. He was well aware of the wicked designs of those attempting to steal them from him. He remembered Everet's warning that he must keep it secure at all costs.

"Please don't be offended, St. Thomas," he said, clearing his throat, "but there are some evil people who are trying steal the Lyricor. Before I show it to you, I must know that you actually possess the philosopher's stone. I need indisputable proof."

He dropped his head, expecting a rebuke from the saint. To his surprise, the monk laughed.

"I applaud your caution, David. Satan has not hidden the fact that he wishes his minions to possess the stone in order to further his evil designs. Meet me tonight at the monument marking the equator. It's located in the village of Mitad del Mundo, about thirty-five kilometers north of here. Your guide knows where it is. Be there promptly at dusk."

The monk stood from the table and smiled. "And now, if you will excuse me, I have other urgent matters to attend to."

That evening, Ted dropped David off in the center of the tiny village of Mitad del Mundo. "Pick me up in two hours," David told his guide as he exited the car.

As he walked across the central plaza, he noted that the structure erected to mark the exact point where the equator was thought to pass through stood about thirty meters tall. It was pyramidal in shape—each side facing a cardinal direction—and was topped by a massive brass globe. He felt a surge of excitement as St. Thomas made his appearance.

"Good to see you again, my dear David," the saint said jovially. "Are you ready?"

David nodded in assent, noting the large backpack slung over the monk's habit and the propane lantern he was carrying.

They began walking in the direction of a small mountain located several miles to the north. After passing through a patch of trees and scrub brush, they entered a large clearing.

David watched in fascination as the saint lit the lantern and changed into the clothing he had brought. The monk donned an ephod made of white linen, covered by a long priestly robe of black bombazine reaching all the way to the ground. Drawn around his waist was a white girdle with Latin words inscribed into the fabric with black stitching. A cap of black sable adorned his bald head, and golden crosses were painted upon the tips of his black leather shoes.

"The Keeper of the Stone must always observe the traditions set forth by the angel," the monk explained. "Now I must draw the protective circles."

The monk produced a can of white spray paint from his backpack, and David held the lantern for him as he marked off the area with parallel lines—about nine feet square. Next, he drew two concentric circles inside the lines and then filled the spaces between the circles and the lines with triangles and crosses. Then he concluded his work by spraying Latin words over some of the lines. The whole procedure took about an hour.

David thought there was something familiar about the circles, recalling that they were very similar to the Circles of Power described in Tom Harrison's memoirs. "What is it that you need protection from?" he asked the monk as the man sprinkled holy water over the drawings.

"Two things," the monk replied. "First of all, Satan will do anything he can to disrupt the ceremony. The circles will protect us from his demons. In addition, the philosopher's stone is very powerful. It draws dark energy from the surroundings and uses it to transform matter at the subatomic level. Mortals cannot withstand the power that is unleashed. The angel can only protect us as long as we stay inside the circles."

The monk produced a round metal sphere from his backpack—about a foot in diameter—and a metal three-legged stand. Affixed to the tripod was a plate with a hole in the center, sized to hold the sphere firmly along its equator.

The monk opened the sphere by unscrewing it at its middle. "The philosopher's stone lies in the bottom half of the sphere," he said.

David's heart pounded with excitement as he shined the lantern into the sphere and caught his first glimpse of the philosopher's stone.

It was small and round—about six inches in diameter—and burgundy in color, with a dull finish. "It's not very big," he mused softly.

"Size is not important," the monk said patiently. He picked up a small pebble and handed it to David. "Examine this pebble carefully. I will demonstrate the power of the philosopher's stone by transmuting this worthless piece of rock into pure gold."

After David had inspected the pebble, St. Thomas placed it directly on top of the stone and screwed the two halves of the sphere together. Then he placed the tripod on the ground about fifteen feet in front of the circles and lowered the sphere onto it.

"The moon has risen," the monk said, looking upward. "It's time to begin the ceremony."

David followed him into the inner circle and watched the sphere with rapt attention as the saint began chanting in Latin. After a few minutes, David noticed a slight darkening of the air around the sphere, as if the very shadows of the trees were being sucked into it.

David lifted the lantern higher in order to get a better view. He watched in fascination as the immediate area surrounding the sphere continued to darken until it became completely enshrouded in what appeared to be a black cloud. He observed its continually changing shape, noting the thin streaks of charcoal grey quickly moving along its black surface as if it were alive.

St. Thomas ceased chanting, and the cloud gradually dispersed until the sphere was completely visible again.

"That was amazing," David remarked. As he anxiously stepped toward the boundary of the circle, the saint gripped his arm. "We must be sure the dark energy has dispersed before walking outside the circles of protection," the monk said.

Approximately a half-hour later, the monk gave the go-ahead. They stepped outside the circle and approached the sphere. "Now you will have the proof you require," St. Thomas remarked proudly as he unscrewed the top.

David gasped as he looked inside. Sitting on top of the philosopher's stone was a round piece of gold, the same size as the original pebble.

The monk removed it from the sphere and handed it to David. "I assure you, it's real," he said, grinning. "You may keep it as a memento of the occasion."

David inspected it in the lantern's beam and then bit into it. It was soft. "I believe you, St. Thomas," he said excitedly. "When am I to receive the stone?"

"Tomorrow at midnight," the saint replied. "As I said, you will need the Lyricor for the angel to make the transfer. Meet me here in the clearing. I will mark the path on our return to the village."

The next night, several minutes before midnight, David returned to the clearing by following the white markings the saint had spray-painted on the trees the night before. He felt jubilant at the prospect of finally returning home and using the stone to heal his father.

St. Thomas was waiting inside the circle when David arrived. "Hello, David. It's good to see you again," he said with an accommodating smile.

By the light emanating from the lantern, David could see that the monk was dressed in the same priestly attire as the night before.

"Did you bring the Lyricor?"

"Yes. Now what?" David asked.

"Just set it down on the ground, about ten feet outside the protection area."

David reached into his backpack, produced the Lyricor, and placed it on the ground in front of him.

"You can't come inside this time," the monk said as David began walking toward him. "The circles will negate the power necessary for the transfer. You must stand next to the Lyricor and activate it when I give the go-ahead." After David had complied with his request, St. Thomas said, "That's good. Now be still while I perform the ritual."

As the monk began chanting, dark shadows formed around the Lyricor and David. To his dismay, feelings of fear and distress overcame him as he was enveloped by the black cloud. He looked down at the Lyricor and was horrified to see that it was completely covered in a shell of blackness.

A million voices thrust themselves into his mind, clamoring in a language he didn't understand. He held his hands to his ears as the bedlam intensified, torturing his mind with pain.

When he looked down at the Lyricor, red numbers began appearing on its surface, shining through the thin black veil covering it. The feelings of dread and anguish swelled until he fell to the ground, crushed by the horrific weight of the unseen supernatural power.

Suddenly, the shadows began to fade. Through the lingering dark mist, David was able to discern a white-robed figure approaching in the distance. A voice came from the figure, saying, "Do not fear the Legion."

A moment later, the shadows completely dispersed, enabling David to recognize who it was. "Boy, am I glad to see you, Everet!" he exclaimed. "I thought I was going to die."

"You're safe now," Everet said with a gentle smile. "The demons used their black magic in an attempt to force the Lyricor into revealing the location of the stone. Fortunately for you, they failed."

David glanced at the circles, but the monk was no longer there. "I feel so foolish," he said sheepishly. "The sorcerer had me convinced that he was St. Thomas."

"Witchcraft can have a very suggestive effect on the mind," Everet said.

David sighed with exasperation. "I get it. They've been casting spells on me for months now, haven't they?"

In response, Everet held his outstretched hand into the air. "I have something for you."

In the moonlight, David discerned a small silver cross attached to a thin silver chain dangling from Everet's fingers. "Take it, David," he said. "The cross will provide the true location of the stone, but you will still need the Lyricor to access it."

"What do you mean?" David asked. "I thought the Lyricor was supposed to give me the location."

"You will understand shortly. You must return home now. Your father is dying. Don't forget the Lyricor when you leave."

"But how can I heal my father without the philosopher's stone?" David asked in a panic as he retrieved the Lyricor. "Please help me find it before it's too late!"

His eyes moistened with tears as Everet turned away in silence and disappeared into the woods.

# Chapter Twelve

David sat down on his couch and began sorting through the mail he had picked up at the post office. He suddenly felt a surge of excitement when he saw a letter from Aaliyah.

"My dear, sweet David," the letter began. "I have given much thought to what happened between us during our short time together. I was going through a really hard time, and you were such a great comfort to me. I made a place in my heart for you willingly. You did not manipulate me in any way. I know that your feelings for me are genuine, and it saddens me at what I must now tell you.

"After you left, I received another letter from my boyfriend, saying that he had made a big mistake and had broken up with the other woman. He went on and on about how there was no other woman like me, and how he had taken our love for granted. He said he wanted me back and that he wanted to marry me when I returned from my mission."

David paused for a moment and used his shirtsleeve to wipe away the tears that had begun trickling down his face.

"At first, I was angry," Aaliyah continued. "What right did he have trying to patch things up after breaking my heart like that? I went back to the falls where we swam together, David, and I thought of all the reasons why I should be with you instead of him. He had no right cheating on me and taking my love for granted, but I knew you would never treat me that way.

"I went back to that same spot every afternoon and thought of you, but after a few days, I began to remember what it was like with Donald. I remembered all the time we had spent together in high school and how much we were in love. I thought long and hard about how I really felt about him. When my anger faded, I realized that I still love him, in spite of the terrible thing he did to me.

"I know how you feel about me, David, and I am so very sorry, but I can't be dishonest with you. I have decided to give Donald another chance. As I mentioned, we have a lot of history together, and that is something that cannot be erased.

"I don't know how to say this any other way, but thank you so much for your kindness and love. Please feel free to write me and let me know how you're doing, okay? Goodbye. Your friend always, Aaliyah."

David crumpled the letter, tossed it onto the floor, and continued to cry. He knew that he would never see her again. After all that had happened with Angela, he had opened his heart a second time—only to have it broken again. After a while he calmed down, went to the kitchen, and poured himself a stiff drink.

"Golly, it's good to see you, man," Alan said, standing from the table and giving David a tight hug. "Welcome back to Chicago!"

"It's good to see you too, Alan," David responded with a weak smile. "I see the place hasn't changed much."

Curley's was packed with customers. The small dance floor was filled with people dancing to a funky blues number belted out by a live band.

"It seems that we've come full circle," David said with a nostalgic smile. "Back here, the place where all my adventures began."

"Hey, I hope this isn't a downer for you, buddy. I didn't think about that when I made the plans."

"I'll have a whiskey with a beer chaser," David said as the waitress approached.

"Make mine a Southern Comfort on the rocks," Alan said, giving her a flirtatious grin.

"Hey there, buddy," David said after the waitress left. "From the way you looked at that waitress, no one would suspect that you have a girlfriend."

"Oh. That," Alan said with a faraway expression. "It's over and done with." He took a deep breath. "I'm back in circulation," he said, his face brightening, "For better or for worse. I guess you're the one with the attachment now. So, tell me about your new woman, buddy."

David lowered his head and stared at the table with a melancholic expression. "I'm done with women for good this time, Alan," he said glumly. "She dumped me." He attempted a weak smile and lifted his shot glass. "Here's a toast to us—the hottest, most available guys in town."

"Here! Here!" his friend exclaimed, lifting his glass.

"So, tell me about her," Alan continued after downing his drink. "Who was this woman who won you over so quickly?"

"Her name's Aaliyah. I met her in the Congo."

"What in the heck were you doing in the Congo?" Alan asked. "Chasing more witches?"

"It's a long story," David replied. "That's not the only piece of bad news, I'm afraid."

Alan gave his friend a sympathetic look. "I heard about Dr. Lucas letting you go."

"I should have kept him better informed. I've been too distracted lately, with my father being sick and everything. I lost focus; you know? I don't blame him for firing me."

"I'm sorry, David. You've been through a rough time. I don't think I could have held onto a high-pressure job like that either, especially under those circumstances. Sometimes there are more important things in life than pursuing a highly competitive and intense professional career."

"Thanks for the sympathy, Alan, but I should have handled it better. Anyway, I'll try and summarize my latest exploits. I told you about the Lyricor, right?"

"Yeah. You said that Tom had written about it in his journal. How he needed it to locate the philosopher's stone and cure his girlfriend. You said that someone had given it to you and that it led you to Nova Scotia."

"That's right. A guy named Everet gave it to me. I used the coordinates from the Lyricor, hoping to locate the philosopher's stone so I could heal my father. I know it sounds pretty weird, but I hope you can understand how I felt, that I would do anything to save him."

"That makes total sense," Alan said. "I'd like to think that I would've had the guts to do the same thing if I was in your position."

"Thanks. Anyway, when I arrived in Nova Scotia, some witches—I think they were from Revic's coven—tried to steal the Lyricor, but Everet showed up out of the blue and stopped them."

"Sounds like you have another friend you can count on."

"Thank the Lord for that. Afterward, the Lyricor directed me to the Congo, where I met Aaliyah. She's a nurse working in a Baptist mission there. I fell in love with her." He snapped his fingers. "Just like that."

"Maybe she's a witch too," Alan joked. "She put a love spell on you."

"Nice try, Alan," David said with a grin. "Unfortunately, the real witches showed up and took Aaliyah hostage. They threatened to kill her if I didn't give them the Lyricor. I made a deal with them, saying I could give them something much better—the philosopher's stone itself. A week earlier, the pastor of the mission had shown me a cross with a red crystal inside which I mistakenly believed to be the genuine article. In return for Aaliyah's freedom, I stole it from him and handed it over to the witches."

"That was very chivalrous of you," Alan remarked with a smile. He ordered another round of drinks when the waitress returned. "Please continue. This is getting more interesting by the minute."

"For you, maybe. Anyway, while I was in the Congo, the Lyricor gave me another new location—so I had a difficult decision to make. I had fallen in love with Aaliyah and wanted to stay with her, but my father's condition was deteriorating After a sleepless night or two, I decided to go to Argentina—the new location. I still wonder what would have happened if I had stayed in the Congo.

"I flew to Santa Fe and met a monk wearing a large cross. I thought he possessed the philosopher's stone, but he ended up not being a real monk at all. He and a group of his buddies—who turned out to be sorcerers—cast a spell on me to trick me into giving them the Lyricor."

"Wow! That's quite a tale. Apparently, there are others who want the stone for themselves. So, what happened with the phony monks?"

"Everet showed up at the last minute and took care of them. He has some fast moves, you know? I owe him my life."

"So, who exactly is this Everet fellow, and why is he helping you?" Alan asked.

"Those are the million-dollar questions. I asked him who he was, but he just walked away without saying a word. After that, the Lyricor gave me a fourth location—Quito, Ecuador. There I met another monk who pretended to be St. Thomas Aquinas. Because he matched the saint's description and played the part perfectly, I believed him. He had me fooled all the way."

"It sounds like the coven was still casting spells on you, using the power of suggestion to make you believe what they wanted."

"Yeah, they threw everything they had at me. The monk said I was chosen by God to be the next Keeper of the Stone. He had me meet him outside of town and bring the Lyricor, claiming that he needed it in order to transfer ownership of the stone."

"That would stretch anyone's credulity. You didn't actually believe him, did you?"

"Of course not. I told him that I needed proof that he actually possessed the stone. He gave me a very convincing demonstration, turning a pebble into this." David reached into his jacket pocket, produced the piece of gold, and slid it across the tabletop. "Check it out, man. It's the real deal."

"Amazing," Alan remarked after carefully examining the object. "It sure looks genuine. I'm guessing that this guy convinced you, right?"

"Yeah. We met at the same spot the next night, and the bastard conjured a slew of demons in an attempt to force the Lyricor into revealing the location of the stone."

"That's really hard to believe. Demons? There's no such thing."

"I swear to God they're real, Alan. I saw them with my own eyes. They were all grouped together in a big black shadow. Or something. They were in my mind too, like a million voices speaking simultaneously. I could feel the evil oozing out of them. I thought I was going to die."

"That was pure witchcraft, plain and simple," Alan said, taking a large swallow of his drink. "Nothing more than smoke and mirrors. They worked on your mind somehow—got you to see what they wanted you to see."

"That could be, Alan, but it sure felt real enough. Anyway, Everet showed up and banished the demons. Afterward, he gave me a cross and said that it would reveal the location of the philosopher's stone."

"Do you have it with you?"

"I wear it around my neck," David said, pulling the cross out from under his shirt.

Alan leaned over the table and examined it. "It looks like any ordinary cross. But what are those markings on the ends?"

"I had them translated. They're the Hebrew letters for the four directions." David took a sip of his drink. "I don't understand it, Alan. How could four directions point to a single location? It doesn't make sense."

Alan leaned back in his chair. "How many locations did you travel to, David?"

"I told you—four."

"You said two in South America, right? Argentina is in the south, Ecuador's to the west. And the Congo—that represents the east."

"And Nova Scotia's to the north," David said excitedly, finishing Alan's thought. "The four directions. But they don't point to anything."

Alan took out a pen and drew something on his cocktail napkin. "Perhaps they're not pointing outward. What if they're pointing inward instead?" He smiled slyly and pushed the napkin in front of David.

David stared at the napkin and breathed in sharply. Alan had drawn four points and connected them—north to south, east to west—the result forming a cross. "The intersection of the lines reveals the true location!" he exclaimed excitedly. "Alan, you're a genius!"

"What are friends for?" Alan gloated, a proud smile on his face.

# Chapter Thirteen

David was relieved to see his guide waiting for him as the speedboat docked at the small fishing village on the bank of the Rio Jatapu, one of the Amazon's numerous tributaries. His guide, a resident of the village, was a middle-aged tracker of native descent named Bruno.

"We can go now," the man said in passable English, motioning to his kayak.

After David boarded, Bruno began paddling upstream into the rainforest.

"You don't have many supplies," David said, noting the two backpacks lying on the floor of the kayak.

"We hunt for food," Bruno said with a grin.

David gave Bruno a discerning stare. The man's hard, lined features, coupled with his strong, athletic build, gave David the impression of someone who had spent most of his life outdoors. When David had first arrived in Manaus, the man who had arranged the expedition mentioned that Bruno had excellent tracking and hunting skills.

David frowned, recalling his mother's reaction when he had informed her that he was leaving for the Amazon rainforest. She had tearfully begged him to stay and spend the last few weeks with his dying father. The doctors had only given him a month to live, but David had been adamant about continuing his search for a cure.

The city of Manaus was located in Amazonia, Brazil—the closest major city to the coordinates David had plotted on his computer. He had taken a direct flight from Miami and had been disappointed to learn upon his arrival that the highway was impassable due to an untimely, copious amount of rainfall. The only alternative route to the equator was to travel east on a dirt road for approximately 360 kilometers to the Uatumã River and then board a speedboat to the Jatapu.

Having completed the first leg of the journey, he was now embarking upon the 400-kilometer trek northwest to the equator. David checked the backpacks as Bruno continued paddling, noting the hammocks, tarps, mosquito nets, fishing equipment, water, and canned meats and vegetables. The kayak itself was a large, white fiberglass canoe, fitted with life jackets and helmets.

He had brought his own suitcase as well, filling it with sundry items such as malaria pills, insect repellent, sunscreen, T-shirts, underwear, a swimsuit, a pair of long pants, and a poncho.

David was quickly captivated by the scenic beauty of the rainforest as they traveled along the river, admiring the green forested hills, the blue-green streams, and the exotic vegetation growing on myriad rocks scattered along the riverbank. He spotted a few squirrels, three varieties of monkeys, several unique and colorful birds—Bruno said they were toucans and macaws—and some larger mammals, including deer and tapirs.

To his delight, several freshwater dolphins swam into view at infrequent intervals. Bruno explained that they were curious about the shape of the kayak's nose, that they were comparing it to their own.

That evening, the men set up camp on the forested shoreline. Bruno explained that the beaches were normally flooded throughout the year, but David's timing was excellent. It was December, the end of the rainy season.

After eating a meal of canned beef stew that Bruno heated over a small fire of driftwood, David strung his hammock between two trees and fell asleep.

Early the next morning, Bruno treated David to a breakfast of fresh black piranha, which he had caught at sunrise. Then they broke camp, boarded the kayak, and resumed their journey upstream.

Sometime around noon, Bruno landed the boat and went into the jungle to hunt for food. David spent the time swimming and sunbathing. About an hour later, Bruno returned with a wild turkey, which he had shot with his rifle. David watched with interest as his guide expertly skinned and cooked the bird over an open fire. After eating their fill, they launched the kayak and proceeded upstream.

They spent the next five days traveling without incident, hunting, and fishing as they went, but on the sixth day, it began to rain. Bruno explained that it usually rained in squalls this time of year, but this rain was unusually persistent.

The next morning, to Bruno's consternation, the rain was still falling hard, and the river had risen several meters. When Bruno told David that he didn't want to resume until the rain had stopped, David was glad for the break, giving much-needed rest to his tired, aching muscles.

After a few hours of sitting in his hammock, David realized that the jungle was affecting his mind. No matter what he did to make himself comfortable, mounting feelings of fear and dread threatened to send him into an irrational state of panic. He recalled Bruno's comment earlier that morning that he didn't like resting, that he always kept busy so that the jungle wouldn't take him over. Now he understood what his guide meant. Unfortunately, all they could do was swing in their hammocks and watch the seemingly endless rainfall.

By the end of the day, David felt completely at the mercy of the jungle, realizing that as long as he was there, he would never find relief from the constant exposure to the elements—the sun that cooked him, or the rain that chilled him to the bone.

David was surprised that he no longer felt sad about Aaliyah. Perhaps it had been a mere infatuation, intensified by the tragic loss of his beloved Angela. Or perhaps the emotional noise created by the jungle was drowning out his true feelings.

By nightfall, David felt as if a huge weight had been placed upon him, a weight that he had been carrying for a long time. He needed to purge himself of it somehow, but being surrounded by a million square miles of rainforest and a labyrinth of never-ending rivers made it impossible.

Mercifully, the rain ended the next morning. As David followed Bruno into the jungle, he realized thankfully that a most welcome feeling of tranquility had replaced the mind-numbing helplessness he had felt the day before.

After a short walk, they came upon a Brazil nut tree. "Looks like we found breakfast," Bruno remarked with a grin. They spent a half-hour collecting the nuts that had fallen to the ground before returning to their campsite. Then Bruno brewed some coffee while David shelled the nuts. After finishing breakfast, they broke camp.

After another week of paddling and hunting, the twosome finally arrived at the mouth of the stream. Because they were still ten miles from the equator, they had no choice but to cover the remaining distance on foot, so they lashed the kayak to a tree, donned their backpacks, and began their trek into the jungle.

The first day of hiking was relatively easy for David. The forest floor was unencumbered with foliage, and the canopy was very dense. It absorbed eighty percent of the sunlight, allowing for little growth below. He admired the huge trees, rising above the canopy to a height of two hundred feet or more. The variety of Amazonian flora and fauna that coexisted on the top layer amazed him, exhibiting even more diversity than the Congo.

As they walked along, Bruno pointed out a variety of monkeys, harpy eagles, and many other species of birds, as well as a myriad of flowers and fruits. David noted that the understory consisted of much smaller trees with large, dark-green leaves, growing only about twelve feet high, many of them covered with lianas, flowers, and fruits.

As evening approached, they came upon a small clearing and decided to make camp. After gathering sufficient firewood, Bruno showed David how to make torches by covering the tips of very straight tree branches with resin he obtained from a particular species of plant leaves that burned slowly when lit.

After dinner, David and Bruno spent the remainder of the evening swinging in their hammocks, telling all the jokes they could remember. David eventually drifted into a deep sleep, calmed by the relaxing night sounds of the crickets and frogs.

The next day, they continued hiking through the endless jungle. They stopped at midday for a lunch of canned pork and beans, which they ate cold, washing it down with warm pop. Bruno explained that since they were so close to the equator, he didn't want to waste any more time hunting or building a fire.

As they ate, David spotted some brightly colored toucans and macaws, and a group of black howler monkeys traveling through the rainforest, swinging from tree to tree high up in the canopy. Bruno identified several other exotic animals: a three-toed sloth, a tamarin, and a giant anaconda hanging from a tree in the understory.

As they continued their trek that afternoon, David began feeling apprehensive again. He remained alert as they walked, vigilantly scanning the surrounding forest and searching for any sign of danger. He attempted to rationalize his feelings, thinking that the jungle was affecting his mind again, but he couldn't shake the feeling that someone or something was following them.

When he mentioned it to Bruno, he said, "I think you may be right. Could be ocelot, or maybe jaguar."

David shivered at the possibility that wild felines were stalking them. "Are we in danger?"

"Not yet," his guide replied with a comforting smile. "Ocelot is no problem—only weighs about thirty pounds—but jaguar much bigger. We are safe during daytime. Jaguar stalk prey at night. We build fire tonight, then throw pepper on it. Should keep cat away."

They set up camp late that afternoon on the bank of a small stream. Bruno instructed David to gather as much firewood as possible, explaining that a large fire would prevent animals from entering their campsite. While David completed his task, Bruno broke out the fishing tackle and caught several fish, which he cooked over a small fire. By the time they had finished their meal, it was getting dark. Nighttime always came early in the jungle.

"Time to make fire bigger," Bruno said.

After they had a sufficient blaze, Bruno said, "I keep watch tonight and tend fire. You sleep now. Don't worry about cat."

David lay down in his hammock but couldn't sleep. The irrational fear that had plagued him during the rainstorm ten days ago had returned in full force. He held his breath for a moment and listened intently to the night sounds of the rainforest, but he could discern nothing threatening.

Just as he was about to fall asleep, he noticed that the forest had become eerily silent. He abruptly sat up in his hammock. "Bruno!" he shouted. "Something's wrong!"

In the waning firelight, David saw a large orange cat with black spots and rounded ears suddenly leaping out of the forest and into their camp.

He screamed with fear as it ran toward him. Suddenly the air was pierced by the sound of gunfire. The jaguar dropped dead in its tracks.

"Close call," Bruno said with a wry smile. "You okay?"

"Yeah. Thanks, Bruno," David replied in a shaky voice.

"No problem," his guide said. Bruno cautiously approached the jaguar and poked its side with his rifle. "Ever eat grilled cat?"

After another day of hiking, they made camp by a waterfall. As David bathed in the spacious pool, some giant otters ran out of the jungle and began playing in the water near the opposite bank. He watched attentively as the six-foot-long mammals frolicked about, humming, squealing, and screeching at each other.

Suddenly Bruno came running toward him, a frantic look on his face. "David," he said breathlessly. "Get out of water. Some men are coming!"

Just as David stepped out of the water, four men walked out of the jungle and approached them. "I think they follow us," Bruno said in an undertone. "Stand still and keep quiet."

A chill of fear coursed through David's body as he watched the men approach, their brown skin glistening in the sunlight. They appeared to be tribal natives.

They presented fearsome images. Their faces were painted red, their ears were pierced with shells, and spines jutted out from their noses. Their arms were girded by armbands of monkey teeth.

David inhaled sharply, noting the blowguns they carried, each about four meters in length. Quivers of poison darts hung from their necks from bright, multicolored woven bands.

Two of them said something to Bruno. He replied in Portuguese, but it was obvious they didn't understand. Then two of them leveled their blowguns at David and Bruno and motioned for David to get dressed. The other two tied the men's hands behind their backs with strong cords of animal skins. The tribesman confiscated their tackle boxes and backpacks and pushed them toward the warriors who were walking back into the jungle.

"Follow them," Bruno said in a low whisper, "and keep quiet."

About two hours later they arrived at a clearing surrounded by several large huts. Five women sat in the center, cooking something in an iron pot. A few small children ran about in the clearing, laughing and playing.

The warriors led David and Bruno into one of the huts, motioned for them to sit on the floor, then left.

"This is where they live," Bruno said, keeping his voice low. "It's called a longhouse."

David surveyed the interior. The longhouse was a large, simple structure of wooden planks covered with straw and palm leaves. The inhabitants' sleeping quarters, sparsely furnished with hammocks and baskets, were partitioned off by colorful blankets. The center space was open, containing only a few items of pottery. There were two doors, one on each side, and next to the doors were benches, baskets, and more pottery.

"It looks like at least ten people live in here," David remarked softly, trying to stifle the anguish boiling inside of him. "Are we going to be okay?"

Bruno shrugged and frowned. "Don't know. We find out soon, though. I try and talk to them again."

Just after sunset, two of the tribesmen entered, untied David and Bruno, and set two bowls of food and two smaller drinking bowls onto the floor in front of them. Although there were no lamps inside the longhouse, a large bonfire burned just outside, providing adequate lighting. The warriors remained inside, guarding them as they ate.

"Monkey meat," Bruno said, tasting a morsel. "Not bad."

David cautiously sipped from the drinking bowl and breathed out a sigh of relief that it was water.

After they had eaten, the tribesmen led the men out of the hut and into the common area, located in the center of the village.

In the light of the bonfire, David witnessed a line of men moving about in some kind of ritualistic dance. Their bodies were painted red, and they made grunting noises as they moved, mimicking the sounds of pigs. The women and children gathered in a circle around them, about forty people in total.

"What the heck are they doing?" David asked softly.

"It's the ceremonial dance of the Queixada," Bruno whispered in reply. "They're imitating wild pigs."

"Why are they doing that?"

"They believe animal spirits give good fortune in hunting. They do other animal ceremonies too."

"That makes sense. Everyone wants the same things in life—health and prosperity. Maybe we're not so different after all."

After the ceremony, one of the tribesmen approached and spoke a few sentences to Bruno.

"Did you understand that?" David asked with a quizzical expression.

"A little," Bruno replied, frowning. "He is village chief. He wants to know what tackle boxes are for."

Bruno turned to the chief and spoke a few words while making hand gestures as if casting a fishing line into the water.

The chief gave him a puzzled look and called for his guards, who promptly returned them to the longhouse. Once inside, the guards tied the captives' hands together again and pointed to some blankets lying on the dirt floor.

"They want us to sleep now," Bruno said with a relieved sigh. He smiled for the first time since their capture. "If they wanted to kill us, they would have done it by now."

"I'm glad to hear that," David said, breathing a sigh of relief. "But we're still prisoners, aren't we?"

"Don't worry—I have idea."

Early the next morning, the guards returned to the longhouse and led David and Bruno to the chief, who stood surrounded by five warriors in the middle of the village.

As they approached, the chief pointed to the two tribesmen holding the tackle boxes and spoke a few words to Bruno in the chief's native tongue. After Bruno replied, the chief barked orders to his men, and they began walking toward the jungle.

Bruno turned to David and smiled. "I told them to take us to nearby stream."

Five minutes later they came to a swift-running stream. The tribesmen untied the companions' restraints and handed them their boxes. "I told the chief I would show him what boxes are used for," Bruno said, opening his tackle box. "I told him if I show him how to feed entire village, he let us go."

He assembled his line and tackle, plopped his line into the water, and pulled out a fish ten seconds later.

The tribesmen gasped with astonishment, and the chief made some remarks in an excited tone. Bruno removed the fish from the line and handed the line to the chief, who tried it for himself. Several seconds later, he caught a fish. They continued to fish—each tribesman attempting the deed on his own—until they caught their fill.

"They didn't tie our hands this time," David remarked as they returned to the village.

"We can go soon," Bruno said with a grin.

The men created a stir when they arrived, proudly displaying their catch to the women and children. After all the excitement subsided, David turned to Bruno. "Are we free to leave now?"

"Yes. We are very near equator. What is it you look for, David?"

David pondered for a few moments before replying. "Ask the chief if he knows of any churches, missions, or monasteries in the area."

When Bruno asked the chief, the man turned very pale. Then, after a long pause, he spoke in a near whisper.

"What did he say, Bruno?" David asked anxiously.

"Understand a little," Bruno replied slowly. "Holy place nearby, but tribe is forbidden to go. Chief says we must stay away—place is cursed. Bad things happen there."

"Ask him exactly what will happen if we go there."

"Forbidden to say," Bruno said after speaking to the chief again. "He says tribe will show us the way if we give them tackle boxes."

David felt giddy with excitement. After all the many travails and hardships, he had experienced during his quest, he was on the verge of success. "I definitely want to go there," he said with a bright smile. "Have them show us the way!"

Bruno spoke a few more words to the chief, and two of his warriors beckoned them to follow. David had trouble maintaining the pace as the tribesmen moved quickly through the jungle.

"Why are they in such a hurry?" he asked breathlessly as they jogged through a grassy meadow.

"They waste no more time than necessary," Bruno replied with a concerned expression.

Noting David's exhaustion, the tribesmen paused for a short break. After continuing for another hour of fast walking, they finally stopped.

"They say holy place just to the west," Bruno said after questioning the warriors. "They afraid to come any closer. They go back to village now."

"Tell them thanks for showing us the way," David said.

"I go with them," Bruno said, to David's surprise. "They say anyone who goes there is cursed. I believe them."

"I'm sorry to hear that," David said with an anxious look, wondering how he would fare in the jungle without Bruno's expertise. "I see that your mind is made up, so I won't try and persuade you, but I would ask one thing—will you meet me back here tomorrow?"

"I will be here tomorrow," Bruno said. "Just head east from holy place. I will find you."

"Thanks, Bruno," David said with a grateful smile. "I'll see you tomorrow."

Without another word, Bruno and the tribesmen turned eastward and ran off into the rainforest.

David's mind filled with anxiety as he listened to the raucous sounds of the birds and animals surrounding him, realizing that this was his first time completely alone in the vast Amazon rainforest. He attempted to quell his trepidation, reminding himself that he was doing this to save his father.

After walking through the forest for another twenty minutes or so, David arrived at a spacious, grass-covered clearing. He stopped at the edge and stared in fascination and wonder.

A white tower stood in the center, rising to a great height, its walls thrusting upward through the canopy. He cautiously approached, stopped about five feet away from the base, and gazed upward. The tower rose to a dizzying height of approximately six hundred meters.

He walked all the way around the tower, noting that it had four tapered sides, each about fifty meters wide at the base, ending in a pyramidal shape at the top. It reminded him of the Washington Monument he had visited as a boy. He remembered that it was called an obelisk.

Upon returning to his starting point, he cautiously moved closer. From two feet away, he could discern faint, mottled, burgundy streaks running through its smooth, polished surface. The obelisk appeared to be made out of marble. He was overcome with curiosity as he noted the strange markings, symbols, and characters carved into its base.

David slowly walked around the obelisk for the second time, touching the surface and viewing the carvings, recognizing nothing familiar. He searched for an entrance, but the surface appeared unbroken, with no doors or windows.

"There must be some way inside this thing," he muttered as he began his second round. Upon reaching the opposite side, he noticed a small indentation—approximately six inches in diameter—one meter above the tower's base.

As he stood there pondering how to gain entry, he suddenly recalled Everet's statement: that he would need the Lyricor to gain access to the stone. He removed his backpack and rummaged through its contents until he found the Lyricor. When he inserted it into the indentation, it fit perfectly.

A moment later, faint lines appeared on the obelisk's surface. Then suddenly, a portion of the wall slid silently and slowly to the right, leaving an open doorway.

Upon entering, David noted the exquisite quality of the workmanship. The room he stood in was octagonal in shape, roughly sixty meters across. The tile flooring was very elaborate, with rows of large purple diamonds containing smaller black-and-white octagons placed end to end. Eight marble columns with carved wooden bases stood at each corner of the octagon, supporting a plaster ceiling covered with more octagonal shapes painted in a variety of pastel colors. A wrought-iron spiral staircase with railings of pure gold and balusters of turned mahogany rose upward, passing through a large octagonal hole in the ceiling. The interior was brightly lit by eight golden candelabra, centered on each of the embroidered, purple velvet-covered inner walls.

David began climbing the stairs, taking in the mysterious purple and gold symbols stenciled on the windowless white-plaster walls.

After about a half-hour of climbing, he arrived at a marble landing, ending in a wall with a large brass door in the center. Like the outer surface of the obelisk, it was covered with strange symbols, embossed into the metal with great precision.

He stood there for a moment to catch his breath, then he mustered his courage and knocked on the door.

It opened silently inward, and David stepped into the throne room of a palace. The walls were covered in burgundy embroidered velvet. The domed ceiling was painted with a spectacular fresco, depicting various gods of antiquity and their worldly kingdoms. At the foot of the throne stood two lions made of bronze. Stylized, flowered chairs of golden velvet were placed along the walls at regular intervals. The tile floor was beautifully detailed, with swirling patterns of peach, purple, and black. A large porcelain globe of the world stood in the right corner. The upper molding was broad and elaborately ornamented, with metal and ceramic detailing of silver, turquoise, and mauve. The lower portion of the walls featured a three-foot-wide border of white cloth, embroidered with patterns of gold thread.

The throne itself was covered by a large awning of fine purple silk with gold embroidery, and it stood on a raised platform of four-tiered blocks covered in red velvet. Rising from each side of the awning were two gold columns, supporting elaborately carved wreaths.

On top of the wreaths were pedestals with sculpted eagles of solid gold nesting on them. Inside each wreath was the capital letter *P*, also done in gold. Adjacent to each column were two more columns, each supporting exquisitely carved golden candelabra featuring candle-shaped incandescent lamps.

The throne itself was covered in plush red velvet, its circular back embossed with an elaborate border and the letter *P* embroidered in gold at the top. Behind the throne hung a huge pleated curtain of light-purple satin with white stars embroidered into the fabric. Directly in front of it stood a small table, also covered in purple velvet.

Sitting on the throne was a man dressed in a white silk robe, open at the neck, covering his entire body down to the ankles. He was young and handsome—appearing in his mid-twenties—and fair-skinned, with blond hair and blue eyes. His feet were shod with leather sandals dotted with precious gems. His right hand held an elaborately carved silver scepter with the letter *P* inset into a gold-leaf circle mounted at the top.

David paused at the doorway, unsure if he should approach.

The man smiled, put down the scepter, and beckoned him to come forward.

When David reached the base of the throne, he stopped once again and knelt to the floor.

The man laughed. "You may stand, David," he said in a deep voice.

"Are you the Keeper of the Stone?" David asked softly.

"My name is Phariel. I am an angel of God, one of several currently residing here in this world."

"Phariel," David muttered, a puzzled expression on his face. "I don't remember reading about you. Are you one of the seven archangels?"

"God has kept my name hidden from the world," the angel replied, smiling. "As the stone's Keeper, I have a great responsibility to keep it from falling into the wrong hands."

"Did you give it to Thomas Aquinas?"

"No," the angel replied, his smile unbroken. "That story is a myth. No mortal has ever possessed the philosopher's stone."

"I guess I'm here on a fool's errand then," David said, his shoulders slumping in discouragement.

"That is not true," the angel said. "I have brought you here for a purpose."

"You brought me here?" David asked. He was baffled by Phariel's words. He had put his life on the line during the course of his travels, battling evil men, women, demons, and the elements, all without any help from the angel.

"Do you remember Everet?"

"How could I forget? He saved my life several times."

"He is my servant. Do you accept the fact that, without his intervention, you would not be standing here at this moment?"

"I see what you mean," David said. "So, it has been your intention to bring me here all along."

"Yes, David. I have selected you to be the next human to receive the benefits of the stone. You are the first since St. Thomas to have that honor."

"I thought you said that he never possessed the stone."

In response, the angel bowed his head and began chanting in a strange language.

As the angel continued to chant, a deep, powerful thrumming sound began emanating from somewhere beyond the surrounding walls.

Apprehension filled David as the floor began to vibrate. He watched in amazement as a purple glow appeared just above the surface of the table.

He watched in wonder as a black dot, appearing in the middle of the energy field, grew in size, gradually expanding into a dark-purple cube the exact size as the table.

The cube, now firmly resting upon the table, began pulsating with a red glow.

The angel stopped chanting and turned to David. "Behold the philosopher's stone!" he exclaimed, his stentorian voice reverberating throughout the throne room.

"That's incredible," David remarked in a hushed tone. "I don't understand. How did it appear out of thin air like that?"

"It didn't appear out of nowhere," the angel replied. "The obelisk is a portal into the fourth dimension. The stone is a tesseract. It has simply moved into your three-dimensional field of view at my command."

He moved his hand over the stone, bathing it in the red light. "The philosopher's stone provides beneficial effects to anyone who comes into contact with its emissions." He beckoned to David. "Come hither," he commanded.

David slowly approached the stone, stopping within an arm's reach of it.

"Move your hands into the field," Phariel said. As David gingerly moved his hands into the glowing red light, he felt a warm tingling sensation spreading throughout his entire body. The sensation increased in intensity, filling his body and mind with indescribable ecstasy. He stood there in a state of complete rapture for an indeterminate length of time, keeping his hands in the red light.

"That is enough for now, David," the angel said, snapping him out of his reverie. "Please step away from the stone."

As David backed away, Phariel produced a thin, round piece of lumber approximately one foot in length and slowly moved it toward the stone. As the wood entered the field, its color changed from brown to gold. After running the entire piece of lumber through the field, the angel placed it onto the floor and began second round of chanting.

As the angel chanted, the philosopher's stone gradually shrunk in size, eventually disappearing from view. The purple energy field vanished along with it, and the thrumming sound ceased, leaving the throne room eerily silent.

David stood motionless, enjoying the blissful sensations that continued to flow through his body.

"Come forward," the angel commanded with a benevolent smile.

As David approached, the angel picked up the golden rod and handed it to him. "A parting gift for you."

David almost dropped it—it was heavy for its size. "Did the philosopher's stone turn the wood into gold?" he asked, a look of wonder on his face.

"Yes. The stone can transmute any object into gold. You are the beneficiary of its other properties as well."

"What other properties, Phariel?"

"You will no longer age as rapidly as other men. The rays of the stone have affected your body on a subatomic level, giving you more vitality, strength, and longevity."

"How long will I live?"

"You will maintain your present age until the effects wear off—in about ten years or so. Then you must return for another treatment, or you will begin to age at the normal rate. To answer your next question, you can theoretically live for hundreds of years, as long as you return within the allotted time frame."

"Can I be killed?"

"Your body has excellent powers of rejuvenation, but you can die if too many of your cells are killed at once—such as from burning, poison, radiation, or lack of oxygen."

David's mind began to whirl—so much had happened so quickly. "Why did you choose me, Phariel?"

"I did not choose you, David. The choice was made by the Most High. No living being—mortal or angel—understands the reasons behind his decisions."

As David attempted to speak, the angel held up his hand for silence.

"Satan and his demons have been trying to gain access to the stone for centuries. He desires to bestow its powers upon his evil minions for the purpose of creating a virtually unstoppable army, powerful enough to rule the entire world."

"That explains all the problems I've had lately."

"Satan and his followers will stop at nothing to possess the stone. This battle is not over."

A sudden chill swept through David as he recalled the immense, evil power the demons had wrought upon him in Ecuador.

"Will I be okay?" he asked in a shaky voice.

The angel smiled approvingly. "You are more powerful now. It will be more difficult for his servants to trick you."

"What other powers do I have?"

"The stone has given you curative abilities."

"I had no idea the stone could do all of that."

"That is why you must not let the Lyricor fall into the hands of Astaroth's servants." Phariel gestured with his scepter. "Go now and use your gifts wisely. Keep the Lyricor safe. You will need it when you return."

David knelt before the angel. "I am grateful for the blessings you have bestowed upon me," he said humbly. "I promise to keep the Lyricor safe."

# CHAPTER FOURTEEN

David tilted his seat back and closed his eyes with a sigh, realizing that it was his seventh airplane flight in the last three months. His thoughts drifted aimlessly, eventually returning to the events of the previous few weeks. On his return to Pittsburgh, he had found, to his great chagrin, that his father had passed away. Although his mother and sister had forgiven him, he couldn't forgive himself. The all-consuming quest for the philosopher's stone had cost him dearly.

Saddened by the loss of his father and laden with guilt at missing the funeral, he had spent the holidays alone in his room, going downstairs only for infrequent meals. He thought that his self-imposed solitude would help put things into perspective, that he might find some direction or purpose, but all attempts had proven fruitless. Having no desire to return to Chicago—there were too many painful memories—he had enlisted Alan's services to clean out his apartment and ship his belongings home.

He had lost so much—Angela, his job, Aaliyah, and now his father—and he blamed himself for everything. The only thing saving his sanity was his desire to honor his father's last wish. It was the least he could do after all that had happened.

On the third day of the new year, David had attended the annual board meeting. During the meeting, Jack Murphy had informed him that the king of Slavania was ramping up his country's oil production and that he had requested the new president of Sholfield Oil to meet with him personally.

In order to accommodate his father's wishes, David had shaken off his depression and accepted the king's invitation to Zoran, the Slavanian capital. He realized that, regardless of his personal feelings, the job had come at the perfect time. He was single and unattached, and his medical career was on hold. Perhaps the change would do him some good.

After successfully making his way through the Zoran International Airport's security, David met Gustav, his chauffeur, who led David to a large, black limousine parked just outside the terminal.

"I hope your flight was satisfactory," Gustav said amiably as they began the short drive to the king's palace.

"It was fine," David responded, noting Gustav's excellent English. "But truthfully, I'm happy to be on the ground again. I've been flying too much lately."

"You are a very busy man, yes?"

"It's probably for the best—no time for boredom to set in."

"Do you see the cooler on your right, David? Help yourself to anything that pleases you. There is a selection of fine liquors in the rack beside it."

"Thank you," David said politely. He opened the cooler. There was a variety of soft drinks, beer, liquor, and wine. "Am I meeting the King today?" he asked, opening a can of root beer, his favorite soft drink.

"Yes, sir. You will be dining with him this evening."

David smiled. How ironic it was that just a few weeks ago he was kayaking down an obscure river in the solitary wilderness of the Amazon jungle, and now here he was, back in the civilized world, on his way to a palace no less, representing his father's company to a king.

A few minutes later, they arrived at the main gate of the palace. When the chauffeur pulled up to the guardhouse, one of the three formally clad guards on duty waved them through.

David stared in admiration as they approached. Crafted in the neoclassical style of its Russian namesake, Alexander Palace stood surprisingly low to the ground. It was only two stories high, but the entire structure was painted in a light-gold color with white trim. On either side of the outer colonnade stood two square porches, reaching to the height of the roof. Tall arches on the front and sides gave access to the entranceways. Two wings jutted out from either side, each fronted by four Corinthian-style columns supporting ornamented pediments. The highly ornamented roof featured cornices, friezes, parapets, and balustrades. The windows were rectangular in shape, longer in height than in width, the first story windows being much larger than the second. A fabulous garden stood in the center of a spacious lawn.

The chauffeur dropped David off at the third entrance, just to the right of the colonnade. "Your luggage will remain in the vehicle until we arrive at your hotel this evening, sir," he said formally.

A butler appeared and ushered David into the building, then led him down a long hallway into a formal reception room.

David gazed at the room in wonder, overwhelmed by its beauty. Sunlight streamed through several large French windows. The walls were covered in white marble, topped by a beautifully molded entablature crafted in the late eighteenth-century style. Cranberry-colored curtains with inner drapery of white lace contrasted with the whiteness of the walls. A dark-gold parquet floor was almost entirely covered by an enormous Savonnerie carpet, and a beautiful crystal chandelier with a ruby-red glass center hung from an intricately carved plaster ceiling. A plethora of fine paintings and tapestries adorned the walls.

The room contained numerous pieces of eighteenth-century furniture, including a roll-top desk, several small tables, high-backed chairs, and two tapestry-covered ivory screens. A number of accessories—including busts of the king, his wife, and his father—several eighteenth-century clocks, as well as many carvings and pieces of statuary of gold and marble, rounded out the décor.

"Please be seated," the butler said in a pleasant tone, leading him to a high-backed, light blue, velvet-covered chair. "The king will be joining us presently."

After David sat down, the butler introduced the other guests. "This is Sven Boskovic—our energy minister—and his wife, Princess Triska, the king's second eldest daughter. I believe you have already met Duke Revic, the finance minister. And this is his fiancée, Princess Stephania, the king's eldest daughter."

"It's a pleasure to see you again, David," the duke said with a friendly smile.

David inhaled sharply. Meeting the duke was an unexpected and unwelcome development. "You too," he said.

His gaze lingered on princess Stephania for a moment. Her long brown hair was surprisingly thick in texture considering its length. Her features were very refined, very Russian, with a wide jaw, high cheekbones, and a pair of almond-shaped green eyes. Her figure was a mystery, obscured by a voluminous dress of azure silk and white lace.

"Pleased to meet you, David," she said formally. "I hope your stay in Slavania will be a pleasant one."

"It has been a pleasure doing business with your father over the years, David," the energy minister said with a congenial smile. "He was a good man. I'm sorry for your loss."

"Thank you." David's mind churned with questions. Was the duke here strictly on business? He recalled that the butler had introduced him as the finance minister.

Presently, the butler re-entered the room. "Presenting King Alexander, the Second, of the House of Premar," he announced in a loud voice.

David followed suit as everyone stood and bowed. He noted the similarity of the king's features to those of Stephania's. David was surprised that the king's tall, thin frame was clothed in a business suit, albeit a very expensive one. The man appeared more like a Fortune 500 exec than a king. To his embarrassment, the king ignored his other guests and approached him with a purposeful gait. He took David's hand in a firm grip. "It's a pleasure to meet you at last, David," he said, smiling cordially.

David's self-conscious reply was interrupted as twelve busboys entered, carrying an expensive cherry-wood dining table and six gilded neoclassical-style chairs covered in yellow silk.

The king laughed, noting David's surprised expression. "We will be dining here this afternoon. I hope that is agreeable, David?"

"It reminds me of how we do things back in the States, Your Royal Highness," David remarked with a smile. "Very convenient for your guests, I would say."

"I'm glad you are pleased," the king responded. "Now everyone, please be seated."

David breathed out a sigh of relief as he watched the others take their places. Everyone knew exactly where they were supposed to sit—Stephania to the right of the king with Duke Revic next to her, Triska on his left with her husband, and David taking the remaining seat at the opposite end of the table.

Then, like clockwork, a bevy of female servers—smartly clad in black tailored uniforms with gold trim—descended upon the guests in a flurry of movement, setting out the dinner service of porcelain and silver platters, crystal glassware, and deep-blue, gilt-edged China. A variety of drinks and sumptuous appetizers were served, including German salads, rare caviars, sautéed mushrooms, and other delicacies.

When the servants had finished their preparations, the king raised his glass of wine. "A toast to my new friend, Dr. David Sholfield," he said, giving David a benevolent smile. "May our relationship be as fruitful as it was with your father, God rest his soul."

"Here, here," the guests responded, smiling and raising their glasses.

"I am also looking forward to having the opportunity of working with you," Sven said, giving David a warm smile. The energy minister was a tall, brown-haired young man with an athletic build. His brown eyes glistened with intelligence, and his handsome features exhibited the high cheekbones characteristic of his Slavic ancestry.

Although Sven projected an amiable demeanor, David surmised that the energy minister was a competent leader in his own right. His pretty brunette wife, Triska, on the other hand, was short in stature, quiet, and unassuming—the perfect complement to Sven.

After the toast, King Alexander turned his smiling gaze to David once again. "Louis Sholfield was one of the finest men I've ever met. Did he ever tell you about the oil spill that occurred when a barge accidentally ran into one of my rigs?"

"No, I'm afraid not," David said.

"He handled the incident exceptionally well. He had the spill cleaned up and the damaged rig repaired in record time. He took care of all the details personally. With all the hubbub that ensued, I never saw him flustered or angry." He gave David an appraising look. "Are you the kind of man your father would be proud of, son?"

David turned red with embarrassment at the king's unexpected probing question. "I hope so," he muttered softly.

"It looks like we will be doing business with your company," the king said with an approving smile, pleased by David's humble response. "I hope you weren't offended by my indelicate question. I needed to see for myself what kind of man is running Sholfield Oil. Further, I'm pleased to announce that our geologists have recently discovered a large area of oil sands in the Pannonian region," the king continued. "The fields are even larger than Canada's, with approximately one trillion barrels of proven reserves."

"That's huge," David responded.

"I'm well aware of the excellent work your company has done on the Canadian project. I believe your company is the best choice to provide the necessary expertise to facilitate our oil production as quickly and efficiently as possible."

"I'll have my engineers consult with your staff immediately, Sven," David responded. His heart raced at the thought of the huge revenues such a massive project would generate. He sipped his wine and grinned. "All of you speak such fluent English. I'm impressed."

"Don't be," Stephania said with a demure smile. "When my father took the throne, he decreed English to be our country's official language." She glanced at her father proudly. "Of course, his decision has proven to be a very wise one."

David felt his heartbeat increase a little as she gave him another smile. She appeared just as warm and bright as she was beautiful. He wondered what she was doing with a bastard like Revic.

The dinner proceeded smoothly, the guests eating their fill while discussing the oil project. It was obvious that no expense had been spared. The three robust main courses featured a myriad of exotic, fresh cuisine, shipped from various lands around the world. After the third course, the guests were treated to several hot and cold dishes of fresh strawberries, jellies, and ice creams. The main dessert—served with coffee—consisted of sponge cakes of varying colors, shapes, and sizes, as well as rich chocolates and candies, all created in the imperial confectionary. David realized that the king desired to make a good impression on the president of the oil company that would be instrumental in leading Slavania into a bright and prosperous future.

At the conclusion of the dinner, the king departed and the butler promptly returned to escort David to his car.

"I would be honored if you would visit us at my residence at a later time, David," Sven offered as David was leaving. "Perhaps I can give you a guided tour of our city."

Upon arrival at the five-star hotel, David was checked in by a gracious concierge. Then he rode the elevator with the bellhop to the top floor and entered the penthouse suite.

After making a brief inspection, he smiled in satisfaction. The suite was everything he could have asked for. With over three thousand square feet of living space, the suite's amenities included a marble foyer, a guest bathroom and bedroom, and a wet bar, complete with its own refrigerator. The spacious main bath—lined in Italian marble—included a whirlpool, a glass-enclosed steam shower, a powder room, and two 40-inch LCD televisions. The entertainment lounge was state-of-the-art, with a 100-inch HDTV, a Blu-ray DVD player, a DVR, and surround sound. The private dining area seated ten, and the well-equipped office featured high-speed internet access, a fax machine, and a multiline telephone. The spacious master bedroom contained a luxurious king-size bed and closets filled with sumptuous linens and robes. The contemporary décor was pleasing to the eye, with purple drapery, cream-colored walls, and matching furniture. David was pleased to learn from the bellhop that room service was available twenty-four hours a day, and that housekeeping came twice daily.

David tipped the bellhop, walked into the master bedroom, and climbed into the bed. Although exhausted from his travels, he couldn't sleep. His mind continued to churn, wandering through recent events. So much had happened, and he'd had so little time to digest it all.

He had spoken to Detective Scott during his short stay in Pittsburgh, learning to his disappointment that there were no new leads in Angela's case.

He then recalled his whirlwind romance with Aaliyah. It seemed strange not to feel sadness at their separation, and no longing for her company. Apparently, it had been nothing more than an infatuation, his true feelings distorted by the tragic loss of his beloved Angela.

The terrible images of his sister and mother grieving over his deceased father abruptly thrust themselves vividly into his mind. Although they had forgiven him for his absence at the funeral, he wondered if he would ever be able to forgive himself. Tears trickled down his cheeks as he recalled some of the precious moments he spent as a child with his father. He realized that his life had changed forever. Nothing would ever be the same, and he was powerless to return it to its former state.

He reminded himself that, in spite of all the obstacles and failures, he had succeeded in his quest, locating the philosopher's stone and, in the process, meeting an angel of God. Phariel had warned him to be careful. Although he had gained new powers from the stone, he was still vulnerable to attacks from Astaroth and his demonic servants, as well as from Revic's coven.

Revic had seemed so calm and collected when they had dined with the king. Of course, he was a very important and powerful man in Slavania and could easily hide his evil deeds from public scrutiny. Realizing that it would take an exceedingly subtle strategy to bring the murdering villain to justice, David resolved to remain in Slavania for as long as necessary.

Finally, there was the beautiful Princess Stephania, the king's daughter. He was surprised at his passionate reaction at the dinner table. Unfortunately, there was absolutely no chance of acting on it, considering her exalted station in life. Besides, how could she possibly be engaged to the foul Revic? Of course, the man was an aristocrat with lands and wealth, obviously intelligent and well-bred, with plenty of panache to impress and deceive. She probably thought he was a great catch. As much as he hated Revic, Stephania's personal life wasn't his concern.

The next morning, David was chauffeured to the airport. Then he boarded a helicopter with the energy minister, their destination being the largest oil sands site, located a hundred kilometers to the north. It was his first business meeting with Sven Boskovic.

After they were airborne, Sven gave David a friendly smile and asked, "So what do you think of our king?"

"He seems to be a good man," David replied with a thoughtful expression. "I'm impressed with his honesty and sincerity. I think I will enjoy working with him."

"I know he likes you," the energy minister said with a smile. "I have a good feeling about the project." His expression turned serious. "Outside of managing the affairs of the kingdom, though, he's not a happy man."

"Really?" David responded with a surprised expression. "He appears, on the surface at least, to have everything any man could ever desire. Why is he unhappy?"

"You haven't met his son, Prince Alexander. Unfortunately, the prince is not well. That's why Alex wasn't in attendance at dinner yesterday afternoon."

"I'm sorry to hear about the prince," David replied with concern. "The king didn't mention anything about him at dinner."

"He doesn't like to talk about it. You're a doctor, aren't you?"

"Yes. I've been out of practice for several months, though. What's wrong with the prince?"

"Lung cancer. It's in the early stages, but the prognosis is unfavorable."

David felt a sudden surge of excitement. An opportunity to use his newfound healing powers had presented itself. It would be the perfect opportunity to set things right. Perhaps his expedition had not been in vain after all. "That's not really my line of expertise," he responded casually, "but I would like to examine him if that's agreeable to the king."

"That's very kind of you, David. I'm sure I can arrange it."

A few minutes later, they landed. After exiting the helicopter, they walked to the edge of the open-pit mine, which was nothing more than a deep gash in the earth.

Sven pointed to the heavy machinery at the bottom. "Those are some of the largest trucks and shovels in the world."

"This is a very big operation indeed," David remarked with an excited expression.

"We've only just begun. We need your company's expertise to help us build the extraction and separation systems."

"That's no problem. The bitumen's going to need some upgrading before it can be refined, as well as dilution with other hydrocarbons to make it transportable by pipeline. I'll have my engineers send you a detailed plan."

"Time is of the essence, David. The king's anxious to capitalize on the find, especially with the recent uptrend in oil prices."

After spending several hours discussing the details of the project with the project engineer and the foreman, the men boarded the helicopter and returned to the city.

"Zoran has some great restaurants and nightclubs," Sven said as they stepped into the black stretch limousine waiting at the terminal. "Take us to Foley's," he told the driver. "Zoran is a very modern city," Sven continued as they drove, pointing to the rows of newly constructed government buildings. "It was founded back in 1991 when Slavania first declared its independence. We have a viable transportation network, including high-speed rail, highways, buses, boats, trams, even trolleybuses. The king wants the city to be a tourist destination as well as the administrative seat. In keeping with his wishes, we've constructed a national museum featuring an enormous collection of world-renowned painters. If you like opera, ballet, or plays, we have a beautiful, brand-new national theater. We also have a state-of-the-art sports arena."

"I'm impressed," David remarked. "Zoran seems like a very well-rounded, cosmopolitan city. I'm certain to enjoy my stay here."

"If you want to shop, we have duty-free flagship stores selling many designer brands. They're located on Canal Street. The cafés on Bana Street are also very popular, serving a variety of continental coffees. I chose Foley's because it has a distinctly American flavor," Sven remarked as the limo pulled into the parking lot of a large restaurant.

David smiled as they entered the flamboyant restaurant and nightclub. It felt as if he had just arrived in Las Vegas.

Sven showed his pass to a formally clad host, and they were promptly led to their table. On their way to the VIP section, David noted the elegant and extravagant styling of the décor. The lounge featured round; mirrored tables surrounded by plush sofas made of silky dark-red fabric lined with white striping. Light-red pillows matched the color of the contoured ceiling and the gold-trimmed brocade wallpaper.

The nightclub featured a walkway leading to a raised dance floor, and a huge indoor waterfall stood directly opposite, surrounded by live pine trees and shrubbery. A large stream of water spilled majestically from the rocks at the top of the structure down into a pool just below the dance floor. It was a spectacular sight.

Moments later they arrived at their table, located in the back of the VIP section. It was designed for comfort, with overstuffed navy-blue sofas surrounded by low obsidian tables topped with crystal spheres containing white candles. Each table was sectioned off by partitions of purple drapery with silver-trimmed, oval mirrors. The black ceiling was dotted with tiny multicolored spotlights, which appeared like stars sparkling out of a nighttime sky.

Just as they sat at the table, a cocktail waitress dressed in formal attire appeared.

"This place is amazing," David remarked with a delighted smile after their orders were taken. "It feels like I'm back in the States."

"I'm glad you're pleased," Sven said, smiling graciously. "Since you're going to be staying in my country for a while, I want you to feel as comfortable as possible." He paused a moment. "I don't see a wedding ring on your finger. If you don't mind me asking, are you unattached?"

"I'm single," David replied, frowning slightly. "I've had some problems in that department lately."

"I'm sorry to hear that. Perhaps my wife can introduce you to the local female gentry."

"Thanks for the offer, but I'm not ready to start dating just yet. I found Princess Stephania to be quite beautiful, though. If I were ready for the dating scene, I think she would be my first choice."

"I would be most happy to accommodate you in that regard," Sven said, laughing. "Unfortunately, as you know, she is betrothed to Duke Revic, whom I must say, doesn't really suit her. And there's an additional obstacle: Since she is a princess, she can only date a titled aristocrat."

David was surprised and irritated by the flare of disappointment he felt at Sven's statement. It was an unwanted, incongruous, emotional response considering he barely knew the woman. He took a deep swallow of his mixed drink and tried to relax.

"Tell me about yourself, Sven," David said, changing the subject. "How did you land such an important position at the palace?"

"I inherited my father's land and title when he died," Sven said. "That automatically made me a duke. I practically grew up with the Alexander family—Prince Alexander was my boyhood friend. We maintained our friendship throughout college. After graduation, I married his younger sister, Triska. When cabinet positions became available, I was appointed energy minister by the king."

"So, everyone in power is a landed aristocrat?"

"Yes. That's how the king maintains loyalty within his ranks. We all own lands and the cities that reside upon them. We collect taxes from the townspeople, businesses, and farms within our respective regions. Duke Revic is the largest landowner—next to the king, of course."

"It sounds like the aristocracy has a vested interest in maintaining a prosperous country."

"That is why we are all in favor of the king. His policies have given our economy a much-needed boost over the past few years. He has even promised us a share of the oil sands revenues."

"What about the queen? I haven't heard any mention of her."

"Unfortunately, she died from lung cancer several years ago. The king was hurt very badly by his loss and has never remarried."

"Isn't that Prince Alexander's diagnosis?"

"Yes, I'm afraid the disease runs on his mother's side."

David spent the remainder of the evening dining and conversing with Sven, enjoying the young aristocrat's company. He had made his first Slavanian friend.

David pulled his new Mercedes into the hotel parking lot and breathed out a sigh as he shut off the engine. The last few days had been hectic—shuffling frantically between Sven's office and his suite, spending untold hours working on the oil sands project. Then yesterday, he bought a car from a nearby dealer, freeing him from dependence on the government limo that had been his sole means of transportation. It was Friday, and he was looking forward to the weekend. Sven had invited him to go sightseeing.

As David stepped out of the car, a black sedan pulled up beside him. The rear door opened, revealing a female sitting in the backseat. He inhaled sharply when he saw she was pointing a pistol at his chest.

"We meet again," Jamie said menacingly.

He hesitated for a moment, considering his options. From the smattering of information Phariel had divulged concerning the effects of the philosopher's stone, he could probably withstand a gunshot. It might weaken him, though, enabling the witches to overpower him.

He decided to play along. Besides, if he displayed his powers, the witches would know that he had found the philosopher's stone.

Jamie stepped out of the car. "Get in," she said in a firm tone, pointing the gun at his forehead.

"Okay," he said, displaying the palms of his hands. "I'll go." He slowly climbed into the backseat and slid over to the opposite side.

The driver, who was none other than Holly, turned around and said with a surly grin, "Hello, David. Give us the Lyricor, and you can go free. You'll never have to put up with us again—I swear."

"I don't have it with me," David said with a frown, noting that both women had abandoned their witch garb in favor of business attire. "It's in my room."

Jamie sat down next to him, closed the door, and pushed the nozzle of the gun into his side. "Give me your room key," she commanded. "I'll go fetch it."

"Why don't you dispense with all the mystery, Holly, and tell me who you're working for?" David asked after Jamie had exited the car. "Could it be Duke Revic?"

"What business is it of yours?" Holly said. She turned around in her seat and pointed her pistol at his chest. "Maybe Jamie and I are doing our own thing. Maybe we want the stone for ourselves."

"If that's the case, I'll pay you a million dollars in cash to forget about the stone and leave me alone," David said with a sincere expression. "I'm a wealthy man. You know that I'm good for it."

Holly burst out laughing. "What kind of a fool do you take me for, dear? The stone will provide us with unlimited wealth."

David remained silent as Jamie returned with his suitcase. "Let's get outta here," she said after rejoining him in the backseat.

Holly drove to the outskirts of town and pulled into the driveway of an abandoned church. The building was very ancient—it had no roof, only crumbling, vine-encrusted stone walls.

It was almost dusk as David entered the church, the witches following close behind, keeping their guns pointed at his back.

"Over there!" Holly exclaimed, pointing to a set of broken wooden pews. "Sit down in the front," she said.

David walked to the front row and sat down carefully, testing the pew's strength. It made creaking noises as he shifted his weight, but remained securely in place.

Holly opened the suitcase and pulled out the Lyricor. "I want you to activate it for us," she said sternly. "Don't try anything, or we'll kill you."

She put the polished white stone on the floor and pushed it gently toward David. Both women remained silent as they stared intently at the stone, waiting for him to respond.

"I don't know how to activate it," David said, giving them a sheepish look.

"That's a load of crap," Jamie said heatedly "It won't do you any good to stall. No one knows we're here and there's nobody around to save you. We'll let you go after we get the location of the philosopher's stone; I promise."

Holly laughed. "C'mon, David. You're way too handsome for me to have to kill you. Please do as Jamie says. Okay, honey?"

"I'm not your honey," David said, giving her a look of contempt, "and I'm telling you the truth. The Lyricor activates itself, and only when it wants to. I really think you two should drop your crazy scheme before someone gets hurt."

Jamie's face contorted in anger as she pulled the trigger back on her Glock 43. "That was the wrong answer, David. You have thirty seconds to comply with our request, or I will be forced to kill you."

David moved suddenly, attempting to seize her gun.

Jamie responded by shooting him in his right arm.

Ignoring the tremendous burst of pain from the bullet, David grasped the handgun and managed to wrestle it away from her. Then he spun away as Holly fired off a round from her pistol, the bullet barely grazing his left shoulder.

He continued to spin, bringing Jamie's gun into firing position. He pulled the trigger, and Holly fell to the ground with a shriek of agony as the bullet penetrated her left leg.

In response, Jamie ran at David with arms outstretched, attempting to regain possession of her gun. But he dodged away from her and she fell to the ground. "You shot her!" she shouted; her face contorted with rage.

As David hesitated, deciding if he should shoot her, Jamie crawled to Holly's side and inspected her wound. "You're going to be okay," she said, ignoring David.

Then Jamie took out her athame, cut a strip of fabric from the bottom of her dress, and used it as a tourniquet, tying it tightly to Holly's wounded leg.

David watched in silence as Jamie silently helped Holly to her feet and helped her walk out of the church. A minute later, he heard the sound of their car starting. He ran out of the building, catching a glimpse of it as it sped away into the twilight. In the ensuing stillness, he heard a metallic tinkling sound as something fell onto the pavement near his feet.

David knelt down and picked up the object, barely discerning in the growing darkness that it was a bullet. He quickly shucked off his suit coat and shirt to inspect his left arm and right shoulder. To his surprise, there were no visible wounds.

# Chapter Fifteen

"Thanks for setting up the appointment," David said with a smile as the limousine approached the hospital.

"It was no problem," Sven responded, returning the smile. "The king was completely amenable. It's a very unfortunate situation, but I suppose he's still holding out hope for his son. And, of course, I am as well."

"You mentioned that you and the prince were boyhood friends," David said. "I understand how you must feel. I lost my best friend back in high school, although the circumstances were different."

"The circumstances don't really matter if the outcome is the same," Sven remarked glumly. "Anyway, if there's anything you can do for him—even if it's just to cheer him up a bit—the royal family will be immensely grateful."

The limo pulled up to the main entrance of the hospital, and the men exited the car and walked into the lobby. "He's on a private floor," Sven said as he led David to a locked elevator. He swiped a plastic card through the reader, and the door slid open.

After making a swift ascent to the top floor, they walked to the nurses' station and Sven spoke to the doctor on duty. After several minutes of discussion, the doctor motioned to David. "This way, please."

When the men arrived at the door to the prince's room, Sven paused before entering. "I will introduce you to Alex, and then, if it's agreeable to him, I will leave you alone to proceed with your examination. Feel free to ask the nurses for anything that you may need."

When they entered the room, Price Alexander, who was sitting up in bed, gave Sven a big smile. "Come here, old friend," he said.

David noted the young man's pale countenance. His features closely resembled the king's, leaving no doubt that he was the king's son.

Sven walked to his bedside and they hugged each other for a few moments. "How is the staff treating you?" Sven asked, breaking their embrace.

As the two friends began a spirited exchange, David quickly appraised the room, noting that, aside from the medical equipment, it held little resemblance to a hospital room. It featured a complete entertainment system, plenty of incandescent lighting, and expensive furniture, including an armoire, several sofas, and a large eighteenth-century-style dining table. The walls were done in purple satin brocade and hung with fine paintings. A lush, purple, and red diamond-patterned carpet completed the décor.

A few minutes later, Alex motioned David to approach. As David walked toward the bed, Alex fixed him in a steely, penetrating, blue-eyed gaze. Then he smiled.

"I've heard good things about you from my father," the prince remarked affably. "I met your father once when I was a boy." He nodded to Sven. "You can leave us for a while. I'm certain David wishes to examine me in private. Thanks for coming, my good friend. It was jolly good seeing you again. I hope they let you off your leash a little more often so I can fritter away some more of your time."

Sven chuckled. "It will be my pleasure, Alex. I will see you again soon."

"It's good to finally meet you, Prince Alexander," David said with a cheerful smile after Sven left the room.

"You can call me Alex," the Prince responded. "And you don't have to sugarcoat my condition," he said candidly, rubbing his head. The chemotherapy treatments had rendered him bald. "I know the prognosis. I've made my peace with it, actually."

David's mind whirled as he attempted to find a reasonable way to express his intent. If he told Alexander about his healing powers, the prince might brand him a lunatic and have him escorted off the premises.

"Oh, c'mon, David," Alexander said lightheartedly. "We both know you're not here to examine me. The doctors have already done everything medically possible." A curious expression appeared upon his features. "So why are you really here?"

As David hesitated, Alexander laughed. "I know you're not here to assassinate me, so how bad can it be? Out with it, man!" He was abruptly overcome by a fit of coughing.

After Alexander's coughing subsided, David said, "This may sound a little strange, but I believe I may have a treatment for your condition."

"I've made it known to my staff that I'm open to any suggestion," the Prince said evenly, "no matter how ludicrous it may be. So, let's get on with it, David! What is it that you want to do?"

"Thank you for being so accommodating," David replied, breathing out a sigh of relief.

"I want to try a little experiment—something I picked up during my travels. Just unbutton your gown at the chest, please."

"Certainly, Doctor," Alexander replied with feigned sincerity.

David leaned over the bed and gently rested both hands on Alexander's exposed chest, noting the scar from the prince's thoracotomy, starkly visible in the bright incandescent lighting. David continued to press his hands gently against the prince's chest for a few minutes and then stepped away. "How do you feel?" he asked with a hesitant look on his face.

"Not bad, actually," Alexander replied with a grin. "There's a pleasant tingling sensation in my lungs. They feel lighter, not so heavy anymore."

"I'm pleased," David said. "I don't want to get your hopes up, but I want to return in a few days to check on your condition."

"As I said before, Doc," Alex replied, "I'm completely open to any and all suggestions. If your treatment actually works, I'll make sure that my father hears about it. He will, no doubt, compensate you very generously."

"That won't be necessary," David said unassumingly. "I'm just glad to be of service." He glanced at his watch. "It's almost suppertime already. It was good meeting you, Prince Alexander."

"Likewise, David."

David walked out of the hospital room feeling hopeful. If Phariel had told the truth about the philosopher's stone, Alexander would be healed, and David would be redeemed from his guilt, free from his unrelenting self-recriminations.

The next morning, Sven called David on his cell phone. "Something's happened," Sven said breathlessly.

David had never heard him sound so excited. "What is it, Sven?" he asked, worried if something was wrong. "Is it the prince? Is he okay?"

"Relax. It's nothing bad. I'm coming to your suite. I'll explain everything there, okay?"

David hung up the phone feeling perplexed. What was so important that Sven couldn't explain over the phone? Did he have good news concerning the prince?

Sven arrived a half-hour later.

"So, what brings you here this morning, Sven?" David asked as they sat down in the great room.

"The king and his staff are keeping this entirely under wraps for the time being," Sven replied. "Everything I tell you must remain in strict confidence. Is that understood, David?"

"Certainly," David said, overcome with curiosity. "Please continue."

"Duke Revic has been arrested."

David tried to calm himself as a jumble of emotions surged through him. Had Revic finally been linked to Angela's murder? He never really believed Revic was innocent, even though the man had an airtight alibi. The duke could easily have commanded members of his coven to assassinate Angela while in transit to Slavania. "What were the charges?"

"He was caught embezzling money from one of his cities."

"Really!" David remarked in surprise. "He was the treasury minister, wasn't he?"

"Yes, he was. It turns out that he had a scheme going with one of his accountants. They were falsifying tax records and expenditures from his largest city. The mayor was in on it as well."

"What do you mean by 'his city'?"

"As I mentioned before, the aristocrats collect taxes from the farms and businesses that reside on their lands, as well as from the general population. All the tax collections and receipts are turned over to the Chancellor of the Exchequer, then he redistributes a percentage back to the landowners—Duke Revic, in this case. The duke was caught falsifying tax records, allowing him to skim money from Horvat, his largest city. God knows what he needed the money for. He's the largest landowner in Slavania next to the king. He has more money than he can spend in several lifetimes."

"So Revic was skimming funds from the taxes of the people living in his city, correct?"

"Yes. All the city officials—the mayor, the judges, the police chief, and the fire chief—were appointed by the duke, so they could all be involved. So far, only the mayor and the duke's accountant have been implicated."

"So, the duke has the ability to appoint whomever he chooses into positions of power, and his mayor collaborated with him in the embezzlement scheme, correct?"

"It's a little more complicated than that. All of the duke's appointees have to be approved by the king, or at least by the House of Lords in sessions of Parliament. The king has the power to veto any of their decisions."

David held up his hands. "That's more detail than I care to know, Sven. Politics has never been my strong suit. So, won't this be a blow to the Crown since the duke was betrothed to Princess Stephania?"

"It complicates matters," Sven replied with a chuckle, "however, the investigation has been ongoing for several years, and Stephania has been cleared of any wrongdoing. She's very popular with the people, you know. We don't expect any backlash to the House of Premar. They've always held themselves to the highest moral standards."

David paused for a moment as he absorbed the news, feeling a sudden surge of anger over Revic's thievery. The man deserved to be punished as the evildoer he was. "I wonder if it would be possible for me to speak with the duke?" he asked softly, masking his anger.

"I remember now," Sven said with a grin. "You had dealings with him back in the States, didn't you? Did he do something to offend you, if you don't mind me asking?"

"I never really liked the man," David replied, frowning. "I'll just say that we had a few disagreements."

"That's perfectly understandable," Sven said with a sympathetic smile. "He's made many enemies over the years. He always struck me as a prideful, arrogant sort of individual. Will you excuse me for a moment?"

He stood from the divan, pulled his cell phone out of his jacket pocket, and walked to the other side of the room. Then, after dialing a number and speaking a few words on the phone, he returned to David. "We can see him immediately if you desire."

"That was fast," David remarked.

"It helps being married to a princess," Sven said with a grin.

A short time later, they arrived at the prison. David noted that the building was quite large—at least six stories high—and was constructed entirely from concrete. The solitary row of windows on the first floor had bars on them.

They stepped into the lobby and were greeted by two guards who promptly escorted them to the elevator. Upon reaching the top floor, the foursome proceeded down a short hallway leading to a thick, metal door. The guards opened it and ushered them down another hallway leading to a solitary jail cell. When they arrived at the steel-barred cell, Duke Revic stood from the bench he was sitting on and approached.

"Tell your wife's sister that I miss her," Revic said with a sarcastic laugh after Sven dismissed the guards. "She won't speak to me."

"You can tell her yourself after your trial," Sven said with a smirk. "You're never going to see the light of day after what you've done."

David could tell there was bad blood between the two aristocrats. He wondered what Revic had done to make Sven treat him with such disdain.

"Don't be so sure about that, Sven Boskovic," the duke said with a haughty expression. "I have friends in high places."

"Be careful what you say, Revic," Sven responded. "If you threaten the king, he might add treason to your list of charges."

David realized that Revic had made a veiled threat to the king's supremacy: The only way the duke could regain his freedom was by overthrowing the king. It was David's first introduction to court intrigue.

"Your blathering has become tiresome," Sven continued. "David desires to speak with you." He turned to David. "I'll be downstairs. Call me on your cell when you're finished, okay?"

"Thanks, Sven," David said.

He waited until Sven was out of earshot and then turned to Revic. "I know you killed Angela, you wretched murderer!" he shouted angrily. "If I could prove it, I would tell the world what an evil bastard you are."

To David's surprise, the duke smiled merrily, showing no sign of anger or intimidation. "Don't be so moralistic, David. You're no saint either, you know. Besides, I had nothing to do with Angela's murder. I was out of the country at the time."

"I don't buy your load of crap," David said in a harsh tone. "You could have easily ordered witches from your coven to kill her."

"I know that you've read Thomas Harrison's writings," the duke remarked, changing the subject. "Did you actually find the philosopher's stone?"

"Don't try and evade the question, Revic. You had Angela killed, right?"

"I swear to you, David, I had nothing to do with that. Think about it. What motive could I possibly have? She was no threat to me, and as you know, I was very fond of her."

"And what about the witches from your coven who have been trying to steal the Lyricor? I suppose that you have nothing to do with Holly and Jamie either."

"I do not," Revic said with a mischievous grin. "Claire has no knowledge of the Lyricor, or the philosopher's stone, for that matter. She never read Tom's journal. And the particular witches you mentioned are not from my coven."

David paused in thought for a moment, remembering that Claire was after the Numericon, not the Lyricor. Was it possible that she had never read Tom's journal? Perhaps Revic had concealed his knowledge of the philosopher's stone. It made sense that he would withhold the information.

"If the witches that attacked me aren't from Claire's coven, then who are they working for? And what about the phony monks who accosted me in South America? You used every available tool at your disposal, even going to the extreme of attacking me with sorcerers and demons."

The duke clapped his hands together and broke into a round of raucous laughter. "I applaud your sincerity, David," he said, eventually regaining his composure. "It sounds as though you're facing quite a dilemma."

"I have one more question for you," David said. "Why did you leave Tom's journal behind?"

"You stole it from me, remember? I had flight reservations for London the next morning, leaving me no chance to retrieve it, so I used my not-so-negligible influence in the king's court to bring you here. It was my suggestion to hire your company for the oil sands project."

"Why didn't you try and steal the memoirs while I was in Chicago? You could have hired a thug to break into my apartment."

"Why go to all the trouble? I simply had you summoned here. The king was quite agreeable to my suggestion of hiring your company for the oil sands project. Now that you're in my country, it's a simple matter to reclaim it.

"You know, David," Revic continued, "I'm quite impressed by your earlier statement that you are in possession of the Lyricor. If you don't mind me asking, how did you obtain it? Tom was never able to find it, as knowledgeable as he was in the black arts. There are some very powerful sorcerers and witches who have spent lifetimes searching for it. The rumor is, it's guarded by a holy man."

David sadly realized that he had inadvertently given Revic a valuable piece of information. Apparently, Revic hadn't previously known that David possessed the Lyricor. If Revic was telling the truth, that meant the witches trying to steal it were not from Revic's coven after all. On the other hand, Revic could be lying, claiming to be innocent of both Angela's murder and the witches' failed attempts to force David into giving them the Lyricor. He suddenly remembered Everet's warning never to tell anyone about the Lyricor. "I hope you rot in hell, Revic!" David exclaimed angrily. He walked away, pulled out his cell phone, and dialed Sven's number.

David returned to his suite that afternoon and immediately searched through his belongings. Sure enough, Tom's notebook was missing. Fortunately, the Lyricor was safe because he always carried it with him. No doubt the duke was responsible for the theft of the memoirs and everything else that had happened. He was feigning ignorance to clear himself of suspicion.

Lingering doubts remained in David's mind, however. For instance, it was true that Revic had no obvious motive for murdering Angela. That made it more likely that the witches were working for someone else.

Just as David finished his breakfast the next morning, there came a knock on the door. "The housekeeping staff's early today," he muttered as he walked to the entrance. When he opened the door, a tall, thin, middle-aged man stood before him, dressed in livery. David noted the king's golden seal embroidered upon the left breast of the man's green jacket.

"Are you Dr. David Sholfield?" he asked in a formal tone.

"I am," David responded.

"His majesty requests your presence immediately, Dr. Sholfield. You are to come with me."

David followed the man out of the building into a very long, white stretch limousine parked in the staging area.

"Can you tell me what this is all about?" David asked apprehensively as they began driving toward the palace. He felt all the more anxious when the man remained silent. Perhaps the king had heard about his visit with Revic and wanted to question him.

Upon arrival, David was shown directly to the king's reception room.

"May I present Dr. David Sholfield to the king," a servant announced in a loud, formal tone as they entered.

The king was sitting at a long, rectangular walnut table, dressed in his usual business attire. On his right sat a man also dressed in formal attire, wearing a curly white barrister's wig.

"Sit next to me, David," the king said with a smile as David bowed. "I have a most important business matter to discuss with you."

As David seated himself, a bevy of servers descended upon them in a flurry, laying out an assortment of beverages, fresh delicacies, and candy. Then they left the room.

The king sipped on his cappuccino and smiled once again. "I wanted to be the first to tell you that my son—Prince Alexander—has been healed."

David felt himself grow faint as the king enthusiastically slapped the table and exclaimed, "Well done, David! My son told me that you were responsible for his cure."

David remained silent for a moment, stunned by the news. Apparently, the angel had told the truth: The philosopher's stone had provided him with healing powers. "Is cancer in remission?" he asked softly.

"Not only that," the king said jubilantly. "There's no trace of it ever having existed. All of the tests show his lungs to be completely normal."

David gulped down a glass of cold water. "I'm glad to be of service, Your Highness," he said in a wavering voice.

"You're more than welcome, son. Now, on to the business matter, I wish to discuss with you," the king continued jovially. "I can never repay you for saving my son's life, but it is my desire to reward you handsomely for your act of kindness. I desire to elevate you to the exalted title and position of Duke of Horvat. I hope you will accept this honor as a small token of my appreciation," he said, his voice filled with gratitude. Then he became silent, smiling gently while awaiting David's response.

David's mind spun as he attempted to digest the news. Becoming a duke was a great honor, but it also undoubtedly carried with it great responsibilities. He didn't know anything about running a dukedom. What would happen when he returned to the States?

He cleared his throat. "With all due respect, sire, I appreciate the offer, but I don't know anything about being a duke. Furthermore, what would happen if I returned to the States?"

"There are no strings attached, David," the king said, chuckling. "You will retain the title forever, even if you decide to return to your homeland. I will personally look after your lands and maintain them in your absence. Of course, you will always be welcome in Slavania. Consider this your second home."

David felt vastly relieved by the king's assurances. "The Duke of Horvat, you say? Where have I heard that name before?"

"Horvat is the largest town in Vojislav—Revic's former domain. I have stripped him of his lands and title. It is my desire that you possess them in his stead."

David smiled. How ironic that he would profit from Revic's fall from glory. Although all the money and titles in the world could never compensate for the tragic loss of his beloved Angela, it was a small measure of justice, unknowingly meted out by the king. "Yes, Your Highness," he replied brightly. "I will most assuredly accept your generous offer."

"I am well-pleased," the king responded with a triumphant smile. "You have my eternal gratitude. But now I have another matter to discuss," he continued. "Because this has been such a joyous event for all of Slavania, I have decided to throw a celebration in your honor. It will be held in the palace ballroom five days hence. You will receive a formal invitation explaining all of the details. Feel free to bring as many guests as you like."

The king nodded to his attorney. "David, I want you to study the papers Chancellor Mundit has for you to sign. He will explain everything and answer all of your questions. I will also assign an instructor to school you in the affairs of your dukedom."

The King stood from the table, David and the attorney following suit after a respectful pause.

"If you will excuse me, I have more business to attend to," the king said. "Before I take my leave, is there anything else that I can do for you?"

An idea crystallized in David's mind, giving him a newfound clarity of purpose, as the intense light from a flashbulb illuminates the surrounding objects in a dark room. "Would it be all right, sire," David asked with an embarrassed expression, "if Princess Stephania were my tutor?"

"No need to be shy, son," the king replied with a chuckle. "It would be my honor." Then he turned away and departed, accompanied by several attendants.

The next afternoon, David was summoned to the formal reception room to begin his lessons under the tutelage of Princess Stephania.

Following the usual palace protocol, a butler introduced him as he entered. He smiled, noting the servants clustered around the table serving beverages. He had never attended classes in such comfort and style.

"We meet again, Princess," he said, maintaining his smile as he sat across from Stephania at a round marble table in the center of the room.

"Hello, David," the princess responded formally. "I hope your stay in our country has been a pleasant one thus far."

"It has been," David said, giving her an appraising stare.

Her long hair was coiffed in an up-style. A pair of glittering, round, emeralds dangled from her lovely ears. Her attractive features were gently enhanced by the subtle use of cosmetics. She was attired in a jacket and dress combination, similar to what a teacher might wear, excepting the exquisite quality and cut of the fabric. Her feminine figure was trim and athletic. She appeared quite beautiful. David found it difficult to tear his eyes away.

"Since you are now officially a citizen of Slavania," the princess began with a friendly smile, "I thought we would start with a short history lesson."

"That would be appropriate," David said. "I'm anxious to learn all I can. From what I understand, before gaining its independence, Slavania existed for many years as a region of the former Yugoslavia."

"Yes. Our ancestry can be traced back to AD 500 when the Slavs migrated from Poland and Russia. Each Slavic group formed an independent state. For example, the Serbs formed Serbia, the Croats formed Croatia, and so on. Unfortunately, they gradually lost political control of their respective regions," she continued, "and by the year 1400, nearly all their lands were controlled by foreign powers. The movement for Slavic unity began in the 1800s, but in 1929, King Alexander the First replaced the constitutional monarchy with a dictatorship.

"During World War II, Yugoslavia was occupied by German troops. Resistance groups formed, eventually gaining enough power to place the country under Communist rule. In 1990, due to internal political pressure, the communist party voted to end its rule, and in 1991, Slavania gained its independence along with the other Baltic nations. Soon afterward, war broke out between the Serbs, the Croatians, and the ethnic Albanians, lasting until 1995."

"It sounds like your people have seen their share of war and oppression," David remarked.

"We certainly have," the princess affirmed. "Because of the external threats to its stability, and in order to consolidate power, Slavania became a mixed monarchy."

"What do you mean 'a mixed monarchy'?" David asked.

"Although we have Parliament with a democratically elected House of Commons, there is also a House of Lords, consisting of the wealthy landowners. They, including the chief judges, are appointed to their positions by the king."

"I think what you are saying is that although the people have a voice in government, the king has the final say."

"Very good, David. Each bill is presented to both houses and debated by both parties. It can only be signed into law by the King's Chancery. The king has full authority to veto any bill, or to revoke any law after it has passed the houses."

"What about succession?"

"We are a hereditary monarchy, with full equal primogeniture, meaning that the next ruler will be the eldest child, whether male or female. At present, Prince Alexander is next in line to the throne."

"And if you were the eldest?"

"In that case, I would rule as queen, and the man I married would be king."

"I see," David mused. "And what if you both were killed, heaven forbid?"

"Then my younger sister, Triska, would rule—with one caveat, however. If my brother is unmarried at the time of the king's death but I am married, I will ascend to the throne."

"Your father seems like a very beneficent man," David remarked, changing the subject. "The citizens must be very pleased with the modernization of their country."

"That is to your benefit, David." The princess gave him a charming smile. "The king favors you highly. I also wish to thank you for saving my brother's life."

"You are very welcome," David responded graciously. Did he detect a hint of approval in her eyes? Suddenly, he knew what he wanted to ask. "Speaking of honors, you're probably aware that the king is throwing a celebration in my honor in a few days. I don't know how you do it in Slavania, but back in the States, all guests attending a formal party are required to bring dates. Unfortunately, I have been so caught up in my work and being new to the country, I have no one to bring."

The princess laughed. "That's not a problem. There are several available young women of title that would be happy to escort you, now that you are officially a duke."

David cleared his throat and hesitated for a moment.

"Is everything all right?" the princess asked with a perplexed expression.

David knew that this was his best chance. If he delayed, some other young aristocrat would surely move in. "I know that you have just broken up with your fiancé, Princess," David began slowly. "If my request is inappropriate, please excuse my rudeness. I have no intention of offending you, but would you consent to be my escort to the ball?"

The princess seemed taken aback by David's request. She frowned slightly and paused for a moment, pondering the situation. "I have to be careful," she replied slowly. "My actions are under constant public scrutiny. It may be too soon after the duke's imprisonment."

"That may be true, Princess," David responded, "but as you said earlier, the king is well-favored by the people, and he is throwing the ball in my honor. Unaccustomed as I am to the workings of your political system, may I venture that my association will do you no political harm?"

The princess laughed. "Well-spoken, David. For one unaccustomed to court politics, you seem to have an excellent grasp of the situation. I will say, although Duke Revic seemed a good man—he always treated me in a genteel manner—I never felt the fondness toward him that a proper fiancée should."

"May I ask why you were betrothed to him?"

"You will soon realize, David, that although we are royalty and have many privileges, our first duty is to preserve the interests of the Slavanian people. Duke Revic was the largest landowner, next to my father."

"I understand," David said. "It was an arranged marriage."

The princess gave him an affectionate smile. "But now it seems that you are the largest landowner."

David felt a sudden, fervent urge to kiss her, sweet and heady, like the taste of strong wine. He resisted the impulse. "May I take that as a yes, my lady?"

# Chapter Sixteen

"Announcing Princess Stephania of the House of Premar, and David Sholfield, the Duke of Horvat," the announcer said in a loud, authoritative tone. Everyone clapped and cheered as the couple promenaded down the wide, red-carpeted stairway of the palace ballroom. David felt chills run through his entire body as he returned Stephania's approving smile. Although the princess was dressed in formal evening wear, her white-trimmed purple gown was in keeping with the current fashion trends. He realized that everyone was dressed in fashionable attire, including the king. No hint of the past, no sign of former tradition appeared anywhere. The aristocrats had left the past behind in their unceasing quest for progress.

The spacious ballroom was the center of an ensemble of parade halls. Like the formal reception room, the walls were covered with smooth, white, artificial marble. The central doors of the apse opened into a terrace overlooking the gardens. Broad columned archways led into halls filled with tables laden with dishes of incredible variety, including copious amounts of vodka and French champagne. The wooden flooring was designed in an elaborate parquet pattern. The furniture was sparse in relation to the size of the hall, with only a few high-backed, custom-designed chairs and small tables placed against the walls, leaving a large open area for dancing. There were two marble fireplaces on either side of the main entrance. An elaborate chandelier of wrought iron and crystal hung from the vaulted ceiling. A chamber orchestra, assembled in the right-hand corner, provided classical background music. The room had an airy, opulent ambiance, David thought.

David felt like a high school boy on his first date as he waltzed around the floor with the princess. After they danced to several traditional numbers—foxtrots and sambas—the princess escorted him through the various banquet halls, introducing him to a variety of aristocrats—dukes and duchesses, barons, and earls, counts and viscounts.

Eventually, they paid homage to the king, who was seated apart from his guests, surrounded by his usual myriad of servants.

"How pleased I am to see you again, David," the king remarked with a boyish grin as they approached. "Please sit with me for a moment."

"Thank you, Your Royal Highness," David said with a polite bow. "The party is sensational," he added as he and Stephania were seated by two attendants.

"Has my daughter explained some of the aspects surrounding your new title?" the king asked.

"Thank you, yes. Some sire. I was thinking of traveling to Horvat and meeting my staff. I have a lot to catch up on, I think."

The king slapped his hand on the table and laughed uproariously. "That's what your staff is for, David," he said after regaining his composure. "You don't have to catch up on anything. They are highly specialized in their duties and very efficient. You'll see—everything will be taken care of quite properly. That's the upside of being an aristocrat."

"That's very reassuring," David said with a relieved smile.

"There is one thing that they can't do for you, however," the king said, turning serious. "Horvat needs a new mayor now that the former one is locked up in prison." He suddenly broke into another round of laughter. "You will have to appoint one."

As David began to reply, the king held up his hand. "I realize that you have no idea who your next mayor should be, so I have asked my daughter to accompany you to Horvat and set up interviews with the most qualified candidates. Of course, since the princess will be present during the proceedings, I will know with certainty that your appointee will be sympathetic to the Crown. Does that sound agreeable?"

David's heart beat a little faster as he realized that he would be spending more time with Stephania—and the icing on the cake was having her father's blessing. What a fortuitous turn of events!

He glanced at Stephania, noting her encouraging smile. Apparently, she was comfortable with the arrangement as well. "I am honored, sir," he said, giving the king a smile of gratitude.

The king raised his glass of champagne in a toast. "Here's to new beginnings. May you prosper in your new lands, Duke Sholfield!"

David cruised along the two-mile-long avenue from the gatehouse to Horvat Castle, enjoying the view from the back of his limousine. The grounds were magnificent, graced with numerous buildings and monuments. Two structures, in particular, caught his eye: a pavilion styled after the manner of a Greek temple, and a large Palladian-style mausoleum. A huge concrete fountain stood about a hundred yards away from the castle entrance. As they approached, David noted the five ornately sculpted figures surrounding it. The landscaping was eighteenth-century, with grass terraces, gardens, and highly decorative parterres fashioned from box hedges, gravel, and flowers. With several ponds and a large lake rounding out the scenery, the place looked like something out of a storybook.

David joyously realized that Horvat Castle was a palace in its own right, constructed in the late baroque style with beige-colored stone, featuring a symmetrical design, detailed ornamentation, many long, arched windows, and a sloping mansard roof. Two spacious wings projected outward from either side of the main structure, which featured a masonry dome. The façade bristled with exuberantly carved ornamentation, including coronets, ciphers, and friezes of seahorses and cherubs. He noted the differing styles of pilasters ornamenting the wings: Doric for the east, Corinthian for the west.

After parking the limo in front of the main entrance, David's valet led him into the great hall where he was met by his housekeeping staff. He stood there for a moment, gazing about in silent admiration. The hall was exquisitely beautiful, including four symmetrical vaulted ceilings, dozens of ornate, marble pilasters, and a series of golden-gilded archways. Beautiful frescoes of cherubs were painted on the ceilings in pastel colors. Daylight poured in through the stained-glass dome. The furniture was a mix of seventeenth- and eighteenth-century craftsmanship. An enormous fireplace graced one of the walls, featuring a rounded marble front with a colorful fresco encircled in gilded woodwork. Three sculpted marble statues stood on the mantel above it. The floor was traditional in style, featuring a pattern of white tile with black diamond centers.

After meeting with his staff—it was impossible to remember the names of all forty of them—David was shown to his bedroom suite on the second floor. The bed-chamber was equally luxurious, with a four-poster king-size bed. The windows were hung with matching silken, turquoise, and cream-striped drapery, and the room was comfortably warmed by a gilded porcelain fireplace. The space was filled with expensive furniture, including four finely crafted cocktail tables, a set of custom-carved chairs, a white oval table with a blue top surrounded by three white chairs, a large walnut desk, and a makeup table with a mirror set in an ornately carved gold frame. The carpet was light-red, imprinted with a gold-crown pattern. Many small paintings hung from glossy, golden-papered walls patterned with pink cherry blossoms.

David lay down with a sigh on the cream-colored silken bedcovers. His first month in Slavania had been a fortuitously eventful one, a complete reversal of his previous misfortunes. Not only had he successfully landed the new oil sands project, but also, he had used his newly acquired powers to heal Prince Alexander, winning the favor of both the king and the beautiful Princess Stephania. His good fortune had continued to shine, as he had become an aristocrat, acquiring lands and wealth. He wondered how much of it was Phariel's doing. Was the angel responsible for his burgeoning prosperity? And not least of all, there was his newfound affection for the beautiful Princess Stephania, who would arrive tomorrow morning, lodging in the royalty suite of the town's finest hotel.

He had learned from the chauffer that Horvat was a city of moderate size, with a population of half a million people. He would begin interviewing his first mayoral candidate at the hotel in the morning. Stephania had reassured him that the man was honest and well-qualified. Having had served on the city council for a number of years, he was familiar with the needs of the townspeople.

David wondered how the princess felt about him. It was true that she had accompanied him to the ball—how much of that was acquiescence to her father's wishes he couldn't be sure—and there was the matter of her brother's miraculous healing. He had to be careful not to mistake gratitude for affection. Nevertheless, he was determined to ask her for another date after the Horvat business was concluded.

"Horvat is a town of many purposes," his driver said as they approached the downtown area the next morning. "See that large, new building? That's the government building. There's the Grand Hotel, where the princess is staying. Over there is the stadium, used mostly for basketball and football games. We also have a newspaper, a library, and a museum, as well as various theaters, restaurants, and markets."

"The city looks very American," David said with a grin. "I feel right at home."

"Yes, most of the construction is recent. Many of the older buildings were destroyed in the war."

Several minutes later, the driver parked in the staging area of the Grand Hotel. From there, David was escorted to a conference room by two guards clad in formal military dress.

The room was small but well-appointed, with red-and-gold patterned wallpaper, blue-and-purple carpeting, and two chandeliers. A refrigerator, a coffee maker, and a counter laden with various breakfast foods completed the amenities.

The princess sat at a large rectangular walnut table occupying the center of the room. Directly across from her sat a middle-aged gentleman with slicked-back brown hair and a thin build. Dressed in a tailored navy-blue pinstripe suit, the man projected a sharp, professional appearance.

They both stood from the table as David entered.

"David, it is a pleasure to see you again," Stephania said in a businesslike tone. "This is Abban Peterka."

"Good to meet you, Abban," David said, shaking his hand. "And you, Princess."

"Abban, we would like you to begin by recounting your political experience," the princess said after they sat down.

"Certainly, Princess," Abban responded with a polished smile. "I've served on the city council for over five years. During that time, I've learned much about the inner workings of the city, having been significantly involved in the negotiations of the mayor's revitalization efforts. During that time, we've seen an increase in the tax base of approximately twenty percent. The budget is in line, with no deficits. Perhaps after the meeting, I can show you some of the new construction projects we're working on."

"That would be great," David responded. "I must mention, however, that I'm concerned about the city's recent embezzlement problems. Have you rounded up everyone who was involved in the subterfuge?"

"Rest assured, Duke Sholfield," Abban said with a confident smile. "The city council, in conjunction with the police department and the king's security forces, has taken aggressive measures to root out all corruption. We believe that everyone involved in the ring has been apprehended."

"We congratulate you on your diligence," the princess remarked approvingly. "Now," she continued, "tell us of your plans and your goals for the city."

"Thank you, Princess," Abban responded deferentially. "My goal is to diversify our economic base by using tax incentives and education. Our university is recognized as one of the best in the region in both engineering and technology. Our plan is to supply an educated workforce to multinational technology-based companies that are looking to expand."

"That sounds like a very ambitious goal," David remarked.

"Slavania has maintained its independence," Abban responded proudly, "And its leaders are known for their forward-thinking. Since English is now our national language, it makes it easier to attract both British and American companies. Several have already begun construction of new plants."

"That makes sense," David said. "That's why Vojislav Revic was in Chicago, correct? He spent several years there, I understand."

"Yes," Abban replied. "Before all this happened, he was influential in bringing the attention of several multinational American companies to our humble city. I have personally worked with all of the top executives of those companies. That is, among many other reasons, why I hope you will seriously consider me for the position."

David and Princess Stephania continued their interview with Abban throughout the afternoon, covering important matters concerning employment, public safety, transportation, and utilities.

"Tell me, David, what do you think of Mr. Peterka?" the princess asked after the meeting was concluded.

"I'm sold," David replied with a serious expression. "I suppose that, for the sake of fairness, we must interview several others, though."

"Not really," Stephania said. "If you feel he is competent and trustworthy, there is no need for more interviews. Personally, I think he is the most qualified for the position."

David felt his heart flutter as he gazed into the princess's beautiful green eyes. He wondered if it would offend her if he asked her out to dinner. She was here on business, after all. The last thing he wanted was to break one of the many layers of social customs that surrounded her like the skin of an onion.

During the ensuing pause, Stephania let her gaze linger on David for a moment. Then an affectionate smile spread across her face. "I see you are unsure how to proceed. It's perfectly honorable for an eligible duke to ask the princess on a date following a business meeting."

He gave her an amazed look. It was as if she had read his mind.

"Thank you, Princess," he responded, quickly gathering himself. "I appreciate your candor. May I have the honor of dining with you this evening?"

She laughed. "The pleasure is all mine, Duke Sholfield. We must be careful, though. The paparazzi has learned of my presence at the hotel and are gathered just outside the entrance, waiting to pounce on us like a pack of hungry wolves. Wherever we go, they will most certainly follow. Perhaps we can dine in."

David felt his belly rumble. It was almost dinnertime, and he had no desire to spend another forty-five minutes or so fending off the press on the way to a restaurant and then waiting for the food to be ordered and served. "That would be convenient, Princess," he responded with a smile.

The couple, accompanied by several royal guards, took a private elevator directly to the princess's penthouse suite.

David smiled appreciatively as he entered the great room. It was surprisingly contemporary, sumptuously furnished in leather and silk, with gilt-framed paintings hanging from dark-blue wallpaper and cherry paneling. A wide-screen television covered one entire wall.

They were promptly ushered into a spacious dining room, luxuriously appointed in a contemporary western style, including a mahogany table large enough to seat twenty guests. Servants fluttered around it, making hasty but ample preparations.

"Please make yourself comfortable," the princess said, beckoning him to sit beside her at the head of the table. "Please don't be intimidated by the formality of the courtiers," she said, smiling at his bemused expression. "They're just doing their job."

David sat down on the gilt-edged chair on her right and sighed. He noted that no expense had been spared—like Alexander Palace, the luxurious accommodations offered the ultimate in comfort and privacy. Unsure of royal protocol, he waited for the princess to begin eating before touching the appetizers on his plate.

"It's quite all right, David," Stephania said with a grin, noting his hesitation. "I know you are inexperienced with our customs, so you needn't worry about offending me. I want you to feel at home, okay?"

David held her gaze, reminding himself that he was in the presence of a beautiful, cultured, intelligent woman. He needed to temper his passion with empathetic compassion, conducting himself honorably as a gentleman, proving himself worthy of her affections.

"Abban made a very good impression of himself at the meeting today," David said, sipping his wine. "He definitely knows what he's doing."

"More importantly, do you trust him?" Stephania asked with a serious expression.

"I do. I don't need to interview any more candidates. How do I go about appointing him as mayor?"

"He has to be approved by the king, of course," Stephania replied. "That won't be a problem. I will simply give my father our recommendation. Then he will send one of his attorneys in a day or so to complete the paperwork."

David's mind began churning in the ensuing pause. So much had happened so quickly. He needed to be careful not to say something foolish, not to unwittingly divulge his secrets to the princess. He decided to turn the conversation to her past, avoiding any reference to his.

"So, tell me, Princess," he ventured in a casual tone. "What was it like for you growing up in a royal palace?"

"What gives you the audacity to think you can put me on the spot like that?" Stephania responded with a stern expression.

Stunned by the sudden change in the princess's demeanor, David stared at her blankly, squirming in his chair, attempting to formulate an appropriate reply.

Noting his agitation, Stephania burst into a round of laughter. "Please forgive me," she said after regaining her composure. "You looked so disoriented—like a little lost puppy. I apologize. And please, call me Stephania."

David broke into a relieved smile, realizing that she had been joking. "Boy, you had me going there for a moment."

At that moment, she appeared as a young, innocent schoolgirl, caught in a childish prank. "May I ask how old you are?" he asked.

"Certainly," she replied with an impish grin. "I'm twenty-two. I was born on February 23, 1985." She smiled again. "If you want to know about my upbringing, my childhood was a happy one, living with my parents in Premar Estate. My mother was tall and blonde. People say that I have her eyes."

David's gaze traveled from Stephania's eyes to her creamy, alabaster skin. "Have you inherited your beautiful complexion from your mother as well?"

"Yes, I have," she said, taking the compliment in stride. David detected no hint of bashfulness or boasting in her response. She seemed very sincere. Of course, her aristocratic upbringing would not lend itself to indecorous behavior. Her demeanor projected a reserved self-assurance, reflecting her culture and refinement.

"My mother was labeled by the media as 'fashionable,'" Stephania continued, "always consummately dressed, but the serious reporters described her as a political powerhouse. She was my father's closest advisor. She always did and said what she believed, brooking no opposition from her detractors, and as a consequence, she was not as popular with our citizens as the king. She was strict with us children as well. Unfortunately, she died in 1992 from lung cancer."

"I'm sorry to hear that," David said. He noted her sad expression. "What was it like growing up as a princess?"

"That was the best time of my life," Stephania replied, her expression brightening. "We went on a lot of summer outings, spending months at a time at the Boskovics' and other dukes' and duchesses' estates. Being surrounded by wealthy aristocrats insulated me from the vagaries of the Communist party in those early years. I was six when my father was crowned king. After that, we moved into Alexander Palace, where I was homeschooled by a governess. When the court was in session, private secretaries, courtiers, landed aristocrats, and royal cousins swarmed the palace. From those experiences, I learned my first lessons in the workings of the court.

"As queen, my mother placed great emphasis on developing our behaviors and tastes so we would emerge as cultivated adults. We were brought up to have exquisite manners, conduct ourselves properly in various kinds of company, to be civilized and well-liked individuals, to never behave unseemly in public."

"That seems like a lot of responsibility for a child to carry," David observed. "Did you ever feel stifled?"

"Not until my adolescence," Stephania replied with a grin. "That is an astute observation, though. Many aristocrats have problems when they become young adults because of the strictness of their upbringings. I'm afraid my brother fell into that category before he joined the army.

"Anyway, when my parents went on trips, I was cared for by a nanny. I grew up listening to classical music, which I still prefer over the other genres."

"It sounds like you had a lot to be happy about," David said.

"Oh, yes. It was a magical time, growing up amongst the wealthy and famous. I met so many interesting people. Life in the palace was joyous and eventful, and although there were many servants, everyone mingled. Mother in particular was a happy woman—always laughing, always mindful of her exceeding privileges. She always made time to visit us at bedtime, bringing lots of cuddles and bedtime stories.

"Now, that is quite enough about me for one sitting," Stephania said. "Please tell me about yourself, David. I'm curious about your metamorphosis from a doctor into an oil baron."

"I'm afraid that might be a little anticlimactic after the tale of your remarkable childhood," David responded.

"I doubt that," Stephania said with an encouraging smile. "In addition to being a doctor, you're the president of a successful oil company and a titled aristocrat. I think you can hold your own in any circle of society."

"Thank you," David said. Once again, he felt a surge of passion, very strong this time, flaring up like a bonfire primed with kerosene. He wondered what it would be like to kiss her.

"Although my family is somewhat wealthy," he continued, clearing his throat, "my father insisted that I attend public school. Although I learned to fend for myself, I had no real direction in my life. I fell in with the party crowd as an adolescent, learning firsthand about sex, drugs, and rock-and-roll. My summers were more productive, though. My father took me abroad and taught me about the oil business, but when I returned to school in the fall, I resumed my bohemian lifestyle."

"It's amazing you turned out so well considering your upbringing," Stephania remarked. "I know lots of people like that—young people with rich parents who never did anything but wander about from one party to the next. Something must have happened. May I ask what it was?"

"You're very perceptive," David remarked. "Yes, something did happen. When I was sixteen, my best friend died from a drug overdose. I found him lying on his bed in a coma, covered in vomit. I didn't know what to do for him, other than call the emergency number. I felt so helpless just standing there, watching the ambulance take him away. The experience filled me with a passionate desire to become a doctor. I wanted to be in a position to help people whose lives were in jeopardy. I thought I could make amends for what had happened."

"Did you blame yourself for his death?"

"At first. Eventually, I forgave myself, though. Becoming a doctor helped me regain my self-confidence."

"How interesting," Stephania said. "You took a bad situation and turned it into something positive." She suddenly took his hand and held it in a gentle grip. "I believe that you are a good person, David Sholfield."

The sensation of her touch was sublime. David didn't want her to let go, to spoil the moment. He wanted to see her again but didn't know how to broach the subject.

After a moment, David knew what he wanted to say. "I have enjoyed our dinner together," he said, standing from the table. "Thank you for the invitation." He quickly pressed on before he lost his nerve. "How about joining me at Horvat Castle this weekend?"

"I'm sorry, David," Stephania replied with a smile. "I already have plans—a fundraiser for the Slavanian National Ballet and Youth Opera. You must understand that my duties as princess include attending a variety of charity events and fundraisers, which are really nothing more than a lot of boring luncheons and dinners." Then she smiled and said, "Father's attorney will be arriving within the next two days with Abban's papers. Signing them will be a simple formality. I can't see any reason why we can't meet during the interim. How about tomorrow afternoon? Would that be suitable?"

"In that case," David said, his expression brightening, "would you have lunch with me at Horvat Castle?"

"I would like that," she said with a tender expression.

The princess clapped her hands, and David was escorted by two palace guards out of the hotel. On the way to the staging area, he was immediately besieged by a throng of reporters.

"Are you dating the princess?" one of them asked. David was surprised to feel a tingle of excitement at all of the attention. Rather than being intimidated by his sudden notoriety, he felt a surge of self-assurance. "No," he replied with a dashing smile. "It was a business meeting."

"Have you appointed a new mayor yet?" another asked.

"No. The matter is still under consideration. I will make a formal announcement as soon as the mayor has been approved by the king."

"Speaking of the king, how does he feel about you spending time with his daughter?" a third reporter asked.

"Thank you, but that's all for now," David replied. Then he made a dash toward the waiting limo.

The next afternoon, David met the princess in the Great Hall of Horvat Castle.

"That is a magnificent fireplace," Stephania remarked admiringly.

"It is," David affirmed with a grin. He nodded to the two valets accompanying her. "You two can follow my valet, Peter, to the changing room. It's just three doors down the hallway on the left."

"Are we still on for horseback riding?" Stephania asked as the servants walked away. "I'm dying to see the rest of the property. The drive up to the main building was quite inspiring."

David let his gaze linger upon Stephania for a moment, noting how her custom-tailored, red-and-black riding outfit enhanced both the femininity of her lovely features and her svelte, athletic figure. "Let's go outside then."

As they walked outdoors, David noted the two palace limos parked in the driveway, with men occupying both vehicles. "My guards are in the first one," Stephania said, noting David's stare, "and my chauffeur is in the other."

"Perhaps they would like some lunch," David ventured. "I'll have Peter show them to the kitchen."

Just then, his valet reappeared. "Make sure they have everything they need," David said, nodding toward the limos.

"No problem, sir," Peter replied, grinning.

"Hi, Tommy," David said to his stable boy, who approached with two brown stallions in tow. As David and Stephania mounted their horses and began trotting away from the building, he recalled the thrill of riding a horse for the first time at summer camp. He was only thirteen then.

"Let's see what these horses can do!" Stephania exclaimed. Then she shouted and kicked her horse in the side, sending it into a gallop.

David's horse responded in like manner, almost throwing him from the saddle. He held on for dear life as the horses sped along, cutting across the drive into an open field. The horses continued galloping for several minutes, finally slowing when Stephania said, "Whoa boy!" while pulling on the reins of her horse. David noted that the field terminated in a line of trees fronting dense woods.

He attempted to mimic Stephania's actions as she deftly dismounted and tethered her horse to a nearby tree.

"I see you're not used to riding," the princess said with a cheerful laugh as David clumsily dismounted.

"I should probably take some riding lessons now that I'm officially a duke," David responded, pausing once again to admire the princess's beauty, noting how carefree and uninhibited she appeared.

"I'll have my polo instructor teach you," Stephania responded. "He's an excellent rider. Then you can sport around with the other aristocrats. It's a skill that will come in handy, believe me."

"It sounds like I have a lot to learn," David said softly.

"Then I will just have to teach you," she said, giving him an affectionate gaze.

David grasped her by the waist in a snug embrace and began kissing her passionately. He was surprised when she didn't pull away. After a few minutes, he became so heated, he finally had to break the embrace, afraid that he might do something improper.

"That was great," he remarked bluntly, trying to catch his breath. "I think it's time to take a break, though."

To his surprise, Stephania laughed and pulled him down onto the grass, and began kissing him again. Although he wanted her more than anything, he couldn't forget that she was a princess and that her father was the king. He pulled himself away a few moments later. "Let's save some of that for later, okay?"

Stephania pouted for a moment, then gave him a tender smile. "I see that you're a gentleman. I approve. Let's have lunch, okay?"

They untied the two picnic baskets hanging from the horses' saddles and began setting out the food. A few minutes later, they sat down on the grass under a large oak tree, sipping red wine while feasting on a meal of grilled chicken, fish, and steak, accompanied by a salad, scalloped potatoes, and other vegetables.

"I asked the chef to cook an American-style meal. I hope that is agreeable, Stephania." He liked the sound of her name on his lips.

"It's most agreeable," she said, taking hold of a chicken breast and taking a large bite out of it.

"You seem to catch on to American customs very quickly," David remarked, laughing.

"Actually, I visited New York City once as a child. My father had his driver show me the sights during the daytime while he was occupied with business meetings."

"Speaking of your childhood, where did you go to school?" David ventured, changing the subject.

"That's right. I never finished my story. Now, where was I? Oh, yes. I was homeschooled by a governess until age nine, and then I was sent away to a boarding school in England. It was one of those fancy manor houses in the country with high ceilings and lots of expensive paneling. It was well-staffed and well-tended.

"The teachers expected us to always have good manners—to put others first in the aristocratic tradition. Of course, that was no problem since my mother had raised me that way. After overcoming my initial homesickness, I grew quite comfortable there, making friends easily while maintaining a good academic record. I had no best friend, though, because there was really no need. My self-confidence in dealing with social matters enabled me to mingle with many students.

"I liked the ballet and became a fairly good dancer. I played hockey and netball in the winter, swimming, and tennis in the summer. I still swim several days a week, my schedule permitting."

"It sounds like you enjoyed your stay there," David remarked, "and received a well-rounded education in the process."

"I was very happy there. Then, when I was twelve, I was sent to a private English school. Only 120 students—all of the children of European monarchs—were allowed to attend. Like the boarding school, it was located in the country and well-run. The school's curriculum included a lot of community service. That's where I learned to work with the aged and infirm, doing chores for them such as shopping and light cleaning. Since becoming Princess, my background in charity work has stood me in great stead.

"That all being said," Stephania continued, "the constant pressure to be well-behaved, pleasant, and polite eventually created underlying feelings of frustration and anger. I felt as though I had no free will, that my every thought and deed was mapped out in advance. My emotional conflicts eventually manifested themselves as an eating disorder. The conflicting desires—my appetite for rich foods versus the concern over my appearance—resulted in binging and purging. I've long since dealt with the problem, however."

"I can understand that," David remarked. "You were under a lot of pressure to conform to the strict protocols of palace behavior, and that was your way of dealing with it. Was it the same with your brother? Last night at dinner, you alluded to his problems with authority."

"Yes, my older brother, Alexander. He rebelled against the strictness of our upbringing, going off on forbidden escapades with people of non-aristocratic lineage, especially on summer breaks. At the insistence of our father, he joined the army. In retrospect, it was the best thing that could have happened to him. It cured him of his childish behavior."

"He seemed a perfectly likable fellow when I met him at the hospital," David said.

"Yes, he's always been a good brother to me. Now—let me finish my story, David, before I wear out my stay. On summer break, I visited my parents at Premar Estate, where I spent most of my time reading romance novels and practicing dance steps on the black-and-white marble floor of Edwards Hall. It was such a relief from the strict rules at the school—I got to wear jeans and no makeup and go swimming in the outdoor pool every day. Rather than the luxurious living quarters that one would expect of a royal, my quarters were simple and comfortable, consisting of just one room with twin beds, a sofa, a full bookshelf, and an Edwardian-style bathroom.

"I loved the summers there," Stephania continued, smiling. "I kept to myself, especially during the frequent arguments between my mother and brother, sneaking off to my room and doing lots of reading. In the evenings, I attended lavish parties attended by political figures from Europe, as well as local aristocrats. There were weekend dinner parties and dances, as well as horseback riding, swimming, and tennis. On winter breaks I enjoyed shopping, skiing, and dancing."

"It sounds like you had done it all by the time you were a teenager."

"Well, not quite," Stephania said, grinning. "In September 2002, I began my studies at Oxford. Because of my previous experience with private schools, I adjusted to college life quickly. I dated around a bit but never had a serious boyfriend. After graduating with an education degree last June, I began dating Duke Revic, becoming his fiancée in December."

"That was an arranged marriage, correct?"

"Yes," Stephania replied, sighing. "I had every intention of putting my own desires aside for my country. It was my duty to marry according to my father's wishes."

"Is that why you're dating me, now that I'm a duke?" David asked hesitantly. "For crown and country?"

In response, Stephania wiped her mouth with a napkin, threw her arms around him, and began kissing him again.

# CHAPTER SEVENTEEN

David walked into the parking deck feeling tired and lonely. After the king's attorney had signed the papers Wednesday morning, Abban Peterka had been sworn in as the new mayor of Horvat.

Stephania left immediately afterward—she needed to meet with her staff and prepare for her fundraiser, which was scheduled for today.

David had spent the last few days working with the mayor and the city council, filling the vacancies left by the former administration. Although he had accepted the mayor's invitation to a celebratory dinner in the town's finest restaurant that evening, he still felt like an outsider.

Thoughts of Stephania constantly filled his mind, pushing out everything else, making it extremely difficult to function. He couldn't wait to see her again, to feel her soft skin, to run his fingers through her silky, auburn hair.

David's reverie abruptly ended as someone shouted his name. Turning in the direction of the sound, he beheld a tall, thin man dressed in a tailored navy-blue suit fast-walking toward him. The man's high cheekbones and light skin bespoke of his Slavic ancestry. His brown eyes narrowed as he smiled. "David, please come here," he said in a perfunctory manner. "I have something that you will be very interested in seeing."

"What do you want?" David asked, taking a step toward the man, feeling an undercurrent of suspicion. His hands clenched instinctively. "Please state your business," he said in a firm tone.

Suddenly, two men tackled David from behind, grabbing his arms as he landed on the ground. In a spilt second, they had his hands handcuffed behind his back. They must have received police training, he mused. He felt uncharacteristically calm, considering the situation. He decided to play along for a while. "What is this all about?" he asked mildly as they led him to a silver-grey Mercedes.

The men opened the rear door in silence, pushed him into the backseat, and sat down next to him, one on each side. The man in the blue suit, obviously their leader, sat in the front passenger seat. "Put this on him," he said, handing the man on David's right a blindfold.

"Where are you taking me?" David asked in an irritated tone after being blindfolded. He felt a sensation of motion as the car pulled out of the parking lot.

The men remained silent throughout the trip, which lasted, by David's reckoning, about an hour. Eventually, the car stopped and the men led him into what he surmised was a building of some kind. He heard the sound of a lock being turned and a door being opened. They helped him down a flight of stairs, and after several more steps, removed his blindfold.

David noted that the room was devoid of any clues. It looked like the inside of a white box, the walls and ceiling having been constructed entirely of plasterboard. He had no idea what kind of building he was in, or who might be inhabiting it.

"Sit down," the leader said, pointing to one of two wooden chairs located in the middle of the room.

"Sure," David responded, trying to sound personable. "What's with all the secrecy?"

The man sat down on another chair directly in front of him, produced a handgun from under his jacket, and laughed.

"You have something my boss wants," he replied bluntly.

"I would be more than happy to oblige," David said, feeling a twinge of anxiety. He took a deep breath and tried to think. If things got nasty, he might have the strength to break the handcuffs and escape, but at this point, there was no reason to provoke the thugs. Besides, he didn't want to deal with the pain of another gunshot wound.

"What is it that you want?" he asked with a friendly smile.

The man laughed. "Search him!" he shouted to his henchmen.

David struggled as they began their search, but before he could break the chain linking the handcuffs, one of them pulled his hand out of David's trouser pocket and hoisted his prize into the air, proudly displaying it to his associates.

"Is this what you're looking for, boss?" he asked with a triumphant grin.

David became filled with anger as he saw the white polished stone firmly clenched in the thug's hand.

The leader abruptly stood from his chair and snatched it out of his henchman's hand.

"Thank you, David. That wasn't so bad now, was it? My boss will be very pleased. Now, I bid you a fond farewell."

As he began walking up the stairs, he turned to the largest thug. "Blindfold him and give him a ride back to town. Make sure you don't let him out of your sight until then, okay?"

"Got it, boss," the man replied.

David waited until he heard the sound of the car engine starting. Then he pulled his arms apart with great force, snapping the chain linking the handcuffs together. Before his captors could react, he lunged at the largest man, toppling him to the floor. They wrestled for a few seconds before his partner grabbed David by the shoulders and lifted him off his companion.

David leapt to his feet, dodged the man's fists, and landed several heavy blows to his face as well as his companion's, knocking them to the ground.

They sat there for a moment, dazed and surprised at David's strength. Then they rose to their feet and charged him.

After waiting until the last millisecond, David sidestepped them and forcefully pushed their heads together as they passed, knocking them unconscious. Then he made a brief search of their clothing, confiscating their driver's licenses and other identification, as well as the keys to the second car.

David slowly walked up the stairs and entered the kitchen, consumed with feelings of anger and frustration. The loss of the Lyricor was a great blow to his confidence. He wondered if Phariel and Everet would be angry with him for his carelessness. He understood the impossibility of gaining access to the obelisk without the device, preventing him from visiting the angel again, preventing him from receiving the beneficial effects of the philosopher's stone several years hence.

In the waning daylight filtering in through the windows, he discerned that he was in an abandoned farmhouse. After rummaging through the cupboards, which were stripped bare, and after making a quick search of the rest of the ransacked building, he walked outside, entered the car, and drove away, leaving the thugs to find their own way back to the city.

"I'm sorry, David, but the IDs you gave me were phony," Sven said as they sipped coffee together in David's dining room. "There's no way of knowing who those guys were."

"I thought not," David said with a sigh. "Thanks for checking, though."

He had not divulged the thieves' intentions to Sven, neither had he mentioned the two men he had left stranded inside the farmhouse. There was no reason to. Surely, they were long gone by the time the police arrived.

He suspected Revic hired them and was now in possession of the Lyricor. Unfortunately, since the former duke was in jail, there was no way of forcing the truth out of him.

"It seems strange that the robbers would pick a newly minted duke for their victim," Sven mused. "Things will go very badly for them when they are apprehended."

"I guess I'm high-profile now," David said with a grin. "Perhaps the thugs have connections in the government, or maybe they're just plain arrogant."

"Perhaps," Sven said. "I heard that the king sent Stephania to help appoint your new mayor. I know that you're fond of her. Did things go to your liking?"

"Everything went okay," David replied casually. Although he trusted Sven, he had no desire to reveal the depth of his feelings for Stephania.

"The press says that it's more than friendship," Sven said with a laugh. "Of course, they always tend to exaggerate things. Tell you what. If you ever want to know anything about Stephania, all I have to do is ask Triska. They confide in each other."

"Thanks for the offer," David said with a grin. "I may take you up on that."

"Listen, David," Sven said, his expression turning serious. "If you ever get into trouble again and need a place to hide, I have a cousin whose friend owns a bakery here in town."

As David began to ask for clarification, Sven held up his hand and continued. "You're a duke now, and you're keeping company with the princess. She's second in line for the throne. Unfortunately, as beneficent as the king is, there are enemies within and without the government.

"Every noble has an emergency escape plan—a sanctuary of sorts. I think it's time you had one as well, so I'm sharing mine with you for the time being. The bakery is called Seibel's. If you ever need help, you can go there. It's a safe house. No one in the government knows about it. Don't forget that name, okay?"

"Seibel's. I hadn't thought about needing an escape plan," David said. "After what just happened, I agree that it would be a wise precaution. Thanks, Sven. You're a true friend."

Just then David's cell phone rang. His heart leapt for joy at the sound of Stephania's voice. He glanced back at Sven, who was walking toward the doorway. "I'll show myself out," Sven said with a perceptive grin.

"I heard about your incident the other night," Stephania said, the relief in her voice coming through loud and clear. I'm so glad you're okay," she continued. "How are you feeling?"

"I miss you," David confessed. "Other than that, there's no damage. I'm unharmed. When will I see you again?"

"How about tomorrow evening? My father has asked that you join us on his yacht. We're going on a cruise. If you want to come along, I can send a helicopter and fly you here this evening."

"How convenient," David replied, chuckling. "I'll start packing my bags."

David hung up the phone feeling jubilant. It was great hearing Stephania's voice again. His misgivings about the Lyricor had all but vanished, as he felt confident that it would turn up eventually. After all, no one else could use it, and he had at least ten years to find it before his powers began to fade.

That evening, the royal helicopter transported him to Premar Estate. After landing, he paused for a few moments, admiring the king's summer home. It was a magnificent, Georgian-style mansion—the white-brick façade and the numerous windows and ornamental entrances gave it an airy, distinguished appearance. The pilot had informed him that it was built upon thirteen thousand acres of land and featured the finest collection of eighteenth-century furniture in the country.

A formally dressed valet led David into the dining room, then they passed through staterooms and private rooms, all very luxurious, spacious, and well-proportioned, with high ceilings and beautiful moldings, the walls hung with spectacular pictures by master artists.

The dining room was no exception, featuring several large ornate chandeliers of remarkable craftsmanship, mounted on a sculptured ceiling. The combined luminescence reflected brightly upon marble floors, exquisite tapestries, silk curtains, and fine rugs. A number of porcelain and silver accessories were placed upon unique tables and cabinets of obvious antiquity, artfully gracing the corners of the room.

After David was seated, Stephania introduced him to the twenty guests present at the king's table. The friends of the king—all of them aristocrats—were seated on his left. Opposite them were the friends of the princess and Triska. He noted that the king's guests were middle-aged or older, while the princess's friends were all young.

"Wow," David exclaimed to Stephania after the introductions were made. "This place is fantastic."

"I'm glad you are pleased," Stephania said, responding with a warm smile. "It's good seeing you again, David."

Just then, the king made his entrance. Everyone stood as he was announced.

David couldn't help staring in admiration at Stephania. Dressed in a silvery, sparkly top and a turquoise chiffon dress with side slits displaying her shapely legs, she looked ravishing.

"And how are you, my good Duke David?" King Alexander asked, giving David a concerned look after they were seated. "I heard about your run-in with some rather nasty individuals."

"I'm fine, Your Highness. Fortunately, I wasn't hurt."

"I'm very glad to hear that," the king responded with a relieved smile. "You have my word that the investigation will be conducted by my personal security staff. Friends of the king must never be treated with disrespect."

He raised his glass. "I would like to make a toast to David Sholfield, the Duke of Horvat, our newest aristocrat. May you prosper in your new country."

"Thank you," David said softly after the guests made congratulatory remarks. "I am honored by the bestowal of such great gifts, as well as your kind regards."

As the first course was served, David turned to Stephania. "Where's the prince? Is he well?"

"He's fine," she replied, laughing. "He's off with his buddies on a hunting trip, which is not unusual."

"He seems very independent," David remarked with a thoughtful expression. "So, tell me about the cruise," he continued.

"It's going to be such fun," Stephania responded with an enthusiastic grin. "We will cruise the Adriatic and visit some islands along the way. The mistral wind blows this time of year—traditionally a harbinger of excellent weather."

"That sounds fantastic!" David exclaimed. "I could use a little relaxation after all the studying I've been doing lately."

There was a lull in the conversation. The king turned to one of his guests. "Duke Crovic, please tell us about your new country manor."

The man replied at length, giving a detailed description of its architecture, followed by lengthy remarks from the other nobles, each bent on contributing his and her insights, attempting to upstage each other, the resulting conversation lasting for more than two courses.

Eventually tiring of the conversations about colonnades, entablatures, and pediments, David concentrated on the sumptuous meal before him.

During the fourth course, a woman seated to his right gave him a friendly smile. "Now David, you must tell me what you think of the artist Vermeer. I'm considering purchasing one of his paintings for my drawing-room."

David recalled what Stephania had previously mentioned about her. Sarah Yoric, the Duchess of Newburgh Heights, was a close friend of the princess. A young, charismatic, red-haired woman with a dimpled chin, freckled skin, and a cute little nose, Sarah had an interesting and contrasting network of friends, running the gamut from fun-loving jet-setters to serious-minded intellectuals.

He paused for a moment, trying to recall what he had learned from his art history class in college. "I must confess," he replied carefully, "I've not studied the Dutch School in detail. I know it's an art of portraiture, the artists using intimate observation to capture detailed renderings of persons and places in their daily lives. Vermeer was the finest technician of those excellent craftsmen," David continued. "None of his works have been equaled in the use of color, tone, and brushwork."

"I'm impressed," Sarah said with an approving smile. "You must have paid attention to your college professors. I've been considering adding *Lady at a Spinet* to my collection, now that it has recently become available. After hearing your remarks, it would seem that my mind is made up."

Stephania gave David a playful nudge. "It seems you have a way with the ladies, Duke David. Should I be jealous?"

David laughed, took a sip of the fine chardonnay that filled his wineglass, and replied, "Not to worry, my dear. There's no one here that could possibly compete with you."

David couldn't remember the last time he had had such an enjoyable time. Here he was, surrounded by nobles and a king, feeling very much accepted, and the icing on the cake was the beautiful princess's obvious regard.

An hour later, the king took his leave and the party broke up. After saying goodnight to Stephania, David was led by a livery-clad servant to one of the exquisitely furnished guest rooms on the second floor.

Early the next morning, David was roused from a sound sleep by a butler who, after waiting for him to shower, led him to the dining hall.

After consuming a sumptuous breakfast, David walked with the other guests to the car caravan waiting outside.

Then, after the king and his entourage were seated in the first of the two royal limousines, a valet led David to the second one, seating him in the rear along with Stephania, Triska, and Sven.

After a stately, seven-mile drive to the marina, the cavalcade arrived at the dock where the guests leisurely boarded the royal yacht.

"Greetings, everyone! My name is Captain Gilevy," the captain announced loudly after everyone was assembled on deck. "Welcome to the *Tyrama*. It is my express wish that all of you find your stay here a pleasant one. The *Tyrama* is a 385-foot power yacht, manned by a crew of sixty who are ready to accommodate your every request. In addition to the master suite, there are thirty cabins, complete with their own bathrooms.

Fifteen of them have queen-size beds. The rest is fitted with twin and double beds."

He pointed to the uniformed man on his right who was holding a clipboard. "Just tell the steward which bedding arrangement you prefer, and he will have a crew member show you to your cabin. This vessel is fully air-conditioned and features a private cinema, an outdoor swimming pool, and Jacuzzi, a luxury dining room, a nightclub complete with a stage, dance floor and gambling casino, a sauna, a massage room, an onboard hospital, a beauty salon, and a gymnasium."

"I can't think of any reason to ever leave this boat," David remarked to Sven. "It has everything one could ask for."

"The king desires his guests to be comfortable," Sven responded with a grin.

After the captain concluded his introduction, twenty stewards appeared and led the guests to their rooms.

"If you need anything," David's steward said, handing him a plastic magnetic card as they arrived at his cabin, "just use the phone in your room. Have a pleasant stay."

David swiped the card through the reader and stepped inside.

The spacious, oak-paneled room featured an ebony floor, which was partially covered by an intricately woven Persian rug. The room held two twin beds with brass reading lights mounted on each headboard, and a night table with a beautiful Tiffany lamp. Contemporary-style sofas were placed around the room at convenient locations.

The bathroom was equally luxurious, with two sinks and a separate shower and bathtub. David noted the fixtures, which appeared to be pure gold and silver.

As David lay down on one of the beds, his mind began drifting, recalling the events of the past few months. After much tribulation, he had finally succeeded in his quest but had been unable to save his father.

After spending several sorrowful months grieving, he had experienced a complete reversal of fortune, landing a lucrative business contract with the King of Slavania.

Using the powers granted by the angel Phariel, he had saved the king's son. As a consequence, the king had made him a titled aristocrat with lands and great wealth. To top it all off, he had begun a romantic relationship with the beautiful Princess Stephania.

Counterbalancing his good fortune, however, were the encounters with the demons and Satan's minions—evil men and women who practiced the black arts—all seemingly bent on his destruction.

His beloved Angela had fallen victim to their corrupt machinations, and although her murder remained unsolved, he strongly suspected Vojislav Revic.

It was of little comfort that Revic had been stripped of his title and sent away to prison. His punishment wouldn't bring Angela back, and it made it impossible to recover the Lyricor.

He considered confiding in his friend Sven. The energy minister had connections in the secret service, and his animosity toward Revic was readily apparent. He could offer Sven the simple explanation that the Lyricor was an expensive artifact that he wanted to be returned. After pondering for a few minutes, he decided not to involve his friend because it was too risky. He would be patient and wait for a better opportunity to arise.

Just then the phone rang—coincidentally, it was Sven. "Please meet us in the dining room, David," his friend said cheerfully. "The king wants to discuss our itinerary over dinner."

The next few weeks flew by as David spent his daytime hours in swimming, playing volleyball in the gym, or lounging on the deck. Whenever the ship made one of its frequent stops at an exotic port of call, he joined Stephania and her friends, touring the quaint tourist towns and engaging in water sports on sparkling private beaches. Her companions were gracious and accommodating, accepting him as one of their own, patiently teaching him the pleasurable arts of windsurfing and scuba diving. At night the guests returned to the yacht, and after a sumptuous feast, gambled and danced the night away, reveling in the music of contemporary hit songs, superbly performed by a live band.

Although David greatly enjoyed spending time with Stephania and her friends, he soon discovered, to his disappointment, that there were no opportunities to meet with her in private. Attendants were always hovering over them, providing some service or other.

At the conclusion of the voyage, David returned to Premar Estate and resided there for the entire month of May, enjoying the constant thrill of association with the popular royal family, his emotions buoyed by the rapid and exciting pace of the palace life. He spent his time horseback riding and playing tennis, and most evenings were filled with dinner parties attended by distinguished guests, including heads of state, visiting dignitaries, and celebrities. Sometimes he attended the theater or the opera. The plethora of activities consumed most of his time, leaving only limited opportunities to be with Stephania.

It was the evening of the last Friday of May, and the couple was in attendance at the opera house, comfortably seated in His Majesty's representative's box. It was intermission, and all of the other guests had left for refreshments, leaving them temporarily alone.

As Stephania stood to leave, David touched her arm gently. "Please stay for a moment," he said with a serious expression. "I have something important to say to you."

The princess sat back down in her purple, velvet-backed chair. "All right, dear. You have my attention."

"We haven't had much alone-time together since we've been dating," he said, gazing deeply into her eyes. "You know how I feel about you, don't you?"

"Of course, dear," Stephania said with a tender gaze. "It's been difficult observing all the palace protocols lately," she admitted with a sigh. "Perhaps we can sneak away this evening and be alone."

"What I want to say is this," David said, ignoring her remark. "I love you with all my heart."

"I know that, David," she replied, giving him an affectionate hug. "And I love you too, dear."

He knelt on the carpeted floor in front of her. "I know we've only been dating for a couple of months," he said affectionately, "but there's no doubt in my mind how I feel about you. I'm hoping that you feel the same way. I know that our relationship is special and I want to be with you for the rest of my life. Will you be my wife?"

In response, Stephania began crying. "Yes, David," she replied after a few moments, dabbing her eyes with a handkerchief. "I feel the same way. There's absolutely no doubt in my mind. No other man has ever made me feel the way you do. I know our love is special and will last forever. I will certainly marry you."

David produced an engagement ring from his jacket pocket and slipped it onto her wedding finger. Stephania lifted her hand and admired it. The band was made from white gold, featuring a large central sapphire surrounded by twelve diamonds.

"It's beautiful," she remarked. Then she pulled David into her bosom and kissed him.

"It is our great pleasure that the King of Slavania announces the betrothal of his daughter, the Princess of Premar, to Dr. David Sholfield, the Duke of Horvat," the king's press secretary announced in a loud, clear tone.

David glanced at Stephania for reassurance as the phalanx of newsmen, who had been patiently waiting on the front steps of Alexander Palace, rushed forward. It was their first press conference as a couple, and he was nervous.

"How did the two of you meet?" one of the reporters asked.

Stephania deferred to David. "I first came to Slavania on business at the behest of the king," he replied with what he hoped was a confident smile. "My company was hired to expedite the oil sands project. I first met the princess at a business dinner."

"How did you feel about meeting David Sholfield?" another reporter asked Stephania.

"I thought he was nice," she replied with a demure smile, "but I was engaged to Duke Revic, so I really had no special feelings for him at the time."

"When did you start dating?" a third reporter asked.

"It was not until after I became a duke," David replied. "The king assigned the princess to help me appoint the new mayor of Horvat. We began dating shortly after our first business meeting."

The couple spent another twenty minutes with the reporters—answering questions and recounting their romance.

Then they returned to the palace and spent the entire afternoon consulting with the wedding planning committee, afterward attending an engagement celebration—a lavish affair thrown by the king at the Zoran Polo Club.

The very next day, David moved into Alexander Palace.

"How do you like being a prince?" Stephania asked, giving him an approving smile as he entered the formal reception room.

David sat down at the large circular oaken table across from her and sighed. "I feel overwhelmed," he replied, giving the room's splendid décor an exhausted gaze. "I have no idea what I'm doing most of the time."

"Relax, darling," Stephania said with a giggle. "We have a whole staff of people to help you every step of the way." She sipped her coffee. "While we're on the subject, you've been assigned a private secretary—Ken Fengliska. You will begin meeting with him tomorrow."

"What the heck do I need a private secretary for?" David asked, shaking his head in dismay. "I already have a business secretary."

"You will be pleased to know that his job is to teach you exactly how to behave like a proper prince in public— how to enter a room, how to exit a car, how to hold yourself while being spoken to, how to pose for photographers without appearing to do so, for example."

"Anything else?" David asked with a wry smile.

"Of course, dear. He will school you in all the ways of royalty—how to treat the staff, butlers, cooks, valets, etc. Additionally, he will test you on your required reading of Slavanian history and politics and the biographies of past royalty."

"Wow!" David exclaimed. "I'm studying for a degree in Slavanian royal etiquette."

"It shouldn't be much of a challenge for a person with your education and intellect," Stephania replied passionately.

She abruptly shooed the servers away and moved close to him. "They won't stay away for long," she said with a conspiratorial grin, "but at least we can enjoy a few minutes alone together."

David pulled her close and kissed her.

After a few moments, she pulled away. "Now that we're properly engaged, David, I think it's only fitting that we meet secretly at night after everyone has gone to bed."

"Now that's the best suggestion I've heard in over a month," David said, laughing. "So, what's the plan, my bold naughty princess?"

The next few weeks were hectic ones for the newly-betrothed couple. David spent the mornings taking instruction from Ken, afterward completing the required reading or lunching with Sven. The afternoons were spent conducting business from his penthouse suite in Zoran. A detective from the Royal Protection Department accompanied him whenever he left the palace.

Stephania spent her time horseback riding, ballet dancing, or staying in the palace answering congratulatory letters. Then there was the planning of the virtually infinite details of the wedding with her staff, headed by Sophia Kelcivic, her private secretary, and the Lady Susan Polemski, a lady-in-waiting who was of great assistance in selecting the wardrobe, guest list, and bridal registry.

In the evenings, the couple attended dinner parties or ate dinner separately in their own rooms.

"Ken says you're ready," Stephania remarked as they sat down to lunch one afternoon in the formal reception room. "It's only taken you three weeks to complete your introductory training. That's some fast learning, David."

"That's what Ken tells me," David responded with a chuckle. But then he frowned. "What do you mean by 'introductory training'? Is there more?"

The princess laughed. "Of course, darling. It never ends. We must continually do everything in our power to bolster public confidence in the Crown."

"That sounds reasonable, I guess. How do we accomplish that stupendous feat?"

"You must understand, David, that we have our separate duties as prince and princess. My duties include: to be the belle of many a ball, to watch polo matches, and to visit the dying. Every event requires a new outfit. I have a special team of advisors for that purpose. I have a private secretary to help organize exhibitions, to write thank-you letters to the hosts, to answer correspondence, and so on.

"I also have many state engagements to attend, including the State Banquet at Alexander Palace, the State Opening of Parliament, the Annual Festival of Remembrance, and the Royal Slavanian Legion. Then there are the arts charity events and fundraisers, such as the Royal Music Hall, the Slavanian Symphony Chorus, dinner at Banqueting House for Duchess of Kervisky, and the March for the Hospices Foundation."

"Okay, okay!" David exclaimed, raising his hands defensively. "I get it. Definitely a full plate. Your charity work is a worthwhile pursuit, though. I think that's one of the reasons behind your popularity."

"That may be true," Stephania said with a smile, "but the important thing is to do all I can to help the helpless, to make life better for people, to relieve suffering and distress. That's why I'm involved in the Woman Help Organization, which provides a way for women of the developed world to help their sisters in the Third World. The female volunteers are responsible for ninety percent of the work related to pure survival, such as crop tending. I also visit the Zoran Mission Hospice and cheer up the AIDS patients there. I've also worked for the CRUSAID Organization, and have started such projects as the Rodney Portivic Ward of St. Mary's Hospital, a neighborhood health center for HIV-positive people, and the Positively Women Group, a self-help group of women who have tested positive for AIDS.

"My travels have taken me to many foreign countries," Stephania continued, "such as Monaco, Australia, New Zealand, Germany, Portugal, France, Germany, and Spain. As a royal, I must make extensive preparations for each and every trip—which clothes to wear, which staff to take, which people to see, what presents to buy, which customs to respect, and so on."

David gazed at her in astonishment. "You are truly an angel. I think I understand why you do all of those things: because it's part of your character. Your celebrity status enhances your ability to bring meaning to the lives of so many. You've been given the gifts of sensitivity, compassion, and awareness. You're a kind and sympathetic individual. Slavania is lucky to have such a princess as you, and so am I."

He then stood from the table, walked to her side, and threw his arms around her.

"No one has ever spoken to me in such a special way," Stephania remarked passionately. "You truly are my prince. Now sit back down, David," she said after smothering him with tender kisses. "We have more work to do. I think you're ready for the Walkabout."

"The Walkabout?"

Saturday morning, David and Stephania began the Walkabout—a three-day walking tour of Zoran Stephania explained that it was a custom borrowed from British royalty for the purpose of unifying the Slavanian citizens to the Crown.

The ceremony began as the betrothed couple stepped out onto the second-story balcony of the capitol building in downtown Zoran, where the princess presented the soon-to-be prince to the people. David, standing arm in arm with the princess, smartly dressed in red and gold—the national colors of Slavania—with his handsome features and trim figure, immediately won over the hearts of the thronging onlookers below.

After the cheering subsided, the couple exited the palace at the street level entrance and began their walk. The crowd followed wherever they went, waiting patiently as they visited the sick at several nursing homes along the way.

As they continued, Stephania randomly singled out people from the multitude, touching the sleeve of an old lady, the hand of a little girl, squeezing the fingers of women who were holding their hands out to her.

Everyone could see that the princess was sincere, that every gesture came from the heart, enhancing her already enormous popularity.

When the rain came pouring down that afternoon, she refused an umbrella, desiring to empathize with those around her. To those who had been waiting for hours in the cold, wind, and rain, she said, "You poor dear. My hands are freezing and yours must be much worse. Thank you for waiting for us. You must be soaked to the bone. You must be freezing. I am. Thanks for coming to see us."

Everyone noted the princess's eagerness to please, her openness to everyone she met. Her compassion, mixed with the glamour of royalty, won everyone over. The hearts and minds of the multitude were touched by her selflessness, that she would take the time to dress up and not mind when the rain ruined her clothes, her hat, and her makeup.

Unfortunately, some were not so admiring. David noted several youths holding placards and chanting, "Go home, American."

When the couple returned to their car on the third evening, they found it spray painted.

A group of college students nearby were holding a noisy demonstration. As the couple appeared, scuffles broke out, and the police moved in and began making arrests.

Following Stephania's example, David remained gracious and kind throughout the entire episode, learning firsthand what it was like to be a prince.

# Chapter Eighteen

"Your Royal Highness," David said with a low bow as he entered the formal reception room.

"Please be seated," the king responded, giving David a benevolent smile.

David seated himself on the opposite side of the rectangular cherry table. There was a flurry of activity as six servers quickly and deftly performed their duties, setting out a variety of appetizers and beverages. A minute later, the king clapped his hands, dismissing them. David realized it was the first time he had been alone with the king.

"I want to tell you, David," the king began with a pleasant smile, "how very pleased I am with your engagement to my daughter."

David's mood was immediately uplifted by the joyous emotions he felt at the king's encouraging words. His favor remained intact. "Thank you, sire," he said humbly.

"Not only is my daughter obviously in love with you but also the majority of the good citizens of my country as well. I have received tens of thousands of letters of approbation. The press conference went well, and the Walkabout has served its purpose, uniting the people more fully to the Crown. This is a good day for us, my son, and you have my full blessing."

"Thank you again, sire, but Stephania must be given all the credit. The people adore her."

"Humbly spoken, my good duke. Now I must bring up the matter for which I have summoned you here this afternoon," the king continued. "The criminals that mugged you have been apprehended."

"That's great news!" David exclaimed. "How did you find them so quickly?"

"It was quite easy, actually," the king replied with a smile. "It seems that when their boss cut them loose, apparently having no further need of them, they panicked, thinking that they were marked for assassination. My security agents were watching the airports and bus stations. We caught them at the airport when they tried to leave the country. They weren't very smart, it seems."

"I'm glad they were apprehended," David said. "Did your agents learn who their leader was?"

"Certainly," the king replied, his expression turning serious. "It pains me to tell you this, David, but they worked for Abban Peterka, your new mayor."

David inhaled sharply. Something wasn't right. He realized that he would need to provide an explanation to the king. He didn't believe for a second that Abban was behind the theft of the locating device. Revic was the likely perpetrator, using misdirection to prevent the king's agents from detecting his crime.

"Are you all right, David?" the king asked with a look of concern.

"Yes, sire," David replied tensely. "It just took me by surprise, that's all. Abban seemed like a good man. Do your men know what his motive was?"

"No, the hoodlums said they were simply carrying out orders, but that's no surprise." He gave David a perplexed look. "Do you have any idea why Abban wanted to rob you?"

David's apprehension increased. He didn't want to lie to the king, but he couldn't reveal the truth and couldn't play ignorant either. He cleared his throat and calmed himself. "I was carrying a large diamond that I purchased from a trader in the Congo," he said with a sincere expression. "The man was in financial trouble, and I acquired the stone at a discount. I showed it to Abban a few days after our first meeting. I thought I could trust him. It's hard to believe that he was involved in this. Perhaps the thugs were lying. Do you have any hard evidence linking Abban to the criminals?"

"Not yet. That's why we haven't arrested him. He's being watched as we speak. This is still an ongoing investigation, so please don't mention our conversation to anyone, David."

David sighed in relief. At least Abban had not been arrested. "Thank you for including me in the loop, sire. You can rest assured that I will keep our conversation in strict confidence."

"It's just a small matter, but you can understand why I wanted to speak to you in private. I suggest that you discontinue the practice of carrying valuables on your person now that you are to become a royal."

Just then, there came a knock on the door. The king frowned at the intrusion. "I told the staff we were not to be disturbed," he said gruffly.

Suddenly the door burst open, revealing the king's son.

"What's the matter, Alex?" the king asked concernedly, noting his son's anguished expression.

Instead of replying, Alexander took a few steps toward the king, drew a silver pistol from his jacket, and shot his father in the chest at point-blank range. David watched in openmouthed dismay as the king toppled out of his chair and fell to the floor with a thud. "Why, my son?" the king whispered with a stunned expression as he lay on his back, writhing in pain from the gunshot wound.

Instead of replying, Alexander grimaced and shot him two more times in the heart. Then he laid the pistol on his father's chest and turned to David, who was still sitting at the table with an expression of stunned disbelief. "Don't just sit there, David," he said sarcastically. "You're a doctor, aren't you?"

David sat there for another few seconds, attempting to will his shock-stiffened body into action. Then he lunged out of his chair and ran to the king's side, and in an attempt to heal him, lifted the pistol off the king's chest and laid his hands directly upon the spot marked by the bullet holes. But it was too late—the king was already dead. He looked up and gave the now-smirking Alexander a look of disdain. "You killed him."

"No, David," Alexander responded with an ice-cold expression. "You did." The prince drew his cell phone out of his trouser pocket and dialed a number. "This is Alex," he said brusquely. "I want the entire security team at the formal reception room at once!"

David glanced at Alexander's hands and noted that the prince was wearing gloves. Suddenly realizing that the only fingerprints on the gun were his, David quickly pushed Alexander to the side and ran out the door.

By the time David reached the palace entrance, four guards were waiting for him. He managed to strike two of them on the side of the head with sharp blows, knocking them unconscious. As the others lunged at him, he sidestepped one and spun away from the other, breaking the man's grasp on his shoulder.

They chased him to his car, which was still parked in the driveway in front of the building. After a brief tussle, David managed to knock both men onto the pavement. Several more guards appeared as he entered the vehicle, then he quickly sped away with tires squealing, breaching the main gate just before it closed. Upon reaching the main road, he headed for the downtown area, driving as fast as possible.

David glanced in the rearview mirror and breathed a sigh of relief—no one was following yet. His anxiety lifted a little as he recalled the sanctuary that Sven had spoken of. At least he had a plan.

Ten minutes later, David entered the city limits. He ditched the car in an alley and proceeded on foot. Spotting a gas station on the street corner, he walked inside and asked directions to Seibel's Bakery. The attendant replied that the bakery was on the other side of town, but that a trolley with a stop two blocks away would take him halfway there.

David found the trolley stop, sat down on the bench, and waited, replaying the king's murder in his mind. Alexander must have perceived David as a threat to the throne. He recalled Stephania's previous explanation: If Alex was single at the time of the king's death and David and the princess were married, they would succeed him as the next king and queen. Apparently, Alexander's aspirations had gotten the better of him. Framing David for the king's murder would prevent David's marriage to Stephania, disqualifying them both for the throne and making Alex the new heir—a vacancy that would have to be filled quickly.

A few minutes later, the trolley arrived. As David boarded, several police cars sped past with lights flashing and sirens wailing. Once again, he felt a rising sense of panic and desperation. The royals were looking for him, and the whole country would soon be on the alert. He tried to calm himself and think. Although Sven had mentioned that he could find sanctuary at the bakery, his friend had not given any specific details. He chided himself for not asking more questions at the time.

David exited the trolley at the last stop and found himself standing in front of a large, public library. He hailed a cab and breathed a sigh of relief when it pulled up to the curb. "Take me to Seibel's Bakery," he said as he climbed into the back seat. "And hurry!"

Fifteen minutes later, he had the driver drop him off a block away so he could appraise the situation before entering the store.

As he approached, a military supply truck careened around the corner and skidded to a halt directly in front of him. He watched, paralyzed with fear, as two men dressed in military camouflage outfits carrying rifles exited the truck and motioned him to get in the back. He slowly walked toward them and climbed in, realizing with a sinking feeling that Alexander had sent the king's soldiers to apprehend him. He wondered how they had found him so quickly. Had Sven been questioned? He sat down on the hard, wooden floor across from the two soldiers. "Where are we going?" he asked, noting the empty interior. They remained silent and motionless; their gazes fixed directly in front of them.

About forty-five minutes later, the truck stopped. The soldiers opened the rear door and motioned for David to step out. He jumped down to the ground and stared in surprise at the same abandoned farmhouse he had been taken to a month earlier.

The guards escorted David through the house, down the stairs, and into the interrogation room in the basement. A man dressed in an officer's uniform—obviously their captain—was seated at a thick wooden table.

The officer motioned to the chair on the opposite side. "Sit down," he said in an authoritative tone. With cold, blue eyes and a square chin, he appeared every bit the professional soldier.

"What do you want?" David asked, his suspicions beginning to mount. Alexander had all the evidence he needed to lock him up in prison, so why hadn't the soldiers returned him to the palace?

"I want to know about the Lyricor," the captain stated unequivocally. "Where is it?"

"You're not really soldiers of the Crown, are you?" David remarked, feeling a chill run down his spine.

Instead of replying, the captain silently nodded to one of his guards. In response, the soldier walked behind David and struck him soundly on the back with his baton.

"I'll ask the questions here," the captain said in an authoritative tone as David slumped over the table, his body racked with pain.

"I will only ask you one more time," the captain threatened after waiting for David's pain to subside. "Where is the Lyricor?"

David felt fear stabbing through his abdomen like a knife blade as he stared into the captain's eyes. There was no doubt in his mind that the soldier would kill him if he didn't comply.

"Please let me explain," he responded in a shaky voice. "I was brought here last month by some strangers. They stole the Lyricor from me. I don't know who they are, or what they did with it."

"That's not good enough!" the captain shouted. "I'm tired of your evasions." He turned to one of the soldiers and said in a commanding tone, "Hold his right hand down on the table," As the soldier complied, the captain unsheathed his military knife and brought the blade down hard on David's little finger, completely separating it from his hand.

David screamed in agony as blood spurted out of the stub where his finger used to be. Then he slowly stood up on wobbly knees, tore off his shirt, and wrapped it around his left hand.

Suddenly, the captain's cell phone rang. David was in too much pain to comprehend the conversation. A minute later, the captain put the phone away, stood from the table, and frowned. "I must take my leave." Then he broke into a round of laughter. "I hope you don't mind if I keep your finger. It will be a prized memento." He burst into another round of mocking laughter, then motioned to his soldiers. They all left the room, closing and locking the door behind them.

Drained by the ordeal, David fell back into the chair and waited for his strength to return, having no will to escape. A few minutes later, still dazed by the pain, he managed to unwrap the shirt surrounding his left hand. When he inspected the wound, he was surprised to find that it had closed and was no longer bleeding. He smiled, realizing that his body was benefiting from the effects of the philosopher's stone.

David remained seated, waiting for his energy to return, wondering how the soldiers had known about the Lyricor. The fact that they hadn't known it had been stolen was proof that the soldiers weren't working for Revic. If they were Alexander's men, it followed that they had learned about the farmhouse from the king's security staff. But why hadn't they taken him to the palace?

Suddenly, the lights dimmed. David glanced up at the ceiling and noticed, to his chagrin, that a thick, black cloud had invaded the room, appearing out of nowhere. Terror surged through him as it slowly began to descend, eventually cutting off most of the light and casting the room in relative darkness. As the cloud swirled around him, his chair slowly lifted up off the floor, elevated by a supernatural force. He tried to jump down, but his body was paralyzed by the malevolent power.

The chair continued to rise slowly until it was about four feet off the floor. Then it began to spin. The chair continued to rotate in midair, its velocity increasing with every turn.

David suddenly felt a strong presence invade his brain, probing his thoughts and memory, sounding like a million voices speaking simultaneously. The voices quickly strengthened in intensity, growing into a tumultuous thunder inside his head. As he cried out in fear and pain, the voices abruptly ceased and the chair fell to the ground with a crash.

David slowly picked himself up off the floor and shook his head, trying to clear it. Although he had a splitting headache, the paralysis had vanished, along with the voices. A feeling of relief washed over him as he glanced around the room, which was now brightly lit.

Sven inhaled sharply as he walked into the security room of Alexander Palace. Three guards were lying on the floor in pools of their own blood. Upon closer inspection, Sven determined that their throats had been slit and that they were all dead. One of them was the security chief. He carefully walked over to the console, avoiding the blood, and replayed the video records. Unfortunately, all of the cameras had been taken offline—only background noise and snow appeared on the televisions.

"Alex," he said, as the prince entered the room. "Thanks for apprising me of the situation. I don't know what to say. I'm so sorry about your father."

"Thanks, buddy," Alexander responded with a feigned grimace.

"Unfortunately, there's no time for grieving. We must find David. Have you checked the security feeds?"

"I have. Unfortunately, there's no record of what happened. The cameras were taken offline, and the king's security detail are all dead." Sven frowned and shook his head

"I can't believe David would do something like this."

"When I came to see Father this morning, I saw David run out of the reception room," Alexander said.

"The prints on the murder weapon have been analyzed, and they're a perfect match."

The prince patted Sven on the shoulder and gave him a sympathetic look. "I know you two were pretty close, after working together on the oil project and everything. Do you know where he might have gone?"

Sven paused in thought for a moment. "I remember now," he said, snapping his fingers.

"I told him that if he ever needed sanctuary, he could use the bakery."

"What bakery, Sven?" Alex asked eagerly.

"Seibel's. He's probably on his way there now."

David tried to kick open the heavy metal door of the interrogation room, but it didn't budge. In a fit of anger, he turned to the wall on his right and kicked a hole in the drywall. His foot hit something hard on the other side. He knelt down and peered into the jagged hole, and there was just enough light to see that behind the drywall was cinder block. Realizing that there was no way out and that he would have to wait for someone to free him, he sat back down and fell into a fitful sleep.

David was awakened by the sound of a lock being unlatched. He opened his eyes and beheld two soldiers walking toward him through the open doorway. He recognized them from the day before. One of them handcuffed him. "Move!" he said in a commanding tone.

David slowly stood up and stretched the stiffness out of his limbs, then the soldiers led him out of the farmhouse and into the same supply truck he had ridden in the day before. After about an hour's journey, the truck stopped. The soldiers removed David's handcuffs and he exited the vehicle, finding to his surprise that they had returned him to the bakery.

As David entered the store, he noted the clerk's frightened expression. "The police have been here looking for you," the young man said in a shaky voice. "Come with me." The clerk hurriedly led him through the stockroom and out the back door.

He pointed at the bakery truck parked next to the building. "Get in the back," he said. "Quickly!" The man slid open the back door, and David stepped inside. He found a space between some cardboard boxes and sat down on the floor. A moment later, the engine started and the truck began moving.

"Leave us!" King Alexander the Third commanded the prison guards who had escorted him to Vojislav Revic's cell. Alexander paused for a moment, then said in an authoritative tone, "Kneel to your newly crowned king, prisoner!"

"Your Royal Highness," Revic responded as he knelt down on the cement floor.

"Rise," King Alexander said. "Now tell me about David Sholfield," he continued in a formal tone as Revic rose to his feet. "I understand you had dealings with him back in the States."

"Yes, Your Majesty. He's a strange one. I know that your father put his company in charge of the oil sands project. By the way, congratulations on your coronation."

"Let's get to the point, Revic," the newly crowned king said brusquely. "As you have no doubt heard, the man healed me of lung cancer. The strange thing is how he did it," Alexander continued, unbuttoning his shirt. "He put his hands on my chest and a week later cancer completely vanished."

He bared his chest for Revic to observe. "The scar from the thoracotomy even disappeared. What do you make of that?"

"If I can be frank, Your Highness, I believe you have read a certain piece of literature written by a man named Thomas Harrison?"

Alexander grinned. "Very good, Revic. When you were arrested, I had my men search your belongings with orders to bring me anything that might be of interest. They brought me Harrison's memoirs along with another book filled with strange symbols."

"Do you think that David found the philosopher's stone, Your Highness?" Revic asked with a sly expression.

"You get right to the point, don't you," the new king responded with a laugh. "You have obviously spent way too much time in the States. To answer your question, that would certainly explain his extraordinary healing powers."

"So why are you here if you don't mind me asking, Your Highness?"

"I want you to tell me what you know about the good doctor. Perhaps you can shed some light on how he was able to find the philosopher's stone."

"David obviously needed the Lyricor," Revic replied. "My guess is that someone helped him, perhaps a holy man. David is not a practitioner of the black arts—not by any means."

"But you are," the king said with a piercing stare. "The other book is a spell-casting book, isn't it?"

"Yes. It's called the Numericon—the witches' book of shadows. It comes in very handy, believe me. I can teach you the fine art of sorcery if you like."

"Are you attempting to give me a reason for your release?"

"I can dramatically increase your personal power, Your Highness. With my sorcery, you will become exceedingly influential in your dealings at court. Your opponents will be unable to resist your will."

"I have already achieved that, Revic. I've replaced all the ministers in the House of Lords with men who are completely loyal. I have the favor of the Royal Army as well. Even the prime minister is afraid to oppose me."

Revic's eyes gleamed as he paused for a moment. "I have the Lyricor."

Alexander inhaled sharply. "What did you say?"

"It was my men who kidnapped Sholfield," Revic replied with a hearty laugh. "He was carrying the stone on his person—a very stupid move on his part. It was a simple matter to take it from him."

"I heard about the incident," Alexander said with a smirk. "The official line is that he was mugged. So that was you."

"Yes, it was," the former duke replied with a haughty expression. "If you release me, I will turn the Lyricor over to you."

"And of course, I will need your skills to use it properly. Is that what you're offering in exchange?"

"Yes, Your Highness. I wish to have my lands and title restored, as well as the office of finance minister. In return, I will teach you the art of necromancy, not only to enhance your already formidable powers of persuasion but also to access the Lyricor."

"Agreed," Alexander said, smiling in satisfaction. "When I obtain the Lyricor from David, I will use it to find the philosopher's stone. Then I will use the stone's great power to overthrow the other European countries and will find a united world order over which I will reign as supreme leader. However, the matter of your embezzlement charges remains. That is somewhat problematic. Any ideas?"

"My guess is that you were the one who framed me," Revic replied with a conspiratorial grin, "ensuring that I would never succeed you to the throne in case I married your sister. Now that you are the king, I imagine you can undo your own work. Am I correct, Your Highness?"

Alexander laughed and shook his head. "No, Revic, that was not my doing. You must certainly have a lot of enemies."

"That's very strange," Revic responded with a perplexed expression. He shrugged. "What about Sholfield's mayor? It would be a simple matter to plant some incriminating evidence on him, yes?"

"A brilliant tactic, Revic! Thanks to the testimony of your thugs, the mayor's already the main suspect in Sholfield's mugging. I'll have some phony documents drawn up to implicate him in the embezzlement scheme as well. I can have the good mayor arrested in a matter of hours."

Alexander broke into a round of enthusiastic laughter. "I'll have you exonerated next week," he said after regaining his composure. "Your title and office will be fully restored. Then we can begin my instruction in the black arts."

"It will be my pleasure, Your Highness."

"By the way, Revic, I know where Sholfield is hiding."

"Really! How interesting. Why haven't you had him arrested?"

"I want him available when we access the philosopher's stone, just in case we need his help. He's much easier to get to in his current location.

If he were locked up in prison and then released on some trumped-up excuse, there would be too much backlash from the press, as well as from the imbecilic prime minister."

"Brilliant thinking, Your Majesty."

# Chapter Nineteen

David climbed out of the bakery truck and stretched his legs. Directly in front of him stood a small farmhouse—a one-story red-brick cottage with a sloping roof. He knocked on the door but nobody answered. "The farmer's probably in the cornfield," the driver said. "Good luck." Then, with a wave and a smile, he turned the truck around and drove away.

David spotted the cornfield, which was about a half-mile away from the cottage. After walking past a large pasture filled with sheep—there were at least twenty of them—he arrived. "Is anyone here?" he shouted into the wall of cornstalks. A moment later, he heard the sound of a tractor approaching. After it appeared out of the field a few rows down, the driver stopped the tractor, stepped down to the ground, and waited as David approached. The farmer was elderly—probably in his early seventies, David surmised. He was bald and plain-featured, dressed in thick denim overalls with a plaid shirt underneath, rolled up at the sleeves.

"I asked for a hired hand and they send me a city slicker," the man remarked with a frown.

David couldn't tell whether the farmer was joking. He smiled and extended his hand. "I'm David. David Sholfield. Good to meet you, sir."

The man didn't return David's smile. "I'm Ladislas Balic," he said brusquely, ignoring David's outstretched hand. "This is my farm."

There was an awkward silence as the man gave him a penetrating stare. "It's time to get to work, boy," the man said in a thick Yugoslavian accent. David could barely understand him.

"What do you want me to do?" David asked hesitatingly. The man was certainly not making him feel welcome.

"Don't you know anything, boy?" the man asked in an irritated tone. He strode back to the tractor, produced a shovel and a bucket, and dropped them onto the ground. "You know how to weed, don't you?"

"I think I can manage," David replied. As he picked up the bucket and shovel, the farmer hopped back onto his tractor and drove away. David noted the farmer's agility. Apparently, the years of physical labor had kept him very fit.

David sweated copiously as he slowly worked his way down the row, shoveling out the weeds as he went. By the time he reached the end of the row, the bucket was almost full and felt heavy. He sat down and rested for several minutes, then picked up an empty bucket and proceeded to the next row.

Several hours later, the farmer appeared on his tractor. "Time for supper, boy," he said brusquely. By the time David reached the farmhouse, he could barely walk. His legs felt as if they were made of lead, and his arms ached from the hard work.

As David walked to the front door, Ladislas motioned to the pump house next to the cottage. "Get in there and wash up, boy. My wife doesn't appreciate no stinkin' city slicker sittin' at the dinner table."

David looked down and noticed, to his dismay, that his dress shirt was drenched in sweat, his trousers caked with mud.

"There are some clean overalls in there," the farmer said. "Be sure you put them on before you come in."

David walked into the small building, noting the granite basin filled with water. A cup was tied to a bracket on the wall next to it. He untied the cup, filled it, and thirstily gulped down the cool, clean water. He repeated the process several times, quenching his thirst. Then he changed into the shirt and overalls that were hanging from a hook on the opposite wall.

David returned to the cottage, opened the front door, and walked into a small green-carpeted living room. The furniture looked handmade, except for the matching dark-brown leather sofa and recliner. David surmised that, like the rest of the farm, the antiques had been handed down from father to son. A widescreen television dominated one of the beige-colored walls. The adjacent one had a built-in fireplace. The entrance to the kitchen and dining room was just to his right.

When David entered, Ladislas beckoned him to sit at the sturdy wooden dinner table. "Sit down, boy, and have a real meal." He motioned toward the woman preparing the food in the kitchen. "My wife, Natasa, will join us in a minute."

David tried not to stare. Young, blonde, and buxom, Natasa looked more like a model than a farmer's wife. Her breasts jutted upward against her form-fitting, button-down shirt, which was open at the chest, exposing her cleavage. Her jeans were also tight-fitting, highlighting the curves of her hips, thighs, and buttocks. She glanced at him briefly, then she looked back at the stove. "I'm glad you had a safe trip, David," she said demurely. She glanced at her husband, who glowered at her and said, "Hurry up with the food. I'm starving."

A few minutes later, she completed her preparations and served the food. David's mouth watered as he smelled the fresh ham, chicken, and corn. Freshly baked muffins and a salad of fresh garden vegetables completed the course.

Natasa served Ladislas first, and the farmer passed each serving bowl to David after taking his portion. Natasa served herself last.

Without waiting for the others, the farmer dug in with gusto, rapidly shoveling heaping forkfuls of food into his mouth. "I'll bet you never ate like this back in the city," the farmer remarked as David began eating. "Not even at the king's palace, did you, boy?"

"It's very good, sir," David replied. He glanced at Natasa and observed that she barely touched the scanty portion of food on her plate. She kept her head lowered, staring downward in silence.

"This is a cottage farm," Ladislas continued. "I own forty-five acres of land. Ten acres of forest where I get my fuel, two acres of vegetable gardens and orchards, and five acres of woodland around the house and barn. Like to keep it that way. The trees act as a natural windbreak, protecting the barn in the winter months—takes less fuel to heat the house. Another twelve acres of open land are divided by fences into plots of permanent pasture and grain crops. I'm using four of them as cornfields. There's a pond in one of the plots. Helps me avoid the extra work of hauling water. The animals go there and drink their fill.

"There's another sixteen acres of woodland in the back of the property where I harvest mushrooms, nuts, wild berries, and maple syrup. I raise honeybees to pollinate the crops and provide honey. I also raise sheep—saves me the trouble of mowing the pasture. Then there's the cow, the pigs, and the chickens."

As David attempted to respond, the farmer held up his hand. "Here's your daily chores, boy: Feed and water the two hogs and thirty chickens. Milk the cow. Muck out the stalls and provide plenty of fresh hay and straw for bedding. After that, you will help me anyway I see fit. Any questions?"

David's mind was reeling from the sudden and drastic changes in his life, abruptly thrust upon him by no choice of his own. "No, sir. I can't think of anything at the moment," he muttered.

"All right. Now come with me," he said, deftly cleaning his plate. He stood from the table and left the kitchen without saying a word to his wife.

David followed Ladislas out to the barn where the farmer showed him how to milk the cow. "You milk her every morning and night," the farmer said after completing his demonstration. "Now follow me. I'll show you your sleeping quarters."

David followed the farmer back into the cottage, through the kitchen, and down the stairs. The basement was sectioned off by two dark-green walls forming a hallway lit by a solitary light bulb dangling from a wire hanging from the ceiling. There were two doorways—one on each side.

David walked through the right doorway, discerning in the half-light that it was a utility room. Several boxes were stacked on the concrete floor. Mounted on the walls were rows of shelves filled with canned goods. Additionally, he saw a refrigerator, a large freezer, and a washer and dryer.

"Your room is on the left, boy," the farmer said gruffly. "I'll be down to wake you in the morning." Then he turned away and walked upstairs.

David returned to the hallway and walked through the left doorway. There was a switch on the right, and when he flipped it, a ceiling light came on. The tiny room was modestly furnished with a double bed, a nightstand, a chair, and a small bookcase. The flat-white plasterboard walls were bare, except for a few clothes hanging on a clothes rack mounted on the wall to the left of the doorway. Another doorway at the opposite end led to a tiny bathroom containing a shower, a sink, and a toilet. He noted that there were no doors in any of the rooms.

After retrieving his clothes from the pump house, David returned to the utility room and found a box of detergent lying on a shelf next to the washer. He filled the soap container, then undressed, threw his clothes inside, and started the wash cycle. As the machine whirred, he returned to the bedroom and lay down on top of the covers, exhausted from his labors in the cornfield.

Thoughts began wandering through his mind, pre-empting much-needed sleep. The farm was a drastic change from the palace, but at least he was safe for the time being. He wondered why the farmer had treated him so unkindly. Perhaps the man was disappointed at not having an experienced farmhand to rely on.

Suddenly the image of Natasa thrust itself into his mind. What a strange contrast she was from the farmer. He was old and grizzled, while she was young and beautiful. Something didn't add up.

He abruptly became aware of an itching sensation on his left hand. He looked at it and discovered that his little finger had partially grown back—almost to the knuckle. He smiled. The regenerative power of the philosopher's stone was working its magic.

David's sense of well-being and serenity was quickly replaced by an overwhelming wave of sadness as thoughts of his lovely fiancée entered his mind. He had allowed himself to fall in love once again, only to have the object of his affection torn from him.

Stephania was not to blame, though. He wondered what the conniving Prince Alexander—who was probably king by now—had done with her. He realized that no matter what happened, she would always be in his heart, her cherished memory forever kept alive by his love. As the weight of the past few days' events fell upon him with a crushing blow, he began crying, blocking the sounds with his pillow, eventually falling into an exhausted sleep.

Hours later, David was awakened by a loud, clanging noise. He groaned, opened his bleary eyes, and beheld Ladislas standing in the doorway, banging on a cowbell with a ball-peen hammer. "Okay, okay, I'm awake," David said, shielding his eyes from the glaring light.

"Hurry up, boy," the farmer said with a scowl. "Breakfast's almost ready."

Fifteen minutes later, still fatigued by the hard labor of the day before, David dragged himself up the stairs and entered the kitchen. His mouth began watering as he smelled the freshly cooked bacon. "What time is it?"

he asked the farmer, who was already sitting at the table, wolfing down hefty portions of bacon, eggs, and potatoes.

"It's first light, boy, and you got chores to do."

David sat down and glanced at Natasa, who was also sitting at the table and nibbling at her breakfast. She remained silent, not acknowledging his presence, her gaze firmly focused on her plate. David shrugged and ate heartily. He knew he would need all the energy he could muster to perform his chores that morning.

After breakfast, David went straight to the barn and milked the cow, mimicking the actions the farmer had shown him the night before. After leading it out to pasture, he met the farmer at the chicken coop—a simple ten-by-twenty-foot structure made of wooden planks. The chickens had already left the coop, having begun their daily foraging.

As the men entered, Ladislas pointed to the three nests along the left wall. "The roof keeps it dark to discourage egg-eating," the farmer explained. "The nests need clean straw regularly. The chickens get fresh water daily. You pour the water into those jugs over there." He pointed to several plastic containers by the door. "The hens get two feet of either sawdust or straw—whatever's available—for bedding. You feed them by pouring wheat into their trough. The eggs should never be washed. Always wear the same clothes when you come in, otherwise, they won't recognize you. Any questions?"

David thought for a moment, though it all seemed simple enough. "Just one. Where do I get the wheat?"

"From the granary," the farmer replied with a frown. "It's next to the pigsty. C'mon. I'll show ya."

The granary was a small building in the center of the barnyard, consisting of five-grain bins, each about ten feet square and ten feet in height. An inner aisle gave access to all five bins. The walls were constructed from wooden planks, and the floor was raised to the same level as the bed of the farmer's pickup truck, allowing easy transfer of the heavy grain sacks.

The farmer explained that dogs and cats lived under the crawlspace beneath, discouraging rats and mice from breeding there. Shuttered windows were built into the wall of each bin, allowing the grain to be shoveled in from wagons. The inner aisle doors were made of individual boards that could be added or removed as grain levels rose at harvest and fell as the grain was used. David thought it was a very efficient setup.

The farmer pointed to the wheat bin. "Grab a bucketful. I'm going to show you how to care for the pigs and chickens, boy."

Next, the farmer led David to the pigpen—a small wooden enclosure raised about two feet off the ground. "The front two-thirds have a slatted floor, allowing most of the manure to drop through," the farmer explained. "The other third is roofed and bedded with straw. Your job is to replace the bedding, feed, and water the pigs, and clean out the front of the pen every three or four days. You shovel the remaining manure into sacks you get from the barn. Any questions?"

"What do I feed them?"

Ladislas threw back his head and laughed heartily. "Are you really that stupid, boy?" he asked, his face beet-red from his merriment. "They eat anything."

He pointed to the corncrib next to the pen. "Feed 'em some corn or wheat. By the way, don't ever faint when you're in the pen. The hogs will kill ya!"

David frowned as he watched the farmer climb onto his tractor and drive away, hoping that he could remember all the instructions. He didn't want to find out what would happen if he screwed up.

David was an hour into his chores when he noticed a dark-blue minivan pulling up to the cottage. His curiosity was aroused as he saw Natasa enter the van. He continued watching as it returned to the main road, eventually turning down a side road leading into the woods. He made a mental note to check it out later.

Two hours later, David's chores were complete. It was still morning. Thirsty from the exertion, he walked to the pump house and drank his fill. Then he sat down on the bench on the opposite wall and rested his aching body. His mouth began to water as he noticed the apples and the beef jerky sitting on one of the shelves. He eventually walked to the shelf and helped himself, then sat back down on the bench, feeling weary.

About fifteen minutes later, Ladislas arrived on his tractor. After gulping down nearly a gallon of water—using the same cup David drank from—the farmer wiped his mouth on the sleeve of his dirty overalls and grinned. "Time to do some more cultivatin', boy."

The next two hours passed by very slowly for David as he walked along with the cornrows, digging out the tough, fibrous weeds. By the time Ladislas returned, he was completely exhausted.

"Time for lunch, boy," the farmer said, chuckling, noting David's fatigue.

"Your city slickers don't know what real work is. Now we're going to see if you're man enough for the job."

David disdainfully watched the farmer ride off toward the cottage, thinking that it was easy for the old man to talk, driving around on that tractor of his all day.

"Alexander the Third, King of Slavania," the king's attendant said formally as the king stepped through the door of the palace meeting room.

The room was resplendent, bedecked with various pieces of silver and gold statuary. The furniture was eighteenth-century, handcrafted by expert artisans. A large painting of Alexander the Second hung in a gilt frame covering one of the red-silk, wallpapered walls. There were no windows. A large wrought-iron chandelier provided the lighting in addition to numerous ornately carved bronze sconces.

The king's two guests—Sven Boskovic and Vojislav Revic—stood and bowed as His Majesty was seated at the dining table by four pretty blonde women.

"Your Royal Highness," the two guests said in unison.

King Alexander smiled broadly. "Please be seated, gentlemen." He gestured to his female attendants. "Refreshments, please."

"A nice touch, sire," Revic remarked as the women hurried into the adjacent kitchen. "They have distinctly Scandinavian features."

Dressed in revealing, red and purple negligees, the young women looked more like high-class prostitutes than servants. "I must admit, sire—they certainly add to the decor," he added with a grin.

"So, you approve of my Swedish beauties," Alexander remarked with a mischievous grin. "Now, be a gentleman, Sven," he continued with a chuckle. "Remember that you're married to my sister."

As Sven began to reply, the king held up his hand. "I'm jesting with you, my good friend," he said, smiling benevolently. "Everything that is said and done in this room is strictly confidential. Feel free to give full voice to your desires."

Just then the women returned, bearing trays of food and drink, making no effort to hide their ample bosoms as they bent over the table, setting out the various dishes and beverages. The effect was very sybaritic.

After spending a half-hour exchanging pleasantries with his fellow aristocrats, the king cleared his throat for attention. "I asked you here this evening to receive your input on several ideas I've been considering. I want you both to be frank and honest in the expression of your opinions."

"Of course, sire," Sven replied.

The king clapped his hands, clearing the servants from the room.

"I want to hear from you first, Sven," the king said. "I'm interested in learning how my subjects feel now that I am their king."

"They recognize and respect your military service in the Bosnian War," Sven said. "For that reason, you possess the absolute loyalty of the army. However, you are holding Stephania in captivity. She is very popular, and her disappearance is causing quite a rift among the civilians, I'm afraid. Do you have a plan to deal with the fallout?"

"A very simple one, I assure you," Alexander replied with a sly grin. "I'll lower everyone's taxes. Our oil profits will provide the funding. Which brings me to the next important question: How is the oil sands project coming along?"

"It's not online yet," Sven replied. "I've replaced Sholfield Oil—as per your request—with a new company called Redoute Services. It's a Canadian outfit with the requisite expertise. They've been instrumental in bringing their own country's oil sands project to fruition."

"Good work, Sven. How much longer will it take to bring it online?"

"Well, at this point I can only guess. Production should commence in about six months. It will take several years to achieve full capacity."

"What you're saying is that we need to be patient. I believe that our current rigs on the Adriatic are still producing significant quantities?"

"Yes, they are," Sven said with a confident smile. "And you will be pleased to know that world oil prices are still rising. Our oil revenues are up over forty percent from last year."

"That's what I want to hear," the king said with a hearty laugh. "That will give me plenty of leverage with the prime minister."

The king turned to the duke. "Vojislav, now that you have been reinstated as finance minister, I want you to craft a bill with the sole purpose of lowering taxes as much as possible, complete with a detailed analysis showing how the cost will be offset by the higher oil revenues."

"Consider it done, sire," Revic replied with a grin. "Thank you for reinstating my title."

"A promise is a promise, my good duke," the king said. "And that brings me to the other business. In my generous and ongoing effort to improve our good citizens standard of living, I have decided to legalize gambling, drugs, and prostitution, using the lucrative revenue streams those enterprises will provide to build up our military forces."

Revic raised his glass. "Bravo, Your Highness. The citizens will certainly recognize and applaud your efforts to provide them with greater personal freedoms and national security."

The king laughed and raised his glass. "Yes, my good duke, I'm sure of it. A toast to my impending popularity among the good citizens of Slavania!"

He sipped his after-dinner brandy and turned to Sven. "What do you think of my plans, my friend?"

"It will certainly increase your popularity," the energy minister replied delicately. "You must be careful how you manage it, though. Both the prostitutes and the clients must be thoroughly screened for STDs, and there are several other issues that must be addressed—for example, drug and gambling addiction."

"That will pose no problem as long as everything is handled under strict governmental supervision," Revic remarked. "I suppose keeping the casinos and brothels all under the same roof would be the simplest way to manage everything."

"Yes, Duke Revic," the king responded enthusiastically. "All gambling operations, including the new casinos, will be completely nationalized. That way, we control everything and keep all of the profits. Just think of all the new jobs that will create!"

The threesome spent another hour discussing the details Then, at the king's command, the blonde women re-entered the room carrying trays of desserts. When they finished, instead of leaving per the usual custom, the servants remained in the room and began hand-feeding the men in a sensual manner—brushing their scantily clad bodies against the aristocrats while smiling seductively.

Several minutes later, also at the king's command, the women stepped onto the table and began a striptease, dancing to exotic Arabian music that emanated from speakers mounted in the ceiling. Several minutes later, the women had completely disrobed. They continued their provocative dancing, pushing their discarded clothing onto the floor with their feet while twisting and swaying their naked bodies to the pulsating music.

Sven coughed. "I'm sorry, sire," he said apologetically.

"As you know, I'm a married man. I think I should probably leave—if I have your permission?"

In response, Alexander laughed uproariously. "Now, Sven," he said after regaining his composure, "you have my permission to do anything you like. Don't worry about my sister. She will never know. As you are well aware, there is not one aristocrat from here to England who doesn't entertain various companions, consorts, and escorts from time to time—it's all perfectly acceptable. If you desire one of these gorgeous beauties, I'll send her to one of the guest rooms and you can spend the night with her. I'll tell Triska that I kept you up all night discussing business matters. It's really no big deal, my friend. Please stay and enjoy my hospitality."

Sven lifted his hands in the air with a sigh.

"If it pleases thee, my king."

David had just finished cleaning the pigsty when he heard the sound of a vehicle approaching. He turned toward the road, reading the sign on the side of the truck as it drove by. "That's odd," he mumbled as it disappeared into the woods. He wondered why the bakery truck had returned. Were they going to relocate him? He scanned his surroundings, looking for Ladislas. There was no sign of him. Out of curiosity, he decided to follow the truck's path down the road. It was time for a much-needed break anyway.

After about a quarter-mile, the road led David into the woods. He continued walking for another few minutes, then stopped about thirty yards short of a large clearing.

He stepped off the road into the woods and cautiously approached, using the trees and brush as camouflage, eventually stopping behind some large bushes near the clearing's edge.

He peered through the branches and saw a small cinder block building—approximately twenty feet wide by fifty feet long—standing in the middle of a quarter acre of cleared land. The building had no windows, just a grey metal fire door on the side facing the road.

Several men were loading boxes through the open doorway into the back of the bakery truck. Ladislas stood next to the truck, speaking in a low voice to another man dressed in a tailored suit and holding a clipboard. David inhaled sharply in recognition: It was the same thug who had stolen the Lyricor.

David remained behind the bushes and listened intently, trying to hear what they were saying, but they were speaking too softly.

After a few minutes, two other men wearing overalls walked out of the building and entered the truck. One of them climbed into the back while the other took the driver's seat. Then the well-dressed criminal smiled, clapped Ladislas on the back, and entered the cab on the passenger side.

David remained hidden until everyone left, then returned to the barnyard.

Ladislas was sitting in his pickup truck when David arrived. "Are you sick of farm work already, boy?" the man asked in a disrespectful tone. "Where've you been?"

"I was thirsty," David muttered.

"Time to get back to work. Got another job for ya." He motioned to the bed of the pickup truck. "Get in."

Apparently, the farmer had deemed him unworthy of riding in the cab, David thought as he climbed into the bed of the truck.

David's mind began to wander as they drove along the bumpy dirt road. It had been a little over two weeks since he had arrived on the farm. He glanced down at his body and smiled in satisfaction. It had responded quickly and favorably to the difficult physical labor, its development no doubt enhanced by the effects of the philosopher's stone making him even stronger and more muscular. If the farmer's goal was to wear him out, the man would be sorely disappointed.

"Come here, city slicker!" the farmer shouted out of the open window after parking the truck in a hayfield. "I mowed this hay three days ago with a sickle-bar mower," he continued as David approached. "Then, yesterday morning, I windrowed it using a side-delivery rake. Your job is to fork it all into the truck."

David quickly worked up a sweat, the hot sun beating mercilessly down upon him as he forked the hay into the truck bed. Even with his conditioning, the combination of heat and difficult labor began to sap his energy.

When the truck bed was full, they drove back to the barn. Since the bed was full of hay, the farmer allowed David to ride in the cab.

Upon arrival, the farmer stepped out of the truck and climbed into the hayloft.

"Okay, boy," he said after properly positioning himself. "Fork the hay up here, and I'll spread it around. That's my job. If it's not done properly, the barn will catch fire."

After several more truckloads, they returned to the farmhouse for lunch. Natasa served them with her usual detachment. As David ate, he speculated upon the purpose of the building in the woods and the role Natasa played in it. Perhaps it was a production facility of some kind.

When they finished eating, the farmer nonchalantly produced a plain white envelope from the pocket of his overalls and tossed it on the table in front of David. "By the way, this came for you today."

As David reached for the letter, Ladislas quickly snatched it away from him. "Not now, boy," he said with an uncompromising grin. "We got more work to do."

That night, after finishing his chores, David was finally allowed to take the letter to his room. Ladislas had kept it next to his plate throughout the entire meal, taunting him with it as they ate.

"My dear, sweet David," the letter began. "How I miss you. Please don't be concerned for my welfare. I am safe. If you haven't already heard, my brother has been made king. Because of your alleged involvement in my father's murder, I am also under suspicion and have been put under house arrest until the matter has been resolved. I wish to put your mind at ease concerning this. I am being treated well. The restrictions are few, but hard to bear. I cannot leave my palace rooms, and I can have no outside visitors.

"Likewise, after my brother was made king, he exonerated Vojislav Revic and restored his title as Duke of Horvat. Unfortunately, that means that you have lost yours, and since you are now a commoner, we cannot legally be married.

"Oh David, I miss you so. I am very concerned about your welfare. Sven visited me several days ago and said you are safe. I hope you are well. I don't believe that you murdered my father. You are a good man, and I know you never could have done this terrible thing. I haven't given up hope for us, David, and I pray that you haven't either. When all of this is resolved, as I am sure it will be, you will regain your title and we will be together again.

"No matter what happens, I want you to know that no one can take your place, that there never will be another man in my life. I am yours forever. I look forward to the day when we are reunited and married as man and wife, to live out our remaining days in love and happiness.

"I don't know when I shall be able to contact you again. I bribed one of the guards to deliver this letter to Sven. He promised me that you would receive it. Have faith, my fair David. We will be together soon. With all my love, Steph."

David dropped the letter on the floor and wept for a while. Eventually, his tears dried as he realized that their situation could be infinitely worse. Both he and Stephania could have been arrested and thrown in jail, and then put on trial for the king's murder—he as the perpetrator, she as his accomplice. He shuddered to think of the outcome of being found guilty. But that had not come to pass. The king certainly knew that David was here. He wondered why Alexander had not sent for him.

Perhaps the king had learned of the Lyricor and wanted to keep tabs on David until he was ready to use it. He had probably already made some kind of a deal with Revic—restoring the man's dukedom in return for the promise of accessing the locating device, and ultimately, the philosopher's stone.

David then recalled the building hidden in the woods. What was Natasa's role there? And what was her involvement with the crook who had stolen the Lyricor? He would return at the next available opportunity.

David spent the entire next day performing the hot, backbreaking work of haymaking, leaving no time to sneak off into the woods.

Afterward, he returned to his room, exhausted from the difficult physical labor. To his surprise, there were several pairs of underwear and other much-needed clothing neatly stacked on the bed.

He smiled, noting the new books in the small bookcase. Natasa must have gone into town and bought the items for him. It was an unexpectedly thoughtful gesture. He wondered if Ladislas knew about it.

He walked to the bookcase, knelt down, and read the titles—works by John Updike, John Steinbeck, and Ernest Hemingway. David smiled wryly, wondering how a farm wife from Slavania could possibly be acquainted with classic American literature.

It was around nine o'clock the next morning. David had just finished cleaning the chicken coop when the minivan reappeared. This time, when the vehicle turned down the lane leading into the woods, he decided to follow it more closely.

David ran all the way there, not stopping until he reached the edge of the clearing, arriving in time to see six people climb out of the van and enter the building. They were all women. He was unable to discern anything about them from their dress or language. They all wore jeans and work shirts, and none of them spoke a word.

After waiting five minutes, David slowly walked to the fire door and tried the handle—but it was securely locked. He ran to the rear of the building, hoping to find something of interest.

About five yards away stood a large propane tank, a water collection tank, and a small shed. Like the building, the shed had no windows. He tried the door, but it, too, was locked. He pressed his ear against it and noted the thrumming sound coming from within. He surmised that it housed a power generator and used propane as its fuel source. He wondered why Ladislas had gone to all the trouble of constructing a building complete with its own power supply hidden away in the woods.

It was the end of July—harvest time for the wheat crop. David arose at dawn and after a quick breakfast, accompanied Ladislas to the field and began filling grain sacks from the hopper of the farmer's combine as it mowed down the wheat.

After filling a sufficient number of sacks, David loaded them into the bed of the pickup truck, drove to the granary, and unloaded them into the wheat bin. Then he returned to the field for another load.

David was grateful when the day finally ended. Although considerably more fit than a couple of weeks ago, his arms felt heavy from the hard work, and his mouth was parched, his thirst exacerbated by the hot July sun that had relentlessly beat down upon him all afternoon.

After supper, he lay in his bed, attempting to read himself to sleep as he had done for the past two weeks. He had finished the Hemingway novels and had begun *Rabbit, Run*, but he didn't feel like reading tonight. His melancholia had resurfaced.

As he put the book on the nightstand, the full weight of his concern for Stephania's well-being and the harsh, new reality of his life on the farm bore down upon him, threatening to flatten him like a metal can caught in the unforgiving jaws of a garbage compactor.

In an attempt to find relief, David turned his thoughts away from Stephania and began pondering the mystery of the building in the woods. He had learned nothing new from his several visits, and Natasa's role remained a mystery.

Natasa herself was a mystery. He wondered why she had married the old farmer—perhaps out of necessity or security. He glanced at his little finger and smiled, his despondency lifting a little. It had regenerated past the knuckle. At its present rate of growth, it would be completely healed in a few short weeks.

It was early Saturday morning, and David had just finished milking the cow. As he stepped out of the barn, he noticed Natasa standing by the door. "Hi," he said in a cordial tone, masking his surprise. "What brings you here this morning?"

"Lad went into town," Natasa replied, glancing furtively toward the farmhouse. "Let's talk," she said with a serious expression.

It was the first time she had spoken since his arrival. Her English was surprisingly good, with just a hint of an accent.

David followed her into the barn, overwhelmed by curiosity. "Where did you learn about Updike and Hemingway?" he asked. He walked to the nearest supporting pole and leaned against it, awaiting her reply.

She laughed. "So, you don't think a simple farmer's wife should know about things like that, eh David?"

"I don't know, Natasa," he replied. "Should you?" His curiosity mounted as he gazed at the beautiful woman. Nothing about her seemed commonplace or ordinary. She exhibited a worldly, educated demeanor, a far cry from the innocence one would expect of a country naïf.

Natasa frowned. "Perhaps it's time to be frank with you, David," she said in a serious tone. "I'm not really Lad's wife."

"Why doesn't that surprise me?" David responded with a wry smile. "That's the first thing I've heard that actually makes sense around here. So, what are you doing with the old man, if you don't mind my asking?"

"We became partners for the sake of convenience," she replied.

"You're losing me," David said.

"We're business partners," Natasa explained. "Several years ago, I developed a gambling addiction and got into a lot of debt. I needed a way to make enough money to satisfy my creditors. I'm a chemist by trade, and my uncle owns a farm nearby.

"He introduced me to Lad and we made a deal: Lad would provide the means to manufacture methamphetamine, and I would use my knowledge of chemistry to produce it. I'm using my share of the profits to pay off my gambling debts."

David felt a surge of disappointment as he made the connection. She was a criminal, supplying illegal drugs to the Slavanian mob. "So, the building in the woods is a meth lab."

"Please don't judge me too harshly, David," Natasa said, noting his look of disdain. "The people I'm indebted to are very nasty characters. If I hadn't found a way to pay them back, they would have killed my family. What would you have done in my position?"

"I think I understand," David replied, his animosity lifting as he began to grasp her situation. "You were boxed into a corner and you did what was necessary to save your family. I'm sorry to have judged you so rashly."

"I brought this upon myself," she said.

"The man with the clipboard," David said. "His boss is the one you owe the money to, correct?"

"How did you know?" Natasa asked with a look of surprise.

"Unfortunately, I had a run-in with the same bastard a couple of months ago."

"You're lucky to be alive," she said.

"It's no big deal," he responded with a shrug. "He got what he wanted."

"We have to keep up appearances, you understand," Natasa said. "We hide our activities from the townspeople by keeping the farm running, even though Lad doesn't need the income anymore. That's why he needed a farmhand."

She moved close to David and surprised him by running her hands through his hair. "Lad's not my husband, David. We sleep in separate bedrooms. We're nothing more than business partners."

"You could have fooled me," David said.

A sudden surge of passion erupted within him, threatening to gush outward like lava from an exploding volcano as he stared at Natasa's full, red lips. It had been a while since he had made love to a woman, and Natasa was very attractive.

"Ladislas seems jealous," David continued, attempting to sort through a maze of conflicting emotions. He knew it was wrong to make love to Natasa. He was still very much in love with Stephania. It was tempting, though. No one would ever know.

As Natasa pressed her body against his, David looked down and caught a glimpse of her full, round breasts, visible through the open neck of her blouse.

"Make love to me, David," she said in a husky tone. "Make love to me right now. I can't wait any longer."

Just as she began unbuttoning her blouse, Ladislas charged into the barn. "I knew I couldn't trust you, boy!" he shouted, his face distorted with jealous rage. He picked up a pitchfork from against the wall and brandished it at David in a threatening manner.

As Natasa stepped away, the farmer pressed the pitchfork firmly against David's chest. "Now sit down against that pole over there," he said in a firm tone.

After David complied, the farmer ordered Natasa to tie David to the pole with a thick chain that was dangling from an adjacent pole.

When she had finished wrapping it tightly around David's waist, the farmer produced a padlock from one of his toolboxes and locked the ends of the chain together. "That'll keep ya quiet until I figure out what to do with ya," he said with a satisfied expression.

David struggled against the chain, attempting to break free, but it was too thick, even with his enhanced strength. "Look, Ladislas. I didn't mean any harm to your wife," he said apologetically. "Just unlock the chain and I'll be on my way—okay, partner?"

In response, Ladislas grasped Natasa firmly by the arm and led her out of the barn.

# CHAPTER TWENTY

David apprehensively peered into the darkness as he heard the sound of approaching footsteps. He breathed out a sigh of relief as a flashlight switched on. "What's going on?" he asked in a concerned tone.

"Be quiet, okay?" Natasa whispered with a grin. "Lad's asleep. I snuck into his room and stole his keys. "I'm getting you out of here."

Natasa unlocked the padlock and waited for a few moments as David shook the stiffness out of his limbs. Then they left the barn and ran to the farmer's pickup truck parked just outside. They entered quietly without closing the doors. Natasa switched on the ignition, put it into neutral, and let it creep slowly down the road. After reaching a safe distance from the cottage, they closed the doors, put the truck into drive, and gunned the engine.

"Thank you, Natasa," David said gratefully as they sped off. "May I ask where you're taking me?"

"My uncle owns a cabin not far from here," she replied breathlessly. "He never uses it. No one else knows about it. You'll be safe there."

"Why are you helping me?"

"For one thing, I don't believe you murdered the king."

"So, you know who I am."

"Of course," she said with a smile. "Your picture is in all the newscasts."

"And the other thing?"

She gave him a naughty look. "I think you're sexy. Unfortunately, you can't stay at the farm anymore." She pouted. "Such a waste."

"I'm flattered," David said with a chuckle. "You're taking a big risk helping me, though," he said, his expression turning serious. "What's Ladislas going to do when he finds out that you helped me escape?"

"Nothing. I'm his cash cow, remember? Believe me, he's not going to throw away ten thousand dollars a month. Besides, the last thing he wants is to piss off the boss man."

"So, what's the situation at your uncle's cabin?"

"That's something I can't help you with. You'll be on your own. You'll be safe, though."

"That's good to hear," David said. "I'm sure I'll figure something out."

"You have a very positive attitude considering the situation you're in," Natasa said, giving him an inquisitive stare. "What aren't you telling me?"

"It's just my nature," David said. "My father taught me to always look on the bright side." He suddenly felt an emotional distance from her, a distance from every other human being on the planet. He could never reveal the secret of the philosopher's stone to anyone.

They remained silent for another twenty minutes, each lost in their own thoughts. Then Natasa made a right turn onto a dirt road leading into a forest. After another five minutes, she pulled over and stopped the car in front of a locked gate. "Here we are," she said.

Natasa switched on the inside light, reached into her handbag, and handed David a wad of money. "Here's a couple thousand, American," she said. "That should buy you some supplies. When you go into town, wear a disguise and tell the store owner you're my hired hand. There's also a suitcase in the backseat with a flashlight and some clothing. The key to the cabin is under the mat by the front door."

"I'm grateful for your help," David said in an appreciative tone, stuffing the bills into the back pocket of his jeans. "I hope I can repay you someday."

"Just keep yourself safe," Natasa said with a wistful smile. "I'm going to miss you, David," she said, exiting the car. After she unlocked the gate and handed him the key, she abruptly threw her arms around him and kissed him.

David walked for five minutes along the unpaved driveway before reaching the cabin, which was in the middle of a clearing. It was too dark to see what kind of shape it was in. He reached under the mat and found the key, and after fumbling with the lock for a few moments, finally managed to open the door.

He entered cautiously, probing the darkness with his flashlight. The single-room interior was scantily furnished with a bed, a table, two chairs, a full-length mirror, and a fireplace. He took some blankets out of the suitcase, lay down on the bed, and drifted into an uneasy sleep.

David awoke the next morning feeling disoriented. He arose from the bed and inspected the interior of the cabin in the dim illumination provided by the filtered sunlight streaming in through the dirty, solitary window. The linens had holes in them and were filthy, as were the mattress and the box spring. He was relieved to find that the antique frame was made of cast iron and would hold his weight.

He continued to scan the interior, attempting to get his bearings. The walls and ceiling were made of dark, wooden planks, the seams sealed with plaster, yellowed from years of neglect. The floor was also made from planks. They creaked when he walked on them.

After a closer inspection, David learned that there was no electricity, gas, or plumbing. The place appeared to be an old hunter's cabin, unused for many years. However, there were two oil lamps—one on the table and one on the kitchen counter.

He rummaged through the upper cupboards but found no food. The place had been stripped bare. The drawers and lower cupboards contained only a few items: an old-style combination can and bottle opener, a kettle, a skillet, a frying pan, a dipper for drinking water, a bowl, two knives and forks, three plates, one cup, and one spoon. He found another key in one of the drawers, probably to the padlock on the front gate.

David noticed a trap door on the floor near the window. He opened it and walked down several wooden steps into a cellar. There was barely enough residual sunlight coming in through the opening to see. The plaster walls were cracked and mildewed. He found only a few items: a garden hoe, a few burlap sacks, a jug for fuel oil, which was about a quarter full, an empty molasses jug, a metal bucket, an ax, and another oil lamp.

David climbed back upstairs, went outside, and attempted to familiarize himself with the surroundings. The cabin faced east into the morning sun, which was already nearing its zenith. The structure was of small proportions, only fifteen feet wide by thirty feet long, with a peaked cottage roof and walls, which were likewise shingled. It looked to be at least fifty years old and was in a moderate state of disrepair.

The cabin sat on an acre of cleared land, surrounded by rolling woodlands. Blackberry bushes, goldenrod, a few shrub-oaks, a sand-cherry tree, and two sumacs dotted the front yard. He could hear the humming of bumblebees, foraging among the bright-red sumac berries. On the south side was an unkempt lawn, choked with weeds. On the opposite side was a field, also overgrown, terminating in a small stand of pines. The backyard sloped upward, merging into a grassy hill. A creek ran along its base.

David jumped over the creek, hiked to the top of the hill, and scanned the area, noting the bluish peaks of the mountains in the distance, thrusting themselves upward from the undulating, wooded terrain. It was a beautiful, tranquil scene.

He sat down on a tree stump—the only one with a smooth top—and took stock of his immediate situation. He had the necessary clothing and shelter, but his only sustenance consisted of a few jars of canned beans that Natasa had thrown into the suitcase. He felt confident using the creek for his water supply, knowing his enhanced immune system would readily overcome any toxins.

Feeling his belly rumble, David climbed back down the hillside and approached the blackberry bushes. He smiled in satisfaction. It was the first week of August, and the berries were still in season. He eventually quelled his hunger by spending a half-hour feasting on the juicy, ripe fruit.

In order to avoid recognition, David decided that he would have to wait until his beard had grown in before going into town. Realizing that the scanty meal would soon leave him hungry again and that the beans wouldn't last more than a day or two, he began hiking into the forest to forage for nuts and berries.

After returning to the cabin for a gunnysack, David walked around the hill and headed northward into the forest, walking in a rough straight line so he wouldn't lose his way.

He felt surprisingly happy as he zigzagged his way through the smaller trees. It was quite peaceful, the sunlight shining down through the leaves, randomly highlighting various bushes, plants, and portions of the forest floor. He noted the pleasant sounds the birds made as they sang their cheerful woodland melodies.

Upon hearing a sound of thunder rumbling in the distance, David ran all the way back to the cabin, reaching it just as the first raindrops began to fall. He watched with dismay, breathless from exertion, as streams of water began to spill onto the floor from the leaky roof. He retrieved the bucket from the cellar and positioned it under the leak, catching most of the water as it fell. Then he pulled up a chair and stared out the window for a couple of hours, watching the rain falling in sheets, listening to the cacophony of the thunder and wind, admiring the lightning as it lit up the darkness in sudden flashes, reminding him of the strobe lights in the disco clubs back in the early seventies.

Melancholia stole over David once again as thoughts of Angela entered his mind. She was his first true love, but fate had not allowed them to be together. He began weeping as the cold, harsh reality that he would never see her again burst upon him anew. There was no possibility for closure. Her murderer—the evil wretch Revic—was free, and in possession of the Lyricor as well.

How he missed his new love, Stephania. He feared for her safety. Had she been hurt, or even worse, killed by her power-crazed brother? What could David possibly do about it, living out his days in exile in a little cabin in a remote farming community? Things had never seemed more bleak and hopeless than at that moment.

The next morning, David ate the remaining blackberries and came to the grim realization that his food would run out within a day. Only one can of beans remained.

After washing the sweat and dirt off his body in the cold water of the creek, David began his second trek into the forest. He walked disconsolately along the almost indiscernible foot trail, wondering how long his body would hold up without food, wondering if the regenerative effects of the philosopher's stone would prevent starvation.

After an hour of diligent searching, David found another patch of blackberry bushes surrounding a small meadow. He hastily picked as many berries as he could reach comfortably, eating some and stashing the remainder in the gunnysack. Noting that the sack was only a quarter full, he resumed his search for another half-hour but found nothing edible.

David returned to the cabin and spent the rest of the day cleaning the place as best he could—hauling out the furniture, then using one of his shirts as a washrag to scrub the floor, the walls, and the counter with buckets of water from the creek.

While the interior was drying, he went outside and washed down all the furniture. Then he returned to the creek and washed the bed linens and his clothing. Unfortunately, because there was no soap, the linens remained stained.

The next day, David continued his exploration, delving farther into the forest, spending several hours searching for food, once again finding only a few blackberry bushes. It was late in the afternoon when he returned to the cabin. Feeling drowsy, he lay down on the bed and took a nap.

Upon awakening early that evening, David decided to make a fire, more for his amusement than out of necessity. The ax blade was still sharp, and after an hour or so of chopping tree limbs, he had enough wood. He carried stacks of branches into the cabin, made a fire, sat by the fireplace, and ate half of the remaining can of beans, eventually drifting off to sleep.

The next morning, David awakened and finished off the remaining beans. He considered going into town, but one look in the mirror dissuaded him. It would be at least another week until his beard had grown in enough to sufficiently camouflage his features.

After bathing in the creek, David decided to attempt the art of spearfishing. He found a sturdy branch and whittled the end to a sharp point with a kitchen knife. Then he waited by the bank, carefully watching for any fish that might swim by. A half-hour later, he was rewarded by a flurry of underwater movement as a fish drew near. Timing its speed, he jammed the stick down into the water at the precise moment. Unfortunately, the fish jerked to the side at the last instant, avoiding his jab and continuing on its way downstream.

"Claire, what a surprise!" Revic exclaimed as he sat in the formal dining room of Horvat Castle, feasting upon the fresh delicacies he had ordered for his supper that day.

The room was resplendent with silver-patterned, crimson-wallpapered walls hung with large, gilt-framed landscapes. Matching high-backed wooden chairs and several tables graced the walls and corners, including a mahogany library table cluttered with various candelabra, and a white serving table featuring an intricately carved gold design on the front. The floor was also made of mahogany. A white-painted, ornately carved fireplace adorned one wall. A large landscape was mounted above it, framed in layered strips of carved Cherrywood. The mauve sculpted ceiling was adorned with full entablature, likewise expertly crafted.

Twelve young women surrounded the duke at the large, round, black-glass dining table, all wearing light-blue silk robes. Unlike the women, the duke was dressed in a black tailored business suit with white pinstripes.

"Please dine with me," Duke Revic said to his former high priestess. Although his tone was soft, his expression held a commanding intensity. Then he dismissed his priestesses with a wave of his hand.

After the young women left the room, Claire sat down opposite the duke and gave him a penetrating stare, her upright posture and unflinching expression brooking no possibility of intimidation. "You look none the worse for wear, Revic. I commend you on your coven members as well. They all look very fetching in their tailored robes."

Revic returned Claire's gaze, noting how her skintight black jumpsuit accentuated her athletic figure. She carried a large, black leather handbag, slung over her left shoulder. "I see you've been keeping fit as well," he said. "By the way, how did you get through my security?"

"Surely you should know the answer to that, my good duke. It really wasn't very challenging for a witch of my capabilities."

"So why are you here, if I may ask?"

"You know why, Revic," Claire replied with a frown. "You've been causing a lot of problems for me lately."

"I certainly have no intention of doing that, my dear," Revic said with a condescending smile. "Please tell me what I can do to help."

"For starters, the Chicago police have been searching for me. They seem to think, for some odd reason, that my coven is responsible for Angela Stockman's murder."

"I had nothing to do with that," Revic responded, lifting his hands in a gesture of innocence. "The police questioned me months ago. If you don't already know, I was on a plane bound for England at the time. I couldn't possibly have done such a terrible thing."

"I'm not buying it, Revic. You could have easily hired someone to do the job."

The duke shook his head slowly and frowned. "I'm sorry, Claire, but there's nothing more I can do for you regarding the police investigation. And you needn't worry. If they had any real evidence, they would have stepped up their search and found you by now. But that's not the real reason for your visit, is it?"

Claire slowly stood from the table and pointed a finger at him. "Give me the Numericon," she said in a loud, authoritative tone. She continued to stare, a look of concentration furrowing her brow.

Revic laughed. "How very blunt, how very American of you, Claire. Unfortunately, your persuasion spell won't work on me. My protection spells are much too powerful. Besides, there's no need for any disagreement between us. I desire to make you an offer, an offer that will please you greatly. We can work together once again as high priest and priestess."

Claire smiled devilishly. "I don't know why, but I'm listening. This had better be good."

"I want you to consider becoming the high priestess of my coven here in Slavania. I've been counseling King Alexander, and we are having much success with our plans. In another month or so, we will control the entire gambling, prostitution, and drug markets in Slavania.

"I've obtained great influence over King Alexander," the duke continued.

"I've been teaching him the craft—at least parts of it. He hopes to learn my secrets and gain power, but he will always remain a neophyte—I'll never reveal anything of true importance. I have complete control of him, and he doesn't even realize it. He's nothing more than a puppet in my hands. At the proper time, I will kill him and marry Princess Stephania. Then I will be made King of Slavania, and together, using our knowledge of necromancy, you and I will extend our power well beyond Slavania, eventually controlling all of Europe. There is nothing standing in our way, my dear."

Claire laughed. "Thanks, but no thanks, Revic. I don't share your megalomania, and I don't trust the demons you would need to conjure to pull off something that big. The protection spells of the Numericon, although quite powerful, would eventually fail."

"I have a line on the philosopher's stone," Revic offered with a proud grin. "It's an incredibly powerful tool. Combined with our sorcery, we would become completely invincible."

"The philosopher's stone!" Claire exclaimed contemptuously. "That's just a myth. It doesn't exist."

She abruptly stood from the table, produced an athame from her handbag, and brandished it threateningly. "Enough of the small talk, Revic. Give me the Numericon, or I will kill you."

Revic smiled, stood from the table, and produced an athame from under his jacket. He pointed it at Claire and chuckled. "I'm afraid you are being very presumptuous, Claire."

The witch backed away from the table as he began walking around it. Then, while muttering an incantation, she pointed her athame at his and slowly lowered it to her side.

Revic attempted to hold his arm straight, but after struggling for a few seconds, it limply dropped to his side, overcome by the supernatural power of the high priestess's spell.

"I see you have become more proficient," he remarked with a grin.

"Drop the athame, Revic," she commanded, standing her ground as he continued to advance.

He maintained his slow walk, closing the gap between them, somehow managing to keep his grip on the athame. He chanted something under his breath and then lunged at her, grasping the handle of her athame and pushing it to the side with his free hand. Then he immediately thrust his athame upward, pushing the blade into her chest with great force.

She gasped as he twisted the blade, and she fell silently to the floor. Revic knelt down and checked her pulse then stood up.

"Good riddance," he remarked with a smirk.

David awoke with his belly rumbling, realizing that he was completely out of food. After having spent the greater part of the previous afternoon in an unsuccessful spearfishing attempt, he had journeyed into the forest in one last failed effort to find something edible. He considered going into town but decided against it. Instead, he would make one final search.

David walked into the forest for about fifteen minutes and then turned left, departing from his usual path. After marking the spot with a piece of cloth, he walked for another half-hour, zigzagging his way through trees and brush, attempting to maintain the same approximate direction.

Finding nothing of interest, he retraced his steps, returned to the marked spot, then continued onward in the opposite direction. After walking for another twenty minutes, he spotted a large clearing through the trees, roughly fifty feet to his left.

David smiled in satisfaction upon reaching the edge of the clearing. He had found a farm. Directly in front of him was a fenced-off pasture with a small flock of sheep grazing inside. A cornfield lay adjacent to it. He waited behind the tree line for a few minutes, watching and listening for any sign of the inhabitants.

Convinced that he was alone, he began walking alongside the fence, eventually finding a gate. His belly began rumbling as he spotted several chickens foraging among the sheep. He ran through the gate into the pasture and began chasing them. Thirty seconds later, he had one cornered. Just as it made an attempt to hop over the lowest fence railing, he grabbed it and snapped its neck.

He held it upside down for a minute, letting the blood drain. Then he slid it into one of the two gunnysacks he had brought along.

After making sure that he had not been spotted, David left the pasture and entered the cornfield. He immediately found several ripe ears, snapped them from their stalks, and dropped them into the second sack. He quickly repeated the process until he had collected twelve ears.

David returned to the cabin, deposited the sack of chicken into the cellar to keep the meat cool, and then ate a few ears of corn to assuage his hunger. Feeling somewhat refreshed, he walked back outside and spent several hours chopping, bundling, and carrying enough firewood back to the cabin to last the night.

The strenuous labor had made him hungry again, so he returned to the cellar, fetched the chicken, and butchered it as best he could. Then, after boiling the meat in a kettle hung over the fireplace, he finally sat down at the table and ate his fill. A few minutes later, he was sound asleep.

That night, David awakened with the unsettling feeling that someone or something was in the cabin. He looked around but saw nothing in the darkness. He found the flashlight under the bed, switched it on, and scanned the room. He breathed out a sigh of relief, finding himself alone. He walked to the window and peered outside.

It was a moonlit night, allowing him to view the dimly lit clearing. He gasped as he saw a woman standing at the edge of the trees. She was dressed in a long white robe and appeared to be holding something in her right hand. David sensed something familiar about her.

He ran outside and slowly approached the woman, keeping the flashlight beam aimed directly at her. Unfortunately, it was too weak and he was too far away to see clearly.

He walked closer, keeping the flashlight trained on her person. As he came near, she turned and ran into the woods. Just before she disappeared into the trees, he caught a glimpse of her long, black, wavy hair, glinting in the moonlight.

He followed her into the woods, quickly losing sight of her amongst the trees. He searched for a while longer but was forced to return when the flashlight stopped working.

David awakened the next morning with the all-too-familiar feeling of hunger. He recalled that there were six ears of corn and half a chicken remaining, all of which had to be eaten that day. The food would not stay fresh for long in the cellar, and soon, he would have to begin another search. When he thought about returning to the farm, he realized that it was only a temporary solution—eventually he would get caught.

He glanced into the mirror, noting that his beard was filling in nicely. Perhaps in another day or two, he could risk a trip into town.

David opened the suitcase, found the notepad and pen that Natasa had included, then sat down at the table to make a list of needed supplies. He decided that canned goods—specifically meat, vegetables, and fruit—would provide the safest and most convenient food supply. He would need some toiletries as well. Additionally, he would need shingles, plywood, nails, and a hammer in order to patch the roof. A small chainsaw would be a practical purchase because he would need a sufficient supply of wood for the long winter ahead. He would also need fuel to power it, and oil for the lamps. A spare flashlight and extra batteries would be a practical addition.

He estimated the cost of his initial order to be around five hundred dollars, with fifteen hundred remaining. He knew that the money would run out. In order to survive, he would need to become entirely self-reliant. Perhaps there was still time to plant a late crop of beans and corn. He added seeds to his list, as well as fishing tackle.

Feeling his hunger intensifying, David cooked half of the remaining chicken and corn, then sat down at the table and ate.

Feeling energized, he spent the remainder of the morning chopping wood. Then he walked through the overgrown backyard and climbed up the hill.

David spent the rest of the afternoon seated on a log, watching the birds, butterflies, and squirrels as they danced their pleasant, tranquil dance of pastoral existence. He watched contentedly as a pair of female deer slowly and silently made their way to the creek, and as several crows flew around the clearing. A half-hour later, a flock of wild pigeons scurried across the field to the safety of the evergreens.

It was the first time in a long time that he had actually rested. He felt strangely happy and at peace. He recalled Stephania's letter. Although she was living in captivity, her brother, as evil as he was, would not execute her. The citizens of Slavania would revolt. There was hope in the air, hope that he would be reunited with the princess someday and that all would be well.

David made an outdoor fire that evening and cooked the remaining corn and chicken. It was a warm, clear summer evening. He decided to remain outdoors and admire the nocturnal beauty of the forest as night settled in. He let the fire burn down, stretched out on a blanket, and watched the stars as they appeared in the darkening sky. The variety of night sounds, combined with the intermittent whispering of the breeze lightly blowing through the trees, soon made him drowsy. He decided to go inside.

David awoke hours later, and after several failed attempts at sleep, got out of bed and walked to the window. Once again, he saw the woman standing at the edge of the clearing, her white, ghostly figure visible in the moonlight. He tried the flashlight, but the batteries were dead. He decided to leave the cabin without it.

As he approached the mysterious woman, this time she remained in place and her features became visible. His whole body began to tremble as he recognized her. "Angie?" he asked softly. "Is that you? What are you doing here? I thought you were dead."

His limbs began trembling violently as terror gripped him in an all-consuming vice. What he was seeing was clearly impossible. It took all his strength to remain standing.

In the half-light, he discerned that her face held a serene expression and that she held a scroll of some kind in her right hand. Without making a reply, she slowly raised the scroll and began unrolling it with her left hand. There appeared to be some sort of design—perhaps an emblem—painted upon it.

She glanced behind her, then turned back to David and quickly rolled up the scroll with a frightened expression. She turned and ran away from him, staying alongside the tree line.

David remained where he was, his body paralyzed with shock and dread as several dark figures emerged from the trees and began pursuing her. He could barely discern their faces in the moonlight. They appeared grotesquely distorted, barely human, reminding him of the demons he had encountered in Ecuador.

He attempted to chase them, but his body, held hostage by fear, refused to move. He stood and watched helplessly, wondering what manner of beings they were as they pursued her into the woods. Perhaps fallen souls, night-walking through the moonlight in human form, monstrous ghouls performing satanic deeds of darkness.

David awoke the next morning in his bed, not remembering how he got there. Realizing that he was out of food, he pondered his next course of action and weighed the risks of going back to the farm versus going into town. He decided upon the former—although his beard was growing in, he was still too recognizable—and Natasa had mentioned that the news media had been broadcasting his picture everywhere.

As David walked through the woods retracing his journey to the farm, he looked upward, noting the deep-blue sky, visible between the dark-green treetops. He peered into the forest, viewing a mosaic of light and shadow, defined by the sunlit leaves and branches. They appeared to be floating in the air all around him. The sound of sweet birdsong comforted him, putting last night's terror behind him—at least for the moment. But lingering questions remained: Why had Angela's spirit contacted him? What message was she was trying to send?

David began jogging, quickly covering the remaining distance to the spot he had marked two days before. Then he turned right and continued, stopping when he reached the edge of the pasture. Once again, he waited for several minutes, carefully searching for any sign of people.

Just as David was about to emerge from the trees, he heard the sound of a young woman screaming. Turning toward the sound, he saw two men in pursuit of a female, running along the tractor path between the fence and the woods.

As they approached, he noticed that the men were clad in denim overalls. The female wore a brown plaid dress and a white blouse. David guessed that she was a schoolgirl. She screamed again and ran into the woods.

Without thinking, David responded. By the time he reached them, the men had her down on the ground. One of them held her arms while the other attempted to pull off her dress.

"Hey!" he shouted.

The rapist ceased his actions and stood up, then glared at David and shouted something in Slavanian. He looked to be in his mid-twenties, standing about five-ten, with brown hair and a husky build. The other man remained on the ground, keeping the young woman pinned down. He was tall and slender, approximately the same age as his companion, with black curly hair.

Without saying another word, the brown-haired man produced a large hunting knife from a sheath attached to his belt and waved it at David in a threatening manner. David quickly sidestepped the man and lunged, grabbing the attacker's knife hand and slamming it against a tree. The man dropped the knife and jammed the fingers of his other hand into David's neck.

As David struggled for breath, the man retrieved the knife and came at him again. Having no time to step out of the way, David blocked the man's thrust by crossing both arms in front of him. The knife missed his chest, but cut his right forearm badly. When the man attempted to make another jab, David grasped the man's right hand, twisted it, and pushed forward with all his strength, sending the blade deep into the rapist's left arm.

In response, his attacker screamed in agony and fell to the ground. As the man lay there, writhing in pain, he managed to pull the knife blade out of his arm, causing a stream of blood to gush out of the wound. The man covered the wound with his hand, stood up, and shouted something to his companion before both men ran off into the woods.

David removed his shirt and wrapped it tightly around his arm, stanching his wound. He turned to the young woman, who still lay on the ground, crying.

"Do you speak English?" David asked as he helped her to stand up.

"Yes," she whimpered between sobs.

"Do you know those men?"

She wiped tears on her blouse. "No, but I know they are farmhands. They followed me when they saw me cutting through the farm on my way to school."

"Should we call the police?" David asked, instantly regretting the question. If the police became involved, he would be identified, thrown in jail, and held there until his extradition.

David breathed a sigh of relief as the girl shook her head. "I'm okay," she replied. "If I tell my parents about this, they will be very angry. They will be afraid of rumors spreading in town. Besides, my brother and his friends will come looking for the men when I tell him what happened. The bad men will leave town. They know what will happen if they stay."

She gave him an appreciative smile. "Thank you for saving me. My family and I owe you a debt of gratitude."

David stared at the schoolgirl. She had blonde hair and blue eyes and was quite young—probably fourteen or so. He wondered if she was related to Natasa. In a sudden flash of inspiration, he realized that she was the solution to his problem.

"I'm glad I could be of help," he said in a thoughtful tone. "Now that you mention it, there is something you can do for me. What's your name?"

"Ivanka. Ivanka Nola."

"Well, Ivanka, I need someone to go into town and purchase some supplies for me. Can you do that?"

"Of course. My father owns the general store. When I tell my brother you saved me, he will gladly help."

That night, David rolled around in his bed restlessly, unable to sleep, his mind dwelling on the day's events.

After gathering a few ears of corn, he had returned to the cabin with Ivanka and given her his supply list. She had dutifully promised to return the next day. At least he wouldn't starve to death—that is if she returned with the supplies. He had given her five hundred dollars.

David decided to go outside and wait for Angela to return.

Sure enough, about an hour after the moon had risen, she appeared at the edge of the clearing. When he approached, she unrolled the scroll as before. It was a cloudless night, allowing him to clearly discern the details in the moonlight.

A coat of arms was painted on the scroll, with the traditional helm, coronet, and mantling. The inner artwork was divided into four sections: The upper left and lower right panes depicted white gryphons on a solid grey background. The upper right pane contained a red-and-white checkered shield, and the pane on the lower left depicted a black phoenix over a yellow background.

"Why did you come back, Angela?" he asked.

Angela smiled enigmatically, then silently turned away and ran into the forest. David pursued, but quickly lost her in the darkness.

After another hour of searching, he gave up and slowly plodded back to the cabin, overcome with grief as joyous memories of their short time together ran through his mind.

David woke up the next morning and checked the wound on his forearm. As expected, it was healing nicely. After bathing in the creek, he walked to the gate and unlocked it, then returned to the cabin and sat down by the window. As he waited, his belly began rumbling. If Ivanka didn't come soon, he would be forced to return to the farm and steal another chicken.

A half-hour later, David elatedly ran out of the cabin as a brown, pickup truck came into view. As he approached the truck, he saw Ivanka seated in the passenger side. A young man—no doubt her brother—was driving.

"Hi, I'm David," he said, giving the young man a friendly smile as they stepped out of the truck. "I assume you're Ivanka's brother."

"I'm Danijel," the young man said, shaking David's extended hand. "I am in your debt for saving my sister, sir."

Danijel was thin and tall for his age, with brown hair and eyes, and a stubble of beard on his chin. Fortunately, like his sister, his English was passable.

David walked to the bed of the truck, looked inside, and smiled to see it loaded with supplies. "Thank you for bringing all of this," he said. "Now I won't starve to death out here." He pointed to the truck bed. "That's a nice surprise. I hadn't asked for a roto-tiller."

"Yes," her brother responded with a smile. "I rented it for you. I noticed that you had seeds on your list. I thought it might make it easier for you to plant them."

"Thanks again, Danijel," David said after they had finished unloading the truck. "You have no idea how much I appreciate this."

The young man smiled again and pointed to the shingles David had stacked in front of the cabin. "My sister and I will patch the roof while you till the field."

After consuming their fill of Ivanka's chicken sandwiches, the threesome worked the rest of the day. By dusk, Danijel and his sister had finished repairing both the roof and the sides of the cabin.

"Would you two like to stay for supper?" David asked as they prepared to leave.

"Thank you for your offer, but we need to be getting back," Danijel replied. As the siblings walked to the truck, Danijel paused and said, "I'll stop by in a few weeks to see how you're doing, okay, David?"

David awakened early the next morning, and after a breakfast of canned beef stew, he went to work and continued planting his beans and corn.

It was a relief not having to deal with the hunger pains anymore. He felt much happier, relieved from the stress of worrying about his next meal, free from all immediate concerns. He was surprised at his joyous feelings, especially after the terrifying and heartrending encounter with Angela's ghost. Perhaps it was a result of good, clean living. He found himself satisfactorily occupied, working with his hands in the fresh country air and the hot summer sun, growing his own food, providing for his own sustenance. It was an ideal lifestyle now that he was physically conditioned for the task.

The next two weeks passed quickly as David hoed his beans and corn. Time was no longer divided into hours by the ticking of the clock, nor marked by the days of the week. The past, present, and future had merged into one great whole of pastoral existence.

He found himself listening intently to the natural world around him as he worked, surprised at how the simple act enhanced the mystery and beauty of the place and engendered poignant feelings of wonder. He began to understand for the first time the unique and wholesome delights derived from the unbiased observation of nature, uncolored by the frenetic concerns and demands of the civilized world.

With his immediate needs satisfied, David had fallen into a simple routine: He began each day with a bath at sunrise, afterward eating breakfast and then lounging in the sunny doorway till noon, gazing at the pines, hickories, and sumacs in undisturbed solitude and quiet contemplation, occasionally roused from his reverie by the sound of a passing vehicle.

David spent most afternoons climbing up the hillside and listening to the wind blowing through the trees, as it started way off in the distance, moving ever closer in a rush of sound until it blew against his skin and through his hair. Then came the cooing of a solitary mourning dove, lulling him into tranquility.

On sunny days, David fished under the sycamores and willows growing near the bank of the creek. He noted with interest the various species of wildlife the water attracted from the woods and fields, recognizing several birds—several yellow warblers, a flock of red-winged blackbirds, and a kingfisher. Once, a great blue heron flew into the water, wading upstream on stalky legs, spearfishing with its long beak.

On another day, David spotted a sandpiper and a few mallards, and then a pair of snapping turtles swimming underwater in pursuit of a school of crayfish, followed by a variety of fish and bullfrogs. Sometimes a muskrat would scramble up onto the bank and spend a half-hour grooming its paws, or a doe would appear out of the brush to drink.

In the early evenings, David took leisurely walks through the woods to the accompaniment of whippoorwills and other songbirds, sounding truly symphonic in their orchestral richness and variety. Then he would shatter the quiet, rustic ambiance with the loud dissonance of his chainsaw, teaching himself the art of converting trees into firewood, improving upon the procedure after several tries.

After spotting a suitable tree, he would place short lengths of small logs along the path where it would fall, so he could trim it without running the blade into the ground. Then, after felling it, he would cut the trunk into logs using gentle pressure, and after cutting off all the free branches on top, he would roll the logs over and remove the remaining branches. Finally, he would split them into firewood using his ax.

David especially enjoyed the sounds a tree made when it fell. As the trunk separated from the stump, a groan would issue from the protesting wood, turning into a high-pitched wail as the tree gained momentum. At the very last moment, it would scream its raw, shrieking death cry, followed by a thunderous whump as it hit the ground.

One morning, while David was hoeing his field, his quiet solitude was interrupted by the clamor of a large military helicopter. When it reached the clearing, it stopped in mid-air and hovered above it.

Feelings of dread and trepidation filled David as he noted the king's seal on its side. As it landed, he wondered if the king would discard him like a piece of unwanted trash after forcing him to access the Lyricor.

Terrified by the thought, he ran into the woods and watched from behind a tree as Vojislav Revic strode out of the chopper, dragging a blonde-haired woman along with him. She was gagged, and her hands were tied behind her back. "Show yourself, David, or she dies!" Revic shouted over the sound of the whirling blades.

"Natasa!" David exclaimed. Without thinking, he ran into the clearing. "Leave her alone, Revic!" he shouted.

The duke laughed. "I'll release her as soon as you board the chopper."

"Okay, I'll go," David responded civilly. He smiled at Natasa as he passed by. "Don't worry. They won't harm you. It's me they want."

David boarded the helicopter and watched concernedly as Revic cut Natasa loose with his athame. "Make sure that you have the next shipment ready on time," he said brusquely, giving her a shove toward the cabin.

# CHAPTER TWENTY-ONE

As David lay in his hammock listening to the night sounds of the Amazon rainforest, despondency threatened to overcome him. He had felt like a prisoner during the past two weeks, although he was free to come and go as he pleased.

His journey had begun with the chopper flying him directly to a military airstrip, where he had boarded the king's private jet. During the long flight to Brazil, Revic had forced him to reveal the location of the philosopher's stone, threatening to kill Stephania if he didn't comply.

Revic and the king wanted the stone for themselves and had decided to bring David along for insurance. After landing in Manaus, they rented a supply truck and a guide and then drove north on BR-174, the solitary highway running through the rainforest between Manaus and Boa Vista.

Pinpointing their location with his GPS unit, the king had parked the truck in a clearing lying directly on the equator, and from there, after Revic had cast several protection spells, the party headed due east into the jungle on foot, hunting and fishing as they went. Each of them carried a backpack filled with army rations and ammunition.

The trek wasn't much of a challenge for the king, who had extensive military training. Alexander, who was an excellent marksman, had killed several boars, a few turkeys, and a deer. The trip had gone smoothly because Revic's sorcery was very powerful—neither man nor beast had threatened them. David wondered why the king had brought along a guide. He certainly didn't need one.

Finally, after hiking for ten straight days, covering a distance of approximately forty miles, they were within half a day's journey of the obelisk.

Thoughts of Stephania wandered through David's mind. He missed her so much—her bright, sunny personality, her smile, her laughter, her loving embrace. He wondered if they would ever be reunited.

His melancholia deepened as he relived for the hundredth time the heartbreaking loss of Angela, recalling the final hours they had spent together at Greenwood Park. He remembered exactly what she had been wearing and how beautiful she had looked, dressed in her rounded neck, pink-striped, cotton blouse with black denim shorts and white jogging shoes. He remembered how he felt when she had smiled that bright, perfect smile of hers and said, "Hi, David," and then bade him sit on the picnic bench where they ate the sandwiches she had made.

He recalled the unending, pain-filled days following her murder, culminating in the strange and frightening appearance of her ghost at Natasa's uncle's cabin. There, she had given him a cryptic message—a scroll with a coat of arms painted on it. But what did it mean?

David was abruptly roused from his reverie by Sal, their guide. The native was a man of few words, providing little companionship on the journey. "The boss wants to see you," he said sullenly. It was obvious that he mistrusted the Slavanians. They had given him the sole responsibility of butchering the meat and cooking the food. When David had expressed his desire to help the man by collecting firewood, Revic had told him to remain at the campsite, ostensibly to keep him out of harm's way.

Feelings of fear and trepidation descended upon David as he reached the small clearing. Several battery-powered lanterns had been secured to the lower branches of the surrounding trees, illuminating the white concentric circles of power that Revic and Alexander had spray-painted onto the ground. Both men, having changed from their camouflage-style army fatigues into priestly robes, were standing in the center of the circles. Revic motioned to them. "Both of you. Step inside," he said in an authoritative tone.

David knew exactly what Revic was up to. "You're going to summon a demon," he said in an accusing tone.

"There's no harm in that now, is there, David?" the duke responded with a malicious grin. "I want to consolidate my power to make certain that the holy man will give us the philosopher's stone. Now, for your own safety, I suggest that both of you stand inside the protection circles."

David turned to Sal, who looked terrified. "We'd better do as he says, okay? It's the safest place to be. If you try to run away, the demon will track you down and possess you."

"Okay," Sal said in a shaky voice. His body was trembling and sweating with fear. "I will do what you say."

When they entered the circle, Revic began his incantations, holding a bible in one hand while waving a magic wand in the other. After reciting the names of power, he said, "I call upon you, Astaroth, the demon of the highest order. Show yourself!"

David peered into the pitch-blackness of the jungle just beyond the ring of illumination, noting the unusual silence. A moment later, he jerked at the sound of a snapping twig, a sound he should have been expecting. A chill of fear coursed down his back as he saw movement—a shadow moving among shadows. The demon had arrived.

"Oh, Great One," Revic said in a firm, unwavering voice. "I give you a gift in return for power over the holy man possessing the philosopher's stone."

Revic suddenly pushed Sal with great force, sending him completely outside the circles. In the half-light just beyond the boundary, David discerned that Sal had fallen to the ground.

Sal began thrashing his arms and legs, screaming loudly as he fought off the demon possession. Somehow, he found the strength to rise to his feet, then ran off into the darkness. His screaming continued unabated, the sound gradually diminishing until it could no longer be heard.

"You bastard," David said, giving Revic a look of contempt. It was clear why the Duke had brought along the guide. Sal was nothing more than a sacrifice—a gift to the demon in return for power.

"You don't care about anyone but yourself," David continued in a voice filled with loathing. "Someday it will all catch up to you."

"Now David," Revic said with a chuckle, "don't get yourself all worked up. I'm simply exercising my role as a dutiful servant of the king, fulfilling my mission to procure the philosopher's stone."

"That's my good duke," King Alexander said with a smile of approval. "It will be a great day for Slavania when we finally possess the stone. And now I think we all could use a good night's sleep."

The men broke camp early the following morning and began their trek through the remaining five miles of jungle. It was midday when the threesome arrived at their destination.

"Have you ever seen anything like that, Duke Revic?" the king remarked breathlessly as he stared in wonder at the massive, white, pyramidal-shaped tower.

"Of course. It's called an obelisk," Duke Revic replied smugly. "They've been around for centuries. The Egyptians used them as symbols of Ra, their sun god. This one is especially large. How tall is it anyway?"

"At least three hundred feet," David replied.

They paused at the edge of the clearing for a few minutes, gazing at it in fascination.

"It looks like it's constructed from marble," the king remarked as they approached. "What do those carvings mean, David?" he asked, noting the unfamiliar symbols and characters carved into its polished surface.

"I understand why you brought me here," David replied, ignoring the question. "You need me to enter the obelisk. What I don't understand is why you killed your father. He was a good man."

"I loved him," Alexander replied with a serious expression. "I didn't want to kill him at first, but the more I thought about it, the more it seemed like the right thing to do. I decided it was my duty."

"Your duty!" David exclaimed incredulously.

"Yes, David," Alexander replied with a condescending smile. "You see, our country is very small, with limited resources. However, once I learned of the oil sands discovery, I knew that the huge profits it would generate would allow me to build up an immense army, an army strong enough to expand our little country into an empire.

When Revic informed me of the philosopher's stone, and that you were the key to possessing it, I knew that my goal was within my grasp. The stone will give me sufficient wealth and power to control all of Eastern Europe. My countrymen will, of course, be the beneficiaries. Unfortunately, my father would never have agreed to the plan. He was too weak. As you can see, my madness has a method."

"Madness indeed," Revic said. He suddenly drew his athame out of its sheath, pointed it toward the king, and began chanting a series of incantations.

Alexander attempted to reach for his handgun, but couldn't move his arm to grasp it. The king stood there helplessly, staring at the duke with a blank expression, his body paralyzed by Revic's evil sorcery as the man advanced upon him.

David found himself locked in place as well—the spell had affected both of them.

The king managed to open his mouth a little and force out a few words. "Why? We need each other."

Revic broke off his chanting and laughed uproariously. "Do you really think I need you? Whatever for? Once you're out of the way, I can marry the princess and ascend to the throne. Besides, I will make a much better king than you ever could, since I possess the great power and strength of will that you so sorely lack."

The duke abruptly stabbed Alexander in the chest with his athame, the blade piercing the king's heart, killing him instantly

After examining the body and confirming that the king was dead, Revic turned to David, pointed the athame at him, and chanted a few more words, using the same cryptic language as before. "Now you will explain to me exactly what's inside that tower."

David felt the circulation quickly return to his limbs—Revic had nullified the paralysis spell. At this point, there seemed no reason to hide the facts from the man—Revic could, through his evil sorcery, force David to reveal whatever he desired. "I suppose you will proceed with your foolhardy ambitions no matter what I say," David responded. "Very well. I will tell you what you want to know. The being in the tower is not just a holy man. He's an angel of God, the Keeper of the Stone. No mortal has ever possessed the stone, and it would be insane to try and steal it. Phariel will never allow it."

Undaunted by David's warning, Revic laughed uproariously. "So, his name's Phariel. We shall see if he can withstand the power of my sorcery."

He gestured at the obelisk. "Enough of all this talk," he said, handing David the Lyricor. "Take me inside!"

David shrugged and led the duke to the indentation in the wall. He inserted the Lyricor into it, and the entrance appeared, just as before.

"Fascinating," Revic remarked as he watched the doorway appear. "Lead the way."

As they stepped through the entrance, the men took in the elaborate surroundings. "This place is amazing," Revic remarked. "What is the significance of the octagonal interior?"

"Does it really matter, Revic?"

"Not really," the duke replied with an arrogant grin. He unsheathed his athame and pointed it at the stairs. "You first."

They made the ascent in silence. When they arrived on the landing, Revic grasped David's left arm in a firm grip and pushed open the brass door, crouching behind him for protection.

David caught his breath as they stepped into the throne room. He had forgotten how beautiful it was—the burgundy velvet walls, the ceiling with its magnificent fresco and lavish entablature, the beautifully detailed peach, purple, and black-tiled floor.

As before, Phariel was seated on his elaborately ornamented, red-and-purple velvet throne, dressed in a white silk robe and leather, gem-studded sandals. He held an elaborately carved silver scepter in his right hand.

"Hello, David," the angel said in his deep, resonant voice, giving David a broad smile. "And who, may I ask, is your friend?"

Revic gathered his courage, pushed David to the side, and took two cautious steps toward the throne. "Actually, he's more of an acquaintance, Phariel—if that is your real name. I am Vojislav Revic, Duke of Horvat of the kingdom of Slavania." He pointed his athame at the angel. "Give me the philosopher's stone," he commanded. He slowly moved forward and began chanting an incantation, his forehead wrinkling in concentration.

Phariel laughed. "I already know who you are and what you want. You are a very rude sort of individual. Your sorcery will not work here. Your demon, who has possessed the man Sal, has abandoned you to your fate."

The angel laughed again, pointed his scepter at Revic, and slowly raised it. As Phariel lifted his arm, Revic's body gradually ascended upward until he was ten feet off the floor.

Phariel twisted the scepter with his wrist. In response, Revic's body turned in a 180-degree cartwheel, leaving him suspended upside-down in midair.

The angel smiled benevolently at David. "He's completely immobile. Take his video cartridge."

David noticed a thin black plastic case hanging from Revic's pocket, suspended by a wire. He unplugged the wire and slipped the cartridge into his pocket. Although he had just witnessed a miracle, he wasn't afraid. On the contrary, he felt completely secure in the presence of the angel.

Phariel bowed his head and began chanting in a strange language. As he continued to chant, David heard a deep, powerful, thrumming sound coming from below, vibrating the floor.

David watched in fascination as a purple glow appeared around Revic. The duke's body began to shrink, gradually diminishing in size until it was just a black dot. Then it vanished completely from sight.

"What happened to the duke?" David asked, feeling a simultaneous mix of apprehension, curiosity, and relief.

"He has passed through fourth-dimensional space and entered the underworld where all the demons reside," Phariel explained. The angel smiled benevolently. "Now go, David. Everet will help you transport the king's body back to your vehicle."

When David returned to the clearing, Everet and several tribesmen were gathered around the body of the slain king. "Phariel asked me to bring them," Everet explained with a grin, noting the perplexed look on David's face. "The chief has agreed to escort you back to your vehicle after the ceremony."

David counted fifteen warriors in total, including the Queixada chief he had met on his previous journey. He noted that they had placed Alexander's body on a handmade stretcher, covered it with large palm fronds, and lashed it to the stretcher with strong, fibrous vines.

The chief smiled and spoke rapidly to Everet for a minute.

Everet turned to David and said, "The chief says that since this man was your king, he will have his medicine man perform a special ceremony."

David sat down at the table of the small debriefing room. Seated across from him were the Slavanian prime minister, Miro Azinovic, and his secretary. With black hair, handsome features, and a trim, athletic build, the prime minister looked very presidential to David.

The prime minister smiled cordially. "Welcome home, David. I hope your stay in the holding area wasn't too much of an inconvenience."

"Thank you, sir. The accommodations were more than amenable, considering my recent stay in the Amazon."

David noted the grey-haired female secretary taking notes as they spoke, typing their words into a laptop computer.

"We have attempted to expedite your release as quickly as possible," the prime minister continued. "The tests performed on King Alexander's body support the evidence shown on the videotape you presented to the Secret Service. You are hereby acquitted of both the murder of King Alexander the Third and his father, the former king."

"Is it that simple?" David asked as feelings of relief spread throughout his body. "There won't be a formal hearing?"

"It's not necessary," Miro replied with a friendly smile. "All charges have been dropped. There is the matter of Vojislav Revic, though. His body has not been found, and there's nothing on the videotape after the king's murder. Do you have any information that might be of use?"

"As I told the Secret Service, I don't know what happened to him," David said, shaking his head. "He disappeared when the tribesmen showed up."

"The Secret Service is treating it as a missing person case for now," Miro said. "Because Revic killed the king, we have released him from his duties and his title. You may be interested to know that the thugs who mugged you rolled over when they were informed that Revic murdered the king. In addition, their testimony enabled us to apprehend the agent who was working for the bastard. The man admitted to framing your mayor, Abban Peterka, who has also been cleared and released."

He pushed some official-looking documents across the table. "All we need is your signature, David, and you will regain your title as the Duke of Horvat. There is also a document reinstating Abban as your mayor if that is your desire."

David skimmed over the documents and signed them. "Does that mean that I'm free to marry the princess?"

The prime minister laughed heartily. "You Americans always get straight to the point, don't you? Well, that brings up the final matter," he continued. "According to our laws of succession, Princess Stephania is next in line for the throne and will be crowned Queen of Slavania. That means that you, David, will become our next king—that is if she decides to marry you."

David stepped out of the limo and walked toward the throng of reporters gathered on the steps of Alexander Palace. As he approached, four palace guards herded them to either side, forming an aisle. As David walked up the steps, the reporters began questioning him.

"How do you feel now that you are exonerated?" one of them asked.

"Great!" David replied enthusiastically. "I never thought it would happen so quickly."

"Are you going to marry the princess now that you're a free man?" another asked.

"If she'll have me," David responded with a broad smile.

"What do you think about Duke Revic's treachery?" a third reporter asked.

"I have no comment. The matter is still under investigation," David replied. "And now, if you will excuse me, I have a very dear friend I need to see."

Ignoring the onslaught of rapid-fire questions from the reporters, David walked into the palace, flanked by two palace guards.

The guards ushered him into the formal reception room, where a hostess seated him at the dining table in the center of the room. Several servants appeared, setting out various dishes of food and beverages.

Upon finishing their preparations, a courtier, clad in silver and gold livery, entered the room. "Announcing Princess Stephania of the House of Premar," he said in the customary formal manner.

David could barely contain himself as Stephania entered the room. Elegantly dressed in a sheer purple silk and velvet evening gown, she appeared even more beautiful than he remembered. With her elegantly coiffed hair, the large sapphires mounted on pendants dangling from her neck on thin gold and silver chains, and the emeralds and rubies mounted in her earrings and bracelets, David thought that she appeared the very epitome of royalty. "Princess," he said with a low bow.

Stephania clapped her hands, and the servants immediately left the room.

She then burst into tears of joy, ran to David, and threw her arms around him, pressing him tightly against her body. "I missed you so, my love."

Tears wetted David's eyes as he held her in a snug embrace. "Me too, Steph," he said.

They held each other for several minutes. Then after a lengthy and passionate round of kissing, Stephania led David to his chair and poured him a glass of wine.

"A toast, my love," she said, sitting down next to him.

After filling her own wineglass, she lifted it into the air. "Here is to you, my sweet duke," she said in an adoring tone. "Never may we be parted."

"And to you, my beautiful princess," David responded with a tender expression. "Here is to our love, always and forever."

After the toast, Stephania put down her glass. "I was so worried about you, David. I didn't know if we would ever see each other again."

"Neither did I," David responded wistfully. "Sooner or later, I thought your brother would kill us. I'm surprised it wasn't sooner. It turns out that he knew where I was hiding the whole time."

Stephania wrinkled her brow and paused in thought for a moment. "There's something about all this that I don't understand, David. What is it that he wanted from you?"

David paused for a moment. He had spent the last few days pondering what to say to her, finally deciding on maintaining the story he had given the Secret Service. He couldn't bear the thought of her safety being compromised. He was certain the demons and their servants were already marshaling their forces, and would soon come after him after consolidating the full might of their horrific, supernatural power.

"Remember when I healed your brother?" he began. "It was a miracle, really. I have no other explanation for it. His remission from lung cancer was not my doing. I have no special healing powers, other than my experience as a doctor.

"Alexander mistakenly believed that I had discovered a cure for cancer during my travels in the Amazon rainforest and wanted it for himself. After

Alexander freed Revic, he reinstated him as duke and flew us there. Once we arrived, Revic attempted, through the use of sorcery, to force me into revealing the cure, which never existed."

"I saw the video of my brother's murder," Stephania said with a serious expression. "He mentioned something called the 'philosopher's stone.' He seemed to believe it was real."

"I made up the story about the philosopher's stone under duress. He threatened to kill you if I didn't reveal the source of my healing powers."

"So, the philosopher's stone is just a myth," Stephania mused. "How could he have believed your story?"

David shrugged. "I think he desire for power got the better of him. He believed what he wanted to believe. Revic was every bit as greedy and ambitious—and that's why he murdered Alex. I'm sorry for the loss of your brother, but at least one good thing came out of all of this. We can be together again."

"Yes, my love," Stephania responded in a sultry tone. "Let's be together again."

It was still morning when David touched down on the landing area atop the oil sandspit in the government helicopter. Sven was waiting nearby in a military vehicle.

"So how are you, my friend?" Sven asked, giving David a friendly smile as he entered the four-wheel-drive vehicle.

David gripped Sven's hand firmly. "Never better. I've just spent three glorious days with Stephania going over our wedding plans. It feels like I died and went to heaven."

"I'm happy for you, David," Sven responded with a broad smile. "You deserve all the happiness in the world. I understand that you lived at the sanctuary for a couple of months. How did the country living appeal to you?"

"It wasn't so bad once my body became accustomed to the farm work. It's been an adjustment returning to the palace—Being surrounded by courtiers constantly waiting on me hand and foot. I'm finally beginning to adapt to the luxurious living."

"You'll have all the luxury you can handle once you are crowned King of Slavania. How do you feel about that, David?"

"It seems like a dream, really. I haven't had time to assimilate it completely. The prime minister wants the marriage and coronation ceremony to proceed quickly, so he's given us only two months. The courtiers say that's one month short of the customary preparation time for coronations, but Parliament is maintaining that two months is long enough for Slavania to be without a monarch. I'm practically living with my personal secretary while he helps me learn all the protocols and etiquette. I can't believe all the petty details you aristocrats have to deal with."

Sven grinned. "Believe me, David, it will be old hat soon enough. Actually, you will come to rely on it. It facilitates things quite nicely when dealing with important matters of State."

Sven pulled the jeep over to the side of the clearing. "We're here," he said. They had reached the bottom of the open-pit mine. David noted three gigantic dump trucks and an earthmover, silently standing guard a few yards away.

When David stepped out of the jeep, he smelled the sharp, pungent odor of bitumen.

Suddenly, twelve people dressed in purple, hooded robes appeared from behind the trucks. When David turned to Sven to question him, he saw that his friend had thrown off his suit jacket and was donning a hooded robe made of black silk.

"What's going on, Sven?" David asked. "Who are these people?"

Sven finished dressing and pulled the hood over his head. "How do you like my new look?" Then he gestured to the others. "Meet my coven. I'm the high priest, by the way."

David stared at Sven in bewilderment for a moment, then swallowed hard as he noted the coat of arms embossed into the left breast of his friend's robe. The inner design consisted of two gryphons, a phoenix, and a shield, exactly matching the one Angela's ghost had shown him. A sensation of numbness overcame him as it dawned on him that Angela's killer was his best friend. He abruptly fainted.

Sven grabbed him by the shoulders and held him upright as one of the coven members brought two metal chairs from the jeep. Then Sven gently sat David down on one and sat himself on the other as he waited for his friend to regain consciousness.

Moments later, David opened his eyes. "I can't believe you killed Angie!" he exclaimed, the color returning to his face. "I just can't believe it! I thought you were my friend. Why did you do it, Sven?"

"What gives you the notion that it was me?" Sven responded, appearing to be taken aback by David's accusation.

"Don't lie to me, Sven. I know it was you."

"I guess there's no reason to hide it anymore," Sven replied with a malicious grin. "Perhaps it's time you knew the truth. I've wanted the Lyricor all along, you see."

"How did you learn about it?", David asked. And how did you know that I was in possession of it? You never read Tom Harrison's memoirs. Revic would never give away that kind of information."

"I learned about it the same way Tom Harrison did," Sven replied smugly.

"You made a deal with Satan!" David exclaimed. He gave his former friend a look of contempt. "You're going to burn in hell for killing Angie. Shurely you must know that."

"Correct on both counts," Sven responded. "I made a deal with Lucifer to obtain the Lyricor. Unfortunately for Angela and you, he required a sacrifice in return. As you probably noticed," Sven continued, "Revic and I hated each other. We belonged to rival covens; you see. We were both vying for the throne as well. When the former king sent Revic to the US, I tracked his movements and learned which coven he joined. It wasn't too difficult—it was the only Wicca coven in the area.

"Two of my witches went undercover and joined the coven to keep tabs on him. When I discovered that he had become fond of Angela, it was the perfect opportunity to kill two birds with one stone, as they say. When my witches killed Angela, that fulfilled the bargain I made with Satan, and they set up the murder scene to implicate Claire and her coven."

"It all makes sense now," David said. "In order to further your aspirations for the throne, you framed Revic's coven for Angela's murder, conveniently placing suspicion on your rival while simultaneously satisfying your contract with Satan. Her murder was also an emotional strike against Revic since he was fond of her."

"You have stated it perfectly, David!"

"And it was your witches who tried to steal the Lyricor from me in Nova Scotia, correct?"

"Very good, David. After I had completed the sacrifice, Lucifer informed me that you were in possession of the Lyricor. There was a man on my payroll—an agent in the Secret Service—whom I put on your case. He tracked your every move using your credit card and cell phone activity."

"So Revic was telling the truth when he said that he had no idea that I possessed the Lyricor until we visited him in prison."

"He had no prior knowledge of it—that is until you inadvertently told him. A stupid move on your part, by the way. So, I sent the witches to the Congo," Sven continued. "After they returned with that bogus stone, I eventually killed them. They were no longer useful, and I didn't want anyone linking me to Angela's murder.

"I tried again in Argentina, using the phony monks and the gaucho assassin. When those plans failed, I played my trump card, sending my assistant high priest—posing as St. Thomas—to meet you in Ecuador. I thought I finally had you. By the way, how did you manage to escape the demons he unleashed?"

"The man who gave me the Lyricor helped me. His name's Everet."

"Everet?"

"I'm surprised Satan didn't tell you about him. He's the angel's servant."

"Interesting. So, the holy man possessing the philosopher's stone is actually an angel of God." Then Sven threw back his head and laughed. "Unfortunately, he won't be of any use to you here. I found the Lyricor on your person after you passed out. That's not very smart, carrying it around with you like that."

"The Lyricor won't do you any good, Sven. It only responds to me."

Sven scoffed. "You don't know the extent of my powers. I can easily make it respond to my commands."

"What about the soldiers who took me, hostage?" David asked. "And what about the captain? You know, the one who sliced off my little finger? Do they work for you as well?"

Sven grinned. "I see that your finger has healed nicely, by the way. But yes—hired mercenaries. When they couldn't pull the information out of you," Sven continued, "I summoned the demon Astaroth. After mining your brain for information, I learned that the Lyricor had been stolen and that you suspected Revic's involvement. That didn't bother me because I knew that sooner or later, Revic would contact you. His sorcery wasn't powerful enough to access it

"Later, when you returned from your little jungle trek without Revic and Alexander, I correctly deduced that the Lyricor was back in your possession." Then Sven glanced upward. "It's almost dusk. The time of power is at hand."

He motioned to his coven. Two of them came forward and quickly bound David's hands and legs together with thick rubber cords. When they finished, Sven pushed David off his chair, laughing diabolically as he fell to the ground.

"You're going to have a little accident," Sven said. He burst into a new round of laughter. "Once you're dead, the only person standing between me and the throne is the princess. And I have plans for her as well."

Sven produced an athame from under his robe, and after chanting several incantations, pointed it at the dump trucks and the earthmover.

David inhaled sharply when their engines started. As the ponderous vehicles began slowly moving forward, he realized that no one was driving them.

The coven members stayed behind the vehicles and began chanting as the trucks inexorably advanced toward David, who lay there writhing on the ground in a vain attempt to break his bonds. He became filled with desperation, realizing that in another few seconds, he would be crushed to death under the massive weight of the heavy equipment.

Suddenly, the trucks' engines shut off and they stopped in their tracks.

David looked up and saw Everet standing over him. He noted the radical change in the man's appearance. His usual attire—the plaid shirt and blue jeans—had been replaced by a saintly white robe. He also wore a large sword slung over his back.

Everet knelt down at David's side, unsheathed the sword, and cut him loose. "It's not over yet," he said grimly.

As David stood up, Everet gripped him by the arm and pointed to the coven. David watched in horror as Sven plunged his athame into the chest of the nearest hooded figure.

"Lucifer, accept thou this sacrifice and kill the infidels!" Sven screamed at the top of his lungs.

The sky, which until then had been cloudless, ominously began to fill with thick, black clouds.

David watched apprehensively as they consolidated into one large, shapeless mass, then he fell to the ground in terror as the cloud descended and began moving swiftly toward them. He heard strange voices inside his mind, reminding him of his previous demonic encounters.

"Those aren't storm clouds," Everet remarked as the swirling black shape approached. "Satan has gathered his demons to fight us."

"What can we do?" David asked.

"If your faith is strong, you will live," Everet replied. "Kneel and pray to God that he will save you." He lowered his head and began praying in earnest, and David recognized the language as Latin.

Following Everet's example, he knelt to the ground and began praying. His body shook with dread as he recalled the encounter in Ecuador. As bad as it was, this was going to be much worse.

The noise level in his mind increased dramatically as a million voices screamed simultaneously, threatening to destroy his sanity.

Everet smiled bravely. "Have faith, David. Phariel will help us."

Suddenly, the terrible voices vanished from his mind, and a mix of emotions—joy, peace, and amazement—replaced the intense fear and anguish. He looked upward incredulously, noting that both he and Everet were surrounded by a huge pillar of fire, the flames leaping upward at least a thousand feet into the air. He knew he was witnessing a miracle.

David watched in astonishment as the dark cloud made contact with the flaming column. A scream of outrage came from the demons as they were repulsed by the flames.

Realizing that they had been deprived of their victims, and had nowhere else to go, the legion suddenly reversed course and descended upon the coven. The coven members ran toward the dirt wall at the edge of the mine, pulled back their hoods, held their hands to their ears, and screamed in agony as the demons invaded their minds.

They fell to the ground, thrashing their limbs as they died from the overpowering, supernatural violence unleashed by the dark horde.

Soon after all the robed figures had become still and silent, the cloud ascended into the air, gradually dispersing as it floated off toward the sunset.

David lay there for several minutes, waiting for the strength to return to his body. Then he and Everet walked to the pile of bodies.

"When the demons discovered that they couldn't possess us, they turned on the coven," Everet remarked. He gave David an approving smile. "Your faith has significantly strengthened over the past few months. As a result, Phariel was able to produce the pillar of fire—a great miracle."

"Yes, it certainly was," David mused softly.

He paused for a few moments, overwhelmed by the powerful, mystical events that had just transpired. "Thank you for your help, Everet," he said. "You saved my life once again. I am in your debt forever."

Everet smiled. "It has been my pleasure to serve you, David."

David's eyes landed on Sven's corpse. The body lay on its back in the center of the pile of the other corpses, his face ashen white, his features contorted with pain.

After a brief search of Sven's clothing, David found the Lyricor.

"I don't know how to thank you," he said, turning to shake Everet's hand. To his surprise, the man was no longer by his side. Once again, the angel's servant had vanished.

# CHAPTER TWENTY-TWO

The wedding and coronation celebration began the evening before with a gigantic party held in Drago Park. There were fifty bonfires, fireworks, and several bands and choirs. The Royal Artillery was present as well, firing salvos from the guns of the King's Army. Thousands of onlookers gathered, causing a huge traffic jam. Stephania and David did not join in the festivities but remained out of sight, safely tucked away inside Alexander Palace.

At four a.m., the route from the palace to the church was closed to traffic, and by dawn, there was no standing room within fifty yards of St. John's Cathedral.

The princess arose at 6:30 a.m. and ate a large breakfast to keep her belly from rumbling during the long morning ahead. The preparations began in earnest as she met with her hairdresser in the royal changing room, who deftly set her hair in an up-style, crowned with tiara and veil. Then her makeup artist spent forty-five minutes applying her makeup and nails. The makeup artist was to remain with her throughout the day, performing touch-up work as needed.

While her six attendants—four bridesmaids and two pageboys—were dressed and prepared, Stephania donned her wedding gown. Designed by the renowned clothing designers George and Elizabeth Thomas, her wedding dress was made of the finest ivory-colored English silk taffeta, sewn single-handed by a professional seamstress, including a frilled neckline overlaid with lace, a bodice with more embroidered lace, and a vast, crumpled skirt laden with tiny pearls and gems. Completing the outfit was a twenty-five-foot train, edged with a lace border, the ivory and white perfectly complementing the princess's skin tone.

While Stephania was being prepared, David's courtiers dressed him in a black tuxedo with white piping. Then two palace guards delivered the gold wedding ring, nestled inside a navy-blue suede bag with a drawstring top.

Meanwhile, thousands of people gathered in front of St. John's in order to get a good view of the wedding procession, many carrying sandwiches, beer, and champagne in celebration of a fairy tale in real-time.

The security was very tight, with hundreds of police lining the route, as well as constables, plain-clothes detectives, cadets, mounted police, and ambulances. Marksmen were stationed upon the rooftops, a helicopter kept watch by air, and a myriad of security cameras scanned the crowd.

As David rode in his carriage to the cathedral, he was moved by the roar of the crowds, the color, the music, the laughter, and the excitement. It was truly a joyous day for the citizens of Slavania.

At nine a.m. the first guests began climbing the red-carpeted steps leading to the west doors of the massive cathedral. Once inside, they were greeted by a full orchestra and a boys' choir, located on either side of the dais, performing a program of Purcell, Handel, and Mozart—music which David had personally selected.

As David entered the cathedral, his eyes begin to tear, moved by the approving smiles of the wedding guests, realizing that they had accepted him as one of their own.

He watched with amazement the arrival of the many distinguished guests, including most of the crowned heads of Europe—the King and Queen of the Belgians, the King and Queen of Norway and Sweden, the Queen of the Netherlands, and the Grand Duke and Duchess of Luxembourg—as well as monarchs from Africa, the Middle East, and Asia.

An hour later, the church was completely filled, the majority of the congregation comprised of servants of the Crown and State, including senior members of the Army and a smattering of other politicians and diplomats. Several of the media were allowed inside—mostly news reporters who frantically scribbled on their notepads since cameras were forbidden in the chapel.

Stephania's friends and relatives sat in the second row, with the immediate members of David's family—his mother, grandmother, and sister, also her spouse and their children—sitting in the front pew.

On the royal pew facing David's family sat the entire household staff of Alexander Palace.

As David began his walk along the nave of the cathedral, he heard a huge roar from the crowds outside as Stephania's coach—an extravagant vehicle of wood and glass, pulled by two bay horses from the palace stables—arrived.

The service began with regal flair as several trumpeters, located in the porticoes of the west doors, gave fanfare to Stephania as she entered the chapel. Then she began her stately, three-minute walk along the lengthy, red carpet, followed by Triska, her bridesmaids, and pages. She carried a bouquet of fresh orchids, gardenias, myrtle, and roses in one arm, the other linked to her uncle, Devon Yorvar, the Duke of Flaric.

Upon reaching the end of her imperial walk, feeling a mixture of nerves and excitement, Stephania stepped onto the raised dais beside Prince David and shared several intimate glances with him.

The ceremony began with a hymn and after a brief introduction given by the Dean of St. John's—the Archbishop Neven Barac of Horvat—who, appearing resplendent in a gold silk cape, guided them through their wedding vows.

Stephania repeated after him, promising her husband-to-be to "love him, comfort him, honor him, and keep him, to have and to hold from this day forward, for richer or poorer, in sickness and in health, to love and to cherish, till death do us part according to God's holy law."

David repeated the vows, and they both said, "I will."

A loud cheer from the crowd outside penetrated the thick stone walls of the church, and they smiled, remembering how their vows were being broadcast live through a public-address system.

After the commotion had subsided, the archbishop closed the ceremony with the words, "I pronounce that they be man and wife together."

After more cheering and a prolonged kiss by the newlywed couple, the prime minister began his address. "This is the dreamy stuff of which fairy tales are made," he began. "Fairy tales usually end at this point, but my feeling is that this one is just beginning."

At the conclusion of the prime minister's address, the coronation ceremony began. The Lord Great Chamberlain—his Office of State filled especially for the occasion—with the aid of the Groom and Mistress of the Robes, enrobed the sovereigns in the first robes of royalty.

Named the Parliament Robes, the luxurious capes were made of ermine fitted with long crimson velvet trains lined with more ermine and decorated with gold lace, enlarged in Stephania's case to fit over her voluminous wedding dress.

Then the archbishop proceeded to seat the couple in a pair of high-backed purple and crimson chairs, located on the left side of the dais. He called for the Recognition of the Sovereigns with the words: "Sirs, I here present unto you your undoubted king and queen. Wherefore all you who are come this day to do your homage and service, are you willing to do the same?"

The congregation responded by loudly acclaiming the sovereigns, then the archbishop administered the oath to each of them as follows: "Will you solemnly promise and swear to govern the peoples of Slavania according to their respective laws and customs?"

After David and the princess answered with the customary, "I solemnly promise to do so," the archbishop asked, "Will you, through your power, cause law and justice and mercy to prevail in all your judgments?"

"I will," they replied.

"Will you to the utmost of your power maintain the laws of God and the true profession of the gospel and preserve inviolable the Church of Slavania? And will you preserve unto the bishops and clergy of Slavania, and to the churches there committed to their charge, all such rights, and privileges, as by law do or shall appertain to them or any of them?"

"All this I promise to do," the couple replied in unison. "The things which I have here before promised, I will perform and keep. So, help me God."

The crimson robes were removed, and after changing into another pair of robes—long coats of gold silk reaching to their ankles, with wide, flowing sleeves lined with rose-colored silk and trimmed with gold lace—the couple stepped onto a mounted platform just to the right of the dais and sat on the King and Queen Alexander chairs.

A canopy was held over their heads—borne by four Knights of the Cloth—and the Dean of St. John's poured consecrated oil from an eagle-shaped ampulla onto a spoon and handed it to the archbishop, who then anointed them on their heads, hands, and breasts.

Then the archbishop invoked blessings upon them, and after the monarchs were enrobed in a third pair of robes—four-square mantles lined in crimson silk, decorated with silver coronets, silver eagles, and other national symbols, overlaid with gold silk scarves richly embroidered with gold and silver thread, set with jewels, and lined with rose-colored silk and gold fringing—the archbishop presented the Sword of State to David, followed by the crown jewels—a hollow, golden sphere set with precious stones, a ring, and a scepter.

As David held the scepter, the archbishop placed the Crown of Slavania on his head and then placed the Crown of Alexander on Stephania's head.

Everyone in the congregation leapt to their feet and shouted, "God save the king and queen!"

After the archbishop and the other bishops paid homage to the newly crowned monarchs, they changed into their fourth and final robes—embroidered ermine capes with trains of purple silk velvet, trimmed with ermine and lined with satin.

The dramatic conclusion to the coronation ceremony commenced as the royal couple—accompanied by the majestic sounds of Elgar's "Pomp and Circumstance"—made their stately walk down the aisle.

As they walked, Stephania kept a firm grip on David's right arm and, with head held high, smiled upon the rows of beaming faces of the congregation.

As they emerged from the cathedral, the newlyweds were greeted by a huge roar from the crowds, packed thirty-deep on either side of the waiting coaches.

David smiled as he heard the jubilant peal of bells from the towers above, mingled with the distant clanging of church bells throughout the city.

The noise and wild cheering continued all the way to the palace as David and Stephania sat in their open carriage, smiling and waving to the crowd as they rode, eventually arriving at the inner quadrangle of Alexander Palace, where they were greeted by more cheering from the household staff.

Then the newlyweds—accompanied by a phalanx of palace guards—entered the palace, proceeded to the second floor, and entered a reception room where they posed for photos with their families and other European royal monarchs.

David was quickly reminded of his new status when members of the royal household called him "Your Royal Highness" and "sire."

In an improvisational move, the royal couple stepped through a pair of large French windows out onto the balcony, receiving an earsplitting howl of joy from the crowds gathered below as the monarchs smiled and waved.

When Stephania bent her head toward David for a kiss, the crowd went wild—cheering, shouting, waving, and laughing, even hugging and kissing the strangers standing next to them.

The couple proceeded downstairs to the main dining room and joined the eighty-some guests for a luxurious wedding breakfast of quenelles, crabmeat, scones, strawberries, French wine, and profiteroles, followed by slices of wedding cake—all ten of them on display.

The two-hundred-pound official cake was a feat of culinary engineering in itself, each of its four tiers standing over a foot high.

After David cut the cake with a ceremonial sword, Triska proposed the toast.

Immediately afterward, Stephania changed into a new outfit—a blue chiffon going-away suit with matching hat, featuring peacock feathers, large pearl earrings, and a choker.

They left the palace in an open landau covered in rose petals and confetti, trailing red and gold balloons with a "Just Married" sign on the back.

As the newlyweds journeyed to the train station, David noted with amazement and pride the vast crowds of onlookers and their obvious enjoyment of the queen's magnificent appearance.

David sipped his after-dinner brandy and sighed contentedly. Stephania had planned their honeymoon as a blend of luxury, simplicity, tradition, and adventure.

They had spent the first five days at Divac, an estate owned by Stephania's honorary grandfather—the Earl Kreso of Mecava. The earl's grandson, Lord Petranovic, and his wife, the Lady Sabina, who normally resided there, had generously moved out, giving Stephania and David the full run of the premises.

Stephania had chosen the location out of sentimentality. Her father and mother had spent their honeymoon there. The estate exuded a robustly romantic ambiance. The Georgian-style mansion was set on five thousand acres of countryside featuring a variety of fruit trees and a number of exquisite gardens. The interior featured four main reception rooms, nine bedrooms, and six bathrooms, all decorated in the aristocratic, country manor-house style. The walls were painted with soft, bright, pastel colors; the sofas and chairs were done in colorful chintz; numerous pictures hung from gilt frames; the furniture was all eighteenth-century French.

David found comfort in the state-of-the-art security system—its closed-circuit automatic television cameras continuously scanning every centimeter of the property.

The nerve center for the twenty-four-hour surveillance system was located in an old cottage, locked away in an impregnable, twenty-foot-square steel room on the first floor, stocked with food and drink to last for months. Additionally, there were medical supplies, an armory, communications equipment, air purifiers, and lavatories.

The formal dining room, which David was occupying, featured a circular mahogany table and a cheerful and elegant color scheme of peach walls, white woodwork and curtains, and chair coverings of ripe plum. A massive landscape dominated one wall. Between two large French windows hung an elegantly framed, charming portrait of an eighteenth-century blonde beauty.

David fondly smiled at Stephania, who was seated opposite him, as he recalled the last few romantic days spent in rustic simplicity—the hikes in the woods, the horseback riding, the picnics, and the fishing.

He recalled her expression of surprise and joyous wonder when he had presented the wedding gifts he had chosen: a diamond necklace with a ruby heart centerpiece, a huge sapphire and diamond brooch, an emerald choker, and a stunning suite of diamonds and sapphires.

A thrill of excitement ran through him as he recalled their initial bedroom exploits on the forty-five-foot square, four-poster mahogany bed. The housekeeper maintained a mountain of cushions upon it when not in use.

"What are you smiling about, honey?" Stephania asked.

David paused for a moment, admiring her beauty as he had done countless times during the past few weeks, noting her sheer, red and purple, silk dinner dress, how it partially revealed her feminine curves beneath, implying the sweet, innocent promise of romance to come.

"I'm thinking how gorgeous you look this evening, my sweetheart!" he exclaimed passionately.

"I want to look nice for my new husband," Stephania responded. She gave him an approving smile. "And you look very handsome tonight in your tailored suit, my dear king."

"Thank you, honey. I'm glad you think so, but I'm not quite used to the idea of everyone calling me a king. I still feel like the same guy I was before all of this happened." He sighed and said, "We've had quite a busy time since the wedding, yes?"

"It was all so sublime and transcendental," Stephania said with a faraway look. "I was so nervous on our wedding day, though. I could barely keep my knees from knocking."

"I felt the same way. I was afraid I'd say or do something stupid and ruin the moment forever."

"You acted every bit in character—as a newly crowned monarch should. You are going to make a great king, my sweet David."

"I'm still trying to comprehend what it's like to actually be a king—to live and to walk and to talk like one. I must confess, it's overwhelming."

"You'll get used to it," Stephania responded with a chuckle. "Everyone thinks highly of you. And look at the benefits! Anything you desire is yours for the asking."

"The only thing I want is lots of time to spend with my sweetheart."

David grew serious for a moment. "You know, no matter how great it is to be king, there will come a time when we must part our ways. Then all the king's men won't be able to put us back together again."

"Please don't think such serious thoughts tonight, my beloved husband." She gave him a consoling grin. "We have all the time in the world ahead of us." She cast her eyes downward. "I know what you mean, though," she continued, her expression turning pensive. "Triska has been a wreck ever since Sven died. It took every ounce of strength she had to put on a good face for the wedding, especially coming only two months after his funeral. It was so very strange and tragic how it happened."

"What do you mean?" David asked. For the first time since the wedding, he felt uneasy.

"According to the autopsy report, Sven and the twelve others who were with him all died from heart failure. It was the coroner's opinion that they died of fright."

Stephania paused for a moment, a perplexed expression appearing upon her features. "They said that Sven had apparently been involved in witchcraft, of all things, and the other dead people who were with him were members of his coven. Triska doesn't believe it, but I've seen the pictures. The evidence is very compelling."

David breathed out a sigh of relief. Neither Stephania nor the police suspected his involvement. Everet had covered their tracks well. "It's hard to believe that she didn't know anything about his dealings with the occult."

Stephania shrugged. "Secrets are not all that unusual with aristocrats—especially the royals. Although constantly involved in innumerable public activities, we are always discreet, always keeping our personal lives absolutely private."

"I guess that makes sense—the last thing you want is to see every detail of your personal life splashed all over the headlines. It seems strange that Triska had no suspicions about Sven, though."

David's joy quickly devolved into moroseness as the reality of his future with his beautiful queen hit home. He could potentially live for thousands of years, but Stephania had only sixty or seventy at best. It was a great disparity, and he couldn't imagine what it would be like living so many years without her.

He realized that, sooner or later, the time would come when his youthful appearance would draw questions—questions that he could not answer.

"How somber you look, David. Come over here and let me wipe that frown off your face."

David gazed affectionately at his lovely wife and broke into laughter. "I have no doubt of your success in that regard."

The next morning, the royal couple flew to the coast, boarded the royal yacht, and began their cruise down the Adriatic, this time with only the crew on board. David had trouble believing it was actually his boat.

The newlyweds spent the next few days sunbathing on deck, snorkeling, and scuba diving, as well as spending time alone in their royal apartments—newly constructed for the occasion, the stateroom having been furnished with a brand-new, king-size bed.

They were ecstatically happy, all over each other, and the crew made every effort to pamper them, catering to their every wish.

They eventually reached the Mediterranean, having visited several exotic ports of call along the way, including some of the smaller Greek islands, lazily soaking up the sun and swimming by day, attending onboard parties held by the crew at night, dancing to live music, watching movies, reading, or playing cards.

After cruising around the cape of Italy, the royal couple headed west to their final destination, the famous town of Monte Carlo.

Located on the French Riviera, the resort was widely known as a playground for the rich and famous, offering all the amenities a king and queen could desire. David and Stephania spent several glorious days and nights there, rubbing shoulders with royalty from other countries.

By day, they toured the city, à la James Bond, in a rented red Ferrari, sampling the fare from numerous posh restaurants.

Most afternoons, Stephania was treated to her own private fashion show, afterward selecting articles of clothing made by famous designers.

The newlyweds spent their nights lounging in the penthouse suite at the prestigious Hotel de Paris, or attending the opera at the famous Opera de Monte Carlo, or playing blackjack in a private room of the luxurious Le Grand Casino with the Prince of Monaco.

Eventually, the royal couple returned to Slavania and continued their honeymoon, spending two glorious weeks at Premar Estate where they gave their final press conference. The media promised to leave them alone after that.

They spent most of their time outdoors—hunting, fishing, hiking, and horseback riding.

Triska and several of Stephania's friends came to visit the second week, and the women went shopping in town, afterward sorting through the plethora of wedding gifts and putting them on display in the town hall.

More than a thousand people arrived to view the huge assortment, which included priceless diamond and sapphire jewelry, large quantities of glassware, bowls and decanters, vases, carpets and rugs, gold, silver, and porcelain accessories, twenty pairs of double sheets, pillow slips, satin-bound towels, facecloths, handkerchiefs, paintings, books, microwave ovens, a tea maker, a vacuum cleaner, and every other thing one could possibly think of.

One night, after a busy evening of entertaining, the couple retired to the drawing-room, sat upon a pair of salmon-colored silk sofas, and shared a bottle of burgundy. The room was both elegant and comfortable, with silken wall-coverings of deep, rich yellow, set off by beautiful paintings mounted in elaborate gilt frames.

David mused that the room was spacious enough for liveried footmen to serve vintage champagne to at least fifty guests. In one corner stood a magnificent grand piano, which he yearned to learn how to play.

They were finally alone together, and David was relishing every moment of it. He smiled contentedly at Stephania. "Were you serious when you said that I can do anything now that I'm king?"

"Of course," Stephania replied with a perplexed look. "What's on your mind, dear?"

"Well," he replied slowly, "we're still officially on our honeymoon, correct?"

"Yes, dear."

"I was wondering if we could extend it for a while longer. I've always wanted to see the Northern Lights. Would you care to accompany me to the Arctic Circle, my darling?"

"Are you jesting with me, David?" Stephania asked with a playful smile.

"No, ma'am! I'm completely serious."

"Really!" Then she gave him an affectionate smile. "If that's what you want, my sweet David, I'm up for the challenge. You know I will accompany you anywhere you decide to go." She shivered. "The North Pole. What an adventurous ending for a honeymoon!"

The outdoor temperature was hovering around 25 degrees below zero when the King and Queen of Slavania—accompanied by their security staff—exited the military transport plane.

David had attempted to dissuade the prime minister from including them, but the politician wouldn't hear of it. Since they were traveling to a military location, they had to adhere to protocol and comply with strict security regulations.

Thule Air Base was a collection of numerous concrete buildings raised off the ground by large cinder blocks. David learned that it was necessary to maintain adequate space between the floor and the ground to keep the permafrost from melting and thus causing the buildings to shift or to sink. The structures were built to withstand extremely high winds and subzero temperatures. All the utility pipes were heated and raised above ground level.

David smiled at the magnificent sunset view of Mt. Dundas, rising upward from North Star Bay, its snowy peak dappled in pink and gold.

After checking in at headquarters, the commander gave the entourage a briefing, explaining that the base was staffed with sixty US military officers, three hundred enlisted men, and two thousand Danish civilian workers. The amenities included several well-equipped hobby shops, clubs, a gym, and a retail merchandise outlet.

The commander detailed their impending journey into the arctic, explaining that they had a six-day window of clear weather.

Since it was the middle of November, the ice sheet was deemed thick enough for safe travel. Unfortunately, gaining access to it was nearly impossible because the edges of the sheet rose upward in sheer cliffs of over one hundred feet high. The only place to gain entry was at Camp Tuto—short for Thule Take Off Camp—located approximately twenty-two miles from the base, where the military engineers had built a three-mile, inclined, gravel access road extending out onto the ice sheet.

The trip was to be accomplished in six days—three days there and back—taking full advantage of the favorable weather conditions. The group would travel by dogsled in a northeasterly direction, covering a distance of approximately fifty miles. Since the temperature could range anywhere from -20 to -70 degrees Fahrenheit, with wind speeds surging up to 125 miles per hour, they would be using four extra dogsleds, each packed with approximately six hundred pounds of supplies.

After the briefing, the royal couple was escorted to the supply depot and outfitted with proper clothing for the journey, including parkas, facemasks, gloves, shirts, pants, and boots, all designed for subzero weather and high-velocity winds.

That evening, Stephania and David dined in the base dining room, modestly decorated in a utilitarian 1960s-style décor, consisting of inexpensive wood-paneled walls, fluorescent lighting, and cafeteria-style tables. They were surprised and delighted by the superior quality of the food, which had been professionally prepared by the Danish staff.

Afterward, the royal couple retired to their sleeping quarters. Like the cafeteria, the room was plain, with more wood-paneling, a few veneer tables and chrome-plated lamps, a desk, two double beds, and a small bathroom. David found the room agreeably warm and quiet.

The next morning, after a hearty breakfast, the entourage commenced their journey, traveling by Humvee to Camp Tuto, where their dogsled teams were waiting for them on the ice sheet. David noted that there was not much left of the old camp. Only a couple of wanigans—boxcar-like structures originally used for transporting goods in bulk—a metal bridge, and some concrete building pads remained.

The view was breathtaking and surreal. The white, snow-covered ice sheet stretched off into the horizon, dotted by an occasional dark-blue glacier, with Mt. Dundas in the background—its white, glistening, snowcapped peak tinted with orange and pink as the sun slowly ascended into a deep-blue sky.

Their six Inuit Mushers—Sam, George, Harry, Pete, Dan, and Rick—finished packing the sleds and then hitched all fifty dogs to them. Ten huskies were tethered to each of the four supply sleds, and five dogs to each of the two passenger sleds.

David's Musher, Sam, explained in passable English that the sleds were made from boards set on long, iron runners, lashed together with strips of animal skin, making the sleds flexible and comfortable.

He warned that the huskies were strictly working dogs and were not to be petted. Unlike their Alaskan counterparts, they did not run in columns but ran parallel to one another on equal length lines of sealskin. Sam explained that the dogs' teeth were filed smooth so they wouldn't chew the lines apart.

By the time the team had finished their preparations, the temperature had dropped to minus 30 degrees. Fortunately, there was no wind.

As the Mushers helped Stephania and David into their sleds, the dogs broke the frigid silence with howls of excitement, followed by a cacophony of barking as they were harnessed.

Each sled was launched individually, Stephania's being the first. One of the Mushers levered the sled forward with a steel-spiked wooden pole—called a peavey—while two others pushed along the sides. With a grating squeak, Stephania's sled abruptly broke loose from the ice, and the dogs threw themselves forward to inch it along.

Eventually, all the sleds were away, quickly gaining speed on the smooth ice sheet.

In the calm stillness—the dogs, intent on pulling their sleds, had stopped barking. David noted once again the surreal beauty of the landscape.

Cobalt-blue glaciers, black rocks, and gravel dotted the whiteness of the plain, with rivulets of frozen water appearing as a light blue color. The ice sheet itself was covered by a thin layer of light, powdery snow, the ice underneath appearing as a translucent blue-green color.

Approximately once an hour, the dogs changed places, tangling the lines. Then the Mushers had to stop and untangle them, afterward checking in with the security staff by satellite telephone—a condition imposed by the Slavanian security staff in exchange for them staying behind.

For Stephania and David, it was a most welcome opportunity to climb off their sleds and spend ten minutes or so pounding their feet and swinging their arms, bringing warmth back into their extremities.

Fortunately, the snow was not deep enough to hinder their progress and they made good time, covering about ten miles in the first three hours. However, their progress slowed later in the afternoon, the Mushers having to maneuver the sleds around some rubble ice and several frozen rivulets.

Nighttime came early—after only six hours of daylight. Travel was not recommended during the ensuing eighteen hours of darkness, leaving the travelers plenty of time to set up camp and relax.

Since the temperature was still dropping—the weather forecast called for a low of minus 58 degrees that night—the first thing the Mushers did was unpack the kerosene heaters. After warming themselves for several minutes, the Mushers set up a portable gasoline-powered generator and several spotlights. Then they switched them on, bathing the campsite in bright incandescent light.

After setting up tents for dogs and humans alike, the Mushers cared for the dogs, checking their feet and shoulders, feeding them with frozen meat chunks, which they swallowed whole. Sam explained that the meat expanded as it thawed in their stomachs, keeping them full longer than if it had been cooked.

The Mushers concluded their preparations by erecting a shower and an outhouse for the exclusive use of the king and queen. Everyone else used a metal bucket.

The shower was an ingenious contraption. A pipe with an attached showerhead ran from a heated twenty-gallon tank into a small tent. Inside was a wooden platform to stand on while showering, complete with a drain that captured the water and sent it back outside through another pipe.

It had been eight hours since the start of their journey—five hours of sledding, and another three hours to set up camp—and everyone was hungry.

After dining on a meal of hamburgers and beans prepared by two Mushers over propane stoves in a heated mess tent, David and Stephania retired to their sleeping quarters. The canvas tent rose to a height of seven feet and was large enough to sleep six. The amenities included a kerosene heater, two sleeping bags, foam mattresses, a card table, and two metal folding chairs.

"This is quite a wild adventure you brought me on, husband," Stephania remarked with a smile. "How in the world did you ever come up with the idea of journeying into the arctic on a dogsled?"

David laughed. "You're being much too kind. It's not exactly the Ritz-Carlton, is it? It certainly would have been a lot easier to drive a truck up here." He grabbed Stephania by the waist and hugged her. "I've always wanted to ride on a dogsled, though. It's very romantic, don't you think?"

"What a naughty husband I married," Stephania replied with a mischievous grin. They kissed for a minute or so.

"I had one heck of a time persuading the security staff to let us travel out here by ourselves," she said, pouting. "They made me promise to report in every hour and bring a ton of supplies. We have enough food to last at least three months!"

"It's nice being on our own for a change, though," David remarked.

"I can think of a few ways to take advantage of the situation," Stephania said, unzipping her parka.

"Hold that thought, dear," David said with a grin. "What do you say we go outside and have a look around? Perhaps we can see the Northern Lights."

The royal couple went outside and walked until they were well outside the circle of light.

David looked up into the night sky and raised his arms into the air. "Look at all the stars, honey!" he exclaimed.

"It's magnificent," Stephania responded in an awestruck tone.

They remained standing in the frigid, arctic night air for another half-hour, waiting in vain for an aurora to appear. Then they returned to their tent, spent a few hours playing cards, and finally turned in.

Sam awakened the royal couple early the next morning—three hours before sunrise.

After everyone had consumed their fill of eggs, bacon, and sausage, the Mushers repacked everything and broke camp. By the time they finished harnessing the dogs, the sun was peeking above the horizon.

The party continued their journey without incident until the afternoon when two dogs from David's team got into a fight as the Mushers were untangling their lines. After breaking up the fight, the Mushers checked the huskies for injuries—fortunately, there were none—and the company resumed their trek, making excellent speed until nightfall.

Once again, David and Stephania walked beyond the camp's illumination after dinner, hoping to see an aurora. This time, to David's satisfaction, they were treated to a marvelous light display.

"So, this is what you came to see, my love," Stephania remarked, hugging David affectionately as she gazed wondrously into the sky.

The aurora borealis shone brightly out of the black, star-studded, arctic sky. The royal couple stood absolutely still, mesmerized by the intricate patterns of light as they flickered and danced, the folds and arches of red, green, and blue continuously changing shape and form.

"What a spectacular sight," David remarked in wonder. "It was definitely worth the effort to witness something as magnificent as this. God is a wonderful artist, isn't he?"

David and Stephania continued to watch the display in the hellishly cold air for the greater part of an hour before being forced to return to the warmth and safety of their tent.

A few hours later, everyone was abruptly awakened by the frantic barking and howling of the huskies.

David and Stephania walked out of their tent and watched tensely as the Mushers pointed their rifles at a huge white polar bear that had wandered into the camp, apparently looking for food.

One of the Mushers abruptly shot his rifle into the air, and the bear stopped in its tracks. It remained in place for a few moments, surveying the camp with its black beady eyes and sniffing the air. Then it abruptly turned around and lumbered out of the camp.

The third day began the same as the previous two, the Mushers spending almost three hours feeding everyone—including the dogs—and repacking the sleds.

Unfortunately, after an hour into their travels, the company encountered a fierce wind blowing out of the east, dropping the wind chill to approximately minus 50 degrees, resulting in very slow progress. The Mushers had to stop every half-hour and light the kerosene heaters so everyone could warm their extremities in order to prevent frostbite.

After approximately three hours of braving the bone-chilling cold, Stephania yelled for her Musher to stop. She climbed out of her sled and pointed to the north. "Look, David!" she exclaimed. "It looks like some kind of a big white tower. It's huge. What's it doing way out here in the middle of nowhere?"

David smiled. "It's called an obelisk."

Printed in the United States
by Baker & Taylor Publisher Services